# A Spell in the Country

by Heide Goody and Iain Grant

Pigeon Park Press

Published by Pigeon Park Press
www.pigeonparkpress.com
Cover artwork and design by Mike Watts – www.bigbeano.co.uk

# Chapter 1 – The Three Witches

## The Good Witch of Northfield

Dee Finch didn't consider herself to be just a good witch. Of course she was a good witch. That kind of thing was in the blood. No, Dee wasn't just a good witch; she was a *good* witch, and that meant being good and doing good; whenever and wherever, whatever people might think. So Dee felt compelled to tell the young man in the shopping precinct that his hat was on fire.

"Your hat is on fire, poppet," she said.

Surprisingly, the young man responded with a delighted smile. "Well, that's the final question answered."

Not the reaction Dee expected. It wasn't as if it was the kind of hat one could set on fire without being instantly aware of it. If, say, he had been wearing a bowler hat, one might imagine a small fire on the crown might go unnoticed for a minute or two. But this was a woolly hat with a minor conflagration where a bobble might be, or where the bobble had recently been.

Dee imagined that the young man - with his baggy rough-knit jumper in a variety of mud shades, a beard that wasn't sure if it really wanted to be a beard and had grown in uneven patches, and a general appearance and aroma suggesting his world contained a good many things of a 'herbal' nature – had absent-mindedly put a roll-up behind his ear, and forgotten that it was already lit. It was the only immediately obvious explanation.

"Your hat is on fire," she said again.

"Indeed," he said. "Let me just—" He flipped through the papers on the clipboard in his hand.

"On fire," she repeated.

"Yep." He clicked his pen and put a tick in a box. "Now, would you have a few minutes to complete the rest of the survey?"

"Survey?"

Dee felt she had lost her grip on the situation. The man's hat was on fire and, on a fundamental level, she wanted it dealt with. But now he was talking about a survey and had a look in his eye which suggested his day had been a long struggle to get people to participate.

"What kind of survey?" asked Dee. "I can't be too long, sweetness. I was only popping out for some safety pins and a bottle of linctus for Mrs Binder."

"It's all about trying to become a better you," said the young man.

"And you do understand what I mean when I say your hat is on fire?" she said.

"I do. Now, can I take your name?"

"Yes. It's Dee Finch. Miss."

Dee returned to the Shelter for Unloved Animals charity shop with a packet of pins, a bottle of cherry linctus, a brochure from the young survey-taker and a great deal to think about.

"Thank God you're here," said Mr Tilbury. "It's been bedlam since you left."

Dee looked up from the brochure. The shop was empty, apart from Mr Tilbury who was manning the till. Clothes hung unregarded on their racks. Books gathered dust on the shelves. The poster of the charity mascot, Terry the Boss-Eyed Tortoise, with the slogan of 'Ugly Animals Need Love Too' still hung slightly askew on the wall. It was so quiet that one could almost hear the creak of time passing.

"Bedlam?" repeated Dee.

"A man came in and wanted to know if we had a book," said Mr Tilbury.

"Yes?" said Dee.

"And then Mrs Binder had to go and have a sit down out back because she said the dust from those cardigans had got right to her chest and set her cough off again."

Dee was polite enough to avoid suggesting that Mrs Binder's cough might have more to do with her twenty-a-day habit than any amount of second-hand knitwear. "I've got her medicine."

"But then Melissa Sacks came in. I think it was Melissa Sacks."

"How could you not know?"

Mr Tilbury pulled a pained expression and gestured uneasily at his face. Dee understood instantly.

"Where is she now, poppet?"

"I put her in the fitting room."

Dee crossed to the tiny curtained off corner of the shop which passed for a changing room and slipped inside. Melissa Sacks sat on the stool, her face like a pink balloon stuffed with ping pong balls. Tears sat on her cheeks; or maybe not her cheeks. It was hard to tell.

"What did you do?" asked Dee, not unkindly.

Melissa Sacks made a flesh-smothered mumble that sounded something like, "Munshumfin pfpf muh fush" and ran a hand in front of her face.

"Yes," said Dee. "But I told you it was just for your lips—"

"Ma moh."

"—Instead of getting those awful, and expensive, filler injections you were talking about."

"Buh ma momad muh ibs a muck-muck Amjamima Momie."

"And they do," Dee agreed. "Unfortunately, Melissa, the rest of your face now looks like Angelina Jolie's lips too."

Melissa Sacks put her hands to her swollen, malformed face, and sobbed.

"There, there, sweetness," said Dee. "We can sort this out."

Dee bit the tips of her thumbs, smeared blood across the woman's brow, cheeks and chin, and intoned a single word. Melissa gasped as her face rapidly settled down into a far more human shape.

"Now, have you got the cream on you?" said Dee.

Melissa Sacks handed over a squeezy tube.

"Is this all that's left?" said Dee. "It's a wonder your face didn't explode."

Melissa Sacks patted her cheeks and prodded her back-to-normal nose. "How did you do it?" she asked.

"Psychosomatics," said Dee and waved away any further questions. "I think I'll be looking after this cream from now on."

"But my lips—"

"—Look lovely," said Dee, propelling the woman from the changing room.

Dee put the half squeezed tube on the till counter, picked up the bottle of cherry cough medicine and went into the back room. Mrs Binder, an octogenarian with the sinewy forearms of a lifelong washerwoman, the lungs of a kipper smokehouse and the bloody minded attitude of a woman who had lived through the Birmingham Blitz without a word of complaint, sat by the open back door. She braced hands against her knees and wheezed, "Is that for me?"

"Something for your throat."

"All I need is five minutes breather."

"I'll just get a spoon." Dee wove through the black bags of donated goods littering the floor and stepped into the kitchenette.

Checking that Mrs Binder wasn't looking her way, Dee unscrewed the lid and poured all but an inch of the linctus down the sink. She opened the herb cupboard in which she kept her emergency supplies and took out few leaves of adders tongue and a vial of turnsole sap. Dee stuffed the leaves in the linctus bottle, added a dash of sap and then topped up the whole thing with Ribena and water.

"I don't need a spoon," called Mrs Binder, and immediately set off on a prolonged and noisy coughing fit.

"You're the boss," said Dee. She gave the bottle thirteen firm shakes before taking it to Mrs Binder. "I couldn't find one anyway."

"Youth of today," tutted the old woman.

In the kitchenette, Dee put the kettle on and washed the incriminating dregs of linctus down the plughole.

*Youth of today*, thought Dee. It was a compliment of sorts, she supposed. She had no illusions about herself. She was racing towards middle age, propelled by the momentum of a personal life featuring more early nights curled up with a good book and a sticky bun than late ones fired by wild dancing and a hot date. She had no one to blame but herself and, truth be told, she wasn't unhappy with her life choices but...

It was that brochure the young man with the fiery hat had given her.

*Three weeks to a better you,* it had said. *Develop your true potential,* it had said.

Dee was a *good* witch, but surely her goodness could extend further than operating a down-at-heel charity shop, brewing up cough mixture for the terminally bronchial, and providing magical cosmetic enhancements for women who really just needed a dash of self-confidence?

Dee took those thoughts home with her. She let them percolate at the back of her mind while she cooked dinner (Friday was macaroni cheese with arctic roll for afters). They footled around in her subconscious while she distilled extract of Jude's Wort in her bathroom laboratory following a recipe by Zosimos of Panopolis. They skulked almost invisibly while she watched a DVD movie double-bill of *Legally Blonde* and Disney's *Frozen* – during which she belted out her own rendition of *Let It Go* whilst simultaneously eating a whole box of After Eight mints. The thoughts slipped with her, onesie-clad, into bed and went to work on her sleeping mind.

When she woke on Saturday morning, she had come to a decision.

She double-checked her thoughts and reasons as she parked the car before cutting through the Northfield indoor shopping centre on her way to work. *Three weeks to a better you.* Three weeks wasn't long, but it would mean leaving Unloved Animals in the hands of Mr Tilbury and his painfully passive ilk. Nonetheless, it was a price worth paying.

Dee opened the shutters and took advantage of the hour in which she would have the place to herself to sort things out. She spent a good while in the back room, packing some travelling clothes for herself and casting the few repair incantations she knew over the racks of recently sorted clothes: instantly darning holes and reattaching a number of loose buttons. She threw a protective ward over the shop till, did a full cash count and wrote out a list of instructions for the other volunteers.

Some of the instructions were practical – the locations of keys, the importance of getting donors to sign up for Gift Aid – but most of them were exhortations to use their initiative. Greet the customers, create new window displays, put up some new posters or at least rehang the existing ones so they were straight. She finished with the words *Give it a go. Good things will happen if you open yourself up to the opportunity.*

As she put the final full stop on the page, two women barrelled into the shop, almost taking the door from its hinges and the glass from its frame. The taller and older of the two slammed the door closed behind them and stared nervously out at the high street through the miraculously intact glass.

"We're not open yet," said Dee automatically.

The younger one – an olive-skinned teenager who looked like she had skipped too many meals – stared at Dee. "She needs shoes," she said.

The taller woman bundled her companion over to the till. The wonky poster of Terry the Boss-Eyed Tortoise fell off the wall for no reason.

"Can I help you?" sighed Dee.

"Is there a back exit to this shop?" asked the woman. There was a wild, slightly panicked look in her eyes. Both woman and girl were breathing heavily. They had been running, Dee guessed. She realised that the woman was barefoot and her feet injured.

Dee wasn't a fan of obvious questions but couldn't help herself. "Are you in trouble, poppet?"

A man with a shaved head peered in the shop window, eyes shaded by hands pressed against the glass. Dee knew that *this* had to be the trouble the pair of them were in. Before Dee could speak, the man threw the door open and stalked inside. It was only then that Dee saw his face was divided equally in two, along the line of his nose: one side perfectly normal, the other a painful and shiny pink, as though he had fallen asleep under a sun lamp.

The taller woman swore.

8

Dee opened her mouth, dismayed to realise her mouth's chosen sentence was going to be: "He should put something on that."

The younger woman snatched up the tube of lip-enhancement cream, still lying on the counter since yesterday. She turned and squirted its contents directly into the man's eyes.

## The Good Witch of Southside

Caroline Black didn't consider herself to be just a good witch; she was a fricking *awesome* witch. However, being fricking awesome didn't pay the bills. Witchcraft, unfortunately, was all about the little stuff, the personal stuff, the one-to-one stuff. Magic invocations didn't bring vocational success. Hedge-magic couldn't make you a hedge-fund manager. Having a witch's cat did not make one a fat cat. Witchcraft lent itself to careers like nursing, social work, residential care, customer service and all those other fields of work which paid a pittance.

And so it was that Caroline Black, after royally screwing up her last job, found herself the most fricking awesome witch to be waiting tables at a city centre cafe. Angelo's was a busy little space directly across the road from the Hippodrome, catering mostly to theatre types and, to a lesser degree, the girls from the local lap-dancing clubs. Most days she found herself reflecting that, with some skilfully applied glamours, she could make a minor fortune as a dancer. However, she always dismissed those thoughts, not out of any moral squeamishness, but because even though she knew she could make it work – she was fricking awesome after all – she also knew in her heart that her days of parading flesh for cash were a decade or more behind her.

Instead she'd scrape by on waitress pay, using subtle charms to extract bigger tips, and stoically putting up with minor customer crappiness; like this woman who wasn't happy with her knife and fork.

"I'm sorry?" said Caroline.

"I just wondered if you had some non-metallic cutlery," said the customer.

"Non-metallic."

"Maybe plastic. I have this allergy thing with iron."

The woman gestured helplessly at her three cheese salad. Her lunch companion, a handsome suit, had a suitably embarrassed look on his face.

"I'll go check," said Caroline, giving the suit a playful smile. He'd be the one picking up the cheque. He'd be the one to press for a tip.

She pushed through into the kitchen. "Angelo, do we have any plastic knives and forks? I've got Magneto out front says she can't use metal ones."

Caroline didn't hear his reply. A badly stacked pile of cups and plates chose that moment to slide off the clear-away counter and smash on the floor. Shards of crockery and uneaten food spun across the floor.

"Are you trying to destroy my kitchen?" yelled Angelo> His real name was Anwar but Caroline was happy to play along with the fiction.

"I touched nothing. This should be cleared."

"May is on her break."

"May's always on her break," muttered Caroline.

She rummaged through the utensils and went back to the customer with the one plastic baby fork she had found. By the time she had cleaned up the mess, binned the debris, helped a woman deal with her tearful toddler and caught up with the waiting food orders, Jess on the till had taken payment from the suit and the no-metal woman – no tip – and an hour had passed.

She was wiping down a table when a voice behind her said, "Can I get a coffee to go? Black, two sugars."

She turned to tell the man that he needed to order at the counter. She stopped herself when she saw who it was. "Ex-Detective Sergeant Bowman." Caroline was both surprised and pleased.

He grinned. Bowman, his head shaved to sidestep male pattern baldness, had a caveman physique and a wide mouth. When he grinned it was like an egg splitting in half. "Ex-Detective Constable Black," he said. "How are you doing, Caz?"

She tilted her head to one side. "Waiting tables, Doug. You?"

"Getting by," he said, with a self-deprecating glance.

In the months since they'd both been fired, Caroline had forgotten how much she liked Doug Bowman. He was a laugh, flirty but not sleazy, and the most straight-talking bent copper she had known.

"So, is this a chance meeting or have I got myself a new stalker?"

"Nah," he said. "Just passing on the way to work and saw you in here. Um..."

"Um, what?"

"Is this job—" he drew little circles with a finger to indicate the café "—a permanent thing?"

"Permanent enough. Why?"

"There's an opening in our company."

"A job?"

"Maybe."

"What kind of job?"

"It's complicated."

"The job?"

"The situation."

"So, dodgy?"

He grinned again. "We could discuss it over a drink later."

It sounded like a pick up line but Caroline knew Bowman better than that. Frankly, the day was shaping up to be a shitty one; she reckoned she'd need a drink by the end of it. "The Proofing House?"

"At eight?" said Bowman.

She didn't care what the job was. It didn't matter.

The Proofing House, five minutes' walk from Digbeth police station had been their local when the two of them had been on the job together. Located on an underlit street between the canal and the railway arches, it had minimal charm, a meagre selection of beers and a clientele that cut a swathe across Birmingham's social and cultural strata.

Caroline, dressed in ballbuster black, entered at half eight, expecting to find Bowman and a drink waiting for her at the bar. Instead, there was no Bowman and the barman, who she knew by sight but not by name, nodded to her and passed over a slip of paper.

SOMETHING'S COME UP. BACK SOON AS. DOUG.

"Bugger," said Caroline.

"He got a phone call," said the barman. "Sounded important."

"Better have been," she muttered.

Caroline hadn't brought either cash or cards with her to the pub – she never did – but she had been looking forward to an evening during which she didn't have to make even the smallest effort to get a drink. Oh, well...

She scanned the pub and then went over to a scruffy twenty-something drinking alone in a booth. With a subtle, accompanying flick of her wrist, she said, "You'd like to buy me a drink."

"I would like to buy you a drink," he said.

"A pint of something European."

"A pint of something European?"

While the cute but crusty zombie went to fetch her drink, Caroline sat down and nosed through the open satchel he'd left on the seat. Glossy pamphlets, a roll of stickers and a fat clipboard of filled-in forms. The guy was either a chugger or had robbed one at knifepoint. Caroline suspected the latter.

"A pint of something European," said the young man.

"Thank you." Normally, this was the cue for her to take both her drink and her leave but she was intrigued. "What's this stuff?" she asked.

"You've been going through my things—"

A curt gesture. "But you don't mind."

"—But I don't mind." He half smiled. "It's the day job. Street surveys. Recruiting people for a three week self-improvement course."

"Is this like some Scientology, culty thing?" she asked.

"Lord, no!"

"I just wondered, what with your hat being on fire and all. Thought it might be something religious."

"You can see it?" he asked, pointing at his flaming headwear.

"Yeah," she said. "Because it's on fire."

"Maybe you'd like to take the survey too," he suggested.

"You said it was the day job. It's night now."

"But I'm below quota. Today's the last day. I did a couple of the suburbs this morning, and the city centre this afternoon, but I've still got spaces to fill."

"Last day? Does your mother ship leave tomorrow?"

"It's not a cult. It's a free three week course at a lovely old house in the country."

"Three weeks? As in residential?"

"Yes."

"And it's free?"

"Yes."

Caroline sipped at her pint. She liked free things. "This survey. Are there a lot of personal questions on it?"

"A few," he admitted. "Some."

"Sounds fun," she said.

Saturday morning arrived with sunlight far too bright for Caroline's eyes, and a side order of knocking at the door. She sat up in bed, groaning. The lump beside her stirred. She placed a hand on the cute but crusty lump. His name was Madison Fray, not that she intended to commit it to memory. "You want to get up, make me a coffee and then leave."

There were mumbles from beneath the sheet that sounded close to agreement. The lump began to move.

Caroline climbed out of bed, pulled on a T-shirt that wasn't hers and knickers that were, and went to the door. Doug Bowman stood on the fourth floor walkway overlooking Sherlock Street and the crappier end of the Gay Village.

"Where the hell were you last night—?" she demanded, immediately following with, "What the hell happened to your face?"

Bowman looked like he'd taken part in a consumer product test in which he'd washed the left side of his face with ordinary soap and the right side with bleach. The skin was raw and waxy.

"Work," he said. She could see him trying not to wince as he talked.

"And this is the job you thought would suit me."

"It pays well."

"It ought to. I've got something for your face."

"I put something on it."

"I've got something better."

She fetched a tub of perfectly ordinary moisturiser from her make-up bag and brought it to Bowman, waiting in the hallway. She dabbed it on his cheek, whispering a cantrip under her breath.

"What's that?" he asked.

"Just a saying from the Old Country," said Caroline.

"Didn't know you were Irish."

"Only on St Patrick's Day."

The spell should have worked, but she could see it wasn't. And that meant the burn, or whatever it was on his face, had been caused by magic. "What *have* you been up to?"

"I said. Work. And I could really use your help."

"And the nature of this work?"

"It's—"

"Complicated. Right."

"Um," muttered Bowman. He was looking at the naked man holding out a cup of coffee to Caroline. She took it without a word. Madison Fray made for the front door.

"You need to get dressed before you leave," Caroline told him.

"I need to get dressed before I leave," said Madison, returning to the bedroom.

"I can see you're busy," said Bowman. He grinned, immediately regretting the pain it caused. "But give me a call when you're free. I could really use your help."

A phoned buzzed in his pocket. He answered like it truly mattered. "Yes ... You do? ... And you have an address? ... Pine Walk. I know it..."

He ended the call. The look on his face hinted things had turned in his favour: there was a vindictive glint in his eye.

"Call me," he told her. He gestured at the flat with his phone. "You're better than waiting tables and this."

Caroline shut the door behind him and sipped her coffee. Madison came up behind her and began to pull up her T-shirt.

She laughed in surprise. "What are you doing?"

His voice was toneless. "I need to get dressed before I leave."

She put the coffee on the window ledge and let him strip his T-shirt from her. "Stop," she commanded before he put it on himself.

She slid her hands down to his naked waist. Automatically, he put his hands over hers. He was a skinny lad – clearly the cannabis and alcohol diet worked wonders. Not necessarily her type, but he was young and affable and, most conveniently, here.

"Tell me about this three week residential thing," she said. "Is it a genuine offer? No catches?"

"No catches," he said.

"And it starts today?"

"Yep."

"Do you have a car?"

"I do."

"And when do I need to be there by?"

"It doesn't start until this evening."

"Oh, then we've got time."

"Time?"

She drummed her fingers on his chest. "Go clean your teeth. I expect you back in bed in five minutes. And today's Word of the Day is 'imaginative.' Go."

## The Wicked Witch of the West Midlands

Jenny Knott was a wicked witch. She didn't have any choice in the matter; it was the hand fate had dealt her. She wasn't a wicked person – she went to great efforts to not be – but she was undoubtedly and involuntarily a wicked witch. She had an imp to prove it.

It was easy to keep most of the wicked witchiness under wraps. She didn't have a hooked nose or a jutting chin; her nose was quite attractive, and if she did have a horsey set to her jaw that was down to some distant aristocratic genes and nothing more. She didn't have green skin; only witches in MGM musicals suffered with that. The inevitable warts were infrequent and easily tackled with liquid nitrogen. And she didn't wear black; she had made a conscious decision to ban it from her wardrobe.

In fact, Kevin Carter-King commented on her clothing choice when they met for Friday lunch at Angelo's in the city centre.

"You're like a summer's day," he said.

"That's cheesy," she replied.

It had been more than fifteen years since they'd shared university digs together but they had managed to keep a gentle friendship simmering all that time. Kevin had parlayed his fifteen years into a thriving freight and haulage company, a big house on the Warwickshire border and an acceptably expanded waistline. Jenny's fifteen years had seen a string of personal failures and an on-going battle with her sorcerous dark side.

"Me or the three cheese salad?" he said.

She rolled her eyes and raised a hand to draw the attention of the dark-haired waitress. She was one of those who pouted all day long and acted as though *doing her actual job* was a rude interruption to her busy schedule. She glared at Jenny.

"Do you have any non-metallic cutlery?" asked Jenny.

"I'm sorry?" sneered the waitress.

"I just wondered if you had some non-metallic cutlery."

"Non-metallic," repeated the waitress.

"Maybe plastic," Jenny explained. "I have this allergy thing with iron."

She gestured at her meal. Kevin smiled sympathetically. Jenny had used the 'iron allergy' line all her adult life and he had heard it plenty of times.

"I'll go check," huffed the waitress and slunk off into the kitchen.

The touch of cold iron was one of the few things Jenny could do nothing about. There were several simple but effective wards against wicked witches and the presence of iron was one. Whether it was horseshoes, fridge doors or stainless steel salad forks, Jenny couldn't abide them.

The two other wickedly witchy aspects that she had little control over were her imp and the effect that—

There was a crash of breaking crockery from the kitchen. An ironic cheer went up from a couple of tables and a toddler across the way burst into tears. Jenny looked around for her imp, peering under the table.

"Lost something?" said Kevin.

"I wish," said Jenny to herself.

The waitress came huffing back, put a child's plastic fork down by Jenny's plate, and huffed off again.

"Charming service in this place," said Jenny.

"It's close to my office," said Kevin. "That's about all there is to recommend it."

The kitchen door swung open and Jizzimus sauntered through, chewing on a wedge of crockery as though it were a slice of pizza. A hairy homunculus with the feet and ears of a cow, Jizzimus had a wide mouth full of needle teeth and little nubby horns on the top of his head. He was also a mere twelve inches tall and, as a rule, invisible to all.

"You 'ear that?" he said. "That strumpet called you Magneto. S'an ice-cream, innit? What she wanna do that for, eh?"

Jenny ignored Jizzimus with ease. She found that chatting to invisible magic folk in public tended to generate the wrong kind of attention.

"How's the job?" Kevin asked.

"I'm between jobs," she admitted.

"What happened to the last one?"

"The place had trouble with shoplifters."

"They accused you?" said Kevin.

"Oh, no. I caught them in the act. A pair of teenagers."

"Bravo."

"And then there was an altercation. It got violent. A broken arm."

Kevin shook his head in dismay. "No one should have to suffer assaults in the workplace."

"It wasn't my arm," said Jenny.

"Oh."

"Classic rumble," said Jizzimus. "Don' forget to mention how I pinned 'im down while you bit 'is fingers." He lay on the floor under a table, hands on his belly, staring up a woman's long skirts as she tried to soothe her crying toddler.

"I'm sorry it didn't work out," said Kevin. "Work can sometimes heap the worst kind of crap on your plate."

"I know," said Jenny.

"There are bits of my work I really don't enjoy," Kevin admitted.

"I thought you were doing well."

"I am. But it's a new Europe out there. The industry's changed. You can't just operate inside your comfort bubble anymore."

"You could always give it up," said Jenny. "Start afresh."

"I could," he smiled. "Unfortunately, I'm addicted to earning huge piles of cash."

"I've imagine you've got a swimming pool at home full of gold doubloons. Swim in it like Scrooge McDuck."

"Shockingly close to the truth, Jen."

"I'm sure it provides some small consolation in those moments of self-doubt."

"It does help," he agreed. "But we were talking about you. Maybe it's you who needs to start afresh."

"No. I need to stop starting afresh and actually stick at something for a while."

"I could always find you a job in our office."

"I don't need charity. I need a new direction in life."

"Then retrain," he suggested.

"As what?"

"I don't know. Teacher?"

"I don't like children," said Jenny automatically.

"What you talkin' about?" said Jizzimus. "You love the li'l bleeders. You'd love 'em even more if you actually cooked 'em first."

Jenny put in an earbud as they walked towards the bus stop. Pretending to be on a phone call was the easiest way of talking to

Jizzimus in public. She sometimes wondered how many delusional people went unnoticed now it was okay to talk to oneself in public.

"For once, it would be nice to go on a lunch date without you in tow," she told her imp.

"You know it don' work like that, guv," said Jizzimus. "*Was* it a date?"

"Not like that. Kevin Carter-King is an old friend."

"Fat friend. 'As 'e really got a swimmin' pool full of gold?"

"No."

"I could fill 'is pool wiv gold if 'e likes." Jizzimus widdled on the pavement. He always tried to spell his name but he was only a little imp and rarely got past the third letter.

Kevin had given her his business card before she left, just in case she did want to take him up on a job offer, but Jenny knew that would be a mistake: a holding pattern rather than a solution.

"I need chocolate," she said. "Lots of chocolate. That child in the café. It cried and cried and—"

"I know a really good way to make 'em shut up."

"Making you shut up. That would be a good trick."

"Bloody cheek," said Jizzimus.

Jenny went into a newsagent and came out with a half-pound bar of Dairy Milk. "Three pound fifty," she muttered in disgust.

"Children are free," Jizzimus pointed out.

"Leave me alone." She unwrapped the purple foil. "Look, go torment a chugger. You like that."

Jizzimus giggled and, with a clippety-clop, scampered away. New Street, the pedestrianised heart of the city, was the hunting ground of various religious evangelists, buskers and charity muggers. One had to slalom to avoid God, contemporary world music and direct debits for charities which clearly spent their money on hiring high street bullies and wheedlers. Actually, Jenny had no problem with the buskers but the rest could take a jump in a ditch.

She took a big bite of chocolate. It tasted good, just not quite good enough. It was the methadone of wicked witches. Delicious but just not quite delicious enough to destroy her other cravings—

"Excuse me."

She turned. It was a chugger with a clipboard, a badly-executed beard and unusual headwear.

"I already gave at the office."

"That's nice to know," he said. "I'm doing a survey."

"Does the survey end with me donating to your charity?"

"No, I—"

"Or buying something from you?"

"No—"

"Or God?"

"Um. I don't think so. Not unless God's running a three week self-improvement course."

Jenny thought about that. "Could be." She tried to draw Jizzimus's attention but he was too busying humping the leg of a Cancer Research chugger.

"Go on then," she sighed. "But I am going to stuff chocolate in my face while we do this."

"Fair enough," he said.

He took her name and a contact number before launching into a baffling array of questions. He showed her pictures of cows and asked her to pick the 'best' one. He showed her black and white photographs of women in Victorian dresses and asked her to rank them in order on no particular scale. He invited her to think of a number between one and a hundred and then asked her to do the same three more times. He showed her woodcut images: a jester, a cat, a leafless tree and a tower, and asked her to match them to famous celebrities. He showed her photographs of several green leaves and asked her to select non-green colours to accompany each. He asked about her sleeping habits, her parents and then asked her to describe her favourite cloud. He seemed pleased with all her answers. Jenny couldn't see why.

By the time he had finished, so was her chocolate bar. Jizzimus had stolen a tabla drum from a street music group and was going bongotastic at the feet of a hellfire preacher.

"All done," said the weird survey man. "I just need to ask, do *you* have any questions?"

"One, I suppose," said Jenny. "Why is your hat on fire?"

"Excellent," said the man. He put a tick on his paperwork, and gave Jenny a brochure with a number stamped on the top.

"Eastville Hall?" she read.

"A lovely old house in the Fens."

"Do I now get to buy a remarkably cheap timeshare?"

"No. That's where the self-improvement course is being held. Your answers match our criteria perfectly and I am delighted to say we can offer you a place."

"And how much does it cost?"

"It's free."

"And how much does it cost?"

"It's definitely free. However, it does start tomorrow evening and I understand that's very short notice."

Jenny smiled politely. "Well, this has certainly been entertaining, but I have other plans."

"We can help with transport if that's a problem," he offered.

"Thanks all the same," she said, waving the brochure to emphasise she still had it. She stuffed it in her jacket pocket and walked away.

"Come on," she called to Jizzimus. "I need more chocolate."

Jizzimus threw the tabla drums into a flower stall, bit the heads off some lilies and caught up with Jenny as an argument erupted behind them.

"You see that?" he said. "You see that, guv? I did that. Mental."

A second large bar of chocolate didn't help.

Jenny sat on the stone steps overlooking St Martin's church and munched mechanically. Jizzimus ran backwards and forwards, bringing her stones for her to throw through shop windows. By the time evening had rolled in, there was a pile of stones, half-bricks and weighty lumps of scrap beside Jenny but, to Jizzimus's annoyance, no broken windows.

"'Ow do you know you don' like smashin' windows unless yuv tried it, eh?" he said.

"I'm not interested," she said. "I'm not interested in curses or hexes or blighting crops or—"

"You did a bit of blightin' the other day," said Jizzimus.

"When?"

"That bleedin' codpiece at the sandwich shop."

"I made his salad wilt. That's not the same thing. And he was being an arse."

"Tell you what. I bet some of the shopkeepers round 'ere are arses too."

"I'm not smashing any windows!" She sighed heavily. "Jizzimus, tell me: am I fighting a losing battle?"

"Yes," he said, placing a lump of masonry in her free hand.

"Kevin's right," she said. "I'm racing towards forty and my life is a mess. I can't hold down a job, a home, any kind of relationship. It's like I've got this terminal condition and I just keep fighting and fighting and I know a day will come when I don't want to fight it anymore."

"Don' put off 'til tomorrow what you can do today," said Jizzimus.

"It's just..."

She popped the last of the chocolate in her mouth, dropping the lump of masonry back on the ground..

She was a wicked witch: something she was never going to shake off. There was the small stuff, mere colouration to her nature: the immunity from drowning, her troubles with iron, the tendency to accidentally cackle now and then. Other stuff was more potent, more dangerous: the curses that came to her lips so easily, the ability to conjure witchfire without even thinking about it, the imp familiar. Then there was the real problem, the big one, the one that would be her downfall one day.

"I could have eaten that toddler," she said.

"Could've. Didn'," grumped Jizzimus.

Children were simply bloody scrumptious. Whereas to ordinary humans they smelled of soap and biscuits and sweat and what-have-you, to wicked witches their scent was delicious beyond compare. They didn't actually smell of chocolate, but something about the aroma of young humans worked on the brain's chemistry in exactly the same way. Except chocolate was to children what milk was to ice-cream; what grapes were to wine. God, children smelled nice.

And when they were sad or angry or afraid, their sweet bodies sang with insanely enticing aromas. That crying toddler: no human cuisine could have possibly compared with eating that little one raw. But Jenny resisted; she had always resisted.

She wanted to cry.

"I can smell him even now," she said. She sniffed at her fingers. She could smell something. Or someone. Not the toddler, but a child. The city was awash with the background aroma of hundreds of thousands of children, but there was one scent in the air: something keen and rich and more striking than any other.

"Can you smell that?" she asked Jizzimus.

"Are you going to eat it?" he replied moodily.

"It's—" She stood and sniffed deeply. "Sour. An older child. A teenager maybe. But it's... Oh, God, that's gorgeous."

"Are you going to eat it?"

"He must be absolutely terrified." She sniffed again. "She. *She's* terrified."

"Fine. Are we going to eat *her*?"

"No," said Jenny. "But we're going to find her."

Two hours passed but the smell did not fade. It swirled about them but Jenny unravelled it, following its twist and turns down into Digbeth and then Deritend; down among dim side streets and the lanes of an ancient town.

"You don' have to 'unt down this one child, guv," said Jizzimus, bored. "We could just go to McDonald's. Get a kid 'n' shake to go."

"We're almost there," said Jenny.

"Yuv already said that."

"She's here."

She stopped in front of a pair of thick double doors in an old brick edifice. The doors were padlocked, iron. Jenny stood on tiptoes and tried to peer through the small grimed windows set high up in the doors.

"Can't see anything," she said.

"The door's only wood," said Jizzimus.

"If there's a girl in there, I'm not going to eat her," she told him.

"What are you gunna do then?"

Jenny looked up at the building. It might have once been a factory, back in the days when the city actually had an industry. Now it was dark and lifeless.

"Maybe she was hiding in there – a game, or she's homeless – and now she's trapped. Kids get trapped in fridges and things, don't they?"

"Mmm," agreed Jizzimus happily.

Jenny tutted at him. She placed her hands against the centre of one of the doors, reached down for the witchfire that came so easily to her fingers. A ball of green flame punched a three foot hole in the door.

"Won' smash windows but will blow up doors," noted Jizzimus.

Jenny spat a splinter of wood from her lips, coughed at the dissipating smoke and climbed through the hole she'd made.

The interior of the building was a ghostly shell. Stanchions of masonry and unpainted patches of wall were testament to the machines and fixtures that had once stood there. The floor was mostly brick dust, scuffed by vehicles tracks and footprints. It took a while for the smoke and dust to clear from Jenny's nose.

"This way," she said.

In the next room, there was nothing but a stack of black plastic crates: wide sturdy things to carry machine parts or some such. Jenny sniffed at them and shuddered at the odours clinging to the empty crates. The fear. The despair.

"I don't like this," she said.

"I know," said Jizzimus. "They're bloody empty."

"What the hell is this place?"

"Whatever it is, they've shut up shop, guv."

She shook her head and pointed to a set of stairs, dimly visible in the gloom. It was night outside and now lightless within. Jenny conjured witchfire at her fingertips to give some illumination.

"Up here."

She climbed slowly, testing each step in turn. It wouldn't do to break a leg on dodgy stairs.

The first floor was a single open space with large windows facing the Birmingham and Fazeley Canal. It had probably once been a workshop, filled with seamstresses or engravers. The only thing in it now was a trunk-sized black crate in the centre of the floor. It stank of fear. Mouth-watering fear.

The crate was bound with canvas straps. As Jenny extinguished the witchfire and pulled at the straps, there was a grunt from within and a frantic thumping.

"It's okay," she called. "I'm here to help."

The interlocking lids flew open and the girl within uncoiled from her confinement. She rolled out onto the floor with a cry. A cloud of child-funk enveloped Jenny and she hated herself for the wave of pleasure it raised in her.

Jenny kept away from young people and was no expert on them. The girl wasn't much shorter than Jenny; might have been thirteen, might have been eighteen. She wore a leather biker jacket and an expression that was an even mixture of terror and fury. She crouched defensively, her hands extended to fight.

"It's okay," repeated Jenny. "I'm here to help."

The girl looked about wildly.

"What happened here?" said Jenny. "I don't understand. Who did this to you?"

The girl shifted and recoiled. Jenny followed her gaze. There was torchlight on the stairs.

"It's the fuzz," said Jizzimus.

Jenny fumbled for her phone. Police. She should call the police. She should have called the police a long time ago.

By the time she got the phone in her hand, the man was in the room. He was a shaven-headed Caveman with a torch in one hand and a what looked like either a Taser or an electric razor in the other. She hoped it was a razor.

"Who the fuck are you?" he growled.

Jenny backed away, struggling to find words. He came at her and slammed his torch into the side of her head. Her vision went black for a moment; she was on the floor. There was a noise, like a kettle whine. Jenny wondered if it was her scrambled brains, or the girl beginning to scream.

Jenny blinked. The man stood over her but he was looking at the girl, pointing his weapon at her and shouting. White electricity crackled at the end of the Taser.

Jenny's addled thoughts wrapped around a sudden hatred. She pointed her hand at him and flung every ounce of witchfire within her. The world turned a fiery copper green.

25

There were hands under her armpits, lifting her. And tinier hands tugging fearfully at her trousers.

The man was on the floor, rolling and hollering and clutching his burned face.

Arm in arm, supporting each other, Jenny and the teenager stumbled towards the stairs and down into the darkness.

The girl spoke only twice to Jenny that night.

The first was when she pulled at her arm as they made their way to Digbeth police station. "No police," she said.

"We need to get you help," said Jenny.

"No police," the girl insisted. She had a slight foreign accent.

"We don' trust the fuzz," said Jizzimus.

Jenny didn't have the power to argue. Her head throbbed. She was sure she could feel blood dripping from her ear. She wondered if her skull had been cracked. She waved down a taxi and they climbed in.

"Pine Walk," she said to the cabbie, gave a twenty pound note to the girl, and fell asleep on the back seat.

Jenny woke again as the taxi pulled up outside her home. The girl had Jenny's head cradled in her hand. The monstrous headache seemed to have gone.

"You'll stay with me for one night," Jenny said as they walked up the path to the front door. "Just one night. And then it's the police or the hospital or somewhere else that isn't here." She opened the door, momentarily pondering the wisdom of letting a stranger into her home. More worryingly, letting a child into her home.

She looked at the teenager. The girl was a blank, emotionless slate. Numb? Shocked? Catatonic withdrawal?

"Why did they have you in there?" Jenny asked. "What were they doing?"

The girl looked at her.

"Have you got family looking for you? Are you local?"

The girl said nothing. Jenny didn't want to have to deal with this alone.

"Cat got 'er tongue," said Jizzimus. "I know a recipe for tongue. Wiv onions."

"You need to get cleaned up," said Jenny. "Washed. You stink."

She mimed scrubbing under her armpits. The girl didn't move. Jenny turned her around and propelled her towards the bathroom. Jenny pulled towels off the rail and turned on the shower.

"I'll find you some clothes." She considered the difference between them. "Small clothes."

Only when the door was shut and she heard the girl moving about and getting undressed did Jenny retreat to the kitchen and pour herself a large glass of wine.

"A child in my home." She shook her head.

"A child of sorts," said Jizzimus. "Def'nitely going off. But wiv some onions..."

"This is a new low for me," said Jenny.

Jenny put the girl's jacket on a chair to air and found a pair of jeans and a T-shirt that wouldn't look too baggy. She made up a bed on the sofa. The girl ate the beans on toast Jenny cooked, drank the glass of water and didn't utter a word throughout. She didn't have a phone or a purse or any ID.

Eventually, Jenny began turning the lights out for the night. Part of her hoped that, when she got up the next day, the girl would be gone.

"I wish I knew who did this to you," said Jenny. "Can't you even tell me your name?"

The girl, laid out on the sofa, beneath a tartan rug, put her hands together as though in prayer but held them an inch or two apart.

"Kay," she said.

"Kay?"

"Kay Wun."

"Hi Kay. I'm Jenny."

Jenny turned off the last light and went to bed.

Jenny was woken by Jizzimus bouncing on her chest. This was not unusual.

"W'time is it?" she mumbled.

"The fuzz are 'ere," said Jizzimus.

"The what?"

Jenny was out of bed and at the window in an instant. A police car and a dark unmarked saloon had just pulled up in Pine Walk. Jenny mashed her tired face with her palms.

"How did they know?" she wondered, and shrugged. "Well, we'd have to get the authorities involved in the end."

There was a thump from downstairs and a gasp.

"Our guest is up then."

A man in a black three-quarter length coat got out of the saloon and walked over to one of the uniformed coppers. He was a big guy with a shaved head and the right side of his face had been burnt a raw pink. She had only seen him for a few seconds the night before and it had been dark, but there was no doubt in her mind.

Jenny's brain tumbled through a whole sequence of incomplete thoughts which included: *What? Who? How? Cop? Dirty cop?* and *Shit!*

"Oh, hell!"

Jenny grabbed last night's clothes from the foot of the bed. One of the uniformed cops was walking up the path. Jenny grabbed her jacket as she ran for the stairs.

"Jizzimus! We can't let them in!"

Downstairs, Kay was up, dressed and pulling on shoes.

"He's out front!" hissed Jenny. "The guy from last night!"

"How?" said Kay, alarmed.

There was a heavy thump at the door. "Miss Knott! It's the police. Open up!" A shadow moved across the gap in the curtains.

"You've got to help me!" said Kay. What was that accent? Spanish? Italian?

"Open up!" shouted the police officer.

Jenny grabbed Kay's hand and pulled her towards the kitchen.

Jizzimus, all twelve inches of him, was braced against the front door, ready for the onslaught. "I've got this!" he said.

Jenny, shoeless, opened the outer door and ran into the yard that backed onto the alley that ran down to Rectory Road. Suddenly, there was a figure in a luminous jacket and a hand on her wrist.

"Not so fast!"

Jenny spun, placed a finger on the copper's forehead and uttered three powerful syllables. The police officer fell to the ground, unconscious.

They ran, through the back gate and down the rough-paved cut-through past St Laurence's church to Rectory Road. As they turned a corner, there was a shout. Jenny's bare feet were already cut and bleeding. She decided to use that to her benefit.

She dragged Kay into the shadow of the church door, drew a semi-circle around them with her bloody foot and held Kay close.

Seconds later, a police officer and the burnt bald guy ran past towards the Northfield shopping centre.

"That was lucky," said Kay.

"Lucky, yeah," Jenny whispered.

Jizzimus came hopping and skipping across the church yard, his hooves sending up little puffs of smoke each time they touched the consecrated ground.

"Bacon-Face and the Day-Glo rozzers are gone, guv," he said.

"We have to get out of here," said Jenny and stepped out of the protective semi-circle. "We have to find somewhere to lie low."

"You've hurt your feet," Kay said to Jenny.

Jizzimus stared at his tiny smouldering hooves. "It kinda tickles. Like a footbath."

Jenny managed to hobble up to Northfield high street. There was the sound of a siren, a couple of streets away. She stopped at a cash machine. She didn't have her purse or her cards.

"Keep an eye out," she told Kay.

Jenny put her hand on the screen and muttered an incantation of opening. The machine spat out a score of banknotes. She stuffed them in a bundle into her jeans pocket.

"It's him!" said Kay.

"Where?" Jenny spun about and stumbled as the big guy, Bacon-Face, slammed into her. She rolled painfully on the pavement.

Kay cried out in pain as Bacon-Face grabbed a fistful of her hair and pulled her head down. Jizzimus scuttled up Bacon-Face's coat and bit his ear.

"What the—?" he yelled, swatting at the sudden pain.

Jenny found her feet as Kay attempted to twist out of his grip. Together, through luck, they slammed into him as one, pitched him off a high kerb and sent him sprawling into the road with Jizzimus still clinging to his head.

And they were running again. A few very early shoppers, stopped, stared and pointed. Jenny was beyond noticing or caring. She didn't even look back to see if a conveniently timed bus had run the bastard over.

They slipped and stumbled onto the high street. Hardly anywhere was open yet and they needed somewhere to hide.

Kay pushed Jenny through the door of a tiny charity shop. Jenny turned to shut the door behind them and Jizzimus came sprinting through the closing gap.

"We're not open yet," said the shopkeeper.

"She needs shoes," said Kay.

There was no sign of Bacon-Face yet. Jenny pushed Kay towards the till. The podgy woman with a dodgy perm behind the till seemed horrified by their appearance.

Jizzimus, bounding with nervous energy, ran under the clothes racks, clambered up the book shelves and ripped a poster from the wall.

"Gotta keep movin', guv," he said.

"Can I help you?" asked the shopkeeper automatically.

"Is there a back exit to this shop?" said Jenny.

The woman stared at Jenny. "Are you in trouble, poppet?" she asked.

A brochure on the counter caught Jenny's eye. She recognised the huge boxy house on the cover. Eastville Hall. Her hand went to her pocket.

"Balls!" yelled Jizzimus in sudden alarm.

The door flew open. It was Bacon-Face, perfectly alive and not squashed by a bus after all.

"Shit!" said Jenny.

The shopkeeper goggled, open-mouthed.

Jenny clenched her fist, prepared to conjure witchfire, but Kay grabbed a squeezy tube from the counter and squirted it directly into his face. And then something truly strange happened; Bacon-

Face's upper face exploded, ballooning into a candy-floss mess of enflamed tissue and distended skin. Blindly, he screamed and lurched forward, arms flailing. Kay and Jenny recoiled from his reach and he went stumbling past until a box of toys – and a helpful shove from an imp – sent him crashing to the ground.

"Oh, no, no, no, no!" cried the shopkeeper. She ran forward to help the man.

"Please," begged Jenny. "We need your help."

"What you did—!" said the shopkeeper.

"He kidnapped this girl," said Jenny.

The shopkeeper froze. "Kidnapped?"

On the floor, Bacon-Face, who now bore more than a passing resemblance to the Elephant Man, yelled and thrashed. He tried to get up and fell into another rack of clothes.

"This young woman's life is in danger," said Jenny. "Mine too, now."

Kay nodded in vigorous agreement.

"The police," suggested the shopkeeper brightly.

"He *is* the police," said Kay.

Jenny picked up the brochure on the counter. "Were you offered a place on this course?" she asked.

The shopkeeper frowned. "Um. What?"

Jenny pulled her own crumpled brochure from her pocket and held it up to show. "It starts this evening."

"I've just packed," said the shopkeeper.

"Please," said Jenny. "Please tell me you're planning to drive there."

It was a long and dull drive east, not made any better by Madison Fray's car which, as far as Caroline could tell, was made in a country which no longer existed and was held together by good karma and beaded seat covers. The car had an eight-track player and a single eight-track cartridge of the soundtrack to *Hair*. Long after Caroline was sure they should have hit the North Sea – and the fourth sing-along of *Good Morning Starshine* had made her *wish* they had hit the North Sea – they were still zigzagging through a flat landscape of tilled fields and drainage dykes wide enough and deep enough to swallow a car whole. Eventually, they passed a sign that declared it was only three miles to Eastville Hall and Luxury Spa.

"Luxury Spa?" said Caroline. "You should have definitely put that on the brochure."

"Sorry," said Madison Fray. "You're not actually in the spa area. Mrs du Plessis has given us the west wing of the house but it's just rooms. None of the Jacuzzis or whatever else it is they have in spas."

"Mrs du Plessis. Interesting name."

"Oh, they've been in the area for years," said Madison with sudden enthusiasm. "They were Huguenots, you know the ones, driven out of France centuries back because of their beliefs. Lots of them settled round here. It was them who drained the fens. If not for them, we'd be underwater right now."

"What clever people," said Caroline.

"Apparently, the locals weren't pleased. The draining of the fen killed off the fishing and duck-hunting. They drove most of the Frenchies out of the area – you know, torch and pitchfork style – but the du Plessis family held on."

He pointed ahead. A mile or more distant, a wide patch of woodland and a large building appeared out of the early evening mist.

"Eastville Hall."

It wasn't an attractive building, thought Caroline as they pulled into the long driveway. It was big, true. It had a stone façade, complete with Doric columns, gable windows and an ornately carved parapet roof. It even had a small dome towards the centre of the roof. But all these grand features had been put together with a magpie's eye. It was a stately home as envisioned by someone who had read of them but never seen one. It was neither beautiful nor grimly gothic and forbidding.

"I think it looks tacky," said Madison. "But I'm just a pleb, so what do I know?"

Madison's car puttered and sputtered past the lines of parked German saloons, Bentleys and Jags and to a long low offshoot from the main building which Caroline suspected had once been stables.

Caroline stretched as she got out. There was a salty tang to the air. She looked across the flat fields to the east and wondered how far from the sea they actually were.

"Boston, ten miles that way," said Madison, pointing. "Skegness fifteen that way. The bar is just over here."

"Read my mind," said Caroline. She passed Madison her bags and went inside.

The restaurant-cum-bar in this minor wing was correspondingly small and cosy. Three women sat together at a small table. A buffet table set out against the wall looked untouched. The dark-haired young man at the corner bar was pouring a glass of fizz.

"Prosecco, ma'am?" he said.

"Prosecco, yes. Ma'am, no," Caroline said, taking the weight off her feet at a bar stool. She took a good, long drink.

"You are welcome to join the other guests." The barman nodded towards the table of women.

"Yeah, let me get a couple of these down me first."

She put the empty glass down. The barman automatically refilled it. His hands, strong-fingered and work-worn, weren't the hands of a barman.

Madison tottered in with her bags and wearily dropped them by the bar. "Evening, George," he said.

The barman's smile for Madison was a fleeting thing.

A tall skinny woman with glasses, spiky grey hair and a computer tablet entered the bar. "At last," she said to Madison, voice frosty.

"Aunt Effie," He went to kiss her on the cheek and was wafted away.

Effie, looked at the women sat in the centre of the dining area. "Three delegates checked in," she said, displeased.

Madison looked at them. "Ah, Shazam's here."

"Sharon, Madison," corrected Effie. "Sharon Jaye. Shazam indeed!"

"I don't recognise the other two," he said.

"No?" Effie sighed. "Norma Looney there has joined us because she's been instructed to. It was either this or disciplinary action. And that graceful stick insect next to her is Sabrina Holder-

Eckford of the Cheshire Holder-Eckfords. Her mother understands the value of what we're trying to do here. And she owes me a favour."

"Right," said Madison.

"Three," said Effie, still plainly unhappy. "Hardly the basis for a grassroots revolution."

"Four," said Madison and gestured to Caroline. "This is Caroline Black."

In a heartbeat, Effie's scowl sprang into a smile of genuine warmth. "Caroline," she said, hand outstretched to shake. "Effie Fray, course co-ordinator. So glad you could make it."

"Happy to swell your numbers from an abysmal three to a positively overcrowded four."

"Quite," said Effie. "But it's not about the numbers, is it?"

Caroline smiled. "It frequently is."

"Not at all, my dear. Although if you could magic up a few more delegates, it wouldn't hurt."

"I'll see what I can do," said Caroline and downed her drink.

The double doors swung open and three women walked in.

"Ta da!" said Caroline.

The dumpy looking one in a wonky cardigan and wild curls, smiled brightly. "Are we late?" she said.

"Not at all," said Madison and closed his eyes as he tried to remember. "Dee, isn't it?"

"Dee Finch," said Effie, tapping her tablet.

"I'm Jenny Knott," said the tallest of the newcomers.

She looked mildly familiar to Caroline, although she couldn't place her and was distracted by the fact the woman was barefoot.

"And this is Kay," said Jenny, gesturing to the timid girl in the biker jacket.

"Kay?" said Effie, frowning at her screen.

"That's right," said Jenny.

"Prosecco, ladies?" said George the barman, pouring three glasses.

"Kay and I would really like to get to our rooms," said Jenny. "It's been a tough day."

Effie was still scrolling around on her tablet.

"Sure," said Madison. "I'll show you the way."

As Caroline watched Madison and the two of them leave, she didn't miss the look of concern with which Dee Finch followed them.

When they'd gone, Dee looked at the glasses of sparkling wine as though she'd just realised they were there. "I'd rather have a cup of tea," she said to George. "I'm a bit parched, poppet."

"Of course," said George.

Caroline picked up one of the untaken glasses of fizz. "Waste not, want not," she said.

Jenny shut the bedroom door, twisted the lock and threw the hinged door guard across. She felt they were as close to safe as they could possibly be. Their troubles were over a hundred miles away and – Jenny had spent most of the journey thinking about it – there was no evidence, no documents to link either of them to this place or this event. Running from the law was never going to be a long-term strategy, but Jenny was willing to take this situation three weeks at a time. All this was assuming that the course organisers or whoever would let Kay stay.

"I have to go out again," Jenny told Kay.

Kay sat, knees under chin, arms folded around her legs, on one of the twin beds. Madison had said they were welcome to a room each but Kay clung to Jenny, and Jenny also thought it for the best.

"Why?" said Kay.

"I need to make sure we can stay here."

"I don't want you to go," said Kay.

Kay found the remote for the tiny television mounted on the wall above the tea and coffee things. She tossed it onto the bed at Kay's feet. "Find something to watch. I won't be long."

Jenny went into the small en suite, scrubbed her face with soap and hot water and regarded her reflection.

"You look like shit, guv," said Jizzimus, dangling by his knees from the shower rail.

"Shut up."

"What?" called Kay.

"Nothing. Talking to myself," said Jenny.

She put a finger to her neck and peered closer at her reflection. A wart coming through. Add it to the list, she thought.

"I'll be back soon," she told Kay as she walked through the bedroom. "I'll bring some buffet snacks."

"Can I help myself to the mini bar?" said Kay.

"Do *not* help yourself to the mini bar! And take your dirty shoes off while you're on the bed. And lock the door when I've gone."

In the corridor, Jizzimus kicked tiny dents in the skirting board. "You do know you're meant'a eat 'em, not be their bloody muvver?" he said.

"Yeah?" said Jenny. "Well, while we're here, you're going to be her bodyguard."

"What?"

"Stand right there. Do not leave your post. If she leaves this room or there's the slightest sign of danger, you come find me."

Jizzimus grumbled and pouted. "Jizzimus Bentwood Flapkin didn' sign up for this."

"You didn't sign up for anything," she said. "You told me you were hatched out of a cockerel's egg laid on a murderer's grave and exist to serve me."

"But this... Should report you to my union."

"You don't have a union," she said, walking away.

"Then I'll start one!" he shouted. She didn't look back.

Jenny expected to find the course co-ordinator woman or her scruffy survey-taking lackey in the bar, perhaps looking for her and ready to ask who the strange girl was she'd brought with her, but they were nowhere to be seen and there was only the barman and the five women sat round a table together.

She asked the barman for a long stiff drink and he duly obliged.

"Free bar tonight," he said, waving away her cash.

"Then I'll be having a few more of these later." She raised her glass to him and joined the others.

"And another of our Brummie friends is here," said a middle-aged woman in practical tweed wearing a sticker on her lapel that said, *Miss Norma Looney*.

"Sorry?" said Jenny.

"I told them you'd driven over with me today," said Dee, an anxious look in her eyes as though she feared she had done wrong in telling them.

Dee knew no more now than she did when Jenny had barged into her shop that morning: two women on the run from a dangerous man; a cop. Perhaps she thought they were fleeing domestic violence. Perhaps she thought they were illegal immigrants. Dee hadn't pried and Jenny hadn't explained.

"That's right," said Jenny. "We were in Birmingham this morning."

"We were just finding out where everyone was from," said Norma.

"Didn't know if anyone was from round here," said the beautiful and slightly squiffy woman with a *Caroline* name tag.

"Ur, I should imagine," said a languorously thin creature called Sabrina, "that if anyone was 'from round here' they wouldn't be in a hurry to return."

"What about you, Cobwebs?" Caroline said to the big woman with huge cow-like eyes and a red drink with an umbrella.

The woman's name tag said *Shazam* and she'd drawn a little black cat next to it. Shazam wore a purple dress of a style that might have been in fashion a hundred, maybe a hundred and fifty years ago, with a crocheted shawl shaped like a spider's web over her shoulders and a black fur stole around her neck. Jenny guessed that Shazam was either a time-traveller, a historical re-enactor or was going through some sort of clothing-based identity crisis.

"I'm from Melton Mowbray," she said.

"Like the pork pies," said Norma.

"And it's where Stilton is made too," added Shazam proudly.

"Ur, how nice for you," said Sabrina coolly. Sabrina prefaced every utterance with a long breathy vowel as though each sentence had to be hauled up from a deep cavern of well-spoken ennui.

"Oh, that reminds me," said Dee. She dipped below the table to bring up a battered pre-war suitcase. "You needed some shoes, Jenny."

Jenny wasn't sure what aspect of pork pies or cheese reminded Dee of Jenny's feet but she didn't make a comment. Dee opened the case and lifted out two pairs of shoes.

"Pumps or mules?"

"I'm not sure you and I have the same size feet," said Caroline.

"I take a one size fits all approach at the charity shop and you'd be surprised how often it works," she said cheerfully.

"Ur, I'm not sure I could wear charity shop shoes," said Sabrina. "Or clothes. Or indeed any items that might touch the skin."

"So, 'things' then," said Caroline.

"Right. Ur, I don't believe I could buy 'things' from charity shops. It's the thought of communicable diseases, you understand."

"Can you get diseases from shoes?" asked Shazam.

"No," said Jenny firmly as she tried the pumps on.

"I always treat shoes in the shop with a spray of liquorice and wild lime," said Dee.

"Ah," said Jenny, who had been wondering why her feet smelled like Bertie Bassett.

Sabrina chortled in her now-empty glass. "Ur, liquorice and wild lime are useful against STIs and not much else."

"I beg to differ, sweetness," said Dee. "I've read that they were used in ages past for treatment of foot diseases."

"Yes. And you are aware that, in antiquity, 'diseases of the feet' was a handy euphemism for venereal disease?" said Sabrina. "Those Biblical kings weren't dying of athlete's foot, dear."

Sabrina clicked her fingers to catch the barman's attention and gestured for fresh drinks all round. Jenny wiggled her toes. The shoes were a perfect fit.

"They're great," she said.

"And," said Dee cheerily, "apparently your feet are entirely safe from syphilis and herpes, poppet."

"My mum got foot herpes," said Shazam.

"Really?" said Caroline.

"From a masseur called Carlos who she met on a package holiday in Faliraki."

"You know," said Norma stiffly, "we didn't have such things in my day."

"Package holidays?" said Shazam.

"Herpes?" said Caroline.

"Charity shops," said Norma. "Things lasted back then. Make do and mend."

"I make nearly all my own clothes," said Shazam.

Without asking, Norma leant over, took Shazam's purple dress sleeve in her hand and rubbed it critically between thumb and forefinger. She grunted and plucked at Shazam's spider web shawl. "Is it meant to have all these holes in it?"

"It's a 'look,'" said Shazam with a certain timid bravado. "And I knit all my own underwear."

"Knit?" said Jenny. "Doesn't that—?"

"—Chafe?" said Sabrina.

Norma made a disagreeable noise. "Too flimsy for my liking. That's the problem with modern clothes." She placed her hands either side of her ample, tweed-clad bosom. "Good fabric. Solid under wiring. Whalebone had its uses you know." She grasped her bra through her jacket and gave a good jiggle. "They don't make them like they used to."

Jenny wasn't sure if Norma was referring to bras, clothes in general, breasts or even possibly whales, and was starting to think that her long stiff drink had gone to her head when the barman came over with more alcohol.

"Thanks, George," said Caroline. She winked at him. "Let's move onto the cocktails after these, eh?"

"Let's move onto the cocktails after these," agreed the barman.

"So, what is this course all about then?" asked Dee.

"Ur, the usual tripe about self-improvement and self-actualisation," said Sabrina.

"I'm not doing it if there's any of that meditation nonsense," said Norma. "If I wanted to sit still with my eyes closed I could just get forty winks at home."

"Maybe it's about discovering your inner woman," said Shazam.

Norma snorted.

"Ah," said Sabrina. "Sweat lodges and running around naked in the woods."

An excited little grin burst through Shazam's lips.

"I'm game if you are," said Caroline, coyly.

"I'm all for getting back to nature," said Dee nervously, "but I'm not sure about the whole naked thing."

"Quite," said Norma.

"Doesn't matter," said Jenny.

"It doesn't?"

"Nope," said Jenny. "Any training course, whatever it is, you always judge on the quality of the catering. And the accommodation."

"I've not even checked out the buffet yet," said Shazam.

"Ur, cheese and ham sandwiches, pork pies and a dozen unlabelled variations on 'pastry surprise,'" said Sabrina.

"That sounds nice," said Shazam.

"I'm sure a sea of brown passes for a king's banquet in – where was it you were from?"

"Melton Mowbray," said Shazam, failing to spot Sabrina's dripping sarcasm.

"In my book," said Caroline, giving Sabrina a cold glare, "I judge a course by the quality of the company."

Sabrina's answering smile was brittle and hard.

"It doesn't really matter, does it?" said Dee. "This course is free. So, I'm sure we'll be happy with whatever comes our way."

"I do like free stuff," said Shazam.

Norma held up her glass and peered into its bubbly heart as she swirled it. "I predict several weeks of tedium, interspersed with pain, mud and the faint prospect of a messy death at the hands of each other."

Jenny stared at Norma, a horrible suspicion forming in her mind.

"*L'enfer, c'est les autres,*" said Sabrina.

"Well, at least it's a change of scene," said Dee. "I just hope they cope at the shop without me."

"What kind of charity shop is it?" asked Shazam.

"The Shelter for Unloved Animals," said Dee.

"I love *all* animals," said Shazam. "Although Mr Beetlebane is my absolute darling."

"Mr excuse me?" said Caroline.

"Mr Beetlebane," said Shazam and stroked the limp and patchy stole around her neck. It stretched out its claws and yawned.

"Christ it's alive!" exclaimed Caroline, sweeping several glasses off the table as she jumped back.

Sabrina leaned in with surprising speed. In a twinkle she had a bunch of glasses in her grasp with hardly a dropped spilled.

Mr Beetlebane meowed, gave each and every one of them a half-second evil eye and then curled up to sleep once more.

Jenny shook her head and sighed.

"Startled you, huh?" said Norma.

"It's not that," said Jenny wearily.

"What then?" said Dee.

She gave them a frank look. "Am I just going to have to come out and say it?"

"Say what?" said Shazam.

Jenny shook her head. "We're all bloody witches, aren't we?"

There was a long, silent moment.

"I've no idea what you're talking about, poppet," said Dee.

"As a joke it's in very bad taste," said Sabrina.

"Really?" said Jenny. "You just cast a restorative charm on those glasses *and* you clearly know your herb lore better than Dee."

"I only know what I read in books," said Dee.

"Yes, but you have an uncanny ability to conjure clothes that fit perfectly."

"Mere conjecture," said Norma.

"Says the woman who actually just did a fortune-telling in prosecco dregs. Impressive, by the way."

Norma couldn't help but give a prim but incriminating "Thank you."

"Shazam," said Jenny.

"I'm not a witch."

"You're called Shazam, for one. It's one step away from Bibbidi-Bobbidi-Boo. You have a black cat. You actually dress like a witch."

"This is purple. Witches dress in black."

"You dress like a purple witch. All you're missing is the pointy hat."

"It's in the car," murmured Shazam.

"Witches, huh?" said Caroline.

"Don't think I didn't spot it," said Jenny. "You had the bar chap completely under your spell."

"I don't need magic to do that," said Caroline.

"But it doesn't hurt to use a little I bet."

Caroline gave a little harrumph. "And what's your party piece then?"

"Staying one step ahead of everyone else in the room," said Jenny.

No one spoke for a good few seconds and then Dee said, "I think that answers our question about what this course is all about."

"Ur, I'm sure there's not much you can teach me about witchcraft," said Sabrina.

"We'll ask them to keep it simple for you," said Caroline. "No witch left behind."

Shazam giggled and then apologised to Sabrina.

"I've been around the block a few times myself," said Norma. "I know Effie Fray of old and she's no guru. You'll need to get up pretty early in the morning to teach me something about the craft I don't already know."

"And speaking of getting up early," said Jenny, pushing her chair back.

"Really?" said Caroline. "It's not even nine."

"It's been a long day," said Jenny. Like a switch flipped, she suddenly wanted to cry.

Dee touched Jenny's arm; that only made it worse. "Sleep well, poppet."

Jenny turned away quickly and then realised she had not taken any food back for Kay.

"Buffet!" she declared loudly to dispel her tears, and piled a plate high with unidentifiable brown food things.

She took deep calming breaths as she walked down the corridor to their rooms. Jizzimus was outside the bedroom door as instructed, practising break dance moves.

"Good evening, guard-imp," said Jenny and threw him a buffet nugget which he caught in his thorn-like teeth. "How has she been?"

"Quiet as a church mouse that's bin poisoned and then stabbed, vicious-like," said Jizzimus.

"Good."

Jenny entered the room and almost dropped the food when she saw that the room and Kay's bed in particular appeared to be empty. A moment later she saw the sheets and bed cover down the side of the bed. Kay had wedged herself into the space on the floor between the bed and the radiator, almost managing to slide under the bed. She was asleep, arms wrapped around her.

"Are you gunna eat that?" said Jizzimus.

Jenny looked at him, unsure if he was referring to the buffet food or the sleeping girl. Both appeared appetising but Jenny knew she would regret it either way. She might have had little to eat that day and too much to drink but unidentifiable room temperature buffet was rarely a good choice.

She put the plate down, undressed silently and slipped into the other bed.

"You smell like Bertie Bassett," said Jizzimus.

"Long story," said Jenny.

She lay in the dark and stared at the ceiling, knowing that sleep wouldn't come soon enough.

Her feet smelled of liquorice but the room itself was filled with the enticing chocolate smell of a young woman, clinging to the last vestiges of childhood. The smell – bitter, edging towards sour – was distracting and unnerving.

"Do not help yourself to the mini bar," she muttered to herself.

"Can't sleep?" said Jizzimus.

"No."

"Could perform my latest rap for you."

"No thanks."

"It's got a funkload of swears in it."

"I doubt it will help," said Jenny and turned over.

# Chapter 2 – The Witches of Eastville

Jenny approached breakfast the next morning with some concern. Meals in general were a concern. If anyone was going to spot her difficulties with iron, it would be other witches, and cutlery was a daily problem. She relaxed somewhat when she realised breakfast was a buffet style arrangement.

"Morning," said Dee. She was tucking into a bowl of porridge topped with everything the breakfast bar had to offer. Marshmallows and chocolate chips jostled for position on a mountain of sunflower seeds and blueberries.

Jenny sat down beside her. "Morning."

"Where's Kay?" asked Dee.

"Still asleep. Yesterday was a long day," said Jenny. She ripped into her croissant hungry.

"She's very young," Dee said. "I get kids her age in the shop sometimes. It's good training if they want to work in retail. Most of them spend at least a week trying to hide in the stock room so they don't have to interact with the public. I can't imagine how she must be feeling, knowing she's here on a course with a load of witches."

Jenny looked down at her plate and sighed, searching for the right way to frame her answer. "Um, about that..."

Dee's eyes widened. "Oh my goodness. She still doesn't know? How could she not know? It's going to come up some time soon. Very soon. Oh dear. Do you think she'll be allowed to stay when the organisers realise she isn't a witch?"

"I don't know," said Jenny. "I'll think of something, I just need to keep a careful eye on her today."

"We both will, poppet," said Dee. "You don't have to do everything on your own."

Their first training session was in a separate building on the far side of grass covered rear grounds. When the seven of them were gathered after breakfast, Madison led them across misty lawns.

Eastville Hall's front aspect overlooked a large and busy garden, but to the rear it commanded a view of a lawn so vast that one might be tempted to call it a paddock, if it had any horses, or a field, if it wasn't so well kept. Over a hundred metres wide, the lawn ran several hundred metres towards a long, brutally maintained hedge lined with beehives. Beyond, a patchwork of fields stretched away to the not so distant sea. The enormous garden was home to a row of greenhouses, two ponds, a small copse, a row of neatly spaced sheds which looked like misplaced beach huts, and their destination.

Madison guided them into a round building: low and slightly decrepit looking, conceivably built as a large summer house, albeit by someone who hated summer and wanted to hide from it. They took their seats in a room which had been arranged as a classroom but looked as though its day job was storing things too shabby for the main house. Garden furniture cluttered one corner. A sad pile of mildewed books and board games gathered dust in another. A flip chart on which was a series of drawings was the only new and dust-free item in the room. The chairs were made of military green tubular steel with canvas seats and, despite their shabbiness, were surprisingly comfy.

Jenny made sure Kay stayed close and generally away from the other witches.

"It looks like our first activity is pin the tail on the donkey," said Caroline with a raised eyebrow. The first diagram certainly looked like an oddly deformed horse.

"I've seen that horse in the Unloved Animals calendar," said Dee. "All sorts of animals end up there."

Jenny tried not to look at Jizzimus as he perched on the flipchart and scrutinised the drawing.

"If I'm honest guv, this needs some improvement. Shall I give it a massive willy or what?"

Jenny stared past him, at Shazam, who had pulled out a small jacket against the cool of the room. It looked as if it had been made by hand, in her trademark black and purple, but the fabric had a curious tufted appearance.

"Ur, what is that ... jacket made from?" asked Sabrina.

"Is it chenille?" said Dee.

"I knitted it myself from acrylic," said Shazam, with a proud smile, "but I wove in cat hair from Mr Beetlebane for added warmth. And to capture his, you know, spirit."

Sabrina pulled a face. "It certainly does that."

"Does spirit mean smell?" Kay whispered to Jenny.

Jenny shushed her. "Best behaviour," she said. "Here comes the course leader. Behave and everything will be fine."

Kay looked baffled. "Why wouldn't it be fine?"

Jenny gripped her hand and wished that wicked witches could pray.

Effie Fray moved to the head of the room and beamed at everyone. She'd dressed in a style that seemed consciously quirky. Red Converse baseball boots, a long corduroy skirt, and a Led Zeppelin T-shirt.

"Hello everyone. The first morning of the course proper and I can't tell you how excited I am to have you all together like this. I'll explain a little bit about what we're all doing here, we'll do some sharing around the room, and then we'll spend most of the day on our first practical exercise."

"Googly eyes and an 'at then, boss?" suggested Jizzimus, capering around the flip chart, pointing at the unfortunate equine. "Go on, we'll all need a laugh if this old windbag's gunna keep on like this."

"First of all," continued Effie, "you'll be fascinated to know what you all have in common. It may surprise you, so we'll take things slowly. I don't want to upset anyone. Just remember: we're in a safe environment here."

She moved towards the flip chart. "Let's consider this diagram for a moment. Anyone know what it is?"

"A poor hard-working pony that got stuck in a thresher," said Dee. "He was within a whisker of being put down, but the Shelter for Unloved Animals stepped in and paid the vet's bills. It's a good news story because he got a lovely new forever home when his wounds were healed, and now he's just left with those scars."

Effie was silent for a moment. "Thank you, Dee. An oddly specific guess, but wrong. Anybody else? Yes, Sharon?"

"Shaz—"

"Yes, *Sharon*?"

"Is it a quagga?" asked Shazam.

"It is indeed!" said Effie with clear delight. "What do we know about quaggas, hmmm?"

"Half horse, half zebra, now extinct," said Sabrina.

"Well, the quagga was a distinct subspecies, but that will do. The key word there is 'extinct'. How do we suppose they got that way?"

"Did they all die?" asked Norma. Jenny could see no trace of sarcasm, but perhaps Norma had mastered the art of keeping a straight face.

"Well yes, they did," said Effie, both pointedly and pointlessly. "But what caused it?"

"Did they all get hunted by tooled-up Victorians?" asked Jenny.

"Yes, that's right," said Effie. "Plus they captured some to put in zoos and menageries. Of course, when it was too late, the last remaining specimens were few and far between; isolated in various collections. They died alone and miserable, probably not even knowing that other quaggas existed."

Dee sniffed loudly and dabbed at her eyes. "Poor souls."

"Yes, poor souls indeed," said Effie. "Now let's move on to what the quagga has to do with us. What if I were to tell you—"

"Is this where you tell us we're all witches?" asked Caroline.

Effie's face underwent a minor malfunction as her thunder was stolen.

"We already know," added Norma haughtily.

"Witches?" whispered Kay. Her head whipped around to inspect the women.

Jenny squeezed the girl's hand tighter.

"Goodness me," said Effie. "And how did that come to light?"

"Little Miss Brainiac over here worked it out," said Caroline, indicating Jenny.

Effie smoothed her skirts and looking thoughtfully at Jenny for a moment. She cleared her throat and addressed them all. "Well that does save us some time. You've obviously all accepted it and taken it in your stride. Very good news."

"Witches," Kay breathed to herself.

"So let's compare witches with quaggas."

"Both hunted by Victorians?" suggested Dee.

"Both got a taste for 'orse dong?" suggested Jizzimus.

"Extinction," said Sabrina.

"Exactly," said Effie. "Witches are in danger of extinction. We have lived in isolation for too many years."

"Are you going to *breed* from us?" asked Shazam, her face alight with both horror and excitement.

"Easy there, Cobwebs," murmured Caroline.

"Oh dear me, no. No! That isn't what this is all about. What? No!" A flustered Effie fanned herself with her notes. "The thing that threatens our existence is ignorance. Ignorance and isolation. Witches are naturally secretive. We like to stay below the radar. The way to fight back against our global and national decline is simply to get together to share what we know and support each other. I guarantee that everyone in this room will know something that all of the others don't. We can learn from each other and maximise our potential."

"I can maximise anything me," yelled Jizzimus, grabbing his crotch and thrusting across the floor in front of Effie. "They should all get a load of me doing my sexy-dance. Tell 'em about it boss, go on!"

Jenny ignored him. Her mental attention was entirely focused on the poor teenager beside her. What was Kay thinking right now?

"Maximising our potential?" asked Sabrina. "Ur, specifically?"

"Well, as we move through the course, we will all explore the different aspects of witchcraft," said Effie. "We can exchange knowledge; hone our skills and share the journey towards becoming a better witch. At the end of the course I hope to be able to guide you all on your next steps out in the world."

Jenny was thoughtful, trying to ignore Jizzimus who had taken the word steps as a cue to change his routine. Somewhere between goose stepping and twerking, and it wasn't pretty. She was happy to stay here for three weeks. Learning some new tricks could be handy, and she looked forward to the peace and quiet of a learning environment. The sooner she thought of somewhere safe for Kay, away from those who would harm her – which included Jenny on some level – the sooner she could relax.

Norma Looney made a facetious noise. "Next steps out into the world, Effie? Witching school?"

"Nothing as ... didactic as that, Norma. The coming three weeks are about learning from each other and providing support *for those who need it*." These last words were said with a hard emphasis that silenced Norma.

"I should mention the generosity of our sponsor at this point," said Effie with renewed cheeriness. "Mrs du Plessis is delighted to be supporting the advancement of witchcraft in a practical manner by extending to us the use of some rooms in her lovely house and grounds. She herself is very busy with the running of her spa business so it's unlikely that we'll see her during the course of her stay, but we should all remain grateful to her."

"Is she a witch too?" asked Caroline.

"Yes ," said Effie, "although she has carved out a niche for herself in the spa business, rather than hands-on witchcraft. She fully supports our endeavours, though."

"Wait up!" said Jizzimus, springing up from where he was lolling on an old tennis net. "Aren' spas the kinda gaffs that have naked people in them? You know: massages, wibbly flesh, baby oil and whatnot? I think I might have to go an' 'ave a quick butchers. See what goes on up there. Try not to fall asleep wivout me entertainin' you. And remember, 'orse or quagga, it still needs a massive cock and balls. You owe it to yourself to liven this party up a bit."

With that, he scampered through the doorway.

"Right, let's get straight into some sharing, shall we?" said Effie, reaching into a box which was near to the flip chart, and drawing out a grey feather. With a clap, she crushed it. Abruptly, there was a ball of fire in her hands.

Jenny leaned close to Kay. "It's okay," she assured the girl. "Just a trick."

"A bloody good one," said Kay.

"The Bennu's Spontaneous Eldritch Light," said Sabrina knowingly.

"Phoenix fire," said Norma.

"Madison had it on his hat when I met him," said Shazam.

"I just thought his hat was on fire," said Dee.

"When I throw it at you," said Effie, "you need to tell us all something about your experiences of being a witch. Here goes!" She pitched the flaming sphere at her audience.

Sabrina caught it and smiled. She tossed it lightly in one hand, like captain of the netball team.

"Ur, I was born into a witching family, as you know, so I've always had a clear sense of my place in the world. I had a governess who was a local witch, so I think I have a good broad appreciation of the craft. I didn't just restrict myself to the classical texts in our family library, although we do have one of the finest collections." She smiled around at them. "I'd be very happy to welcome any of you to one of the oldest and most noble houses of witchcraft. Mother's very keen." She looked at Shazam. "Ur, phone first."

Sabrina threw the flaming sphere at Shazam. She looked thrilled to be next up, but spent a moment or two with a worried frown, keeping the flames away from her cardigan.

"Sharon." Effie was patient. "The flame won't set anything else on fire."

"Oh. Good. Right. Well I always felt drawn to the Dark Arts as my mother used to call them. She got very cross with me if she caught me reading about the occult. Or true life crime. Or celebrity marriages. Anyway, it wasn't until I did a test on the internet that I really knew for sure that I was a witch. Up until then I just thought I had a way with animals."

"A test on the internet?" Effie raised an eyebrow.

"The internet!" huffed Norma, as though the word conjured up all that was wrong in the world.

"Yes, the *What Kind of Witch are You?* test. I expect you've all done it. I'm an *All Powerful Child of Diana* apparently. I have an affinity with animals and I am guided by the moon."

"Is that so?" said Effie politely.

"I bought the amulet so that other witches will know which sort I am," she said, fishing a crescent pendant from deep within her ample bosom. She held it up for them all to see.

"The website with the *What Kind of Witch are You?* test. Was it the same website that had the amulets for sale?" asked Jenny.

"Yes. And this bracelet. And this ring. Oh, and the herb hunter wall chart," said Shazam. "They have some great deals. There's a flash sale on crystal balls coming up. You should all take a look."

Jenny looked at Shazam, seeing the muddle of insecurities and a desperate need to find her people. Jenny had her own problems, but she'd never had the craving to belong. She was curious. *Were* these her people? It really didn't feel as if there was much that connected them. The flaming globe was tossed to Caroline.

"Yeah, I'm not sure what I want to say. I didn't do a test like Cobwebs here. I've been a witch all my life but it's not *who* I am."

"Then what are you?" asked Sabrina.

"I'm a people person," said Caroline. "People tend to do what I want them to. I used to think it was because I was charming and persuasive,; then I realised I could be persuasive without being charming. I'm a bit of a master, if I'm honest with you."

"And are you?" asked Sabrina.

"What?"

"Honest."

"Less often than you'd think."

"Thank you, Caroline," said Effie. "Remind me to talk about ground rules in a few minutes."

Caroline gave her an easy smile and tossed the flaming ball sideways to Jenny.

*I'm a wicked witch. I first realised I was a witch when I blighted my geography teacher's hair in revenge for a poor essay grade, causing him to go bald overnight. On my fifteenth birthday, I got my first wart, my own imp and a Celine Dion CD; I still have the imp. Nowadays, I spend much of my time avoiding children and trying not to blast things with witchfire.*

Jenny spoke none of that aloud. Instead she said, "I'm afraid I don't have any interesting stories to tell. I grew up with some unusual abilities, and worked out that it wasn't just puberty. I can't say that I've ever managed to use them for anything earth-shattering, it's just part of who I am."

She quickly threw the sphere to Dee, wanting to avoid any more exposure than was necessary.

"You dint mention me, guv! Shall I get the ball back so's you can say you've got the sexiest imp in these parts? Or any parts! Get a load of my parts!"

Jenny raised her eyes to the ceiling, thankful that only she had witnessed Jizzimus's return.

"They should be 'ad up, calling that a spa. No naked babes. No naked anybody, just some borin' dance class in the swimmin' pool and some chicks in peep'ole underwear."

Jenny's concerted effort to avoid looking at Jizzimus failed. Her eyes formed the question she was burning to ask.

"Oh. Maybe I mean paper underwear. Yeah paper. Sorry guv," Jizzimus dissolved into raucous laughter.

Jenny returned her attention to Dee.

"Yup, mended things since I was this high. I had five little brothers so things were always getting broken. I hate to see anybody upset, so if I can do a discreet little fix for someone to put the smile back on their face then I do. Animals as well, I can't bear to see our furry friends in distress. I did go too far when I was very young, mind. I fixed the tail on a neighbour's new cat, but nobody told me that Manx cats don't have a tail. I thought he looked better."

Dee looked as if she had many more things to tell but thought better of it and passed the charm to Norma.

Norma looked at the flaming orb. "Is this how we have discussions these days? Whatever happened to people simply talking?"

"It's just a fun way to help us make sure everyone gets involved," said Effie. "Why don't you tell us about yourself, Norma?"

"You know all about me, Effie," said Norma archly. "As for the rest of you, all you need to know is that I've been around the block when it comes to witching. Don't mind telling you it can be tough out there, but a good solid knowledge of herbs should always serve you well."

Jizzimus chortled loudly. "Sounds like somebody's got somethin' to hide! What do you reckon it is? Let's beat it out of 'er later. Think she murdered that sheep wiv 'er bare hands so she could pinch its coat?"

Jenny tried not to smile. Norma's bulky Aran cardigan did look like an entire sheep's worth. Jenny saw Norma stand up and carefully place the sphere into Kay's hands. Jenny was already leaning over, preparing to create some sort of diversion when Kay started to speak.

"I once accidentally blew up a cow," she said.

Jenny could hear her own jaw drop. Kay looked around with a shy half-smile.

"Oh Kay, surely you mean—" Effie stalled, opening and shutting her mouth with a frown. "What exactly *do* you mean?"

"I was trying to help," said Kay. Jenny still couldn't identify her faint accent. "The cow had intestinal gas, and the vet was going to perforate its stomach to let it out. I thought that sounded horrible, so I made the gas go out all in one go. I didn't really know what that would look like. I was only eight."

The room was momentarily stunned. Jenny assumed they were all processing the double whammy of hearing Kay speak for the first time and trying to picture a cow actually exploding. Jenny didn't know what to say. It was a ridiculous assertion, but it was so ridiculous as to be faintly plausible. People will believe a big lie sooner than a little one.

Effie gently took the sphere from Kay.

"Right, that was lovely. Thank you all for sharing. We've all learned something there."

"Sure," said Caroline. "Sabrina's open to house parties. Cobwebs here can fit the moon down her cleavage. Brainiac's hit puberty. Norma's been around the block a few times. The teenage wonder has a thing for bovine demolition but Dee could probably put it back together again if she wanted."

"And you have a big mouth," said Sabrina smoothly.

"Big and beautiful," agreed Caroline.

"Okay," said Effie, blithely. "I think we need to get stuck right into something practical if we're all to really get to know each other. You'll be pleased to know that it's a hands-on problem, and you'll get out into the fresh air as well."

"'S not fresh out there, I've seen to that," said Jizzimus, raising a buttock cheek and letting rip in case Jenny wasn't keeping up.

"I'm going to divide you into two teams and you'll spend the rest of the day on this," Effie continued. "The task is simple. There is an amulet for each team, hidden in the local area. You'll need to locate it with a mixture of witchcraft, common sense and teamwork."

Effie counted each point off on her fingers with exaggerated movements. "You'll hear me talk about those things a lot, because one of the barriers we're trying to break down here is the old-fashioned image of the witch being a loner. It's my firm belief that in the modern world we can learn from other industries and apply sound principles of collaborative working, so it's key to the success of this task that you work together. You will almost certainly need to leave the grounds to succeed at this challenge. By the way, the grounds are entirely at our disposal. There are some outbuildings that we might use when we move on to some private study, but we must not enter the stable yard along the other side of the house. Some of the buildings there are not safe."

"An unstable stable?" smirked Caroline.

"Quite."

"Is it a stable or isn't it?" asked Shazam.

"The stable is not stable in the sense of a building that won't fall on you, Sharon," said Effie. "Right, let's form those teams. Dee, Caroline and Jenny, over here. Norma, Sabrina, Sharon and Kay over here."

There was a scraping of chairs as everyone stood and shuffled to their side of the room. Jenny approached Effie and spoke to her in a whisper.

"Can I suggest a swap? How about we have Kay on this team and move Caroline onto the other team?"

"Oh lovely!" said Caroline. "I can't wait to work with you either."

"Ears like a bat, that one," said Jizzimus, echoing Jenny's thoughts.

Effie was firm. "You will remain in the teams that I have allocated." She held up two sheets of what Jenny thought was glossy paper. "I'm going to give each team a piece of parchment. You need to work out how it's going to help you. Shouldn't take more than a couple of hours. Meet back in the annexe restaurant for lunch."

Kay took a sheet for her group. Jenny tried to reach out to her, whisper some words of advice or comfort before she was abandoned to the other witches, but Effie slotted the sheet for Jenny's group into her outstretched hand. It was a piece of genuine aged parchment, sealed in plastic laminate. Kay turned away and the words never came.

"Good luck," said Effie. "One team can use the breakout area to study the paper, so you can discuss your plans in private." Effie waved at what looked like a cupboard door.

Dee opened the door. It was a cupboard, containing a wooden tea trolley. Caroline flicked the light switch. Jenny squeezed in with them, placing the laminate on top of the trolley. Jizzimus scampered in and she shut the door.

"Hmmm. Interesting," she said, staring at the parchment.

"I've got no idea either," said Caroline.

"Who knows where to start with this old fashioned writing?" Jenny muttered. "I'm not even sure I can read the words. Most of the letters look like *f*s."

They all peered closely. The original parchment was damaged in parts, and faded in others. The lettering was all present, but written in a dense and difficult style that made Jenny recall school lessons long ago when their English teacher made them study Chaucer.

"That first word is definitely *herb*," said Dee, poking a finger at it. "There's a little picture of a plant as well. So *herb*. I'm not too sure after that."

Jizzimus was rootling through the junk at the back of cupboard. "Let me know if you need a parasol, boss," came his voice, "or a wasp's nest, or a strimmer."

"Strimmer?" said Jenny before she could stop herself.

"You can see the word *strimmer*? asked Dee.

Jenny coughed. "Of course not. Let's see which letters we can work out, eh? Shall we start with those and see if we can make out any more of the words? Let's start with *h* shall we? There seem to be quite a few and those are clear." Jenny found a dog-eared notepad on a shelf and laid out a series of blanks interspersed with the occasional *h*.

"Ooh, I love a game of hangman," said Dee. "Tell you what, I think I can see which letter is *e* now I've looked at it for a few minutes, shall we add those in?"

Twenty minutes later they had written out a series of words that almost made sense.

"I'm still not sure *quotheth* is a word," said Dee.

Jenny and Caroline wiped spit from their faces, while Jizzimus sang the word over and over again in his own game of tongue-waggling karaoke.

"I think we assume that it is and try to glean something about the meaning," said Jenny. "Let's run it through as best we can. From the top." She cleared her throat.

"*Herb coney bane that merry is I spied,*
*When follow'd I the hag at end of day.*
*So slily in a ditch she gan it hide,*
*With fayryye wondrous wise to light the way.*"

"Oh, now you've said it out loud, I get it," said Caroline. "It's fairy. Like magic I suppose. I thought it was fay rye. Yeah, carry on."

Jenny continued.

"An amulet full layne in privity!
Here quotheth not a word for man to find
The place in which this thing ylodged be,
To all but worthy woman shall be blind."

"Wow, it sounds like a poem when you read it out," said Dee.

"It is a poem," said Caroline. "Just not a very helpful one."

"No it's not," said Dee. "Coney Bane is one of the old names for Pied Deadnettle."

"I was so about to say the same thing," said Caroline, deadpan.

"But it's really rare in England," said Dee. "We'll never find any of that."

"What?" said Jenny. "You mean it's a plant? Surely then if we find the plant then the amulet's close by? What sort of place does it grow in?"

"It's associated with boggy ditches," said Dee. "We just need to look around and find some of those."

Caroline and Jenny stared at her for a long moment.

"Dee, we're in the fens," said Jenny. "You'd be hard pressed to walk a hundred yards without seeing a boggy ditch."

"Oh. Right. We'll just have to use our noses then," said Dee. "It's a very pretty plant but smells like a week old corpse. Used as a contraceptive in years gone by."

"Was it effective?" asked Jenny.

"If it makes you smell like a week old corpse," said Caroline, "what do you think?"

"Well, let's go take a look."

They trooped out of the cupboard. The other group had already left.

"There are some wellies by the front door if you need to borrow them," chimed Effie. "Best of luck."

As they stomped across the muddy field, each of them sniffed the air. Dee led the way: the only one who stood a chance of spotting the herb.

"Shall we try a finding spell?" she suggested, pleased to be in a position to do something practical.

"Finding spell?" said Caroline.

"Yes."

"Never needed one of those," Caroline smirked. "The things I want tend to be available when I need them."

"A finding spell—" Dee was saying.

"And by 'things' you mean 'people'?" said Jenny.

"You see, we could—"

"Well, yes," admitted Caroline. "That's where my talents lie, after all."

"I've noticed," said Jenny. It occurred to her that they'd been ignoring Dee. She looked at the third witch. "Finding spells?"

"Well," said Dee, finding herself with the metaphorical floor. "We need to conjure the thing we're after. Really concentrate on it. Picture it in your minds—"

"But we don't know what it looks like," said Jenny.

"A bit like a broad bean plant."

"Nope," said Caroline. "Don't know what one of those looks like either."

Dee sighed. "Stumpy thing with perky leaves and black and white flowers. Got that?"

Caroline and Jenny nodded.

"Now think of the smell. Week old corpse. Really stinky. Hold all of that in your mind while I make the sigils." Dee murmured something softly under her breath as she made a complicated set of movements in the air with her hands. "Right. If there's any within half a mile or so, we should see a faint glow in its direction."

They all scanned the horizon.

"Is that the sun or is that glow?" asked Caroline, indicating.

"The sun's over there," Jenny pointed out. "Maybe we should go and take a look."

The ground was very muddy underfoot, and the field they were crossing had recently been ploughed. It was hard work to cover what had originally looked a short distance. Dee was encouraged to see that the glow was getting brighter.

"How did you learn that spell?" asked Caroline.

"Self-taught," said Dee.

"Rubbish! What about the spell words and those gestures?"

Dee sighed. "If you must know, it's just my own little ritual that gets me into the right frame of mind. I sing the chorus to *Fixer Upper* and draw the bendy thing from the album cover of *Tubular Bells*. It works for me."

"*Fixer* what-what?" said Jenny.

"It's from *Frozen*," said Dee. "It's kinda catchy."

"If you're a seven year old girl with a princess complex," agreed Caroline.

"Don't be mean," said Jenny.

"Sorry," said Caroline. "I'll ... *Let It Go*."

Jenny groaned and the trio plodded on.

"You know what I can't imagine," said Caroline.

"How you don't get bigger laughs with your killer material?" Jenny replied.

"I can't imagine coming from a family where magic and witchcraft are openly talked about."

It took Jenny a moment. "Ah, like the Holder-Eckfords, you mean."

"I bet tea time at Sabrina's is all about cursing the cucumber sandwiches to make the edges curl up."

"Touch of envy there, Caroline?" Jenny asked.

"Envious of posh gits with a silver spoon shoved up their arse?"

"I think it's a silver spoon in the mouth," said Jenny.

"You're right," said Dee.

"It's up the arse?" said Caroline.

"No, it's weird that some people didn't have to discover witching for themselves. Adolescence is hard enough when you have no clue what's going on in your life. I learned not to ask questions when I figured out other people couldn't do the same things."

"Oh, I never considered it a problem," said Caroline. "More of a gift."

"I think I must have worried for us all then," said Dee. "I was about thirteen when I put two and two together. I spent a lot of time in the library, reading up on superstitions surrounding witches. Gave myself the heebie jeebies, I can tell you."

"You didn't believe all of those things about running water and spinning wheels did you," said Caroline.

"Why wouldn't I? It's like all those ridiculous myths you hear in the playground about sex."

"Like you can't get pregnant standing up," said Jenny.

"Or the first time," said Caroline.

"Or if you sneeze after doing it."

"Or that it's actually medically damaging if a guy doesn't get any."

"Ha! The old blue balls thing," smiled Jenny.

"Although, it did happen to Dean Morley."

"Dean Morley?"

Caroline gazed into the distance. "Wouldn't take a hint. Wouldn't let it go. Took a Doc Marten to the goolies to explain what 'no' means."

"*Anyway*," said Dee, feeling her point had been diverted long enough, "I was all over the place, trying to figure out what was true and what was false. I was supposed to go on a school trip to France and I faked appendicitis to get out of it." She exhaled heavily at the memory.

"What were you frightened of?" asked Caroline.

"I don't know. Turning to dust. Bursting into flames. Faking appendicitis seemed only sensible."

"But what did you tell them when you got to the hospital?" Jenny asked.

"What could I tell them? That I had faked the whole thing because I'm a witch and I was afraid of crossing running water? No. I had my appendix out."

"Oh no, Dee, that's terrible," said Jenny, failing to conceal her smile.

"Wasn't my last trip to the hospital either," said Dee. "That same summer I tried to learn to fly a broomstick. I knew by then how crucial it is to really picture what you want to do; really feel it. I was convinced that if I jumped off somewhere high and I *felt* the wind rushing past me, and *felt* the broomstick lifting me through the air then the magic would kick in and I'd be flying."

They'd all stopped walking. Caroline stared at Dee. "I've never heard of witches flying," she said. "Is it possible?"

"No," said Dee. "I sprained my ankle jumping off the shed. Followed it up with two broken arms when I jumped out of a bedroom window."

"One experiment wasn't enough."

"Well, the first time wasn't exactly with a broomstick..."

"No?" said Caroline.

"Vileda SuperMop. Second time, I saved up my pocket money for a real hawthorn and birch besom broom." Dee's eyes glazed as she took her own turn looking back. "It's no fun breaking both your arms. Gives you a lot of thinking time. Too much thinking time. I came up with the idea that manmade structures didn't have the right energy, so for my last attempt I jumped out of a huge oak tree. Broke my leg that time."

They all stood for a moment before Dee turned away and stomped ahead. "Come on, let's get on with the task in hand!"

"It's the other side of that hedge," said Jenny. "Shall we walk round it?"

They looked at the thick hedge stretching into the distance on either side.

"I can't see a way round it," said Caroline.

"Only one thing for it then," said Dee. "We'll need to go through. A stout stick and a determined attitude should do the trick."

"Is there a spell for making a hole in a hedge?" Caroline asked.

"I don't know one," said Dee. "If there was a wicked witch around she could blast a hole with witchfire."

"Witchfire?" said Caroline.

"Wicked witches?" said Jenny in a disbelieving tone.

"No such thing," said Caroline.

"There are," said Dee.

"Says the woman who jumped off the shed on a kitchen mop."

"Experiences which have made me sceptical of witch lore. But I do believe wicked witches are real."

"And you don't mean just, like, witches who park in disabled spaces, or put random apostrophes before the letter *s*?"

"No. I mean bad-to-the-bone, hardwired-into-their-genes wickedness."

"None of this is helping us get through this hedge," Jenny pointed out.

Caroline ignored her. "So – what? Green skin, warts on their noses, cackling and building gingerbread houses?"

"No, nothing so silly as that," said Dee, thinking back on some of the accounts she'd read. "They have demon familiars, and eat innocent virgins, and—"

"Bollocks," said Caroline.

"Oh, I don't think so," Jenny interrupted. "Is this stick stout enough?"

Dee looked at the twig in Jenny's hand and the dense hedge in front of them. She approached it tentatively, shaking her head. "Could be scratchy."

"Like a drunken bitch with four inch nails who thinks you're trying to steal her boyfriend," said Caroline.

"Nice simile," said Jenny.

"Thank you."

"I wonder if we could just stomp through with our wellies?"

"Let's give it a go," said Dee. "How hard can it be?"

They all plunged into the prickly hawthorn with various noises of discomfort.

"As a rule of thumb," said Dee conversationally, her cheek starting to drip blood, "the age of a hedge in centuries is equivalent to the number of species in a ten yard stretch. Which makes this a fairly young one. It's pure hawthorn."

"Well that's just great," muttered Caroline. "Does anybody know how to untangle hair when you can't use your hands?"

"I think we just need to move forward," said Jenny. "I've already lost a pocket off my jacket."

"I think I've lost a pint of blood."

Fifteen minutes later they were on the other side. They collapsed onto an expanse of grass, comparing the damage the hedge had inflicted on them and their clothing.

Dee scrambled to her feet and looked around. It was very different to the ploughed field. Everything was carefully tended and organised into separate planting areas. Some plots were bare, but most had vigorous and well cultivated plants growing in neat, well-spaced rows.

Jenny stood next to her "Are we in an allotment? I have this horrible feeling I know what we've found."

All three of them walked forward to where the glow was perfectly clear. It hovered in an ethereal, misty green cloud over a set of plants in a central plot.

"We found broad bean plants, didn't we?" asked Caroline, hand on hips. "We pictured them and we found them. Bloody hell!"

"I don't understand why the smell part didn't work." Dee was plaintive. "Broad beans don't smell like a week old corpse."

Caroline looked sheepish. "I'm going to put my hand up here. I don't know what a week old corpse smells like."

"Nor me," admitted Jenny.

"Right, dears," said Dee. "I see. We need to start again. This is obviously not where the amulet is."

"While we're on the subject of things that we don't understand," said Caroline. "What *exactly* does an amulet look like?"

"Well, it's a sort of pendant," said Jenny. "Isn't it?"

"I don't think so," said Dee. "An amulet doesn't have to be worn around the neck."

"So, it's just any kind of talisman," said Caroline.

"No, poppet. Talismans aren't amulets. Well – all amulets are talismans but not all talismans are amulets." Dee frowned. "I think."

"So, it could be a brooch," said Jenny. "Or a bracelet."

"Shazam said that her keyring was an amulet," offered Caroline.

"That'd be the one from gullible-wannabe-witches.com."

"Oh, leave poor Cobwebs alone," said Caroline.

"You've got a soft spot for her," Dee noted.

"You're not the only one who takes pity on dumb, defenceless animals."

Jenny let out a long, exasperated huff. "To clarify. We don't know where this amulet is."

"Correct," said Dee.

"Or what it looks like."

"Correct."

"Or indeed what form it might possibly take."

"Indeed."

"And when we do find it, we probably won't know we've found it."

"Um..."

Jenny threw her hands up in the air. "That's it. I quit."

"What?" said Caroline. "We've barely started. And look what we've achieved."

Dee looked at their mud-spattered, liberally torn clothes and scratched faces. Even with her usual cheery optimism she struggled to find much achievement in view. "We know where it's not," she said, without much confidence.

"I'm heading back," said Jenny.

Dee nodded. "You're worried about Kay."

Caroline frowned. "Yeah, what's the deal with you two? Is she your apprentice or something?"

"Something," Jenny agreed.

"She'll be fine with the others," said Caroline. "We can't just give up. That means the others will automatically win, and I absolutely refuse to accept that."

"We don't stand a chance anyway," said Jenny.

Caroline was having none of it. "If anyone can find an unknown thing which we've got no way of locating, then it's me!"

"Why's that?" asked Dee.

"Because I'm frickin' awesome!" yelled Caroline, stomping back towards the hedge.

"You carry on," Jenny said. "I'm sorry to— I'll see you back at the house later on, okay?"

"If we're not back by tomorrow, sweetness," said Dee. "we'll probably still be in this hedge."

"Good move, boss. Ditchin' the slow team," said Jizzimus as the other two witches exited back through the hawthorn. "We gunna go and eat the littl'un now?"

"We're eating nobody. I just want to see that she's all right."

Jizzimus kicked at a potato plant and blew a raspberry.

Jenny scanned the perimeter of the allotment. "Can you see where the entrance to this place is? There must be a road or a path. We can follow it round and get back to the hall."

Jizzimus climbed up a runner bean cane wigwam support and peered around. "Good news and bad news. Which do you want first?"

"Just tell me," sighed Jenny.

"The entrance is over that way, but it's got a massive gate on it."

"Iron?"

"Iron. And I can see it's padlocked from 'ere."

"What's the good news?"

"I can see a rabbit in the lettuces!"

With a whoop Jizzimus leapt down and gave chase to the startled animal. Jenny was impressed a rabbit could jump as high as it did before it pelted away, Jizzimus just behind it. He returned a few minutes later, dejected.

"Got away, did it?" asked Jenny.

"Jumped a dyke into a field over by the road," grumbled the imp. "Tha's cheatin'. Takin' effin' liberties."

"Could I get out that way?"

"If you can jump like a rabbit. It's a big dyke."

Jizzimus was right; it was a *very* big dyke.

Anywhere outside the Fens it would have qualified as a small canal. Fortunately it wasn't presently filled with water. Even so, the bottom was a sticky, boggy morass. Beyond was a short field in which cows mooched and grazed, a line of trees, and a blessed glimpse of tarmacked road.

"They do that thing in Holland where they jump dykes using a big stick," she said thoughtfully.

"You got a big stick, guv?"

Jenny liberated the largest bamboo cane she could find on the allotment.

"Oh, that'll do it," said Jizzimus with the kind of encouragement that offered no encouragement at all.

But Jenny thought she could clear it. She could visualise it. She could see herself doing it. She focused, backed up a way and ran at it, wanting to give it her all.

Jizzimus yelled, "Strawberries!" at the crucial moment of jumping off. It was too late to stop her forward momentum. She did not stop, did not leap, but stumbled. Mostly upright into the bottom of the ditch and found herself up to her knees in mud.

"Jizzimus!" she growled.

"Wha'? I jus' seen some ripe strawberries. You want some, guv?"

Jenny heaved forward with a grunt. She slipped further down into the mud; it gripped her thighs. She stopped moving.

"I thought you liked strawberries?" called Jizzimus. "What are you doing down there? Those kiddies ain't gunna eat themselves."

"I'm in trouble," she said, slow and calm.

"Nah, you're only in trouble if you get caught eatin' 'em."

"I'm stuck, Jizzimus!"

He approached the edge of the dyke, chin already covered in strawberry dribble. He scratched one of his cow ears thoughtfully. "'Ave you tried movin'?"

"I daren't move. I'll sink even more."

It didn't matter; she was sinking anyway. Jenny thought rapidly. She knew how to stabilise the situation. She spread her hands on the mud and unleashed a brief but powerful blast of witchfire at her surroundings. There was the stench of hot compost on a summer's day, but it did the trick. The mud surrounding her was baked to a solid mass; the vegetation in her immediate vicinity charred and wilted. Only the sturdiest plants on the edges of the blast remained. One caught Jenny's gaze: it was similar to the broad bean plants she'd seen in the allotment. Was it from a dropped seed or was it the elusive Coney Bane?

66

"You made a right mess of this place," said Jizzimus, nodding in approval. "It smells brilliant, guv. Like cow fart pie wiv slurry custard."

He was right. The smell of baked mud was bad enough, but there was another stink: so ripe it was probably just like a week old corpse.

"I think we found Coney Bane," said Jenny. "The amulet might be nearby."

"Nah. Nothing here apart from this bit of old tin." Jizzimus, held up a square silver medal.

"That's it! Can I have it please?"

Jizzimus clippety-clopped across the baked earth and passed her the amulet. It was either really ancient or just badly-made, and stamped or engraved in a grid format across it, the words:

*SATOR*
*AREPO*
*TENET*
*OPERA*
*ROTAS*

"Wha's that then?" asked Jizzimus.

"No idea, but it's what we're after. Now, if I could just get out of here and—" Jenny heaved and twisted. No good: she had baked herself in solid.

"Seems like you're stuck there for a while, boss."

She wiggled and levered her bamboo cane from the earth and started to prod the ground about her. "It will take a while, yes."

"It's a good job you've got me to keep your spirits up! Which do you want first? The hits of Neil Diamond, Mary Poppins or a bit of opera?"

"Maybe, if a certain little someone bothered to help, with his sharp claws and solid little hoofs, then I might be willing to listen to them all."

"Fairy snuff," said Jizzimus. He began to hammer away with his tiny hoofs.

About an hour later Jenny crawled out of the ditch. She was barefoot, and there wasn't an inch of her that wasn't thickly caked with mud. She looked like a troll from a zero budget stage production of *The Hobbit*.

Jizzimus continued his loud faux-cockney singing as she tried to chip the worst of it off. He'd cycled through the promised repertoire and was now working through the songs from *Oliver!* As she walked towards the trees which lined the junction of road and field, his lusty rendition of *Oom Pah Pah* kept the cows out of their path. It was only when he paused to take breath that she heard the sound of a distant car.

"Quick!" She tried to move faster, but the ground was rough and her aching muscles would not obey. She saw a Land Rover come into sight: a silhouette between the anorexic trees.

"Bugger! We're going to miss it. It's the only sign of civilisation we've seen since this morning."

"Leave it to me, boss," said Jizzimus, and scampered ahead.

Jenny huffed and wheezed and cursed – especially where she trod barefoot on an unnoticed thistle – towards the road. She propelled herself through the trees and tripped over the much narrower ditch that lined the road. She found herself looking up at a parked Land Rover and a familiar if puzzled face.

"George, isn't it?"

George, the barman from Eastville Hall, held a rock in one hand. He was considering the smashed side window of his vehicle. "Did you see this? Came straight through the window."

"I thank you," said Jizzimus, taking a bow from the Land Rover's bonnet.

"That's terrible," said Jenny. "I can't imagine how that happened." She got back on her feet.

George studied her face. "It's, um... Don't tell me. Jenny?"

Jenny made to curtsey in playful acknowledgement, but embarrassment, lack of skirts and a thick coating of claggy mud stopped her. Instead, she did a ridiculous jiggle.

"You look like you've been on an adventure," said George.

"Dragged through a hedge backwards," she replied.

"Either that or you've been given a *really* vigorous massage and mud pack at the spa. Are you hurt?"

Jenny ran a quick diagnosis. She had aches, scrapes or injuries in at least seven different places – not counting those places the ditch mud had insinuated itself, causing emotional distress if not actual physical harm. "Here and there," she admitted.

"Come on," he said. He took her hand and guided her into the front passenger seat.

"I couldn't presume," she heard herself saying.

"Yes, you bloody could," he grinned. It was a handsome grin.

He ran round to the other side and started up the engine. Jizzimus swung in through the smashed window and jumped on the rolls of plastic and tubs of chemical cleaner stacked in the back.

"Been to Skegness to get some supplies," said George. "It's amazing how quickly we get through this lot."

In the back, Jizzimus squeezed himself into a roll of plastic sheeting and pulled faces, using the plastic to deform his already ghastly features.

George accelerated smoothly off the verge and down the lane.

"How far away are we anyway?" Jenny asked.

"Eastville? About five minutes?"

"Oh," said Jenny, hearing the disappointment in her own voice. "I thought it would be further. Feels further on foot. Much further."

"I bet it does," said George taking a look at her. "The Fens may be flat but they can be treacherous. Muddy out is it?"

"One of the activities. It was quite challenging, I got stuck in a ditch."

"I'd have thought a group of witches would be able to tackle most things."

Jenny pulled a face. "Oh you know about the witch thing?"

"Yes. So please don't do Jedi mind tricks on me or anything."

Jenny laughed. "Oh, mostly it's all about herbs and things."

"And not eatin' children," mumbled Jizzimus from within the plastic sheeting. "Even though they're delicious and come free wiv the room."

Dee sighed at Caroline.

"I know you've got blisters, poppet, but I think you can come down and have a look with me. There's magic been here: the ditch is all dried out. We're definitely getting close."

"It's not just the blisters. My legs are so stiff, they just won't do what I want them to."

"I'll help. Give me your hand and just go for it."

Caroline stepped awkwardly over the edge of the ditch and landed heavily on top of Dee. The two of them toppled over into stinking slurry.

"I thought you said the ditch was dried out!" cried Caroline. She stood up, caked in what Dee suspected wasn't just mud.

"That bit over there is," said Dee. "I think this is full of run off from the cow field."

Caroline turned. "I haven't seen any – ah—!"

A cow stood on the edge of the ditch, nudging at Caroline with curiosity. She fell over again in fright before scrambling to the dried out area indicated by Dee.

"Magic. Yes. This is not the work of cows," Caroline looked back nervously to where several more cows had gathered. They watched the two women in the ditch, chewing slowly.

"Well I never," said Dee. "There's Coney Bane growing here as well. We're definitely in the right place. All we need to do now is find the amulet and get out of here."

They looked around for several minutes, but could see nothing.

"Dee, you know how we said that the amulet could be anything?" said Caroline slowly.

"Yes love. We need to keep an open mind."

"Well, what if the amulet is a cow? There's nothing else here."

Dee stared at her. "A cow? *A cow?*"

Caroline ran dirty fingers across her brow. "Sorry. It's ridiculous."

"No," said Dee. "No, it's not "I remember reading that some witches had animal familiars that were also some sort of super-amulets. Isobel Gowdie, instead of having a lucky rabbit's foot, had a lucky rabbit."

"Four times the luck," said Caroline. "Especially for the rabbit."

"So, we're going with the theory that one of these cows is the amulet," said Dee.

"You got anything better?"

Dee shook her head. "How do we know which one is the amulet?"

"Maybe it doesn't matter," said Caroline.

"Of course it matters."

"Does it?"

"Yes, poppet. We need to pick the right one."

"Ah," said Caroline "That will be one of those test of character things. You know—" She put on a deep and portentous voice. "— *Choose wisely, for while the true cow will bring everlasting glory, the wrong cow will bring...*"

"Sour milk?" suggested Dee.

"Yes. Something like that."

"So, maybe we need to get out of this ditch and inspect these cows to see which is the most—"

"—Magical?"

"Um. Yes."

George pulled up around the side of the house, near the witches' lodgings.

"I'll drop you here and take the supplies round to storage," he said.

Jenny climbed out and went inside the house, wondering where to start searching for Kay. Effie was near the reception desk; she stepped out to welcome Jenny.

"Well done! Excellent to see you're all back. And clearly having got in touch with nature, I see." She looked past her. "Where are the others?"

"We ... er. We split up," said Jenny, suddenly realising that this might not go down well with Effi., "But we did find the amulet." She held out the silver medal.

Effie shook her head imperiously. "Was there a good reason for your team to split up?"

"I wanted to check on Kay. I was worried about her," said Jenny.

"You were specifically told that teamwork was a key part of this exercise! I'm very disappointed you couldn't even stay together. I'm marking you down for this."

"There's marks?" said Jenny.

Effie tapped on her tablet. Upside-down Jenny could see a table onto which Effie had entered school grades next to names. *Sabrina Holder-Eckford: A; Sharon Jaye: A; Kay Wun: A;* and *Norma Looney* had been awarded an *A+*. And now, *Jenny Knott* was being awarded a *D-*.

"Kay's back?" said Jenny, belatedly realising what the table showed.

"Kay has been back for some time *with her team mates*," said Effie. "Enjoying the much deserved rewards of *working together*." Effie gestured at the entrance to the restaurant/bar area.

Jenny, dismissed, approached the door. She heard Sabrina's voice from beyond.

"Ur, it's well-known in our family. It's part of who we are."

"I reckon she's talkin' about some inbred disfigurement thing," said Jizzimus, listening at the door. "Like wonky knobs or cross-eyed tits."

"It's been handed down for generations," said Sabrina.

"Or maybe it's the family torture dungeon," said Jizzimus.

"Traditional values: I'm a big fan," came Norma's voice. "No point in messing about with something that works."

"Hmm. Could still be either," mused Jizzimus.

"All I'm saying is that Jamie Oliver says we should add a twist of lime, and I think it really adds something," said Shazam.

"Wonky knob," declared Jizzimus with finality.

Jenny pushed the door open as Shazam passed her glass to Norma.

"Jenny!" called Kay. "We're just having some elderflower cordial."

In the one-and-a-bit days Jenny had known the girl, she had never sounded so excited about something so dull. "Elderflower cordial?" smiled Jenny.

"It's the correct drink for a witch, no?"

"And wonky nobs," said Jizzimus.

"It would be correct without the lime," said Sabrina archly.

"Hm, no. I think she's onto something," said Norma. "I like it."

There was a large pitcher of cloudy liquid on the table in front of them. A partially mutilated lime was the only nod to decadence.

"Not much of a party, guv," said Jizzimus. "Might work as a marinade for the kiddie, though."

"I think it's this one," said Dee.

Caroline inspected the chosen cow. "Why?"

Dee tipped her head and gave the cow a wistful look. "I just think Daisy here has a certain ... sparkle to her."

Caroline shook her head. "Course she does. Right, let's get her home."

Dee thought for a moment. "I've absolutely no idea how to herd a cow."

"Well, I can make people do things, and you know all about animals," said Caroline. "I bet we can work something out. So what motivates a cow?"

"I think they're motivated by the usual things," said Dee, not elaborating. "And they're nosey as well. They want to know what's going on."

Caroline leaned as close as she dared to Daisy and whispered, "Something interesting is happening behind you."

The cow turned and nosed its way past its neighbours to look behind them. Dee was impressed.

"That actually worked! How does a cow understand English?"

"It's more the idea you need to get across. As I said the words I also tried to imagine there was something really interesting to a cow just over there."

"Right then." Dee clapped Caroline on the shoulder. "There's a gate over there. I reckon the road must go back to the hall. Let's get Daisy home."

Jenny tried the elderflower cordial. She thought what it really needed was a shot of gin to help her forget the trials of the day. Norma slumped back in an armchair, snoring gently.

Shazam nodded towards Norma. "Sometimes I play a game with Mr Beetlebane when he's asleep. It's called Cat Jenga. You have to see how many things you can balance on top of him before he wakes up."

"Oh, that is droll," drawled Sabrina.

The entire group turned towards Norma, their eyes casting around for small light objects. Shazam went first: taking a small piece of knitting wool from her bag and forming a bow which she dropped onto Norma's head. Kay sidled over and a balanced a drinks coaster onto the shelf formed by Norma's bosom. Sabrina coughed, drawing their attention, then fixed her eyes on a menu from the bar. It rose up, floating across to Norma, where it fluttered lightly down and settled across her face. Shazam and Kay applauded, impressed.

Jenny leaned close to Kay. "Does nothing today strike you as ... odd?"

"They didn't have any Rice Krispies at breakfast. Everything else, but no Rice Krispies."

"I mean, about today's activities... These women..."

Kay pulled a face. "Norma did a magic map reading," she said. "She saw where the amulet was before we even left the hall. I think that's what made her very tired."

"No, I—"

"Boss!" Jizzimus stood in the window, jumping up and down. "You've got to see this!"

Jenny looked out. There was something large peering in the window.

"Your two bleedin' mates have brought a cow. Now it's a party!"

Dee and Caroline looked even more mud splattered than Jenny, as if they'd been swimming in it. A small, concentrated throng of witches ran outside, Jenny carried along with them.

"Whose cow is this?" demanded Effie.

"It's, er, yours?" said Dee.

Effie peered at it, as though it might conceivably be her cow and she needed to check. "I don't own a cow," she said.

"It's the amulet," explained Caroline.

"We brought it back for you," added Dee.

"The amulet," repeated Effie in a flat voice. "Does it look like an amulet? At any point did you stop and say to yourselves, 'this is a cow, not an amulet'?"

"Aha!" said Caroline. "That was the trap, wasn't it?"

"Trap?"

"Yes. Because couldn't something be both a cow *and* an amulet?"

"No."

"Because didn't Isobel Gowdie have a—"

"A cow that was an amulet? No, she most certainly did not."

Caroline grimaced. "Well, we thought outside the box and here we are. If we're wrong then we're wrong; but we score highly for initiative and creativity." The words were accompanied by the subtlest of hand movements.

"Stop that immediately. I will not be manipulated. Teamwork! I could not have made myself any clearer when I said that this initiative was about teamwork. Jenny, would you like to show your teammates the amulet?"

With an embarrassed smile, Jenny fished out the medal and held it up. "I found it after we split up. Sorry."

"So you left us behind and nicked the actual thing we were supposed to be looking for?" hissed Caroline. "You undermined our chances in every way possible!"

"Yer in trouble boss," said Jizzimus. "You might as well go on that murd'rous rampage yer've been promising yerself."

The rest of the witches gathered around in interest. Unlike Effie, they kept themselves at a distance and safely away from the cow's rear end. Even Norma had woken up and wandered outside, leaving the title of Norma Jenga champion unclaimed.

"Well," said Effie. "I'd like to say that this concludes this morning's activities, but there remains the small matter of returning this cow to the field where it belongs. Can I trust you ladies to take care of that?"

"We've just brought it here," said Dee, with the whine of the truly knackered.

"I'm sure, with initiative and creativity, you will be able to take it back again with no trouble."

"But this is Jenny's fault," protested Caroline.

"Yes. But you must tackle all challenges as a team," said Effie with prim *schadenfreude*.

Jizzimus leapt onto the cow's back with a whoop of delight and scurried along its spine, lifted the tail and probed with his fingers.

"Imps .ave been messin' wiv cows for years, boss," he said grinning. "We know exactly how to give someone who stan's behind one a *really bad day.*"

As he squeezed, the cow let out a low bellow of annoyance. Its tail quivered as an explosive mess erupted from its hind quarters. A fine spray of cow dung, almost mist-like. Pervasive and penetrating, Jenny thought.

For a few moments everyone was dumbstruck. Everyone except Jizzimus, who cackled with delight and danced on the cow's back. "Best day *ever*! Did you see what I did boss, did you see it?"

Effie screamed through tightly-clenched, horror-stricken lips. When she regained control of herself, she wiped the muck of her tablet and stabbed viciously at the screen.

"F! F! F!"

"The word is 'fuck'," offered Jizzimus helpfully.

Effie turned and walked back into the building without further words, trying to keep movement down to a minimum. The rest of the witches were torn between amusement, indignation and general bewilderment.

Jenny, Dee and Caroline met each other's' eyes and started leading the cow back down the lane. As they went, Jenny could hear Norma ask, "Why is there a coaster stuck in my cleavage?"

They hadn't gone far when Jenny felt a hand slip into hers. Kay smiled at her.

"So, anything strike you as odd about *your* day?" she asked.

76

"I think the cow kind of wins that one," said Jenny.

"That cow looks sad."

"I think that's just their natural look."

"We should make it happier."

Kay skipped ahead and brushed a hand across the cow's ears.

"What was that?" asked Jenny.

"Look," said Kay.

The cow raised its head and gave a series of sharp, bark-like sounds.

"Is this cow laughing?" said Caroline, eyebrow raised.

A sparkling rainbow nimbus developed around the animal's head.

Jenny stopped walking and looked at Kay, conscious that her mouth was, yet again, hanging open. "You're a witch!" she said.

"We're all witches, poppet," Dee called back to her.

"But why on earth didn't you say?"

Kay put a hand on the cow's flank and looked back at Jenny. "You never asked."

# Chapter 3 – Witches Brew

It was odd, Caroline reflected as she walked across the rear lawns to the summer house cum teaching hut for the morning's seminar. It was odd how quickly all six of them had fallen into a routine. Mealtimes, lessons, exploratory visits to the local marshes, field and woodland, more lessons, private study or magical research in the teaching hut or the rows of individually allocated sheds at the far end of the garden – because Effie did not want the witches practising untried magic or charms in their living quarters. And even though certain relationships still had rough edges to be smoothed off, they were, by and large, getting on with one another. All in all, it was quite enjoyable, even if the fenland retreat had so far been a complete sexual desert...

"Ooh, hi tech," said Shazam as she sat.

Effie had set up a screen and a computer projector in the classroom, *and* there were printed notes on the students' chairs.

"We're in for a treat today," said Jenny. Caroline was pretty sure she was being sarcastic.

The title on the screen, in a square, no nonsense font, was *The Business of Witchcraft – How to Make Witching Pay*. Effie stood proudly beside it, dressed in that self-consciously kooky look she was determined to rock. Today's T-shirt was a Jimi Hendrix print asking the all-important question, *Are You Experienced?*.

"All here. Five, six, seven. Kay, there are seats near the front. You don't need to get anoth— Oh, you have." Effie smiled brightly. "Right, ladies, today I want to discuss one of the key points of this course: the fact that you're all criminally underselling yourself. I'm going to be brutally vulgar and ask how much did you earn from witchcraft in the last year?"

All around Caroline, women gasped, tensing up.

"Um, well, I'm between jobs," said Jenny.

"I'm not even eighteen," said Kay.

"Charitable work is its own reward," said Dee.

"The rewards of witchcraft are mostly ... intangible," said Caroline with a salaciousness that made Shazam blush.

"Ur, I couldn't even begin to guess the stock dividends we've received this year—"

"Not earnings in general," said Effie, interrupting Sabrina. "How much does *witchcraft* make you?"

"Well, it's a dashed impertinent question," said Norma.

Effie nodded. "It is. And I'll admit that I myself am probably no richer as a witch than I would have been if I were a mere *woman*."

"Witchcraft isn't meant to pay."

"And yet—" Effie clicked the remote. An image of a medieval illumination of dead eyed medieval folk doing something indecipherably medieval flashed on screen. "In times gone by, witches were respected and revered and handsomely paid for their services."

"Um," said Shazam. "Don't you mean persecuted and burned at the stake, Miss Fray?"

Sabrina smirked. "Ur, I think you'll find that hanging was the preferred method of execution."

"I'm not talking about the persecution suffered by innocent women, non-witchfolk almost all, at the hands of religious zealots," said Effie. "I wish to discuss the high rewards witches reaped from their socially beneficial work."

"That's just danger money, really," said Caroline.

"Ur, I'd certainly want large cash sums up front if I thought Matthew Hopkins might try stringing me up," said Sabrina.

"If I may return to my point—" Effie looked at Dee, who was sitting attentively with her hand in the air. "Dee. We're grown women. We don't need to put our hands up."

"I have a question," she said.

"Is it about earning money from witchcraft?"

"No. Sorry. But maybe you can settle an argument."

"Yes?"

"Are there such things as wicked witches?"

Sabrina sniggered.

"That's off topic, Dee," said Jenny. "Let's get back—"

"Well, it's sort of relevant," said Dee, rearranging her cardigan assertively. "It's wicked witches that have given the rest of us a bad reputation."

"There are no such things as wicked witches," said Effie with assurance.

"There are," said Norma flatly.

"I mean, there are obviously sisters who use their powers for something other than the public good—"

"I don't mean that," said Dee.

"No, wicked witches do not exist," said Effie firmly.

"You're wrong," said Norma, firmer still.

The gazes of the oldest women in the room locked furiously.

"Are we gonna see a witchy smackdown?" Caroline heard Kay whisper.

The room darkened, although a boring person might argue that it was just a cloud passing in front of the sun. When Effie spoke, it was in a quiet voice of jaw-lockingly controlled fury.

"In ages past, there *may* have been certain twisted creatures who, whilst *superficially* appearing to be like us, were in truth magical or demonic creatures which might narrowly and glibly be described as evil or wicked. But that age has *passed*. And anyone foolish enough to bandy around words like 'wicked' and use them to persecute, harass or harm women is likely to find themselves in trouble with both the law and *their fellow witches*." The air crackled.

"You and I have seen things," said Norma darkly.

"And done things," replied Effie.

"I was only asking," said Dee, very, very quietly indeed.

Abruptly the light returned to the room and Effie looked round at the assembled witches with a sudden smile. The presentation flipped to an image of a bearded man with an enormous frilly collar.

"But witch lore and myth are topics for another time, yes? This morning's seminar is about the payments you should expect to receive for your services. For example, did you know that King James I here paid Agnes Sampson eighty pounds to help him with, um, marital performance issues? Now, I've done some calculations and as this next graph shows ... yes, that's equivalent to more than two hundred thousand pounds in modern money."

"That'd buy a nice sports car," said Caroline.

"Bugger that," said Shazam. "That'd buy a house."

"Ur, wasn't Agnes Sampson garrotted and burned at the stake?" commented Sabrina.

"Point is," said Effie. "The *point is*, witchcraft should be able to make any one of us wealthy and self-sufficient."

"That's olden times," said Jenny. "The world's moved on since then, hasn't it?"

Effie sped through a number of slides to a corporate logo. "Possibly the most successful tech company in history. How many of you have their phones or tablets or i-wotsits?"

There were several hands in the air.

"Why?" asked Effie. "They're more expensive than any of their competitors."

"Ur, they're the best," said Sabrina as though it was the most obvious thing in the world.

"Really? How do you know?"

"Everyone knows," said Shazam.

Effie pointed at Shazam, her point made. "'Everyone knows.'"

"Witchcraft?" said Jenny.

"There's an entire coven in Silicon Valley."

"Witches help sell products?" said Jenny.

Effie nodded. "You know that irritating *I'm lovin' it* thing they do on the burger commercials?"

"Really irritating."

"It helped boost their market share by five percent."

"Witchcraft?"

"Witchcraft. And do I even need to mention a certain 'Secret blend of eleven herbs and spices'?"

"And you said witches were in danger of dying out," said Norma with a scoff.

"Oh, but they are," said Effie. "With few exceptions, witchcraft is being commoditised and exploited. I'm sure you've all heard of – what do they call it? – cultural appropriation. Well, this is magical appropriation. It is taking the benefit of witchcraft, applying it to areas for which it was never meant, and then not giving the rewards back to the original witch."

"So, why are you showing us this?" asked Caroline.

Effie picked up a booklet of printed notes. "We're going to change that. Our focus for the next few days is going to be on creating our own witchy product or brand, and planning how to market it for our own benefit. Now, if you'd all turn to page two, there's a lovely quote from that delightful hoover-salesman James Dyson which I think sums the whole thing up..."

At least, thought Dee charitably as she struggled to follow the lengthy notes and lecture, it was nice to see Effie Fray had a passion. It didn't matter Effie's passion was for turning the least business-minded section of society into the corporate sharks of tomorrow, or that the tool she was going to do this with was a set of ideas and principles openly cobbled together from sources as diverse as a gas-fitters manual, a BTEC Child Care course textbook, the Operating Manual for Spaceship Earth, and snippets of wisdom from the likes of Gerald Ratner, Anita Roddick, PT Barnum and General Leopoldo Galtieri. It didn't matter because the whole activity was doing Effie the world of good. So Dee told herself.

She could see that the lecture, and perhaps the entire course, was a way for Effie to get stuff off her chest. Wide-eyed and innocent though she knew herself to be, Dee suspected what they were all witnessing was a rebound reaction to some recent trauma. Without a doubt, women of a certain age had done stranger things after a divorce or bereavement. Setting up your own intensive programme for unfocused and directionless witches was no madder than moving to rural France, joining a commune in the Western Isles or getting a tattoo; or buying a scooter and starting a torrid affair with a pipe-smoking geography teacher.

By the time Effie had come to the end of her rambling lecture, Dee had already painted a mental image of Effie trapped in a boring and sexless marriage to a Pringle-jumper-and-moccasin-wearing man who knew the price of everything and the value of nothing. He'd seen the writing on the wall and had abandoned his ever-patient and forgiving wife in search of adventure and lost youth. Dee had even given him a name.

"And so this brings us again to our four guiding principles." Effie pointed to the items listed on the screen. "Find a need and fill it. Operating expenses will be higher than you expect. Open up your mind to any marketing opportunity. Face the future – and embrace it. F.O.O.F. If you forget all else, don't forget your foof. All ideas should be foofy."

"Amen," said Caroline, stifling a yawn.

"Your tasks then," said Effie. "I want each of you to independently design, devise or produce a product or idea that might create a sustainable income for you."

"What kind of product?" asked Dee.

"I think that wholly depends on your individual specialisations. It could be a charm, an enchantment, a potion or an even more intangible service. What it needs to be is something that will make money, and is based upon your skills and knowledge of witchcraft. I also want you to carry out a SWOT analysis of your finished product and present it to the whole group."

There were a number of groans at this last one.

"Like a presentation?" said Jenny. "Standing up in front of people?"

"Yes," said Effie. "Cheer up, Jen. At least this task doesn't rely on teamwork. Not your strong suit, eh?"

Of all the laughs at that, the loudest was from Kay. Jenny scowled at the teenager.

Dee could see, plain as day, that Jenny and Kay had fallen into the roles of mother hen and less-than-gracious child, even though she guessed they weren't related and hadn't even known each other for long. It was cute to observe, but made Dee all the keener to ask certain questions.

"As an enticement," Effie was saying, "Mrs du Plessis is offering a day at the spa for the two who create the most promising product."

"Oh goody," Sabrina whispered, just loud enough for them all to hear. "Like good puppies, we're performing for treats."

Effie either did not hear or chose to ignore her. "Although this is not a secret project, let's respect each other's privacy and stick to the workspaces we were allocated earlier in the week." She gave a final nod of dismissal and they responded with scraping of chairs, stretching, yawning and a general shuffling towards the door.

Outside, the mid-morning sun played peekaboo through the wide clouds. A pair of wading birds flew eastward along the edge of the lawn.

"They are real," whispered Norma.

The others had either gone up to Eastville Hall or their work sheds and Dee hadn't realised Norma was there.

"Pardon? Oh. Wicked witches... Yes, I didn't mean to cause a ruckus in there."

"That wasn't a ruckus," sniffed Norma. "That was just two old friends not seeing eye to eye."

"Oh, right. I was asking about them because you do hear rumours."

"More rumour than fact," agreed Norma. "But that doesn't change the truth. They're real, they're a danger, and there are some who'd rather stick their heads in the sand than face reality."

Dee looked around suspiciously. The door to the teaching hut was shut, Effie still inside. "You've seen them? I mean: for yourself, with your own eyes?"

"Met them," said Norma. "Barely escaped with my life."

"Cor."

Norma leaned in even closer, to the point where Dee needed to turn sideways to avoid being sumo-barged by Norma's titanically scaffolded bosom. "I've got a book you might like to read," she whispered.

Those exact words had been whispered to Dee once before. Back then the book in question had been *The Female Eunuch* and the whisperer had tried, three nights later over a glass of red wine, to involve Dee in a husband-murdering plot with *Thelma and Louise* overtones. Dee had since learned to view conspiratorial book lenders with scepticism.

"A book?"

"A book about witch hunting."

"Oh, I've read most of those already," said Dee. "I read the *Malleus Maleficarum* when I was thirteen."

"This one's different," said Norma.

"Oh?"

"It was written for witches by a witch. A proper witch at that, a personal heroine of mine. I had hoped to meet her one day but..."

85

"But?"

"Died. Disappeared. Who can tell with these Nordic types? Probably went off to play with the elves. Anyway I'll lend you my copy of her book if you'd like..."

The dozen or so sheds along the far edge of the lawn, now serving as witches' work sheds, were remnants of an earlier age. Their original purpose was uncertain. Perhaps they had served as the clubhouses of a vigorous bowling or croquet club. Perhaps they had been placed there by a previous owner with enormous foresight who was simply waiting for rising sea levels to bring the seaside to Eastville. Or perhaps they had simply been the garden sheds for a gardener with *a lot* of tools.

Whatever the case, Jenny's work shed, whimsically painted with green and white stripes like a giant mint, brick built to knee height and wooden panelled above, was a fine space for her to think, read, and learn those witchy skills of potion-making and herbalism which she had mostly avoided her adult life.

Jenny inspected the wart on her neck in a small wood-framed mirror. She had zapped it earlier in the week and it had blistered nicely.

"Just tell 'em you're a wicked witch," said Jizzimus. The imp was filing his tiny horns to sharp points with one of Jenny's emery boards.

Jenny looked at him. "And then what? They'll either kick me out or have me sent to ... witch prison, or whatever."

"*Or*," said Jizzimus, pointing the nail file, "you can roast 'em wiv witchfire and cackle madly as you dance in the ashes."

"I can't do that."

"It's easier than it looks, guv. The trick is in the breathin', innit. A good cackle comes from down 'ere, in your balls."

"You don't breathe with your balls."

"Nah, but I knew this yogi guy who could drink tea through 'is knob. I've been practisin', but no success yet."

Jenny considered asking the imp if he'd been practising in *her* tea but she didn't want to hear the answer. "I meant, I can't tell them,

86

and I'm not killing anyone. We're laying low; for Kay's sake and mine."

Jizzimus glowered at her before, holding the emery board like a guitar, he did a Chuck Berry duck walk along the table. "Well then, boss, you'd better start dreamin' up some killer product so Lord Sugar don' kick you off the course."

"I was trying to, but a certain imp keeps interrupting me with nonsense about cackling and knobs and—"

"Porn!" yelled Jizzimus.

"What?"

"Imp porn!"

"What?"

"No one's done it before."

"I don't think there's much of a market for it," Jenny said kindly.

"There's an 'ole internet community out there wiv an 'ole in their life that can only be filled by dirty movies of imp action. An' oo am I, Jizzimus Long-Dong Silver, to deprive 'em, guv?"

Jenny sat down on the workbench. "Putting aside the fact that presenting imp porn to the world would be an admission of what I am, you've forgotten that you are invisible to the rest of humanity."

"I can make myself visible if I want to. Look." Jizzimus closed his eyes, clenched up with a little grunt and then leapt up in a star jump. "See!"

"Yes," said Jenny slowly. "I could see you before though, couldn't I?"

"Sure, sure. But anyone else oo was 'ere would now be rubbin' their eyes and goin' 'Fuck me! What the shittin' 'ell is that? An', if you don' mind me sayin', what a fabulously hung beast 'e is. I'd like to see some of that on a pay-per-view porn channel.'"

Jenny couldn't help smiling. The more foul-mouthed he became, the more child-like he appeared. She picked him up. He made a show of resisting for a moment. "What am I to do with you?" she sighed.

"Get me a jar of lube, a fluffer an' a camera crew, boss."

A thought struck Jenny. "What makes you invisible?"

Jizzimus shrugged. "Dunno."

"I mean..." She picked some crumbs of horn filings off the table. "Are these invisible, or is it just you?"

Jizzimus pulled a dumb face. "Why?"

"I might have an idea."

There was soup for lunch in the restaurant. Caroline regarded its brown, vegetable depths critically.

Next in line, Shazam said helpfully: "It's soup,"

Caroline reluctantly ladled a dollop of it into her bowl. "I was merely wondering what kind," she said.

"Ooh, it's got little cubes of ham in it," said Shazam. "Very continental."

At that moment, Caroline spotted the thick, elbow length rubber gloves Shazam was wearing. "Is this a new look?" she asked.

"Hmmm? Oh, no. I've been transforming my shed into a contaminant-free laboratory environment. I'm going to do some precision potion-making."

"Ah," said Caroline, thinking about the unscientific plastic tubing and bucket arrangement she was planning in her own work shed.

"But I do think they look elegant," said Shazam. "Like Audrey Hepburn in that *Breakfast at thingummies* film."

Caroline wanted to point out that Audrey Hepburn would only have worn such gloves if she'd been tending to a pregnant cow. Instead, took her soup, crusty cob and spoon to the table where the others were sitting.

"All I'm saying—" Jenny broke off some bread to dip in her soup "—is that it's good to iron out some of the bugs before we get carried away with our plans. A bit of pre-emptive SWOT analysis."

"Ur, and you're the business guru who will show us the error of our ways, are you?" said Sabrina.

Jenny shrugged. "I did a few months of temp work for a friend, Kevin Carter-King. He runs this—"

"That's the company with all those lorries," Shazam piped in. "Like Eddie Stobart or that Norbert Dangerous-angle."

"Oh, we saw one of those Carter-King trucks going by the other day," said Dee.

"Yes, we did," said Caroline. "As we were leading a cow through a muddy field because our team mate had abandoned us and got the amulet without telling us, I believe."

Jenny coughed uncomfortably. "Anyway, those months gave me a bit of an insight into marketing and strategy, and I'm merely offering my services – a little mutual support – if we're all willing to share."

"But you might steal our ideas," said Norma.

"My product idea is awesome," said Kay and put a pebble on the table.

Everyone peered at it. It was a red clay lozenge of a stone and appeared to glow very dimly.

"That looks interesting," said Jenny encouragingly. "What is it?"

"A work in progress," said Kay and swept it out of sight again.

"Ur, maybe you ought to share your idea first," suggested Sabrina.

"Very well." Jenny put an empty jam jar on the table.

Everyone was less dumbfounded than nonplussed.

"I think I preferred the glowing pebble," said Norma.

"Can you see it?" asked Jenny.

Dee put her eye right up to the glass. "No, poppet."

"Exactly!" said Jenny.

"Okay," said Caroline. "Who had Jenny in the *First Witch To Go Completely Cuckoo* sweepstake?"

"The reason you can't see it is because it's invisible. I'm going to make a cloak of invisibility."

"Ooh, that'll be nice," said Shazam.

"Might be a wise fashion choice for some," said Sabrina.

"Can't be done," said Norma flatly.

"That's fighting talk," said Kay. "What's your big idea?"

"I'm not saying, Miss Wun. And, for your information, in this country, young ladies speak to their elders with a bit more respect than that."

"I'm making a hair tonic for gloss and shine," said Shazam. Her own hair was a Fifties-style bouffant homage to the philosophy of bigger is better. Caroline thought if it was any glossier or shinier, it would be blinding.

"You use some of the stuff on your hair already?" she asked.

"Not for me," laughed Shazam. "I'm making it for pets." She ran a rubber-gloved hand over the near-dead cat hanging around her neck. "Mr Beetlebane is looking a little threadbare these days. He could do with a sprucing up. My tonic will transform and revitalise."

"I'm going to cure PMT," said Caroline with deliberately ridiculous pomposity.

"We've all tried that, sweetness," said Dee.

Norma hmphed. "No one even had PMT until *Cosmopolitan* invented it. All in the mind."

"To be honest," said Caroline, "I'm going to play it safe and just distil some soothing essential oils. Thought I might go out and track down some evening primrose."

"For stress relief you could also try borage," suggested Dee.

"Or cleavers," said Sabrina.

"Cleavers?" Caroline frowned. "Sounds dangerous."

"She means sticky-willy," said Dee.

"Oh, *goose grass*," said Shazam, understanding.

"And, of course," said Sabrina, "the important thing to remember is that the season and time you harvest your herbs is as important as what you harvest."

"Is it?" said Caroline.

Sabrina rolled her eyes. For such a languorous woman, rolling her eyes took a full two seconds. "Ur, would it help if I showed you how and where to pick herbs?"

Caroline, who harboured a desire to punch Sabrina on the hooter simply for being a stuck-up little rich girl, bit down on her class envy. "That would be ... really helpful."

"See?" smiled Jenny. "A bit of mutual support."

"Can I come too?" asked Kay.

"And me," said Dee.

"Ur, I thought you were an expert herbalist, Dee."

"I never said I was an expert," said Dee. "And any opportunity to learn..."

"Anyway, what are you working on, Sabrina?" asked Jenny.

Sabrina pointed to a pair of silver rings on the table. "Ur, I'm working on a way of imbuing objects with permanent PK potential."

"Pardon?" said Jenny.

"Pick them up."

Jenny tried. She grabbed one and then the other and huffed as they refused to lift from the table surface. "What...? Are they stuck?" She gave up.

Norma, intrigued, leaned in and also tried to lift one.

"Ur, they're not stuck to the table, I assure you," said Sabrina.

Shazam reached over and tried to lift the other. With a grunt, she managed to lever it a couple of inches off the table and slide her other hand under it.

"It's so heavy," she said, impressed. "How does it work?"

"Well, it's about the application of direction-specific gravity to the— No!"

Sabrina reached out as Shazam turned the ring over to inspect it. The ring flew up out of her hands and struck the ceiling with a firework crack. Mr Beetlebane yowled in surprise and leapt from Shazam's neck. Little lumps of plaster fell onto the table. A triangular piece plopped into Caroline's soup and sank.

"*Nustoti!*"

At Sabrina's command, the ring Norma was tugging at suddenly came away with ease. Up above, something rattled in the damaged ceiling; the other ring fell down through the hole it had made. Sabrina caught it, examined it and placed it back on the table.

"*Veikti!*"

Norma's hand and the ring she was holding slammed down.

"A lifting weight of one hundred and fifty pounds," said Sabrina. "Applied in a specific direction."

"And a delightful addition to any dinner table," said Caroline, fishing in her bowl for the lost lump of plaster.

After a lunch that tasted more than a little chalky, Caroline continued with her own preparations. She walked across the lawns with a half dozen lengths of plastic piping under one arm and a pair of large tubs under the other. She heard the distant sound of a large saw buzzing somewhere by the stable block and wondered if there might be more useful equipment over there, even though it was out of bounds. Having done the briefest of research, she hoped she was carrying the makings of a rudimentary still, through which she'd extract the essential oils of various plants.

Caroline was reluctant to admit it but, although she was a fricking *awesome* witch, her personal awesomeness was based upon natural skill and spontaneous charms. While she could bend wills, charm souls and warp the world to her bidding, she knew next to nothing about the technical aspects of witchcraft. She was a lumbering musclebound Neanderthal surrounded by weaker but wilier, tool-using homo sapiens.

And, speaking of musclebound Neanderthal's and tools she'd like to use...

George – sometime barman, sometime gardener, all time eye candy – was carrying a pair of freshly-sawn tree posts to the nearby borders, a pair of amber-tinted goggles around his neck.

Caroline clicked her teeth softly; a hundred yards away George looked up, on a whim, and saw her. She gave him a wink and a wave. He smiled back, wiped his brow and, tree posts slung casually over his shoulder, ambled across.

"Easier to herd than cows," Caroline said to herself, continuing on to her work shed, safe in the knowledge that George was following.

*Svarta Norn,* or *The Black Witch* by Gunnfríður Vilhjálmsdóttir was a fascinating read. Dee had been reading Norma's book for hours, when she should have been planning, crafting and concocting. Eventually, seized by an exciting thought, she took the book over to Norma's shed and knocked. Something mechanical whirred within.

"Go away," came Norma's commanding voice. "Too busy."

"It's me. Dee."

There was a massive, pained sigh. "Come in if you must."

Dee opened the door.

Norma stood framed by the doorway, wearing a black and yellow striped, all in one body suit. Her face was covered by something that looked like a veil. She was also wearing a pair of deely-boppers on her head. Dee wanted to ask why, but was distracted by a loud droning she couldn't place. It was punctuated by a staccato series of battering noises.

"Come in quickly," said Norma. "I need to close the door."

Dee stepped inside and saw that Norma had brought one of the garden beehives into her shed. Bees filled the air between the hive and the table. On the table was an old-fashioned typewriter. Bees poured through the air, aimed for a key on the typewriter and dropped heavily onto it, striking letters one by one. Dee prided herself on a love of all creatures, but chose to keep a wary distant from the cloud of bees.

"Before you even ask, it works," said Norma.

"It does?" said Dee.

Norma pushed her veil back over the deely-boppers and pointed at the paper slowly emerging from the typewriter. "Yes. Apiomancy. Fortune-telling through the flight of bees. I might need a new z key soon though: they're quite keen on that one. You've come with questions about the book."

"I have," said Dee.

Norma ran her finger down a few lines. "You're surprised about the cold touch of iron, the power of certain berries and other links between wicked witches and the fairy folk?"

"I am."

"But you're particularly interested in Vilhjálm's Potion of Seeing."

"Yes."

"Even though Vilhjálmsdóttir makes it quite clear it cannot be made."

"Yes. If there was a potion which let you see spirit beings then you'd be able to see witches' imps and detect the wicked witch in an instant."

Norma tapped another line. "And even though you know it's impossible, you're going to persevere."

"Am I? That's nice."

Norma stood in the centre of the room, turned around three times, waggled her deely-boppers, stamped her left foot three times, then her right foot twice. As if in answer, the bees fired back several lines' worth of text. Norma read them.

"Caroline Black will prove essential in your plans," she précised.

"How?"

Norma tutted loudly at something on the page. "That's no way to set up a still!"

Dee looked around. "What? Where?"

"She's like a man that one. Does all her thinking with her knickers."

"I think you've lost me, poppet," said Dee.

Norma did another peculiar dance and waited for the bees to reply. "You will succeed."

"With the potion?"

Norma nodded curtly. "But you won't be happy with the results."

"Why not?"

Norma lowered her veil again. "If I told you everything, Miss Finch, then there'd be no surprises."

Caroline fixed one end of the plastic tube onto the top of her pressure cooker. The free end flailed around, threatening to topple the pot. George stepped in and held the cooker steady.

"So, what are you going to be brewing up in this?"

"Some evening primrose. Sticky-willy. Bits and bobs."

George hung the tubing over the rusted hook in the centre of the ceiling, giving the whole contraption greater stability. "I know this kind of thing isn't very technical—"

"It's fairly technical," pouted Caroline.

"—but I haven't got round to setting up one of my own yet."

Caroline gave him a look. "Fancy yourself as a warlock, do you?"

He laughed. "No, Miss Black."

"I answer to Caroline or, occasionally, mistress."

He blushed. She liked that. "I meant," he said, "stills can be used for purposes other than distilling oils."

"To be honest, I hadn't thought of that."

"We had a real bumper crop in the orchard last autumn."

"Ah, cider." Caroline fought to get the further coils of tubing inside the tub that would act as the cooling pot.

George made a doubtful noise. "That was the plan. Here." He crouched beside her to help draw the tubing out the hole in the base of the tub. "Making cider should be simple." He fiddled in the opening with his fingertips. "Chop up your apples, mash them down, let the natural yeasts ferment."

"But...?"

"Ah-ha!" He grasped the tubing between thumbs and forefinger and tugged it through. "Yes, well, I currently have in the stable ten gallons of something that is technically cider but tastes like apple-scented drain cleaner."

Caroline bent the piping towards the collection jar. "And does your employer – pass me that epoxy resin glue stuff – does she approve of you brewing crap cider in her stable?"

"Mrs du Plessis doesn't lower herself to inspect sheds and stables. I keep it hidden behind the gas canisters just in case."

"Being a bit of a naughty boy, then?"

"You missed a bit," he said. Lacing his fingers over hers, he spread a blob of rubber cement around the pipe to seal the hole. "It's a moot point. As I said, the cider is quite undrinkable. However, with a working still – which is exactly what this is shaping up to be – all ten gallons of it could be transformed into a tasty apple-based spirit."

"Moonshine?"

"I'm sure we can come up with a classy name for it." He wiped his hands on his jeans as he stood. "But, of course, this is for distilling evening primrose and sticky-willy."

"That *was* the plan," she said.

"Was?"

As Jenny locked up her work shed for the evening, she was greeted by the sight of someone in an outfit which implied interests in both beekeeping and bondage.

"Shazam?"

The larger woman lifted off her rubberised helmet. It came away with a wet pop to reveal a pink and sweaty face. "Ooh, I'm fair glowing." She fanned herself with the helmet. A sweat-sodden thing around her neck miaowed in possible agreement.

"Are we expecting a chemical attack?" asked Jenny.

"She's 'eard what happens to you after eatin' too many vegetables," said Jizzimus.

"I've created a sealed environment in which to carry out my herbal product development. You can have a look if you like."

Jenny followed the squeaking rubber woman to the next shed and peered in the window. Plastic sheeting had been taped across the floor, angled ceiling and walls. It had all the precision of a neatly packaged birthday present, albeit one wrapped from the inside.

"Nice," said Jizzimus. "You could do your shed like that, boss."

"Hmmm," said Jenny, interested.

"Perfect li'l slaughter'ouse. String up the kid from that wotsit in the ceilin' an' you can get blood all over wivout 'avin' to worry about the cleanin' up."

"And you're sure the hazmat suit is essential?" Jenny asked Shazam.

"Sabrina said you can never be too careful."

"Did she, now? And are you going on the herb gathering walk later?"

"Maybe," said Shazam, with a damp, rubbery shrug.

"But perhaps leave the diving suit in your room when you do."

They walked together up to their wing of Eastville Hall. With evening beginning to settle, lights in the larger, grander windows of the house permitted glimpses of elaborate plaster cornices, four-poster beds, velvet drapes and other finery that did not extend to the witches' little annexe.

"I could use a day in the spa," said Jenny.

Shazam, trying to gently wring out her cat, sighed in agreement. "A facial. One of those Swedish massages. Or just to lie back in a sauna or Jacuzzi."

Jizzimus, who was no doubt in favour of giving a woman a 'facial', and regarded himself as a connoisseur of certain aspects of Swedish culture, opened his mouth. Jenny nudged him with the side of her shoe and sent him sprawling before he could speak.

"A day off would be enough," said Jenny.

They regarded the choice of vegetable stir fry or cauliflower cheese at the self-serve buffet.

"All aboard to Trumpton!" shouted Jizzimus. "Stopping at Parpington, Fartmouth and Bum-Flap-on-Sea."

"Vegetables don't make me fart," Jenny hissed at him.

"'Ow would you know?" said Jizzimus. "You do it in your sleep."

She growled at him, irritated.

"I don' mind," he said. "I just sit on top of you an' pretend I'm in an earthquake zone."

George brought the first container into the shed. Caroline had offered to help him carry it, but the unstable stables were strictly out of bounds. His biceps bulged as he hefted it up to pour the contents through the sieve and into the pressure cooker.

"You can really smell the apples," he said as the frothy piss-coloured liquid poured through.

Caroline blinked furiously. "Yes, I can also feel it."

"I told you it was a bit ... sharp. I had an Uncle Frank who was in the navy. Caught gonorrhoea from a girl in Southampton."

He'd lost Caroline. "Ye-es?"

"He always said the best way to teach my brother and me about the importance of using protection was to show us what happened if you didn't."

George jiggled the can to get the last golden drops out. A dribble of glutinous apple pulp plopped onto the mass already collected in the sieve. "Looked just like that," he said.

Caroline shuddered, lifted the sieve weighted by apple dregs aside and put the lid on the pressure cooker. "Do you tell that to all the women?" she asked. "Or just the ones you don't ever want to have sex with?"

"Did I say I wanted to have sex with you, Miss Black?" he said, not unkindly.

"Not out loud, no."

"Cheeky," he said. "Anyway, I said *he* had gonorrhoea. Not me."

"Guilty by association," said Caroline, carrying the sieve outside.

Night had fallen. The seaward sky was a steely blue blanket sprinkled with stars. Caroline wasn't sure where to dispose of several pounds of fermented apple mush but had no intention of hauling it up to main building. Telling herself that it was biodegradable and possibly even good for the soil, she tossed it against the side of the shed next door.

Back inside, she sealed the cooker, set the temperature and ushered George out. "And now we let nature take its course."

She looked at George and squeezed his muscly upper arm. "Another time and I'd be telling you to take me back to your place."

"Again: cheeky," he said, this time a little more serious. "I've not got anything against the older woman—"

"Whatever!" she interrupted. "I've got a night-time herb expedition to attend."

They gathered on the lawn by the teaching hut: Jenny, Kay, Caroline, Dee and Sabrina. Sabrina wore stout wellies and a potholer's head torch, carried a wicker-basket full of empty jam jars in one hand and a knobbly walking stick in the other. She looked ready to tame the wilderness, one jarful at a time. Jenny, whose clothing choices were still limited to those that Dee had magicked up for her, wondered if her white-soled plimsolls were going to survive the night.

"Ur, first," said Sabrina, "we must regard the moon."

Dutifully, they turned to look at the moon.

"And what kind of moon is that?" asked Sabrina.

"New?" said Caroline.

"Wonky?" said Kay.

"Gibbous," said Dee.

"Waxing gibbous," said Sabrina with a nod. "And in conjunction with Mars, you'll note. There are certain herbs that should be harvested only under a waxing gibbous moon."

It was only when Jizzimus failed to deliver some obvious dirty remark about his 'moon' that Jenny realised he was nowhere in sight. For half a second she worried, before deciding to savour his absence.

Caroline, who was scribbling notes in a little pad, raised her pencil. "What difference could it possibly make?" she asked. "Isn't a plant a plant whenever you pick it?"

Sabrina smiled as she shook her head. Nobody could express condescension like Caroline. "Ur, we are engaged in the esoteric craft of herbalism and potion-making. If you're going to think a plant is just a plant then you might as well take up homeopathy and try to cure illnesses with bottled water containing the 'memory of plants'."

"Melissa Sacks, her mum got an infected ulcer on her foot and used homeopathic remedies to treat it," said Dee.

"Did it work?" asked Jenny.

"Well, she says that they decided to amputate her foot before the remedies really got chance to work, so the jury's out on that one."

"Ur, shall we begin?" Sabrina led them toward the end of the gardens and the field beyond.

"Those shoes are going to get ruined," said Kay, falling into step beside Jenny. She didn't need to speak for Jenny to know she was there: Kay was a walking cloud of sweet and sour child funk.

"Just what I was thinking," said Jenny.

Kay frowned. "I'm surprised you wanted to come along."

"Why?" said Jenny.

"Just didn't think it was your thing."

"Oh? What is my *thing*?" Jenny plucked a weedy flower from the edge of the grass and peered at it. It probably wasn't a herb.

Kay gave her a look. "I don't think you have a thing."

"Ouch."

Kay slipped through a gap in the hedge ahead of Jenny. "Some people might think you're only here to 'protect' me," she said, drawing quote marks in the air.

"Is that so bad?"

"You're not my mum, you know."

The comment stung Jenny unexpectedly. She didn't want to be a stand-in mum and yet, perversely, she felt aggrieved that Kay might reject her as such. "I feel a bit responsible for you."

"Why?"

Up ahead, Sabrina's headlamp and Dee's torch swung around like drunken fireflies. Jenny's foot sunk into something soft and squidgy. She didn't look at what it was. "Well, I found you in that warehouse. I rescued you. That makes me responsible."

"That's stupid logic," said Kay. "Dee rescued both of us when she agreed to bring us here. Is she responsible for both of us? No."

"Have I done something to upset you?" asked Jenny.

"No. But you could trust me to go for a walk without having to hold my hand."

Jenny shook her head and kept her mouth closed until she was sure of what she wanted to say. "Kay. Listen. I'm not trying to be your mum. But you're a young person—"

"I'm an adult."

Jenny laughed. The scent in her nostrils told a different story. "You still need someone to look out for you. Do you have a family somewhere?"

"Why are you asking me that?" Even in the dark, Kay's sudden, defensive attitude was obvious. "Do you want to send me back?"

"What? No. I mean, not unless you want to go. Do you not want to...?" Her words died away as Kay stomped off ahead.

Jenny sighed irritably to herself. "Fucknuggets," she whispered.

"You got nuggets?" slurred Jizzimus, stumbling through a hedge.

"Where have you been?" said Jenny.

Jizzimus mounted her leg then tried and failed to climb up. "I could really murder some nuggets, guv," he said.

"I haven't got any nuggets."

Jizzimus gave up on his climbing attempt and fell to the floor with a mutter of, "Nugget 'oarder."

"Are you drunk?" said Jenny.

"As a skink," he replied happily.

"Skunk."

"Them too. It was great, boss. Someone left this big pile of fuzzy apple mush next to one of the sheds."

"And you ate it?"

"Well, I 'ad to!" he said with passion. "What if someone else et it first, eh? Eh?"

"Why would they want to?"

"Well. There wuz some rats, 'oo were eying it up."

"Nice." Jenny looked ahead. The torches were quite distant now and no one had come back for her. No one appeared to have noticed her absence. "Come on," she told the imp. "Let's get you back."

She bent down and scooped the tiny drunkard up in her arms.

"Can we order chicken nuggets from room service?" asked Jizzimus.

"No."

"Can we cook some ourselves?"

"No."

"Could we steal a car and go get some drive-by takeaway?"

"It's called drive-thru."

"Not the way, I do it, boss," yawned the little horror and rolled over to sleep in her arms.

Having to deal with a remorseful and vomitous drunk at three in the morning is guaranteed to disturb your sleep. This is doubly so when only you can see or hear them. This is triply so when the remorseful drunk is only twelve inches high and is both too small and too drunk to reach the toilet bowl.

Jenny wasn't sure what time she finally got back to bed but, whatever, she slept late. When she awoke, the sun was already high and shining in through partly opened curtains. Kay was gone. Jenny sat up and felt a lump in the sheets. There was a pendant and a piece of paper on the foot of her bed. She picked them up.

The pendant was a pebble. In fact, it was the pebble she had seen Kay present as evidence of her work at lunch yesterday. It glowed with an orange light so feeble it was only visible when Jenny cupped her hands about it. A hole had been drilled through the top and a strip of leather threaded through.

The note simply read *For you,* with a wonky smiley face drawn next to the words.

Jenny uttered the kind of deeply sentimental "Aw" she'd never make if anyone else was present. The irritation and disappointment of the night before instantly melted away.

The reversal of mood was only partly undone by the discovery of Jizzimus in the shower, fast asleep and surrounded by the mess he had made in the night.

Dee had spent the morning facing continual frustration. It was made all the more annoying by Norma having predicted it. Her attempts to brew Vilhjálm's Potion of Seeing as described in *Svarta Norn* had hit a barrier and that barrier was the identification of one key ingredient.

Dee asked Sabrina about it during the otherwise informative herb-walk but Sabrina shook her head and questioned both the spelling in the book and Dee's pronunciation. In the morning, Dee had gone to Norma's hut to see if the older witch could provide any clarification but, even as Dee raised her hand to knock, Norma called out, "I told you it can't be done."

Dee had turned away and now, in desperation, sought out the help of the other witches. Kay had smiled politely and shrugged. Caroline laughed at her for even thinking that she might have the vaguest idea. Shazam's shed had been shrouded in plastic sheeting and, when Dee knocked, a very muffled voice had shouted something about a "critical stage in the process." Driven more by a desire for completion than hopefulness, Dee knocked on Jenny's work shed door.

"Coming," called Jenny. She appeared around the side of the shed in a slow jog. "Overslept," she explained.

"Sorry, poppet," said Dee. "Didn't mean to disturb you."

"Nothing to disturb," said Jenny.

"How's the cloak of invisibility coming along?"

"It's more a hanky of invisibility at the moment. How's the potion-making?"

"I'm struggling with a herb."

"Hard to find?"

"Hard to identify." Dee opened the book. "It's given here as *rœtadruncen*."

"What is that? Latin?"

"It's an English translation of an Icelandic book, but I think this recipe could be written in medieval Gaelic or old English. I don't know."

She looked at Jenny. Jenny did a double take.

"You weren't expecting me to offer any kind of wisdom, were you? I would have thought you'd be better off asking someone like—" She stopped herself. "You've asked everyone else already, haven't you?"

Dee was sheepish. "Sorry, sweetness."

Jenny shrugged gamely. "Well, I haven't the foggiest. *Rat. Rata.* It sounds like your potion calls for a rat."

Dee pulled a face and looked at the book again. "Shockingly, my dear, that's not the worst suggestion I've had."

"From the mouths of babes and fools." Jenny opened the door to her work shed. "If it's any help, someone told me there were rats sniffing around some spoiled fruit down by one of the other sheds."

"Oh, thank you. Well, I'll let you..." Dee tucked the book under her arm and set off.

"What's it going to be anyway?" Jenny called after her.

"What?" said Dee.

"The potion."

"Oh. A potion to make invisible spirits visible. Going to see if I can spot some wicked imps."

Jenny's mouth became an *O* of shock. Dee understood at once.

"Think it'll let me see through your invisibility cloak?" She smiled. "Shouldn't worry. It's devilishly hard to make." She went on her way.

Rats, she thought. It was, genuinely, the best option she'd so far been given. Rat was an ancient word. The Old English for rat was probably *ræt* or *rattus* or something like that. But did the recipe call for the hair of a rat? The toe? The heart? The entire tooting thing? If it did, that raised a new issue for Dee because she was a friend to animals, fair and foul. Rats were definitely on the cute end of the Dee Finch Huggability Scale.

"Nonetheless," she said. With a mind-focusing blast of Disney song and a *Tubular Bells* hand wiggle, Dee cast a finding spell.

She walked along the line of sheds. There was an eldritch glimmer from near the wall of Shazam's plastic-wrapped shed/biohazard laboratory.

There did indeed appear to be the smeary remains of fruit splashed against the shed wall and on the ground; apple by the smell of it. And it had certainly been popular. There were gnaw marks up the damp wall and even a hole bored some way in. And on the grass, as though auditioning for the role of dead rat cliché #2, was a dead rat: flat on its back, paws in the air, with its tiny tongue hanging out of the side of its mouth.

"Aw, poor thing," said Dee, ignoring that pragmatic part of her brain which was cheering because her rat-killing dilemma had been swept away by good old natural causes.

Natural causes?

Dee whipped out a handkerchief and picked up the corpse. It was wet and stank, quite clearly, of apples and alcohol.

"Did you drink yourself to death, you silly sod?" she said.

The rat stayed silent on the matter.

Jenny was frantic.

"This is not good! Not good!"

Jizzimus, nursing a hangover, lay on the worktable of her shed and groaned. "Give it a rest, boss. There's nuffin' to worry about."

"Nothing? Didn't you hear her? She's going to make a potion that will allow her to see invisible creatures. Like you! And then what?"

"Imp porn?" suggested the little fiend.

"No, you pillock. It means we're rumbled and I'm out of here. Or worse."

Jizzimus gave a tiny shrug. "You 'eard 'er though. She says it ain' gunna work. She's gunna fail."

"Of course she'd say it's not going to work!" Jenny shouted. "She's British, for Christ's sake! Have you learned nothing all the time you've spent in this bloody country?"

The imp raised a finger. "Toad in the 'ole isn't 'alf the fun it sounds."

"Shut up! This is serious!"

There was a knock at the door. Kay poked her head round. "Hi," she said. "I just wanted to ... I heard..."

Jenny cast about, flustered.

"Eat 'er," said Jizzimus. "Eat 'er now, while no one's lookin'."

"Sorry. I was just talking to myself," said Jenny.

Kay's smile was polite. "Quite loudly."

"Sometimes I don't listen to myself and I have to ... you know." Jenny shook herself. "Hey—" She took hold of the pebble pendant hanging from her neck. "This is lovely. Thank you."

Kay shrugged. "You like it?"

"It's really cool."

"You're not just saying that to be nice?"

"It's a friggin' stone," muttered Jizzimus.

"No," said Jenny. "Listen, about last night..."

Kay held up her hands. "I snapped. I do that. Um, my bad. I'm just not ready to—" She fumbled for words. "We've all got secrets and stuff. Give me time."

Jenny nodded. "Sure."

"I made us one each." Kay held up a similar pebble, hanging from her neck. "I thought they might help you – us – stop worrying."

Jenny gave her a questioning look.

"They glow when you're in danger," said Kay.

"Oh." Jenny looked at hers. "It's glowing right now."

"Yeah, but not much. I mean there's always some danger. Falling trees. Meteor strikes."

Jizzimus sat up in fright. "Meteors? Meteors!"

"Aren't you more likely to be killed by a donkey than a falling meteor?" said Jenny.

"Shit! There's fallin' donkeys now!" Jizzimus dived under the table. Kay glanced over as a plate rattled.

Jenny made a show of testing the floorboards. "I think we might have rats."

"'Oo you callin' a rat?" came a muffled voice.

105

Caroline spent the afternoon hanging herbs up to dry in her shed and trying to ignore the fact that the place in general, and the still in particular, smelled of apple-scented urinal cake.

George knocked on the open door. "My, what's that enticing aroma?"

"It's not my perfume, if that's what you're thinking," said Caroline.

"I've got a couple of hours off." He stepped inside. "I thought I'd pop by and see how our little experiment is going."

"It's certainly borne fruit." Caroline waggled her elbow at the collecting jar while she finished pegging up sprigs of rosemary.

George regarded the five inches of clear liquid. "Do you think it'll taste okay?"

"I think the bigger issue is whether it will make us go blind. Shut the door. Get those two jam jars off the side and let's see."

"And if we go blind?" said George.

"We'll just have to feel our way, won't we?"

Dee tipped some of her potion into a separate pan and placed it on an electric hot plate she'd set up on her workbench. She watched it boil.

"Right." She consulted the book. "I've got my *'holleac in haligwater'*, I think. So now..." She regarded poor dead Mr Ratty lying to one side. "Now *'hwill brimum an rœtadruncen'.*" She hesitated with the wooden tongs. It didn't help that she'd christened him Mr Ratty.

She shut her eyes enough for her to pretend she wasn't looking at the dead rat, picked him up and plopped him into the pan. Mr Ratty floated. Dee submerged him with the tongs but he bobbed right back up again.

With a sad mewl, she placed the lid on the pan and hummed a few bars of *Whistle While You Work* to calm her nerves.

Caroline watched George take the first sip. He took in a mouthful, immediately clamping his lips together as though trying to hold back something unspeakable.

"How is it?" she asked.

He nodded vigorously; which might have been enthusiastic approval or the first signs of total neurological shutdown.

"Is it good?" She waved a hand in front of his eyes to check he was still with her Lacking any meaningful response, she took a sip herself. The apple spirit burned where it touched, killing off all sensation in her mouth. She coughed as the fumes invaded her throat. "Wow," she breathed.

"I think my dongue's gone numb," said George.

She took another sip. Once she could breathe again said, "It doesn't taste very appley."

George had to drink some more to be sure. "Nod much," he agreed. "Id's nod bad though."

Caroline gave it some thought and topped up their drinking jars. "Goes down smooth," she said, letting the phrase do its subliminal work.

"I can'd feel my mouth," said George.

"Let's see if we can't do something about that." Caroline put her jar to one side and kissed him.

He didn't resist, he didn't pull back; but when she stopped, he said, "Caroline. I'm very flattered but—"

"Stop," she said. He fell silent. "George, I'm afraid you've got to face up to some truths."

"Truths?"

She nodded. "You're quite probably the hottest man within ten miles of this place and I absolutely and fully intend to have my wicked way with you."

"Yes, it's just—"

She cut him off with another kiss: longer and more energetic. Some buttons may have popped off his shirt beneath her fingertips. "I'm used to getting my way," she breathed, eventually.

"You're using your powers on me," said George.

She laughed. "Mind control is like hypnotism. It's like alcohol." She pressed a jar to his lips. He drank. "It only guides: strips away inhibitions and worries."

He swallowed hard. The spirits, or perhaps something else, turned his face red.

Caroline tugged at the remaining buttons. "I can't make you do anything, you don't secretly want to do anyway."

Dee paused in the act of dusting away a cobweb from the corner of her shed – having already gently escorted Mrs Spider outside – and looked over at the pan on the hotplate. It felt as though it was humming to her, murmuring with contentment. Perhaps it was cosmic vibrations. Perhaps it was magical resonances. Perhaps it was a distant seismic shock.

Whichever, the pan was definitely calling for her attention. She went over and, with only a moment's hesitation, lifted the lid.

The rat corpse was gone. The potion had transformed from a watery grey to an iridescent turquoise. As she stared, wisps of light shifted in its depths. It was like looking into a shallow tropical sea and seeing, against all probability, lightning flash across the sea bed.

"I've done it," she whispered in delighted surprise. "I've only gone and flipping done it!"

"Oh God, she's done it!"

Jenny held the pebble pendant in her hand. In the last few seconds, it had shifted from the glow of a dying firefly to a fierce orange light.

"What?" said Jizzimus.

She showed him. "Danger."

The imp dropped into a startled crouch. "Is it the donkeys?"

"It's the potion!" said Jenny.

"We should do somethin' about it!"

"*I* said that!"

"Did you, boss? Cos I'm sure it was my lips movin' and everythin'."

Caroline lounged on a pile of dustsheets in the corner of her shed. "Go on, give us a twirl."

George, stripped to the waist, gave an obedient if mildly embarrassed three-sixty. He staggered a little. Caroline laughed, although even sitting on the floor, she felt quite unstable. That apple-vodka hooch was powerful stuff.

George was a powerfully built guy, far broader and more muscular than Effie's beanpole nephew, Madison; though not narcissistically sculpted like some of the gym bunnies she'd known in her time on the police force.

"How long have you been working for this Mrs du Plessis then?" she asked.

"Since was eighteen, I when I left college."

"Only a few months then."

"Ha ha." George took a swig of spirits.

"So, it takes years of mowing and pint-pulling to get a body like that, huh?"

"A body like this?"

"It's a compliment," said Caroline. "Get over here."

He sat beside her on the dustsheets. "It's not just gardening and bar work," he said. "I'm the odd job guy. Lots of fetching and carrying."

"Working your fingers to the bone." She gave him a peck on the lips, took his hand in hers and guided it to her breast.

"You want to do this?" he smiled, "in a shed?"

She twitched her nose. "Well, matron probably won't approve of us bringing boys back to the dorm after lights out. Believe me, I'm quite happy to paddle my own canoe, but it's much more fun with two. Besides, the first time I let a boy, er, into my canoe, it was behind the school bike sheds. Not a million miles away from this. It's almost nostalgic."

"I'm wondering if we've both had a bit too much to drink," said George.

"We're fine." Caroline gave a magical turn of her wrist. "This is exactly the right place and time."

"This is exactly the right place and time," said George and kissed her.

Caroline squirmed as his hand tickled down her stomach. She pinched him in retaliation. "Of course, we didn't get very far behind the bike shed. No sooner did we get down to it than we were interrupted by old Mr Marsden, the woodwork teacher, who—"

There was an urgent hammering at the shed door. Caroline and George looked at each other.

"Nostalgia's overrated," she said, alarmed. "I mean, if that turns out to be Mr Marsden—"

The hammering came again.

"He must, like, be in his nineties by now," Caroline whispered.

"Are you in there, Caroline?" It was Shazam.

"Um. No?" replied Caroline.

"Please open the door. I need your help."

Caroline huffed. "Define 'need'."

"Please! It's an emergency!" whined Shazam.

"Fine." Reluctantly, Caroline tried to sit up but it was difficult with a man's hand down the front of her jeans. She slapped George's hand and he withdrew it.

"But this is exactly the right place and time," said the magically confused gardener.

She flicked him on the forehead with her finger. "This won't take a moment."

"This won't take a moment," he said.

"You just stay here."

"I'll just stay here."

"In fact, hide under these sheets. I don't want anyone to see you."

"In fact, I'll hide under these sheets." George pulled the dustsheets over his head. "You don't want anyone to see me."

"Exactly." Caroline straightened her top as she stood. With the slightest moonshine-induced wobble, she made for the door.

Shazam stood on the step in a hazmat suit and wild-eyed panic. Caroline put a steadying hand on Shazam's shoulder; although who she was steadying was debatable.

"What is it, Cobwebs?"

Shazam, panting, tried to push sweat-matted hair away from her forehead. "My potion! It's gone wrong!"

"Wrong how?"

"It's not the right colour!"

Caroline's internal emergency-o-meter immediately reset to zero. "Not the right colour? That's it?"

"And the pH balance is slightly out!"

"Slightly out? Jeez, Cobwebs. You said it was an emergency."

"It is! I've worked so hard on this. Effie's going to mark me down, maybe kick me off the course."

"No one's getting kicked off the course."

"Are you sure?"

Caroline sighed, stepped outside and shut the shed door behind her. "Fine. Show me."

Shazam waddled to the next shed at remarkable speed in her awkward suit. She pushed the door open, thrust the plastic sheeting aside and ushered Caroline through. Caroline stared. Shazam had, in the small space, managed to set up what Caroline could only think of as a 'proper' laboratory. Tripods, pipettes, thermometers, apparatus clamps and all manner of oddly shaped glassware.

"It's terrible, isn't it?" said Shazam.

"It's ... amazing," said Caroline.

"What?"

"Seriously. I've got two tubs, a pressure cooker and some tubing in my shed. This is like *Breaking Bad* meets *Willy Wonka*."

"The potion, Caroline! The potion!" Shazam pointed at a deep pan sat on top of a tripod and Bunsen burner. The contents were a pale beige.

"What colour is it meant to be?" asked Caroline.

"Manila envelope."

"Well, it's sort of Manila envelope."

"No!" wailed Shazam. She thrust a colour chart in Caroline's face. "Look! Manila envelope! It's too pale. It's more of a Rich Tea biscuit."

"These are real colours?" said Caroline, trying to focus.

"Please help!"

"Okay." Caroline put a comforting hand on Shazam's arm. "Let's go through this step by step. When did you notice something had gone wrong?"

Shazam took a deep, de-stressing breath. "We left it to steep overnight and this morning, when it should have been ready, it looked a bit off. So I thought we'd try it."

"On Mr—?" There was nothing around Shazam's neck. "Where's your cat?"

"Hiding somewhere. I put an application on Mr Beetlebane's neck. He didn't like it and shot off."

"Ah."

"So I tried some on myself."

"You did what?" said Caroline.

"Just a bit," Shazam whispered.

"That might have been dangerous!"

"It did tingle when I put it on my scalp – actually, it's still tingling – but I feel fine. Lots of famous scientists test out their inventions on themselves."

"And how many survive the experience?" Caroline took a metal rod and gave the beige tonic a tentative stir. "So did you leave the lid off overnight when you shouldn't have? Or didn't when you should've?" The rod snagged. "Or did something extra fall in?"

"I don't see how that's possible," said Shazam. "The pan was open, but there was nothing anywhere near it. The whole room is sealed against possible contaminants."

"Apart from down in that corner."

"What?" said Shazam, looking around in confusion.

Caroline tried to raise the heavy lump from the potion. "Down there. Your plastic sheeting's all ripped up. I guess that's how Beetlebum got out."

"What? No! He's just hiding somewhere," Shazam dropped to her knees to inspect the hole. "This wasn't there before."

The lump broke the surface. Caroline almost lost it again in surprise.

"Something's torn right through here." Shazam was indignant. "Broken right through the wood. Weird, it smells of apples and vinegar. I wonder what it was?"

Doing her very best to not touch it, Caroline transferred the drowned rat from the pot to the workbench surface. "Shazam," she said.

"Yes?"

"Now, I don't want you to panic."

Shazam got to her feet. "Why would I...?" She gaped at the sodden rodent cadaver in horror. "How—?"

"I'm guessing it was thirsty and fell in."

"But..."

"If it's any comfort, his coat looks really thick and glossy."

Shazam put her hand to her mouth. "Oh God. I put ... *that* in my hair."

"It'll wash straight out."

Shazam shook her head. Her usually florid complexion had turned near white. "I'm going to be sick—" She barged out of the shed.

"Oh, dear, poppet," said Dee, approaching the scene.

As Shazam doubled over, Dee patted her back. "What on earth happened?" she asked.

Shazam vomited onto the ground, splashing Dee's shoes.

"That's right, sweetness," said Dee. "You let it all out."

"Potion cock-up," Caroline explained. "Think we'd best get her back to her room." The pair of them took an arm each and guided the larger woman back up towards the hall.

"We all cook up a bad batch from time to time," said Dee sympathetically as they walked.

"Somehow a rat ended up in the pot," said Caroline. "And Shazza here tried a bit before she realised."

Shazam tensed and threw up again.

"Well, that's funny," said Dee, "because it was putting a rat in my potion that made it work."

"S'not funny," mumbled Shazam.

"Not funny, no," agreed Dee. "Peculiar. Particularly since it apparently gorged itself to death on a pile of fermented apples someone had dumped."

"Really?" said Caroline, as innocently as possible.

Jenny peered round the corner of the shed. The sun had not yet set and she watched the three witches, arm in arm, making their way back up to the main house.

"Okay," she said, heavily. "Let's do this."

"No, no, no, no, no!" admonished, Jizzimus. "You can't say it like that, boss. Think what we're about'a do."

"I am!"

"We're gunna sneak over there. We're gunna smash in the front door of 'er li'l sanctum, an' then we're gunna steal that potion what she's been workin' on day an' night."

"I know."

"So, guv, it ain': 'Oh, I suppose we should do it, mope, mope, mope'—"

"I don't sound like that."

"It's 'Let's fuckin' do this! Yeah! Yippe-ki-yay-melon-farmers!'"

"I'm allowed to feel bad about this! Dee worked really hard on that potion."

"Well, don't you go harshin' my buzz, guv." Jizzimus combat-rolled across the grass towards Dee's shed.

Jenny tiptoed after him.

"She's looking pretty washed out," Dee said as they lowered Shazam onto her bed.

"I'll be fine," breathed Shazam. "It's just the shock of seeing..." She clutched her stomach and said no more.

"Maybe," said Dee. "But I'd say if you make a single but significant change to a potion like that, it could have a profound effect."

"It's just hair tonic," argued Caroline.

"I might fetch some of my general cure-alls nonetheless," said Dee.

Before she could go, Shazam grabbed her arm. "Find Mr Beetlebane, please," she croaked. "He'll be worried when he sees I'm gone."

"Of course," agreed Dee.

Dee hadn't locked her shed door, which was just as well: Jenny didn't have the time or the nerve to work around an iron padlock.

"The trusting fool!" hissed Jizzimus as the door swung open. "If she's lax about security then this is all on 'er, ain' it?"

"No, we're the bad guys in this scenario," Jenny reminded him.

"Yeah." The imp swaggered inside. "We're the bad dudes."

The potion was unmistakeable: Jenny could smell the magic coming off it. Dee had decanted most into two cork-stoppered bottles. Jenny picked them up.

There was a good few inches of the potion left in a pan on an old electric hotplate. Jenny looped a cloth through the steel handle and dragged it onto the floor where the contents spilled out. Jizzimus gave a start and jumped out of the way.

"There's a bloody rat in it!"

A pathetically limp and bloated body of a rat lay in the puddle on the floor.

"Can't believe I gave her the secret ingredient," muttered Jenny. "Did the nasty rat scare you, Jizzi?"

"Course not. Jus' surprised me, is all."

"It's all right. You're allowed to be afraid of a rat."

"Call that a rat? More like a hamster. I've seen and faced down bigger rats in— Oh, sweet mummy! Save me!" He crouched between her legs as a cushion in the corner of the room unfolded into something black and hairy and *toothy*.

"That's not a rat," whispered Jenny.

It was far too large: its body a good three feet long; a sinuous tail and powerful legs making it look even longer. Its snout was also too short, its ears too pointed and erect. It seemed trapped somewhere between a rat and a cat.

"Mr Beetlebane?" said Jenny. The rat-cat Frankenstein stretched. Both fangs and large rodent incisors, Jenny noted. "What has she done to you?"

"I think it wants to play," trembled Jizzimus as Mr Beetlebane padded/crawled towards them.

"It can think what it likes." With two bottles under her arm and an imp clinging to her calf, Jenny backed out and shut the door behind her. A second later, something prodded the door before beginning to gnaw at it.

"It's unstoppable," said Jizzimus.

"We're going," said Jenny. As she turned towards her own shed, she saw torchlight bobbing along the grounds towards them. It was at head height.

"Sabrina," said Jenny. She turned around. "This way."

"Why?" said Jizzimus.

"If she sees us with two bottles of potion, which Dee later mentions are missing, we'd be kind of rumbled."

"Circumstantial evidence," said Jizzimus but followed her nonetheless.

The next shed, Caroline's, was in darkness. Jenny tried the door; it opened. They slipped inside. Jenny pressed herself into the shadows and watched the head-torch wearing Sabrina pass by.

"Can I smell apples?" she said eventually.

"I thought it was me," said Jizzimus. "I've been sweatin' cider all day."

In the gloom, Jenny could just make out a contraption of canisters, buckets and hosepipes. "Caroline's built herself a distillery."

"An' she's got a man under these blankets," observed Jizzimus.

George Slingsby, barman and occasional lift-giver to witches, lay semi-naked on the floor underneath a coarse dustsheet. He looked at her but didn't move.

"Ah – what are you doing?" asked Jenny.

"I'm hiding under these sheets," said George. "Caroline doesn't want anyone to see me."

Jenny shook her head. "That woman..."

She could feel the glamour around him, like a web. Unpicking it wouldn't be difficult. All it took was the curl of a finger, a pluck here and there... She crouched beside him and—.

George's eyes widened; he blinked hard.

"You okay?" she asked.

He blinked again. Jenny put her hand on his chest and felt the heartbeat in his warm chest. "Well, you're not dead."

George found his voice. "How long have I—?"

Jenny shrugged. "I don't know. I'm not the one who's been doing Jedi mind tricks, am I?"

"She told me she could never force me to do anything I didn't secretly want to do."

Jenny was amused. "Really? So, you secretly want to lie on the floor of a shed without your shirt and wait for a witch to come along and ravish you?"

"Well – I guess it depends on which witch it is."

Jenny blushed.

"Woo hoo!" Jizzimus was inspecting Caroline's still. "Looks like the gardener wants to get 'is 'ands on your shrubbery."

"I didn't mean to embarrass you," said George. He attempted to sit but Jenny still had her hand on his chest and didn't feel particularly inclined to remove it.

"You barely know me," she said.

"We don't have to know someone to like them. Besides I've been watching you." He grimaced in embarrassment. "Not in a creepy, pervert way. I mean I've seen you about. You've always got a troubled look about you."

"I think 'e's confusin' troubled wiv constipated." Jizzimus twiddled a nozzle on the still.

"Maybe I've got troubles," said Jenny.

"And I'd like to help you with them," said George. "Or at least take your mind off them."

His hand was on her thigh. He was a good looking guy, Jenny reminded herself. A nice guy too. And, yes, she would like something to take her mind off her troubles...

She leaned over George and kissed him.

"S'okay, I won't look," said Jizzimus. The nozzle opened and a tiny trickle of spirits dribbled into his hands. "Sorry, did I say won't look? What I meant was I won't take pictures an' post 'em on Instagram. Course I'll look. Otherwise, 'ow will I be able to give you marks out of ten, an' pointers for next time?"

Dee had given Shazam a light sleeping draught. She and Caroline stayed until Shazam started snoring.

"I think it was just shock," said Caroline. "You know: finding a rat in her potion."

"I hope so," said Dee. "If she'd had an adverse reaction to the potion, we'd probably have seen it by now." She shut the clasp on her bag of general remedies. "I don't know about you, sweetness, but I think I could use a cup of tea."

Exercise and concern had purged much of the alcohol and drunkenness from Caroline's system. "A cup of tea sounds great," she said. "Or maybe something a little stronger. However I, um, was in the middle of something in my shed. I need to attend to it."

They left the sleeping Shazam and walked down to the end of the annexe together. As they entered the restaurant, they found Sabrina: pot-holer's torch on her forehead, a strange beast curled up on her lap.

"Is that a badger?" asked Dee.

"It's a bloody ugly badger if it is," said Caroline.

"Ugly animals need love too."

"Ur, I found it outside your shed, Dee," said Sabrina. "And it's not a badger. I think it is a feline-rodent hybrid of some kind. A magical experiment?"

Caroline recognised the patchy fur. "Oh, Christ! It's Mr Beetlebum!"

The cat-rat thing looked at her and tried to miaow but didn't have the right vocal chords.

Caroline and Dee looked at each other.

"The rat in the potion!" said Dee.

"She tried it on the cat first!" said Caroline.

"And then herself!"

As one, they ran back to Shazam's room.

The bedsheets were thrown back. A hulking creature, seven feet of bristling black fur, stood in the ruins of Shazam's hazmat suit.

Foot-long whiskers twitched as it sniffed the air; pink claw-like hands raking in agitation.

"Ooh my, you've changed," said Dee.

"It's not a particularly good look," Caroline heard herself say.

The Rat-Shazam thing squeaked at them. It sounded like a badly played trumpet.

"Easy now, Cobwebs," said Caroline. "Everything's going to be fine."

"Your coat looks lovely," added Dee. "Very shiny."

Rat-Shazam swung round, evidently distressed. Her fat rope of a tail slammed into the dressing table, cracking the mirror. She gave another bugle-blast of alarm and with two frantic head-butts forced the window open, leaping out into the night.

"Crumbs!" said Dee.

Caroline dashed to the window. Shards of glass crunched under her feet. Rat-Shazam was bounding along the side of the building, down the gardens, thankfully away from Eastville Hall.

"We've got to get after her!"

They tripped over each other as they barrelled into the corridor. Caroline, longer legged, raced ahead: down towards the restaurant and the outside door. She slid to a halt when she saw a cat in Sabrina's arms; Mr Beetlebane returned to his miserable, moth-eaten original form.

"It wore off?" said Caroline.

Sabrina shook her head. "A simple disenchantment was all it took."

"Good." Caroline grabbed and steered her towards the door. "Because you're going to need it again."

Even though the shed was dark and the night warm, Jenny automatically pulled a spare dustsheet up and over to cover their nakedness. She kneeled over George. The pendant Kay had given her, its glow dimmed again, hung between them and cast just enough light to pick out the shape of his face, the glint of his eyes.

She brought her mouth down to his.

Jenny tried not to think about exactly how long it had been since she'd had sex. It had been two years, seven months and eight days since her third and final date with James Morgan. James, who liked to start a fitness app before sex. Unbelievably, the app had *Intimacy* as one of the listed activities for calorie burning. She felt decidedly out of practice: struggling to simultaneously co-ordinate her own lips, hands and hips. She closed her eyes and just tried to 'go with it'; that just made her hyper-conscious of her every clumsy action.

George gave a sharp intake of breath. At least she was doing something right.

"Jenny."

"George."

"Your pendant..."

"Huh?" She opened her eyes. The pebble was burning with a hundred watt glow.

"It's kind of blinding."

She pushed herself upright, accidentally elbowing him in the ribs and trapping her ankle under his knee. "This isn't good!"

"Just take it off," he assured her.

"No. I mean this isn't good!"

Jizzimus tore himself away from the still and scrambled onto the table to look out of the window. Outside, something cried like a tortured bugle.

Caroline propelled Sabrina onto the lawn. "There! There!" she shouted, pointing.

In the dark night, the giant Rat-Shazam slammed into a shed, smashing two walls as though they were nothing more than thin balsa wood.

"What the flaming dickens is that?" cried Sabrina with more gusto than Caroline had ever heard from the world-weary woman.

"Trouble for us if we don't fix it. *No!*"

The rat-witch tumbled sideways and crashed through the wall of Caroline's own work shed.

"What's all this racket?" demanded Effie Fray, striding down from Eastville Hall.

"It's Shazam," said Dee.

There were shrieks from down the garden. Two pale and butt naked figures appeared from the wreckage of Caroline's shed. Caroline recognised one instantly and the other seconds later.

Sabrina raised an arm and took aim at Rat-Shazam. "*Capattin po!*"

The were-rat fell, rolled, and rapidly transformed into something somewhat smaller and much less hairy.

Dee and Effie ran forward to help Shazam. Caroline's attention was held entirely by the fleeing backsides of the naked witch and gardener. They were so intent on getting away they didn't look back.

"Jenny Knott, you are a man-stealing cow, so you are." The sight of the pair of them was too entertaining for Caroline to muster much venom.

"Have I missed something?" said Kay. The teenager was pulling on her leather jacket as she approached. "What are you doing?"

"Just regarding the moon." Caroline nodded towards the rapidly fleeing naturists.

"Ah," said Kay. "I see it's in conjunction with Uranus tonight."

"Good one, kid," said Caroline. "Good one."

# Chapter 4 – Fire and Water

It was hardly surprising that Sabrina and Shazam were declared winners of the product design challenge.

While Kay's danger stones had a clear and practical use, her presentation was a thirty-second inaudible mumble into the oversized collar of her jumper. Caroline had the *chutzpah* to deliver a presentation, but since her shed had been completely destroyed and, as everyone knew, her project consisted of a bunch of dried herbs, some powerful apple hooch and one naked gardener, she was entirely without a tangible outcome. The naked gardener, once he was clothed again, removed said apple hooch to his stables and nothing more was said about it. Dee, similarly bereft of product, had stumbled through a confused explanation about her Potion of Seeing going missing and her inability to recreate it. Norma had refused to deliver a presentation, declaring she wasn't "some common peddler, hawking her wares in the street."

Jenny had made it through her own presentation, although it hadn't been pretty. She'd gone into a downward spiral when she realised she was saying "Er" and "Um" too often. She became so self-conscious about her lack of eloquence that she started to pepper her sentences with "Oh shit!" and the occasional "Bollocks!" as she stumbled through the slides. The poor presentation was compounded by the inadequacy of her product: an invisibility cloak which was a mere one inch square and could only make itself invisible, not its wearer. Its only conceivable market might be cloak-wearing insects who wished to appear naked on command. The world was unsurprisingly lacking in insect flashers.

Sabrina's presentation was, by contrast, polished and confident, and her magical lifting rings were genuinely innovative. Shazam did not deliver a presentation and Effie did not ask for one. In Effie's word's, Shazam's transmogrification into a shambling rat-woman beast was "demonstration enough."

"Thank you, ladies," she said after the last presentation. "A good job all round. You'll find that public speaking gets easier with each attempt, so we might try to fit in another opportunity later on the course."

There were many heartfelt grumblings at this news.

"I can see you've been working hard on your projects, with a somewhat varied degree of success. However I think we can all agree Sharon has genuinely broken new ground with her transformation potion, so she will take one of the prizes. The other will go to Sabrina for her lifting rings."

There was a small ripple of applause.

"Oh thank you!" squealed Shazam. "A day in the spa! I do feel a bit out of sorts after that business with my potion. It sounds like just what me and Mr Beetlebane need."

"Ur, surely you're not taking the cat?" said Sabrina. "I'd like to think that a spa has certain standards."

"Standards?" said Shazam.

"Vis-à-vis pets and other vermin."

Shazam looked crestfallen. "What? I can't go if Mr Beetlebane's not allowed."

Caroline rolled her eyes. "Nice work, Sabrina."

"I'm sure we can work something out," said Effie diplomatically. "I'll accompany you up to the Hall and see what can be done, Sharon." She smiled brightly. "Now, as we discussed this week, Sabrina's family have access to the Pendle Library of Witchcraft in Cambridge, and I'm pleased to say that access has been extended to us for the duration of this course. And so, on Monday, we will be taking a little trip to Cambridge."

"That does sound fun," said Shazam. "Spa days. Trips."

"It's like a dream come true," said Caroline dryly.

"Furthermore," continued Effie, "Mrs du Plessis has kindly offered us the use of the house's mini-bus. Apparently, Monday is some sort of changeover day or they're having new supplies delivered or somesuch, so I think it probably helps her if we're all out of the way."

"Can any of us drive a mini-bus?" asked Norma.

"Not a problem," said Caroline. "Unless Mrs du Plessis is lending us George to chauffeur us around?"

Both Jenny and Effie gave her reproachful looks.

"But today is Sunday," said Effie. "We can sort that out tomorrow. Perhaps today you deserve the rest of the day off. To indulge in *innocent* pursuits."

Effie hustled Shazam and Sabrina across the lawn. Dee latched eagerly onto Norma as she left. Jenny, Caroline and Kay were the only ones left in the dusty teaching hut.

"So," said Caroline. "I think it's time we had the talk, don't you?"

Jenny tried to summon a facial expression that said she had no idea what Caroline was talking about, but she was distracted by Jizzimus settling on the arm of Effie's chair.

"This is gunna be good," grinned the imp. "Sock it to 'er guv."

"Is this about George?" sighed Jenny.

"I should think so."

"Well, I'm ready to hear an apology, Caroline."

"You're ready to ... *what?*" Caroline sputtered a little. "*You* hopped into *my* bed with the man that *I'd* undressed while I tended to Cobweb's emergency. I'd say that's a bit rude, wouldn't you?"

Jenny was agog. "Seriously? Have you no moral compass, woman? Did you trade it in for a sense of self-righteous entitlement?"

"I don't think I'm the one being self-righteous, Miss Goody-Two-Shoes."

Jenny clenched her fist. She could feel her cheeks starting to burn with anger and the tingle of witchfire beneath her skin. "Kay," she said, as calmly as she could, "you don't have to stay and listen to this."

"I'm fine," grinned Kay, settling back into her chair.

"What I saw," Jenny said carefully, "was a man with an enchantment cast over him, left naked in a shed. A man who really didn't know what he was doing there when I released him. You can't treat people like that, Caroline It's manipulative."

Caroline gave Jenny a long, smug look. "So, are you saying that you never used any kind of manipulation on a man to sleep with him?"

"No."

"You never thought about what underwear you might put on? You never took extra care with your make up?"

"That's not—"

"You never played the oh-so-innocent otherworldly witch who's only trying to help?" Caroline affected a whiny falsetto.

"I do not sound like that!"

"To be fair, you do a bit," said Kay.

Jizzimus clicked his fingers and pointed at Kay. "What she said, guv."

"You're meant to be on my side," said Jenny.

"No one's on your side," said Caroline. "You're all alone in your little Kingdom of So Wrong It's Embarrassing."

"You're deluded," said Jenny. "You've lost all perspective. Even if I did any of those things to ... to woo a man, they are not the same as magical entrapment! Nothing like the same."

"It's just a spectrum, Jenny; different degrees of the same thing. People have been manipulating their way into each other's' knickers for centuries; and people like you have been disapproving of it for just as long."

"How can you possibly say that putting a spell on someone is in the same ballpark as a push-up bra or eating a breadstick suggestively?" Jenny tried to ignore Kay, but from the corner of her eye she could see the girl peering at Jenny's chest, a question on her face. "No, Kay! It was a 'for instance'. Where would I find a push-up bra round here?"

"I bet Dee's got one in her suitcase," said Kay. "I might ask, I've never tried one. Have you two finished shouting? I'm bored now and we've got the day off."

Caroline laughed, wagging a finger at Jenny. "I would put money on you being the sort to do breadstick blow jobs. You wouldn't believe how many times a waitress sees it during a shift. It's entry level stuff; you know that don't you?"

"Well I'd put money on you being the sort of waitress who just can't bring herself to be nice to the customers," said Jenny, trying hard not to rise to the bait.

"You clearly don't know how to nice to your friends. You don't steal a guy after your mate has called dibs."

"This isn't about George. Not just him—"

"It is. He's the only shaggable bloke in this part of the fens."

"—It's about how you treat men."

"Just promise that you'll keep your hands off, George."

"You won't get within a mile of him!" yelled Jenny, incensed. "Now he knows what you're playing at, he'll run when he sees you."

"We'll see."

"You haven't listened to a word I said, have you? It's wrong. Mind control is just plain wrong!"

Caroline gave her forehead an exaggerated whack with her palm. "Christ, I get it now. How could I be so blind? You're annoyed that you can't do it, aren't you?"

Jenny was momentarily speechless.

"Time for a bloodbath?" suggested Jizzimus. "We can take 'em both. We kill 'em, messy as you like, stomp on the squishy bits and you get a tasty snack afterwards. It's a win-win, guv!"

"I think I'd better go," said Jenny. There was a tightness at her throat as she rose and walked out.

"Guv, wait! You can't walk out like that. Not wivout a witty partin' shot! Tell 'em yer off to see whose bed the gardener's tending today. No?"

Jenny shook her head as she strode away from the classroom. She wasn't in the mood.

"Or ... or tell 'er that the only reason 'e might be attracted to 'er is because gardeners is used to 'andlin' dirty hoes."

"Okay," she admitted. "That is a good one."

She turned to deliver her stinging retort but the door to the teaching hut was already closed and the moment had passed.

Dee pointed at a puddle on the floor of her work shed. "Look, can you see the residual magic?"

Norma bent forward, with difficulty. Her undergarments were not made with flexibility in mind. "All I can see are a few damp patches and stray rodent hairs. I would advise in future that you bottle up your potions at the earliest opportunity, so as to avoid this sort of mishap."

"I filled two bottles," said Dee, casting about forlornly, "and there's no sign of them. I know we had a beast on the loose and everything, but they wouldn't just vanish."

Norma nodded. "I think I understand, Dee. There's no shame in a learning journey you know. Some of the greatest witches think like scientists. I believe it was Edison who said he hadn't failed a thousand times, he had successfully found a thousand ways that didn't work."

"No. I made the potion. It worked, I'm sure." She looked at Norma's gently judgemental face. "I know you don't believe me, but I really had something here."

"Then make some more, Miss Finch."

"I did but it hasn't been the same at all."

"Interesting. Have you been able to identify any differences?" Norma sniffed at the contents of a jar.

"Rats. Somehow it's the rats. I got some more, but they must be different."

"Where did you get them from? Freshly killed, were they?"

Dee cringed. The death of an animal was something she really didn't want to be responsible for. She reached into a mini fridge under her workbench and lifted out a small, pale corpse. It was squashed and only the tail identified it as a rat. "I phoned a local pet shop. They keep frozen ones for people with pet snakes. I had them send me half a dozen, but they're not working. I don't think they're the same as wild rats"

"Could be a freshness issue," mused Norma. She took the rat and held it to her face, inhaling deeply. "It's a fact that freezing alters the cell structure. You might ask the groundsman if he'll set you a trap; get some fresh ones. Why are you so keen to get this potion working, anyway? The competition is over."

"Scientific curiosity. The challenge."

Norma put the rat back into the fridge and dusted her hands on her tweed skirt. "Yes?"

"And," said Dee, "I want to find wicked witches by spotting their imps."

"Why would you want to find wicked witches? They're best avoided, trust me."

"I suppose because I've never seen or met one."

"You still doubt they exist?"

Dee shrugged, avoiding the question. "And I want to help them."

"Help them?"

"I bet nobody's ever reached out and tried to really understand them."

Norma inflated her gigantic chest and reared in indignation. "Understand them? What's to understand about something that's *wicked*?"

"I don't know if I believe in wickedness. Aren't 'good' and 'evil' just words we use to describe stuff—?"

"They are wicked, Miss Finch. Like murder, theft and queue jumping. It's not just words. It's fact."

"Ah, but you've only got to look back in history. People have said the same about foreigners and dogs and ... and rhubarb. We live in more enlightened times: we know *everything* has its place in the world."

"Are you mad?" exploded Norma. "Seriously Dee, I can understand your enthusiasm for the underdog as well as the next person, but that is a completely absurd comparison to make. I can tell you about wicked witches, if you want."

Dee leaned closer. "Yes, please."

"No, better still, I will *teach* you about wicked witches."

"That'd be nice."

"There's much to know; and by the time I'm done, you'll be less keen to meet one, believe me!"

Dee smiled.

"Which way, kid?" Caroline asked.

Kay looked down the road and shrugged. It was flat and featureless fields in both directions. There was a metal barn on the horizon to the right, and a distant suggestion of trees and a church to the left. They looked equally unenticing for a Sunday morning walk. Caroline steered them left.

"Don't worry about Jenny and me," she said.

"I'm not."

"That was just a little something we needed to get out in the open. We'll be fine."

"But you both want the same man," said Kay.

"George? Oh, Jenny can have him. I might have him too, mind, when she's not looking." Caroline winked. "How about you, kiddo? Many boyfriends?"

Kay shook her head with a small frown.

"A girlfriend, then?"

"No. Neither," said Kay. "I never really got a chance to do any of that stuff. It wasn't easy being a witch where I grew up."

"Where was that? I'm guessing from the accent it's nowhere local."

Kay hesitated.

"Is it some big secret?"

"No. The thing is, I will tell you and then—"

"What?"

"The British are a very judgemental people."

"Are you calling us racist?"

"No," said Kay. "Well, some. But I mean that you make stereotypes. For example, the French, you think they are all—"

"Accordion-playing onion-farmers in stripy jumpers."

"Exactly. And they're your neighbours and friends!"

"Friends is putting it a bit strong, I'd say."

Kay plucked a long piece of grass, pulling at the seed head as she dawdled. "I'm from Portugal."

Caroline nodded politely and thought.

"No comment?" asked Kay.

"Don't think so."

"You think of Portugal and what comes to mind?"

"Not a lot. Package holidays. Costa del Sol. That sort of thing."

"That's Spain."

"Then I've got nothing."

"Right. But if I was to tell you I lived in up the mountains in the north of the country, you'd imagine stone huts and backward and superstitious peasant farmers who cuddle their donkeys to keep warm at night."

"No," lied Caroline.

"And what makes it worse, my family and neighbours *were* superstitious peasant farmers."

"And the donkey-cuddling?"

"They'd deny it. They sold the donkey to buy the first tractor in the village when I was six. In the mountains – I dunno – it's much easier to believe in witches. I believed in them before I even knew I was one; otherwise I'd have been more careful. When people realised I was a witch – and this was when I was only ten – nobody would welcome me into their house."

"Whoa, hold up there," said Caroline. "I don't think people would welcome *any* of us into their houses if they knew we were witches. Luckily for us, when people see something weird happening, they automatically assume reality TV or a flashmob. Definitely not witchcraft. You had it tough then?"

"You have no idea."

"So you what, ran away?"

Kay shredded the last of the grass seeds and threw them up into the air. "No. I was sold."

Caroline stopped and stared at the girl. "You are shitting me."

"Nope. My father locked me up, said it was for my own protection, and sold me."

Caroline couldn't believe it. "Who to?"

"A man from Porto." Kay met her eyes briefly before walking on. "So that's me. No boyfriend. No teenage years to speak of at all. I don't think I did them at all. Tell me about yours, Caroline."

"My teenage years?" She popped her lips and smiled. "That's quite a long story. With parental advisory for explicit content."

Kay pointed down the featureless lane. "I think we've got time for a long story."

"I'll tell you, sure, but it's not too late you know. You're still young enough to do all of those things."

"I'm in the middle of rural England with a bunch of old women. You're not exactly going to come to the skate park with me, are you?"

Caroline put her hand on Kay's elbow and stopped her. "I'll ignore the 'old' comment. Skate park, no. I don't imagine there's one within a hundred miles, but we can do something. We'll walk into town, or whatever that place is up ahead and we'll be teens. Arrogant, awful teens."

Kay rolled her eyes.

"Perfect," said Caroline. "You're a natural!"

Fifty yards down the road, Caroline snapped her fingers. "Ronaldo! The footballer. He's Portuguese, isn't he?"

"Very good," Kay conceded. "A thousand years of history and that's the best you can do."

Jizzimus tripped over a fallen branch and came up spitting leaves. "Hold up a minute, would ya! Jeez boss, I'm only a little feller. D'you even know where we are?"

"In the woods!" Jenny snapped. "What more do you need to know?"

"That there's a burger bar an' a strip joint in the next clearin', but I bet there ain't. Listen, there are much better ways to work off a bad mood than chargin' off like a bull wiv a chilli up 'is fundament."

Jenny shook her head. "What wise advice do you have for me, O sage and ever-creative imp!"

"Tha's better. Bit more respect. I like it." He rubbed his tiny hands together. "Blast that bush there. Go on, nuke it."

Jenny turned to see a scrawny bush. "That one?"

"Yeah."

She thought about it. "It is encroaching on the path. I'd be doing a public service, really."

"Whatever. Do it!"

She summoned a ball of witchfire and blasted the bush, with much greater ferocity than it actually needed. A small, scorched crater remained.

"Way to go! Bloody great that. Do another one!" Jizzimus bounced on the spot. "That one there, it's bigger. I know you want to, guv."

He was right: she did want to. Jenny incinerated the second bush. It went up with a satisfying *woomf* which blackened and curled leaves on the surrounding trees. More than one squirrel considered relocating to a less dangerous wood.

Jenny gave in to her base urges. She blew stuff up for a few minutes. It felt good.

"See if you can get this one, right up to the top!" Jizzimus pointed to a tall pine tree.

Jenny took a deep breath and summoned an extra-long blast. She didn't exactly know where witchfire came from, but on some level it helped if she held her breath. She felt mild elation as the topmost branches flickered briefly with flames.

"Enough for now I think." She sank onto a log while Jizzimus inspected the damage. Bottles clinked in her jacket pocket. She pulled them out. Dee's Potion of Seeing. They buzzed mildly with magic. Jenny knew that she needed to dispose of them or someone would be sure to notice.

She looked around. "Maybe I should bury them."

"You reckon it works then?" Jizzimus settled onto the log beside her.

"I think it probably does. Just look at it," said Jenny.

"You can't tell by lookin'. Giz some." He took one of the bottles, unbunged the cork and tipped the whole lot into his mouth. He smacked his lips a few times. Jenny looked at the other bottle. With a small shrug she opened it.

"It's like Jägermeister wiv a hint of piss," said Jizzimus after careful consideration. He saw Jenny hesitate with the bottle at her lips. "When I say piss, I mean, er, strawberries, obviously."

Jenny swigged from the bottle. Jizzimus's initial observation was accurate. It had a powerful alcohol kick with herbal overtones, but you couldn't ignore the foetid animal tang. She spluttered.

"Go on boss, get it down yer. I've 'ad a 'ole bottle, so I'll be able to see better than you."

She swigged the rest of the potion, gasping at the foulness of it. "Now we should be able to see invisible things."

"Can't see nuffin' boss," said Jizzimus, looking around.

"Maybe there's nothing around here." Jenny stood. "Let's keep walking. We'll either get to something we *can* see, or the stuff will make us blind and insane."

"Brilliant!" shouted Jizzimus.

"I'm telling you, I heard an explosion," said Norma.

"An explosion, poppet?" said Dee.

"An enormous *woomf* sound. Over there."

"Maybe it was a dog."

"I said *woomf* not *woof*."

"An asthmatic dog?"

Dee and Norma walked together through a shaded woodland. More accurately, Dee was scampering to keep up with Norma as she stormed across the countryside. The subject of wicked witches was something that seemed to light a spark of terrifying passion in Norma. She whacked her fist into her palm for emphasis each time she made a new point.

"Wicked witches are a distinct subspecies, Dee. I am convinced that if scientists were able to test a wicked witch, it would be possible to isolate the very DNA of *evil*."

"Cor, imagine that!" said Dee, scuttling forward to open a gate. Norma didn't slow down at all. Dee wondered if she would have just battered through like a tweedy sledge hammer.

"I know you've got this idea in your head that you can help them or save them, but believe me they are simply wicked. They are born wicked and they spend their lives in pursuit of wickedness."

"Ah, so they are born evil then."

"Absolutely."

"And their behaviour is fixed from birth."

"Yes, I suppose."

"So, they don't choose to become evil."

"Well..." Norma hesitated, seeing a philosophical trap up ahead.

"So, being a wicked witch is more like an illness than a moral choice."

"No, Miss Finch!" said Norma loudly. "Born evil or not, wicked witches set themselves apart by the evil acts they choose to commit."

"But what sort of thing do they do exactly?" asked Dee.

"What do they do? What do they *do*?" barked Norma. "They eat children. Torture them if they get the chance. You'll have heard of wicked witches from history?"

"Er, will I?" said Dee, casting about for a reference. "Like in Snow White, yeah?"

"I'm not talking about fairy tales, Dee, there are wicked witches that the world knew and feared. We can go right back to Greek times, when the witch Circe terrorised the people of the Mediterranean."

"Isn't she a myth?" Dee was confused. "Aren't myths the same as fairy tales?"

"Not at all," snapped Norma. "If you want a more modern example, look at Elizabeth Báthory. A seventeenth century European noblewoman who did unspeakable things to local girls as part of her rituals."

"Yes, but what things?"

"Unspeakable things! *Sanguinem veneficae bibit*! I can see that you're hungry for details. Let me show you something. See this scar?" She pulled back her sleeve, exposing her forearm.

"Slow down, Norma, I can't see anything while you're going this fast."

Norma stopped and held out her arm. Lines of pearly scar tissue wound up it. Dee tried to imagine the wounds when they were fresh. They must have been horrific.

"A wicked witch did this to you?" she whispered.

"Yes. Which is why I'm going to pass on my knowledge to you, Dee. If you're going to persist in this obsession then you need to know what you're dealing with." Norma looked around the clearing in which they were standing. "This place is as good as any. Let us begin."

Dee stood attentively while Norma found a spot that she liked the look of and set down her capacious handbag. She started to rummage in its interior.

"So let's talk about the basics. We can start with the wicked witch's well documented fear of iron. It pays to protect yourself, Dee. Do you have any items of iron about your person right now?"

133

"Ooh, let's have a look," said Dee. She took out a large sized men's hanky and spread it upon the ground. She upended her handbag and poked through the contents while Norma peered over her shoulder.

"Dog biscuits? Surely you're not wasting valuable space on such things? In the fight against evil, you must ensure that everything you're carrying has a purpose."

"You never know when you might meet a dog, and where would you be if you didn't have doggy snacks on you?" Dee held up a nail file. "Is this iron? It's a good one, this, came out of a gift set from Boots."

Norma rolled her eyes and indicated Dee should keep looking.

"I've got some keys, would they count?" She held up a clattering bunch of keys of all sizes, suddenly thoughtful. "I hope they don't need to read the meter at the charity shop while I'm away. Or find the spare teabags."

Norma returned to her own bag and reached inside. "An insider tip for you. Get some nails from a hardware store. Very cheap and the iron content is high. Here's a couple of mine to get you started."

"Brilliant!" Dee looked at the two large nails. "What do I do with them, then?"

"You improvise! We'll be doing some practical exercises momentarily, but a well-equipped handbag will hold everything that a witch might need if she's to improvise." Norma reached into her bag, producing a roll of duct tape and a multi-tool. "I shall demonstrate."

Caroline and Kay strolled into Stickney. It was too small to be a town but Caroline, a self-confessed city girl, felt it lacked any of the necessary charm to be called a village. It was just a string of ugly modern houses clinging to the single road running through it. It didn't even have a village green. However, it did have a few of the essential ingredients for a teenager's day out.

"Here we go. First lesson. A car's coming," said Caroline, glancing behind them.

"So?"

"We walk down the middle of the road."

"But he'll hit us," said Kay.

"Nah. He's seen us. We walk down the middle of the road and make him wait."

"Why?"

"Because we can. We're teenagers Damn! We need some bubble gum. To do it properly, we wait until he's really mad, honking his horn mad, and then we turn and blow a massive bubble. Oh, hang on."

Caroline drew a line down her own forehead with her thumbnail and muttered a cantrip. She felt an electrical shiver come over her.

"Jesus, Caroline," said Kay, startled. "Is that what you looked like as a teenager?"

Caroline looked down at the illusory body she had given herself. Hell, she thought with a mixture of pleasure and wistfulness, I used to be so damned *perky*. "It's what I think I looked like," she conceded.

They walked on, slowing their pace and taking up the narrow road with their exaggerated swagger. Kay grinned nervously at Caroline.

"No smiling! Sulky duck face, like we practised."

Kay followed Caroline's lead, affecting an exaggerated pout with eyes raised to the heavens. The car squeezed past them after a few minutes, the driver gesticulating and shouting.

"Well that was fun," said Caroline.

"Is that what being a teenager's about?" Kay sounded under impressed.

"Partially."

"I thought it would be more about boys and booze and stuff."

"We'll get to it. I think we've got everything we need up ahead. An offy and a chip shop." Caroline rubbed her preternaturally young hands. "That's a teen adventure playground, right there."

Jenny could see something through the trees ahead: a large brown brick building at the edge of the woods. It looked like a church; but the degree of movement surrounding it made Jenny doubtful. If a slightly lopsided Victorian church had been dropped into the middle of New Street station, it would have looked pretty much like this.

"Can you see them too, boss?" asked Jizzimus in a whisper.

"Yes, I can see them," said Jenny as they drew closer. "But they're people. I can see people without a potion."

"Oh yeah? Even those ones as 'ave 'ad their 'eads chopped off?"

Jenny halted and took a longer look. There were a great many people, but it was a strangely mismatched group. Some of them looked as if they had plundered the wardrobe of an amateur theatre company for oddly sized and hopelessly worn out garments from different historical periods. There was also, as Jizzimus pointed out, a headless torso, carrying

135

his head under an arm in the manner approved by theatrical ghosts everywhere.

"Ghosts?" Jenny murmured.

Jizzimus gave a muted squeal and ran to her leg, clutching it tightly, eyes closed. "Maybe they're jus' really, really good cosplayers."

"I've never seen a ghost before."

"Come on, guv, let's jus' back away quietly. They'll never know we was 'ere if we go quick."

"What are you frightened of, imp? I just want to have a look at them."

"But they could 'urt us."

"I don't think so. Remember this is a Potion of Seeing. Ghosts must exist all around us; we just don't see them the rest of the time."

Jizzimus let out a whimper of distress. Several of the ghosts stopped their aimless wanderings to stare at them. Jenny walked forward, Jizzimus still clinging on. The figure closest to her was a man in baggy tweed. It wasn't like the tweed Norma favoured, but something coarser, looking as though it might have been repurposed from potato sacks.

A troubled look creased his face. He gestured frantically to Jenny.

"You can see me?" she asked, moving cautiously.

He nodded.

"You can hear me as well?"

The man nodded, his mouth shaping silent words.

"But I can't hear you." She tutted in realisation. "It was a Potion of Seeing. I guess hearing is another matter."

"Guv, that's enough!" whined Jizzimus. "We don' need to encourage 'em."

Jenny ignored him, concentrating on the ghost. "If you want to say something, you'll need to act it out. Do it with sign language, or mime or something."

The man looked thoughtful for a moment. He nodded to Jenny. He held his hands out in front of him at waist height, in a gripping motion.

"Gangnam style?" asked Jenny. "You want to know—"

The man shook his head in irritation and then moved his feet under his outstretched hands.

"Oh you're digging!" The man nodded. "Something to do with digging. Have you buried something?" He nodded vigorously. "Right. So you've buried something important, and you want to tell me about it?"

The man nodded again and changed stance. He mimed the curvaceous outlines of a woman, and pressed hands to his heart, staring dreamily at the sky.

"Lovely woman? Your sweetheart? Your wife?" Jenny was starting to enjoy the game. Jizzimus made loud huffing noises to indicate that he didn't approve.

The man nodded vigorously at *wife*.

"You've buried your wife?" The man scowled in distaste. "No. You've ah … buried something that you want your wife to have?"

The man jumped with excitement and nodded again.

"Good," said Jenny. We're getting somewhere. Now all you need to tell me is what it is. Tell me what you buried, and maybe I can dig it up."

The man beamed. He held his hands in front of him and opened his palms.

"A book?"

He gave a curt nod and frowned in contemplation. He held his hands to his face and splayed his fingers, so they stuck out either side of his face. He wiggled his fingers and darted his head about.

"You're a prawn!" yelled Jenny. The man looked perplexed.

"Prawn? said Jizzimus. "What you been smoking boss? That's a bleedin' mouse or a rat, that is."

The man pointed to Jizzimus at the word *rat* and beamed.

"So it's a book about rats?" said Jenny slowly. The man's expression was unimpressed. "A rat book?"

The man made a stretching motion with his hands.

"Raaaat…" It hit her. "You mean a ration book?"

The man bounced on the spot, nodding and clapping, with a huge grin on his face.

"I think I understand," said Jenny carefully. "I'm guessing you died in the nineteen forties or maybe fifties, and you want to get your ration book to your wife so that she can use it? Right?"

He gave her a thumbs up.

"Right. Just that there's something you need to know there. I'd be happy to go and dig up your book, wherever it is, but thing is, rationing ended ages ago. Your wife can buy as much food as she wants now."

The man looked at her in disbelief.

"It's true. The shops are full of food; tons of choice. Any vegetables you'd care to name. Infinite variety of cheese."

"Penis-shaped pasta," said Jizzimus.

"Frozen ready meals."

"Penis-shaped lollipops."

The ghost held her gaze as a change crept across his face. The troubled look evaporated and his eyes glistened with moisture. His smile was one of genuine pleasure.

"'E's fadin' away. Where's 'e goin'?"

"I think we solved his problem," said Jenny. "The thing that was shackling him to this earthly plane. He's moved on." The ghost faded to nothing. "It's nice to think we helped a troubled soul, don't you think, Jizz?"

"Whatever floats yer boat, I s'pose. You might want to look who's comin' along next though, boss."

"Eh? Who?"

"All of 'em. Every last bleedin' one."

Dee watched, wide eyed, as Norma stepped back and appraised the last of her creations. She'd used a combination of natural resources, minor spells and a *lot* of duct tape. Around the clearing were several different stations, although Norma hadn't yet explained what they all were.

"I think we're ready to begin," said Norma. "Pay attention. I've created a fully immersive battleground for you to learn some valuable techniques. You'll be pitted against the worst that a wicked witch can throw at you, so you'll need to be prepared. Have you fashioned any defences for yourself?"

"Well, I did what you suggested and I found a stout stick," said Dee, holding up a length of tree branch. "But when I came to attach the nail to the end of it I dropped it in the leaves, and I can't find it. To be honest, I was a little bit worried about tetanus."

Norma's eye twitched slightly. Dee wondered if it was tiredness or a lack of patience with her student. "Very well. You can try to defeat a wicked witch with a simple stick, although I'd like to think you might equip yourself more effectively in a live environment. Let's walk you through what we have here."

Dee followed Norma to the first station. To the naked eye it appeared to be a rabbit tethered to a tree stump with strands of ivy, but the rabbit sat up on its hind legs in a very unrabbitlike way.

"Here we have a wicked witch's imp," said Norma.

"Oi can smell yer mother's fanny!" it screeched.

Dee was taken aback. "It's very *rude*. And why on earth does it have an Irish accent?"

Norma shrugged. "Must be an Irish rabbit. Right, what do we know about imps?"

"Um, they grow bigger if the witch is really wicked," said Dee, stepping back as the imp snapped and lunged at her. "They are normally invisible to humans, even witches."

"Yes, very good. We'll work on techniques for subduing an imp a little later." Norma, walked on.

"We're not going to hurt the bunny are we?" asked Dee, her voice quavering with concern.

Norma rounded on her. "Dee, are you taking this seriously? The war against wicked witches is not something to be entered lightly. If cute fluffy animals have to suffer to win that war then we must be prepare ourselves to take whatever action is necessary. Do you understand?"

Dee's nod wasn't very convincing.

Norma deflated slightly. "No, Miss Finch. It will not be necessary to hurt this rabbit. It should come out of this exercise with nothing more than a slightly extended vocabulary."

They approached the next station. Dee found it profoundly disturbing. Norma had used an extraordinarily large mandrake root to mimic the form of a child. It was bound tightly, with just its face showing. It was remarkably expressive, considering its vegetable origins, and Dee's heart went out to the poor mite.

"A captive child," explained Norma. "The wicked witch's next meal unless we can intervene. The taste of a child is irresistible. They will do anything they can to sate their craving. A single witch will eat an entire child in one sitting, given the chance."

Dee's stomach flipped and she swallowed uncomfortably. "Lovely. What's next?"

"This?" Norma walked to the next station and clapped her hands together as she admired her creation. "This is our wicked witch."

It was remarkable. Norma had constructed it from fallen tree branches, selecting those with fungus growing on them to add a certain warty character. It was fastened together with duct tape, herbs and creepers, and even had a crazed hairdo formed from a bird's nest.

"Does she have a name?" asked Dee.

"A name?"

"Yes. If we're immersing ourselves in things, we could give her a wicked witch name like Elphaba or Bellatrix or—"

"Lesley-Ann Faulkner."

"Um. Or Lesley-Ann Faulkner. It's a name, I suppose. It's definitely a name."

Norma cast a brief spell to animate the dummy. Its head snapped up and dead eyes locked onto Dee. Lesley-Ann Faulkner was a frightful vision indeed.

"Right, Dee," shouted Norma, "it's time to pit your wits against the wicked witch. Make no mistake, she's coming for you!"

Dee whimpered slightly and gripped her stick. Norma was fiddling around in her handbag. She pulled out a can of hairspray and a butane lighter.

"We mustn't forget the witchfire," she said, igniting her makeshift flamethrower. "Come on Dee, how good is your firefighting?"

Caroline and Kay went into *Peek-a-booze* and surveyed the shelves.

"We're looking for the cheapest cider," hissed Caroline. "If it mentions apples or has a name like a folk band then it's no good. We want industrial strength chemical fizz." She tried to suppress the memory of her cider-based adventures with George. "Ah – this one's for us!" She picked up a can. "*Liquid Lightning.* Eight percent."

"Don't we want a bigger number than eight?" asked Kay, unimpressed.

"Eight's a big enough number, trust me," said Caroline, and thumped down a pair of cans on the counter.

"You got ID?" asked the shopkeeper, hands flat on the counter as he regarded them.

"I'm eighteen," said Caroline.

"Date of birth?" he asked.

Caroline added seventeen years onto her actual birth date and reeled it off smugly.

"What day of the week was that then?" he asked, tapping on the screen of his phone and fixing Caroline with a challenging stare.

"Monday."

"This app says Thursday. Sorry, can't let you buy that." The shopkeeper stood upright, hands on hips.

Caroline huffed and rolled her eyes. "Right. Fine. We'll just take some fags then."

"No, you're not having fags. Now hop it, the pair of you."

"Oh, what?" whined Caroline. "But we really are old enough!"

"Yeah!" said Kay. "One day we'll even be as old as you, *old man!*"

"Yeah!" agreed Caroline, pleased her young colleague was getting into the swing of it. "You're so old that your birthday candles caused global warming."

"Hey!"

"Yeah," said Kay. "You're so old, you have to scroll down to find the year you were born."

"Yeah. You're so old, if you acted your age, you'd be dead."

"I don't have to stand here and listen to this!"

"We could fetch you a chair if you like," said Kay.

The shopkeeper threw them out and it was brilliant.

Ten minutes later they were sitting on a low wall outside the chip shop, eating from a packet of chips placed between them.

"So, teenagers always have words they use to be different to all adults," said Caroline. "There'll be a word that means 'good' and a word that means 'bad'. It doesn't matter what word, but it must sound like complete nonsense to anyone over twenty."

"It made learning English very difficult," said Kay. "Since when did 'bad' mean 'good'?"

"Well, you had 'wicked', which went from meaning bad to good. Then 'bad' became good. Then things were 'sick' if you liked them. Then 'ill' became better than 'sick'. Not sure whether 'dank' is the new 'bad' or is just bad. And good things might be 'deadly', or I might just be making that up."

"So what are the words to be using now?" asked Kay, raising a fat squishy chip and dropping it into her mouth.

"Christ, I dunno. Stuff used to be 'wicked' in my day. We're best off inventing our own and pretending that it's normal. So these chips, they're like ... stinking."

"Oh, I thought they were quite nice."

"No, I mean we take the word *stinking* and use it to mean really good, see?"

"Right," said Kay. "So the guy in the shop, he was a bit of a biscuit, wasn't he?"

"He was," agreed Caroline. "Complete biscuit."

Caroline spotted three youths coming along the road towards them. They made no indication they had seen the girls which meant, Caroline knew, they were acutely aware of their presence. They all wore similar clothes, made from sagging polyester and emblazoned with sportswear brands.

"Boy alert," she said quietly to Kay. "Duck face would be trying too hard in this situation. What we're looking for here is mute superiority to their ignorant, immature ways."

Kay nodded in understanding. "Are we going to snog them?"

"What? No." Caroline was momentarily flustered. "I mean, you can if you want, but I am not interested in locking faces with a teenager, or becoming the first witch to go to prison for child sex offences."

"A'right?" said the first of the youths. They stopped in front of the wall. Caroline flicked her eyes up in brief appraisal and then continued to study the chips.

"Nice chips?" asked the second.

"Stinking," said Kay, and popped one into her mouth.

The boys glanced at each other in confusion. "That's my uncle Joey's chippie, that is," said the first one, frowning. "They're usually all right."

Caroline and Kay giggled at each other and rolled their eyes.

"That's what we said, they're *stinking*/ It's like you don't know English round here," said Caroline.

"Where you from, then?" asked the first one. He had curly hair styled into an unlikely quiff. "I'm Brandon."

"You wouldn't know it. Miles away. Where we come from, nobody says Brandon anymore." Kay scooped up the last fragments of chips.

"What? No, I mean it's my name," said Brandon, confused.

Caroline spluttered with laughter. "Imagine that! Imagine being called Brandon!"

Brandon glowed red and stared at his shoes.

"What are you doing here, then?" said the third boy. He had mousy hair that fell across his face. "You on holiday?"

"Maybe," said Caroline.

"Is there anything that's actually fun around here?" asked Kay, balling up the chip wrapper and pitching it towards a bin. It missed and rolled across the tarmac.

"We know all about fun," said mousy hair boy.

"Sounds a bit creepy," said Caroline. "You say that to all your victims?"

The two other boys laughed and slapped him.

"I'm not creepy."

"Ignore Toby," said the second boy. "I'm Connor. Do you have a problem with either of those names?"

He met Caroline's gaze. Ah, she thought, the quietly confident one. Underneath the rampaging acne, there was an interesting and potentially handsome face. The teenage Caroline would have definitely gone for Connor.

"Got any booze?" asked Kay, slipping off the wall.

The three lads eyed each other. Toby nudged Brandon. "Um, yeah!" said Brandon. "We got booze and, you know, wheels."

"Wheels, Kay," said Caroline in sarcastic awe.

"Want to come and see?" asked Connor.

Jenny and Jizzimus had formed the deceased into queues for processing. The imp had been coerced into helping by the promise it would make the ghosts go away faster. An alphabet scratched into the dusty earth beneath a massive yew tree had proven invaluable in deciphering the needs of the more recently expired. Unfortunately a good many of the older ghosts appeared to be illiterate, and attempted to mime their requirements.

"Right boss, quick win 'ere," said the little imp, his hoofs fizzing gently on the churchyard's consecrated ground. "Yer can lose six of 'em straightaway if yer tell 'em how World War Two ended up."

"World War Two? The Allies won. Germany doesn't rule all of Europe. Well, not exactly. American defeated Japan – in the war at least. In terms of business, technology and, well, everything else, I guess Japan is sort of on top. And, um, Russia helped win the war in Europe and then Stalin died soon after so they don't have a power crazy dictator in charge anymore. Although—"

Several ghosts faded out of existence. Jenny glanced at her imp.

"Fella there hid the last piece of a jigsaw he was doin' wiv his sister. Feels a bit guilty."

"We've got the sister's phone number and where the piece is?"

"Yeah."

Jenny addressed the ghost. "We'll be sure to let her know, Next?"

"Far as I can tell, this 'un hid a load of gold in a field somewhere. Bashed up crosses, bits of posh swords an' the like. Wants 'is brother to take care of it."

Jenny studied the ghost's appearance. He looked like he had died a very long time ago. He wore a helmet with a nosepiece, a sword at his side, and a woollen cloak fastened with a brooch at his shoulder. She recognised its design.

"Was this in, um, Mercia, I think it was?"

The ghost nodded.

"It's called the Staffordshire Hoard," said Jenny. "I don't know about your brother, but everyone can go and see the gold. It's in a museum. Everyone's very impressed with it. It's worth millions."

The ghost gave a small shrug and faded away.

"Nice work, boss. He was a bit scary wiv 'is mask and 'is sword," said Jizzimus.

"You are a wimp."

"In a world of giants, guv. I'm brave for my size. I think we've done 'em all now."

"We've got six letters to send, and four phone calls." Jenny counted them off on her fingers. "A tree to blast with witchfire and a greenhouse to throw a stone at – you can do that one, Jizz. We need to lobby the BBC to bring back Terry Wogan, in spite of him being dead. Have I missed anything?"

"No, boss, we can defini'ly go now."

Jenny trudged away from the church. "It's nice to help others."

"I think yer confusin' 'help' wiv 'chew the flesh off'."

"Although I'm finding the whole experience quite trippy. It's like being on Class A drugs."

"'Ow would you know if you haven't done any?"

"You know what I mean."

"I know what you mean, boss. Jus' suggestin' you should try some to compare, like— Bloody 'ell!" he swore, pointing ahead.

There was the ghost of a young girl on the path up ahead. She beckoned to Jenny.

"You don't 'ave to 'elp 'em all, you know."

"It's only one."

It's fine to jus' walk away."

"She looks really unhappy."

"She's dead. What you expect, eh?"

It was a fair point but the young lady looked very unhappy indeed. While the other ghosts had worn miserable expressions and born the wounds which accompanied their deaths, this one looked pale and colourless, despite the power of the Potion of Seeing.

"Let me see what she needs," said Jenny and walked towards her.

Seeing they were following, Jizzimus grumbling all the way, the girl turned off the path and headed for a huge drainage dyke. It looked like one of the Fens' superhighways: fed by other dykes criss-crossing the flat landscape. Straight and featureless, the water resonating with still depths.

"Jesus H Shitfister!" exclaimed Jizzimus.

Ranged along the far side of the dyke was a whole line of ghostly maidens, all dressed in insubstantial smock-like dresses; all pale and bloodless, like finalists in a Miss Doomed Gothic Heroine of the Year competition.

"Okay, that is freaky," admitted Jenny.

"Not as freaky as that," said Jizzimus. The imp and the entire line of girls pointed at the water.

"What's the matter?" asked Jenny. Then she saw it.

Below the surface was a malevolent face, grinning up at her. It struck her dumb with fear. It wasn't just the distorted humanoid form and features: a blend of melted snowman and "look, mummy, look what I made." It wasn't just the expression of pure malice. It wasn't just the rotting, misaligned teeth it exposed as it leered at her. No: it was the scale of the creature. It was crouched on the dyke bed but was easily the size of a transit van. It was close enough to grab her if it wanted to.

"We need to get out of 'ere right now," Jizzimus murmured.

The monster stood up in the dyke, thigh deep, water cascading off its grey, wrinkled hide. It twisted its body to face the ghosts and released a deep laugh.

"What the fudge is it?" whimpered Jizzimus. "Oh, cunk!"

The creature turned and reached out for Jenny with a paw like a back hoe. Automatically, Jenny's hand became a ball of green witchfire. The beast hesitated before grunting in amusement and backing off. It waded down the channel, pushing a foot-high bow wave before it.

"Nuff of this boss, we don't 'ave to mess wiv the likes of 'im."

"What is it?" asked Jenny.

"Buggered if I know. Let's talk about it later, back at base, eh?"

"Come on," she said. "We need to follow it."

"No, we funkin' don't!"

Jenny looked at the line of anguished ghosts. "We have to find out what it is and where it's going. That thing's trouble."

Caroline looked into the farm shed. "Those are your wheels?"

"It's my uncle's, actually," said Brandon.

Kay put a hand on the rusted engine hood. "Massey Ferguson 135."

Caroline gave her a look.

"First tractor in my village," said Kay.

"Come on," said Brandon. He climbed up into the driver's seat.

"And where do we sit?" asked Caroline.

Toby pointed to the low trailer hitched to the rear.

"But it's filthy!" said Caroline.

Connor slipped off his jacket. "You can sit on this."

Caroline's lips quirked. "Smooth."

"Better than donkeys," said Kay.

"Stick some iron in the bitch!" howled Norma, as Dee lunged at Lesley-Ann Faulkner, the animated, wicked witch creation. Dee was waving her branch, although it was now more of a stump as she'd snapped off most of it. "Use what you can! Anything you can find."

Dee hid behind a tree for a moment to check inside her handbag. A pen? She fetched it out, only to see a pair of walkers approaching: a man and a woman One wearing a beard, the other a crocheted bobble hat; both showing more bare leg than Dee cared to see.

"Er, Norma, we've got company."

"Focus Dee, focus! Don't let your surroundings distract you."

"But...!" Dee thrust at Lesley-Ann Faulkner with her pen. She struck the creature's arm. There was a piercing shriek of pain and Lesley-Ann Faulkner retaliated in a frenzy. Dee looked around for a fresh stick. Her search took her past the halted ramblers, who were staring at her in alarm. Dee saw their rucksacks.

"You've got camping gear," she yelled. "Gimme a tent peg. Now!"

"Are you mugging us?" asked the woman, more interested than alarmed.

Dee bared her teeth and roared. *"Nooooow!"*

The man shucked his rucksack and unzipped a small side compartment. He took out a metal tent peg and held it out to Dee, like one offering a titbit to a dangerous animal. She snatched it from his hand.

"Thank you. Now hurry up and get out of here. It's not safe!" She sprinted after Lesley-Ann Faulkner with her new weapon, a bloodthirsty cry yodelling from somewhere deep inside her.

She barely heard the interchange between Norma and the dumbstruck walkers, but "Sorry about my friend" and "Been taking mushrooms" filtered through the redness that clouded her vision.

"Your wheels are, you know, all right," shouted Kay over the roar of the diesel engine. Somehow Toby had performed the minor miracle of getting served in *Peek-a-booze* and they all had cans of *Liquid Lightning* to drink. Caroline was pleased to see Kay was smiling.

Kay stood on the plate behind Brandon and Caroline and the two other boys sat in the trailer, having their spines rearranged by the total lack of suspension.

"Where are we going?" yelled Caroline.

"We got a special place," Toby replied. "It's quiet, like." They were driving up a track of compacted mud that ran between trees and a bank which looked like a drainage dyke.

"I can see why you'd need to get away from the hustle and bustle." Caroline realised she was slipping out of character: back to her normal, sarcastic self. The cider was pretty strong.

"Nobody goes down to Lizzie's Bath because it's supposed to be haunted," shouted Connor.

"They say that to keep kids away from the water, duh," Toby yelled back.

"Lizzie's Bath?" asked Caroline.

"It's cool," Toby laughed. "We, er, go there all the time with girls."

A look passed between Connor and Toby; Caroline almost laughed out loud. She was willing to bet that the three of them had never so much as kissed a girl. The closest they'd probably got was practising with a pillow.

"This is it," called Brandon. The track curved slightly as they approached a large drainage pond.

The tractor's tortured roar changed tone as they bounced across rougher ground to the far side of the pond.

"This is it?" Caroline had to shout even louder.

Brandon nodded. "Our little watery paradise,"

"Our foetid pond," added Connor.

Kay looked around. "Great place! So what do you do here? You know: with girls?"

"Skinny dipping!" Toby yelled into the silence as Brandon turned the tractor engine off without warning. The other two stared at him, open mouthed. Mortified, Toby hiccupped and took another swig from his can. "Done it a few times, like."

Kay climbed down and went to the edge of the pool. She stared at the water. "It looks a bit murky. I don't think I fancy doing anything except paddling."

Caroline looked down. The edge of the pool was a gently sloping, gritty bank which could almost be beach-like if you squinted. And held your nose. It did seem to invite paddling. Was it the cheap cider or the company of teenagers making it seem such a good idea?

"A quick splash around couldn't hurt," she said, and slipped off her shoes. She rolled up her jeans up as far as they would go. Kay was wearing

147

a skirt and flip flops: she was in the water in moments. The boys hesitated on the bank; then there was a blur of trainers being thrown aside. The chill of the water took a few minutes to subside.

"You think there are leeches in here?" asked Kay.

"No," said Caroline.

"Henry Mitchell said he saw a dead sheep in here once," said Brandon.

"Hey Brandon," called Toby. "What's pond weed?"

"Huh?" said Brandon.

"You are!" laughed Toby and splashed water up the front of Brandon's jeans.

"Aargh! Die you bitch, die!" Dee had pinned Lesley-Ann Faulkner to an oak tree with the tent peg through her arm. The ramblers had been disinclined to hang around and reclaim it. The twiggy creation lashed and screeched, twisting to get to Dee.

"You need to finish her off," advised Norma, watching from nearby.

Dee thought that Norma really could have helped a little, rather than stating the obvious. "Yep, trying." She needed some magic suited to the occasion. The trouble was, she wasn't equipped with magic for this type of situation. Which, she realised, was rather Norma's point. She needed to be creative. What spell might subdue Lesley-Ann Faulkner? Dee mostly specialised in mending and fixing spells.

"Can I mend you?" she said to Lesley-Ann Faulkner. The thrashing thing wasn't much help.

Maybe turn it back into a tree and subdue its murderous rage. That would show Norma the power of love to combat hate.

Dee concentrated and ran through a couple of fixing spells, murmuring and signing rapidly. Lesley-Ann Faulkner began a rapid transformation. The arm pinned to the tree fused to the wood, her head snapped back, absorbed into the trunk. The rest of her body followed. Suddenly there was quiet, apart from the popping of a number of acorns which, charged with positive magic, had attempted, quite badly, to spontaneously turn into oak saplings..

"What have you done?" cried Norma.

Dee dared to a little victory jig. "Think I've nailed it, sweetness. I think I've nailed it."

She turned to bask in the glow of Norma's praise, but all she could see on Norma's face was unconcealed horror.

"We might want to run," suggested Norma.

"Why?"

The tree behind Dee began to creak and groan.

Jenny paused in her pursuit of the shambling water troll thing and sniffed. "Children," she groaned.

"Good idea," said Jizzimus. "Let's knock this malarkey on the 'ead and go grab a snack."

There was laughter up ahead. The channel cut through some hedges and a veritable forest of nettles. She couldn't see where the creature was heading but she could smell it. The delicious wafts of child scent filled her nostrils. "It's going for the kids."

"S'not right, boss," said Jizzimus. "There'll be none left for you. T'ain't right, when they smell so tasty."

Jenny ignored him. She hurried on, not daring to let the creature out of her sight. The sounds got louder. Boys, by the sound of it. Unwashed teenagers by the ripe, intoxicating stink of it.

Dee backed away from the tree. "No, it should be fine. Lesley-Ann Faulkner's anchored to that tree now."

"Or," suggested Norma, backing away even faster, "the tree has now become part of Lesley-Ann Faulkner."

"What's the difference—?" Dee heard the cracking detonation of a tree wrenching itself from the ground, and an impossibly deep roar that turned her stomach to jelly. A quick glance confirmed that Lesley-Ann Faulkner had indeed been mended and was supplemented by a mature oak tree. Lesley-Ann Faulkner, from her root-toes to her leaf-fringed head was such a size that she could kill them both with a whack from a lower branch.

"And you had to make her an oak tree!" said Norma. "Couldn't have found something smaller or weaker! Couldn't have nailed her to a balsa tree!"

"I think you only find them in South America," said Dee. The arboreal discussion ended abruptly as Lesley-Ann Faulkner swiped at them.

Dee swiftly joined Norma in a sprint down the path. "Your witchfire?" puffed Dee. "Can't you burn her?"

149

"It's a travel sized hairspray, Dee. Size of that thing, I'd want a tanker full of napalm at the very least."

"Can't you just dispel the enchantment?"

"My enchantment, yes," wheezed Norma, her face crimson and her eyes bulging. "Not yours. I made Lesley-Ann Faulk—" She huffed with exertion. "—Lesley! You made the super-deluxe version."

Crashing sounds coming from behind them indicated Lesley-Ann Faulkner was in close pursuit. Dee wondered which would give out first, her legs, her lungs or her heart. They were all proving to be strong contenders.

Dee had always loved nature. It seemed really unfair that it was now trying to kill her

"Can you hear something?" Kay said.

Caroline listened. "Not sure I can hear anything above this lot." The boys were now all completely soaked, but continued to splash water at each other as they hollered. "What did you hear?"

"Like something being smashed by an angry elephant," said Kay.

Caroline wondered if Kay had sneaked another can of cider while she wasn't looking, then she heard it too. She scanned the water and the more distant trees to see if she could discern what was happening.

From the opposite weed-choked end of the pool, a small but unsettling wave rippled out.

"You don't have crocodiles in this part of the world, do you?" she said.

The grey shambling troll-thing had a fair turn of speed. Jenny struggled to keep pace.

She battled her way through the forest of nettles, oblivious to the stings and came out at the high lip of a broad pool in which five teenagers, three boys and two girls in various states of partial undress, splashed around.

"The troll's headin' straight for the buffet!" said Jizzimus.

"Get out!" Jenny yelled to the kids. "Run!"

The words died in her throat when she realised one of the girls was Kay. The other girl, a beautiful dark-haired creature who looked oddly familiar, put her hand to her eyes to shade them from the sun.

"Jenny? Is that you?"

The invisible troll-beast burst into the pool. The teenagers couldn't see it, but the wall of water pushed before it was obvious. They scrambled for the shore but one of the boys was too slow. The beast grabbed him by the shoulder and plucked him from the pool.

Caroline saw Brandon being hoisted into the air by an invisible force. He writhed, twelve feet above the foaming water, and screamed.

Kay was already on the bank and running back to the tractor. The two other lads, dopey Toby and cute Connor, hovered in the shallows and stared dumbfounded at their dangling friend.

"You need to run to a place of safety," Caroline said.

"We need to run to a place of safety," chorused the two boys and were gone: up the bank and into the trees.

Brandon swung back and forth in the air. Caroline was utterly nonplussed. It was as though he had been grasped by some invisible being. His T-shirt hung oddly and she was certain his shoulder shouldn't look like that.

She wanted to fight back, wanted to help but her magics – her natural gifts – were of zero use against something she couldn't see; something she couldn't seduce with words. She had nothing.

There was the abrupt, throaty roar of the tractor firing up. Caroline looked round.

"What are you doing?" she yelled.

Perhaps Kay didn't hear her over the thrashing water and chugging engine. The young woman had a grimly determined look on her face as she accelerated the Massey Ferguson into the pool and at the unseen menace. The water slowed the tractor but it churned its way forward, slamming into something at the centre of the pool.

Brandon jerked in the air and fell into the water. Caroline saw Kay dive after Brandon and then they were gone from sight. "Kay!"

Jenny's stomach flipped with fear as Kay disappeared into the water. The troll-thing had been knocked back by the tractor but was now combing the water in search of the teenagers.

Jenny was about to dash down the bank to help when she heard what sounded like trees exploding. She saw Dee and Norma run from the line of trees above the pool and down towards the water. Their clothes were in disarray; they both looked terrified.

And bursting from another section of the woods, heading straight towards Jenny, came a creature she could only describe as 'a really angry tree'.

"Jizz, I really don't know what's going on here."

"Yer don't say."

As the tree thing bore down on her, Jenny dropped into a crouch and pumped a blast of witchfire into its mid-section. It roared and skidded to a halt, batting at its burning leaves.

Down in the pool, four figures flailed, unaware of the invisible thing that towered over them.

"Jizz, I need you to distract that troll," said Jenny.

"What? Me?"

"Now!"

"Yes, boss." He leapt down into the water.

Jenny ran to the right, putting the tree between her and the pool, and summoned a massive surge of witchfire, scorching its trunk and singeing a significant number of branches. Its roar turned into a howl of pain. As she had desperately hoped, it turned and fled from her. Down to the pool.

Jenny followed, giving it an enthusiastic blast every few seconds. She heard the sound of the tractor engine starting up and the screech of tortured metal. She kept blasting the tree thing with witchfire and it plunged without hesitation into the flame-quenching waters.

Straight into the troll-thing that was currently ripping the front wheels off the tractor.

Dee hauled a young man out onto the banks of the pool as Lesley-Ann Faulkner, all aflame, hit the water with a massive, steamy hiss. Dee, who rarely coped well with multi-tasking, struggled to comprehend what was going on.

Here she was with a gangly youth in her arms. The gangly youth clearly had a dislocated shoulder; he mumbled, on the edge of conscious.

Over there, Norma, Kay and a teenager who bore a suspicious resemblance to Caroline, clambered up another bank.

And there, in the centre of the pool, Lesley-Ann Faulkner appeared to be engaged in a life-or-death wrestling match, or some form of supernatural ballroom dancing, with a giant but invisible assailant while – and this was the odd part – a driverless tractor with much of its front end missing, attempted to cut in between the two of them.

"What the hell is that?" Caroline, drenched and filthy, pointed at the fiery tree monster.

"That, Miss Black, is Lesley-Ann Faulkner," said Norma, attempt to wring pond water out of her tweed skirts.

"Who the buggering fuck is Lesley-Ann Faulkner?"

"It's just a name," said Norma. "Dee said we had to give it a name."

Out in the pond, the violent and invisible force lifted the tractor and, with a titanic swipe, used it to slice Lesley-Ann Faulkner in two. The tree groaned, its upper half fell away into the pool, and was still.

Kay looked at Caroline. "Did this kind of stuff happen when you were a teenager?"

Jenny's heart leapt to see Kay and the others unharmed. She was further cheered to see the troll thing, bleeding from various cuts, one eye permanently closed and bloodied, and a large splinter of branch impaling its hand, turn and flee back up the dyke it had come from.

Jizzimus, wet and stinking but otherwise unharmed, bounded up to Jenny.

"You should 'a' seen me boss, driving the tractor. I'm a natural! Call me Farmer Geddon."

"You're a natural all right. We can't let that thing get away."

"I think we should absolutely let it get away," said Jizzimus.

Jenny began running back along the bank. "Then we need to know where its lair is. We need to know *what* it is."

Dee reset the boy's shoulder, cast a generic healing ward on him and, because she thought he, she and the world in general could do with a

153

break from his pained moaning, put him to sleep with a magical hand-jive and incantation that might or might not have been borrowed from a Disney movie. That done, she schlepped through the mud, stepping over the steaming remains of Lesley-Ann Faulkner, to reach the other witches.

"I," said Caroline-the-teenager, "am very, very confused."

"Have you been drinking?" asked Dee.

"Wait just a second," interrupted Norma. "Miss Black: has Miss Wun been drinking as well?"

"Maybe," said Kay happily.

"What on earth were you thinking?"

Caroline huffed. "Kay is old enough to drink. If you tell her she's not supposed to she'll just want to do it more. We had a chat and there were some things she wanted to try out. Things she missed when she was a teenager."

"Is that what the glamour's for?" said Dee.

With a click of her fingers, Norma removed Caroline's enchantment. "There. Back to your normal annoying self."

"Listen, I wanted to help Kay. You know I wouldn't let anything bad happen to her."

"So where did the tree monster come from exactly?" Kay asked.

"That was me and Norma," admitted Dee.

"Mostly you I think, Dee," said Norma haughtily.

"We were doing, er, combat practice and it got out of hand. Reckon your flame thrower set the woods on fire as well, Norma. Good job really."

"Simply not possible!" snapped Norma, "I did *not* start a fire!"

They all turned to stare at the charred trees and still-smouldering Lesley-Ann Faulkner.

"The evidence would suggest otherwise," said Caroline.

"I don't care what the evidence suggests," said Norma.

"Biscuit," said Kay.

Dee reached forward and plucked a handful of charred acorns from the tree. They fizzed with raw magical potential, creaking with the urge to grow up, to become something much, much more.

She put them in her pocket.

As Jenny gave chase along the wide dyke, she drew near to where the ghostly maidens waited. How many youngsters had the creature killed? How many years had it been skulking and ambushing the unwary in these waters?

"They're fadin', guv," said Jizzimus.

Indeed, the girls were becoming translucent: disappearing in the noon sunlight.

"They jus' wan'ed you to give that bastard thing a pastin'," said the imp. "Their business is done."

Jenny smiled for only a split second. Jizzimus was wrong. "No," she said. "It's the potion. It's wearing off!"

Up ahead, limping between grassy banks, the troll-brute was also fading away. Its grey flesh paled like dissipating cloud.

"No!" shouted Jenny.

She paused for a second to hurl witchfire, but it was too far away. The creature cried out – in pain or defiance, she couldn't tell – and hurried on to where the dyke ran under a hedge-lined road. The creature, just on the cusp of visibility, pushed itself through the wide pipe which carried the dyke under the road, and it was gone.

Jenny had no intention of giving up the pursuit. She pressed on, barged through the hedge and came up onto the narrow road. She gasped and panted and surveyed the area. The dyke continued ahead but there was no sign of the beast, no tell-tale ripples. The fields of yellow-flowered rape beyond swayed in the breeze, not with the passage of a monster.

"We lost it," she panted.

"Cockcheddar," said Jizzimus supportively.

She slumped to a crouch in the road and shook her head. "Jizz."

"Yes, boss."

"It's been a funny old day. What do you reckon Kay and Caroline were up to?"

"Chugging industrial-strength cider and tonguing local boys."

Jenny nodded. "Probably. But I'm damned if I know what Dee and Norma were up to in the woods."

"Indulging in a Sapphic orgy boss, that'll be it. I might keep an eye on 'em for you."

His tongue waggling leer actually made Jenny laugh out loud. She was about to tell him to stop when a car shot round the bend in the road. Jenny came to her feet; not fast enough. The car swerved, caught her upper leg. She was flipped over, her face smacked against something hard. That was all she knew.

# Chapter 5 – Sand Witches

"It's true," said Caroline as they crossed the lawns to the teaching hut. The sun shone brightly on its ageing paintwork.

Dee gave Caroline her most confused look. Dee was a dab hand at looking confused. "Sold?"

"To a man in Porto."

"Like a people trafficker?" said Dee.

Caroline shrugged. "It's what she said." She watched Dee closely. "What do you know about it?"

"What makes you think that I know anything, sweetness?"

"Your face is an open book. With lots of pretty pictures."

"Curse you, face," said Dee. "Fine. All I know is what happened the day we came here. A man was chasing them."

"Kay and Jenny?"

Dee nodded. "Jenny had rescued her from some man. Jenny said he had kidnapped Kay. The only reason they're here is because they're trying to lay low."

"So what's Jenny got to do with this kidnapping plot?"

"Nothing. I think. Jenny just stepped in and helped her. And she's been trying to help her ever since."

That gave Caroline pause for thought. She had imagined Jenny was some mother hen type: over-protective and controlling; but, in the light of this new information…

"Do you think they're in danger?" she asked.

"Jenny seems to think so. She said the kidnapper was a— Sh'up!"

Dee nudged Caroline. Kay sat on the doorstep of the teaching hut ahead, slumped like a discarded marionette.

"Morning, kiddo," said Caroline.

"Ugh," replied Kay with feeling.

"Oh dear. What's the matter, poppet?" asked Dee.

"Too much *Liquid Lightning* yesterday?" suggested Caroline.

"It hurts," said Kay.

Dee rummaged through her purse and pulled out a jar of leaves. "We'll have you sorted in no time."

Caroline put a gentle, restraining hand on her. "No. This is all part of the magical teenage experience."

"My wee smells of apples," said Kay. "Is that normal? Am I going to die?"

Caroline hoisted Kay to her feet and guided her indoors. "Not today, kiddo."

Inside the hut, Effie stood at her teaching position, wearing a *Fairport Convention* T-shirt and an impatient expression. "If you'd care to take your seats, ladies."

Norma and Shazam were already seated. Shazam's large hair was looking especially bouffant today. Mr Beetlebane, equally bouffant, seemed unwilling to settle on her lap.

"How was the spa, Cobwebs?" asked Caroline as she guided Kay to a chair.

"It was wonderful," said Shazam. "I've never felt so pampered. We had a something-something massage and hot stone therapy. And then we went in the sauna but Mr Beetlebane didn't like that as it made him go all poofy. And then we had a ying-yang algae seaweed wrap."

"For lunch?" said Kay, looking green.

"And then I had a rhassoul mud massage and a detox scrub. It was amazing."

"You definitely have a healthy glow about you," said Dee.

Like boiled shellfish, thought Caroline.

"And did Sabrina enjoy it?" asked Dee. Sabrina was absent from the hut. So was Jenny.

"Where's Jenny?" said Caroline.

"She wasn't in the room last night," Kay mumbled.

"I have some unfortunate news," said Effie. "*If* you could please be seated."

Jenny woke slowly, fighting it all the way. She remembered the car accident, felt the physical memory of it in her legs, her head and her spine. She didn't want to wake into a world of screaming agony or life-altering injuries. To her surprise, she came round with only the numbest of pain in her legs, and a dull throbbing ache in her head. She opened her eyes, prepared to see a hospital ward, life support machines and saline drips. Instead, she was lying in a large and luxurious bed in a room of equally large and luxurious proportions. The bedlinen had a subtle smell of lavender. Either the NHS wasn't half as bad as people claimed, or someone had brought her to a five star hotel to recover.

Jizzimus sat on the damask top sheet, watching her. He looked genuinely worried. Jenny wanted to hug the horrible little homunculus.

"You all right, boss?" he said. "Blink once for yes, twice for no."

"How long have I been out?" she croaked.

"All night long."

A shadow shifted in the corner of the room. There was a woman who hadn't been there before. "You've been asleep since yesterday afternoon." She pushed heavy curtains wide and the room filled with morning light. "I thought a sleeping draught would help you heal. How's the head?"

"Sore."

The woman had sparkling amber eyes and a vaguely aristocratic bearing, and though she looked middle-aged, time had softened her features rather than worn them. Jen suspected that a punishing detox diet or the world's subtlest plastic surgery played a part. Either that or a genetic heritage to die for.

The woman placed a hand on Jenny's forehead. "May I?"

The woman muttered softly and the throbbing in Jenny's head subsided. A witch then, thought Jenny. "Where am I?" she asked.

"My home," said the woman. "The nearest hospital is in Boston and we don't need to bother them over a pair of broken legs."

"Broken legs!" Jenny sat up and threw the sheets back, flinging Jizzimus off the bed and onto the dressing table.

"All mended now," said the woman.

"Yeah," said Jizzimus, untangling himself from a hairdryer cord. "Before you looked like someone had given you an extra set of backwards knees. Could'a been useful, if you ask me."

Jenny stared at her bare legs and wiggled her toes. There were some fading bruises but no indication of broken bones, past or present. "Um. Thanks," she said.

The woman shrugged. "Well, I did run you over. Not entirely sure why you were sitting in the road though."

"I was chasing ... something."

"Something?"

Jenny frowned. "Yes. I saw a creature."

"Creature?"

"A monster. In the dyke."

"A fish?"

"No. Definitely not a fish. It had arms and a face. The thing was twice my height."

The woman smiled at her charitably. "I did hit you *quite* hard."

"I'm not making it up."

The woman nodded. "I've lived on the Fens for most of my life, Jenny, and I don't think I've seen any monsters."

The woman knew her name. Jenny hadn't given it to her, and her purse and all her ID were over a hundred miles away in Birmingham. Jenny abruptly re-evaluated the opulence of the bedroom around her.

"Is this Eastville Hall?"

The woman nodded.

"And you're Mrs du Plessis."

"Natasha."

Jenny shook the offered hand. "I'm taking up one of your guest bedrooms. I've not turfed out a spa client, have I?"

"We're rarely full."

"I'm on the course thing Effie Fray is running."

"I know," said Natasha. "I do sometimes glance out of the window at the comings and goings on the rear lawns."

Natasha du Plessis's smile made Jenny blush to the roots of her hair. Natasha smiled even wider.

"I think it's good to ... let your hair down every now and then. And I think this course for witches is a bold and interesting experiment."

"She means she thinks it's a load of codspunk," translated Jizzimus.

"We're really grateful that you're allowing us to use your facilities," said Jenny.

"Happy to help. Just remember, there are other ways to become the best witch one can possibly be."

"I think I'd just settle for being a happy one."

Natasha's face darkened a second. "Don't settle for second best, Jenny. You have potential."

Jenny held back a scoffing laugh for fear of offending.

"Anyway, I am glad to see you are on the mend," said Natasha. "But I have duties to attend to." She rolled her eyes. "The burden of management. Go back to sleep. I will have some breakfast sent up." She left, closing the door softly behind her.

"Breakfast in bed," said Jenny reflectively. "At least some things are looking up."

"What you talkin' about?" said Jizzimus. "I bring you brekkie in bed all the time."

"Yelling 'It's sausage time!' while I'm asleep, then slapping me in the face with an undercooked banger does not constitute breakfast in bed."

"You're spoilt, guv. Tha's your problem."

"So," said Effie, managing to imbue the single syllable with a sense of disappointment, annoyance, resignation and optimism, "it appears that, having one day at Eastville Hall to reflect on matters, Sabrina has decided not to continue with this course."

"Did she say why?" asked Dee.

"I merely received the message that it 'wasn't for her'."

"She means it was beneath her," said Norma, in tones suggesting she harboured similar thoughts.

"Did she say anything to you yesterday?" Dee asked Shazam.

"You know she doesn't talk to me much," said Shazam. "Though she did insist on separate treatments after Mr Beetlebane got a bit bitey in the sauna."

"This is obviously very sad," Effie continued, "and I will be getting in touch with Sabrina to discuss the matter. On a more immediate and practical note, this does mean that, given it relied on Sabrina's family contacts, our planned trip to the Pendle Library is off."

"Oh, that is a shame," said Norma.

"I think that Sabrina throwing in the towel is more of a downer than a cancelled trip to Oxford," said Caroline.

"Cambridge," corrected Effie.

"Whatever."

Norma huffed. "This ridiculous love-in residential holds few points of genuine interest for a professional witch such as myself, but a chance to visit the Pendle Library of Witchcraft was one of them. I was particularly keen to read the scholarly articles on the Peatling Magna incident in two thousand—"

Effie interrupted: "That is no longer possible. So, I thought we might spend today looking at another aspect of the course: astrology, divination and other forms of fortune-telling."

"This is my point entirely!" spat Norma. "What could you possibly teach me about fortune-telling?"

"Nothing at all, Norma dear," said Effie blithely. "Which is why I thought you might be able to lead much of today's teaching."

"Oh, yes," said Shazam. She pulled a slender catalogue out of her handbag. "I could do with some guidance. I'm looking to buy a new crystal ball and deck of tarot cards, and I wasn't sure what to go for. I've been using my Woodland Faerie Folk deck of late but I'm not sure if it has the right magical oomph."

"Oomph?" repeated Norma.

"Mmmm, yes. Celeste says I should perhaps try a Dreaming Angels pack, or maybe a Tranquillity Gems, but I'm not sure."

"Celeste?" said Caroline.

"Yes. She runs the One Stop Sorcery shop where I get all my things."

Norma reached over, snatched the sparkly purple catalogue from Shazam's hand and scrutinised it, her expression furious. "Bloody Americans and their ridiculous nonsense! They're not real witches. If they weren't ten thousand miles away, I'd give them a piece of my mind!"

"Oh, they're not based in America. Their main shop is in Skegness." She pointed at the mail order address sticker on the front of the magazine.

"Skegness?" said Kay.

"That's about fifteen miles thataway, isn't it?" said Dee.

"Fifteen miles," blustered Norma. "Ten thousand miles,"

Caroline cleared her throat and looked at Effie. "Do we still have the minibus booked for today?"

"Today's plan is fortune-telling, Caroline."

Shazam let out a sudden, "Ooh, ooh, ooh!" as though she had sat on a ice cube.

"What?" said Effie.

"And we could visit Zoffner the Astute."

"Who?" said Caroline.

Shazam gave them all a gently patronising head shake. "The world's greatest psychic. I'm surprised you've not heard of him. He's co-owner of One Stop Sorcery and gives audiences at his monastic cave."

"Cave?" said Dee.

"In Skegness?" said Norma.

"Minibus," said Caroline.

"Well, I'm certainly not going," said Effie. "I was going to drive to Cambridge, now I'm afraid I will need to stay and make a call to Mrs Holder-Eckford to discuss Sabrina's departure. I'm not sure anyone else is licenced to drive a minibus."

"I'm an ex-copper," said Caroline. "Minibus, police van, same thing."

Effie sighed in defeat.

"We're going for a trip to the seaside?" said Dee, smiling.

"To a supposed witchcraft shop and 'the world's greatest psychic'," said Effie firmly.

"With a fish and chip lunch," said Caroline.

"And donkeys," said Dee.

"Where's Jenny?" said Kay.

"Ah, yes," said Effie. "The second piece of unfortunate news. It appears that Jenny, while you were off enjoying your innocent Sunday morning pursuits, decided to pick a fight with a passing motorcar. She's all right—" she added, holding out a calming hand towards Kay, "—in fact she's recuperating right now in one of the luxury suites at Eastville Hall."

"Jammy Jenny," drawled Caroline.

"Yes," said Effie. "But I wouldn't recommend it as a way to get your room upgraded."

Within in an hour of waking, Jenny was up and about. Partly testament to Natasha du Plessis's healing skills, partly to how bored one can get in a bedroom with no books, no TV, no phone and only an imp for company. An imp who regarded a game of 'guess what animal I'm pretending to hump' as the height of entertainment.

"I give up," Jenny said. "No idea."

"Aw come on, it's easy, guv. Look."

She ignored his lewd mimes, got up and dressed. There was a blood-edged rip in her jeans and a large tear in her top: evidence of vanished injuries . She grunted at a slight ache as she slipped her shoes on. "Let's explore," she said.

"Fairy snuff," said Jizzimus, bounding out of the door ahead of her. "But I told ya: this place is jus' old ladies in paper knickers getting mud packs. Once you've seen one colonic irritation, you've seen 'em all. By the way, it was a camel."

Jenny looked up and down the corridor. "Camel?"

"I was 'umping its 'ump," said Jizzimus. "Tha's funny, that is. Comedy gold."

The wallpaper looked so expensive, Jenny was afraid to touch it. The carpet felt so rich and plush she felt she was vandalising it just by standing there.

"I can show you where the acupuncture place is," said Jizzimus. "We can practice on some old biddy. I reckon they're so full of gas an' dust that they'll deflate if you prick 'em jus' right."

"I've never been to a spa before," Jenny told him.

"That's cos you learned 'ow to wash yourself. An' you don' need to pay some 'ired flunky to do it for you."

"It's nice to be pampered," she said.

"I pamper you."

"When?"

"I do your toenails."

She looked at him. "You gouge toenail cheese from under my toenails and eat it on toast. That, I can categorically confirm, does not constitute pampering." She walked ahead, inspecting the doors of the rooms they passed.

"Dun't like Sausage Time. Dun't like Cheesy Feet Friday," muttered Jizzimus. "Dunno why I bovver sometimes."

Jenny knocked at a door with the words *Treatment Room* on a brass plate. When there was no reply, she eased it open. Inside was a curious mixture of plush décor and clinical equipment. There was subtle recessed lighting, a large portable lamp on a wheeled base and a green cubicle curtain. Jenny reached out a hand to pull back the curtain and then hesitated.

"Go on," said Jizzimus. "It might be the Wizard of Oz be'ind there. You know, the bastard git out of that 'orror movie."

"What if it's—?"

Jizzimus was already pulling the curtain aside. Behind it stood an adjustable hospital bed in which a woman with cropped ginger hair appeared to be asleep. Her arm was elevated by a stand clamped to the side of the bed. An intravenous tube ran from the woman's arm to a machine. Was it a dialysis machine? A blood transfusion device? Whatever treatment the room was used for, Jenny was fairly sure she didn't want any.

"Look," said Jizzimus. "They're even pumpin' stuff into people who are too lazy to drink. Reckon you could suck on that gubbins like a straw guv? It could be mojitos or blood or summat nice."

"Shush," said Jenny. "We're trespassing."

The woman's eyes snapped open and locked with Jenny's. There was a cold accusatory look to the gaze which made Jenny more uncomfortable than she wanted to admit.

"Sorry! I didn't mean to disturb you."

The woman's free hand moved with surprising speed and latched onto Jenny's wrist.

"I was just looking for the exit," said Jenny. "I didn't mean to—" She checked the medical wristband the woman wore. "Lesley-Ann, is it? Mrs Faulkner? I'm sure you need your rest. Sorry for interrupting."

Jenny pried the woman's fingers away and backed out of the room, Jizzimus scampering after her.

"That woman looked seriously unimpressed," she hissed.

165

"She jus' don't wanna share 'er mojito, does she? Let's see if there's some spares in 'ere, shall we?" Jizzimus tried to yank open a door; it was locked. "Key's in the door boss. Shall we?"

"No, come on. There's definitely stuff we're not supposed to mess with here. Let's go and find the others."

Jenny found the entrance hall and the currently unmanned reception area. They nipped out through the open front door and then hurried towards the annexe. A minibus was coming down the drive. Caroline was at the wheel, and it looked as though everyone else was in the back.

"Hey!" Jenny shouted, giving Caroline a wave. The minibus crunched to a halt.

Dee threw the side door open. "Jump in. You're just in time."

Jenny clambered in. "Where are we going?"

"Skeggy!" said Shazam from the back row.

"We're off to the seaside?" said Jenny. "I'm a mess. Look at this." She poked a finger through the huge rent in her top.

Dee slammed the door. Caroline crunched the gears and pulled away. "Then it's also a shopping trip for you," she said.

"Oh, I'm sure we can mend that," said Dee. "Slip it off a minute, poppet."

"Um. No. I'm not taking my clothes off in public," said Jenny.

"Again," Caroline added.

Dee leaned across and, with a snatch of sung incantation, encouraged the ripped threads in Jenny's jeans to knit back together again.

Meanwhile, Kay asked, "What happened to you?"

Jenny was about to explain when Norma cut her off with a sharp "Ah, ah, ah!"

"Today's focus is fortune-telling and divination," she said in her best schoolmarm voice. "We shouldn't need to ask Miss Knott anything. Her past, present and future is there to be read. And how shall we read it?"

"I've got my Woodland Faerie Folk deck," said Shazam.

"*Pfff!* Put them away. Better still, throw them out the window."

"But ... but they're pretty," said Shazam, very quietly.

"Tea leaves!" said Norma. "There has never been a more reliable tool for augury."

"Hang on," said Caroline, patting her pockets with a free hand. She clicked her fingers. "Damn it, I've left my teapot back in my room. However, I predict that Norma is going to be getting a bit hot under the collar today, based on the fact I can see her woollen vest peeping out from her blouse."

"Facetious," said Norma, adjusting her garments. She pulled a number of sealed plastic cups from her mighty bag. Brown leafy sludge sat in the bottom of each. "A good witch also travels prepared."

She passed a cup to Jenny. "Swirl and throw away the tea."

Jenny did as asked, pouring the dribble of tea out of the window.

"Now, let everyone see."

Jenny passed the cup to Shazam.

"Right," said Shazam. "Now, I've read the chapter in Zoffner the Astute's book. Let me see... The present is represented by the leaves near the rim."

"Very good," said Norma in a tone she might use to congratulate a dog which had learned how to do calculus.

"Um, this looks a bit like a snake. That could mean adversity. Did something bad happen to you, Jenny?"

Jenny nodded politely. You didn't need to read tea leaves to see something bad had happened.

"But what?" insisted Norma.

Shazam poked a lump of tea. "It looks like a fat Michelin man. Did you have a puncture in your tyre?"

"Er, no."

"Next!" said Norma.

Shazam passed the cup to Kay. "I'm more of a coffee person," said Kay and quickly passed it on to Dee.

"A witch reads tea leaves," said Norma.

"I believe some do use coffee grounds," said Dee.

"Coffee," said Norma distastefully. "I'll have no dealings with foreign muck. It's British tea for British witches, and that's the end of the matter."

"Surely, our tea comes from India," said Caroline.

"Yes," Norma conceded. "But it's *British* Indian tea and that's what's important."

167

Dee put her eyeball right up to the cup. "The man thing is in a dense clump of leaves. That's a dark sign. And ... and there's this stain leading from it down to the base. Whatever it is, it will have impact on your future."

"But what is it?" Norma demanded.

Dee attempted to peer closer, an act that would be impossible without getting tea leaves in her eye. "Going out on a limb here, sweetness," she said, "but did you have a fight with a giant invisible monster of unspeakable evil?"

Jenny gave her a frank look and said nothing.

They passed through villages with names like Friskney, Wainfleet St Mary and Wainfleet All Saints and the landscape – pancake flat and dyke-edged fields punctuated with the occasional building – did not change one iota.

Abruptly, Norma yelled, "Stop!"

Caroline slammed on the brakes and they slid, dust flying, into a small layby. "What is it?"

"Out! Out!" Norma all but pushed them from the vehicle.

"Are we on fire?" asked Shazam, trying to settle her unsettled cat.

"Look! Look!"

Norma dragged them to the rear of the minibus and pointed at a sad, squashed lump at the edge of the road.

"Oh, poor badger!" said Dee.

"Haruspicy," said Norma. "The reading of entrails."

"What?" said Caroline.

Norma crouched. There was a pocketknife in her hand. "It's much the same principle as tasseography," she said, merrily sawing open the dead creature's belly. "It's about shape and form and opening oneself up to the realm of *what might be*." Norma peeled back skin and flesh and let a pile of innards slip out onto the dusty ground. "Now, who can foretell a future in what we see here?"

"I can foretell I will not be eating lunch today," said Shazam.

"Come now. What meaning can we see here? What does it show us?"

"That it's really bad to stand next to a busy main road?" suggested Jenny.

To emphasise her point, a tractor and trailer piled high with hay bales rattled by at speed.

"Be serious, Miss Knott," said Norma.

"Oh, I am," said Jenny, stepping onto the verge as far back from the road as possible.

Kay crouched over the badger and poked at it with a stick. "I see animals. Donkeys. A cat."

"My cat?" said Shazam.

"And a monkey."

"Very good," said Norma. "What else? Pay close attention to the liver. It is the most communicative of all the organs."

"I see ... blood."

"Badger blood by any chance?" suggested Caroline.

"Girls' blood. A woman drenched in girls' blood."

"Where do you see that, exactly?" said Norma.

"And I see a passionate encounter. Some full-on snogging."

"Is it Jenny again?" said Caroline.

"No," said Kay. She looked at Norma. "It's you."

There were claps and cheers and laughs.

"Enough of that!" snapped Norma. "What are we? Witches? Or a drunken hen party?"

"We could be both," said Caroline. "We can multi-task."

The sun was shining and, although none of them had actually seen the sea yet, there was a seaside tang in the air and the caws of evil-eyed seagulls wheeling above them when they got out of the minibus in Skegness.

Norma inhaled deeply until her magnificent corsetry creaked. "There's nothing like the smell of the British seaside to clear the sinuses and soothe the soul."

"A stick of rock and a bag of chips comes a close second." Caroline locked the minibus and pointed across the car park to a nondescript shopping centre. "By my reckoning, the shop is through there and up to the left somewhere. Now, our ticket runs out at five o'clock so we all need to be back here by then."

"But, surely, we're sticking together," said Norma.

"Oh, I suspect some of us might wander off to inspect the sights," suggested Caroline.

"Not on my watch. This way, ladies!"

Norma marched them through the shopping arcade and out onto a busy high street. The street thronged with elderly shoppers, fat and uncontrollable children, and holidaymakers showing off more tattoos, orange-peel skin and back body hair than they would fifty miles further inland. Norma cut a path through them like an arctic ice-breaker, and the witches hurried to keep in her slipstream. She stopped halfway up the high street, outside the Coin Fountain arcade, and backtracked twenty yards to a narrow archway between two fast food outlets. A cracked Perspex sign advertised *One Stop Sorcery: through the alley and turn left* with an accompanying arrow for people who didn't know which way was left.

"It's very atmospheric," said Shazam. "Like Diagon Alley."

"I think it's more like they can't afford to rent a place on the actual street," said Jenny.

Norma led a snake of witches down the less-than-fragrant cut-through into a backyard of fire escapes, commercial dumpsters and blocked drains. A multi-coloured bead curtain and electric purple door frame did little to elevate the One Stop Sorcery shop above its surroundings.

The arrival of half a dozen customers caused an almost apoplectic fit of surprise in the woman behind the counter. "You're not a coach party, are you? Coach parties have to book in advance."

"Just browsing," said Norma firmly. "This way, ladies."

She herded them through the book section. Copies of *Interpreting Your Cat's Dreams* and *Nixies, Knuckers and Naiads: Communing with Water Spirits* caught Dee's eye but Norma swept them on, violently batting aside a selection of dreamcatchers and corralling them in a nook of gemstones, jewellery and geodes.

"Right," she said, "what tools does a witch need to ply her trade?"

"A decent chemistry set," said Dee.

"Perhaps."

"Fuck-me shoes and a little black number," Caroline smirked.

"I said witch," said Norma.

"A familiar," offered Shazam.

"Wicked witches have familiars," said Norma. "Anything else is imp-envy."

"Then what?" asked Kay.

Norma gave a meaningful shrug. "Very little. This—" she gestured to the shop around them "—is window-dressing. Utterly superfluous. A good witch, an honest witch, needs nothing but her wits and intuition. She can brew all manner of potions from wayside plants. She can read the future in a cup of PG Tips. She can bewitch, ensorcell and heal with mere words. The junk in this place is the commodification of the occult: a cheap and tawdry attempt to make a witchcraft a merchandisable enterprise. I would warn all you vain and gullible witches to stay far, far a— hang on, is that a Gaja Mani?" She broke off and crossed to a shelf.

"A what?" said Shazam.

Norma had picked up a pearly, egg-shaped stone. "It's a bezoar. If I'm not mistaken, this one was taken from an elephant. They are very rare and powerful. And it's only ninety pounds."

"You were telling us about the cheap and tawdry commodification of the occult," prompted Caroline.

"Yes but – look – they've got an offer on. Three for two hundred pounds."

"Do you need an elephant stone?" asked Dee.

"Need?" said Norma and then pulled a face. "*Want*. Go browse, ladies. I've given my *caveat emptor*. Go."

Jenny sat on an upturned crate in the courtyard outside One Stop Sorcery. With her head in her hands, she tried to focus on breathing calmly and maintaining her self-control. She didn't feel she was succeeding.

Jizzimus put his tiny hands on her knees and stared up at her with concern.

"S'okay, boss," he said. "Just keep breathin' and when you feel it comin', give a big push."

She goggled at him. "What?"

"You look ready to drop a sprog, or lay an egg, or whatever you people do."

"I'm just trying to collect myself. I don't feel very well."

"Oh, I thought you was 'aving a baby. Or a crap."

She raised her eyes to the heaven. "It's funny," she said.

"Everyone enjoys a good crap," he agreed.

"I didn't realise how easy it had become at Eastville Hall. Sure, there's Kay, but she's nearly an adult. Apart from her, there have been no children around at all. But here— Can you smell it?"

Jizzimus sniffed long and loud, filling his lungs. "Rotten seaweed. Out of date toffee apples. Seagull shit."

"And children. Lots of children."

"Feelin' peckish, eh? We could slope off an' go grab one."

She growled in her throat. She should have thought of this: it was summer, holiday season. The delicious stink of children was everywhere. Children with their families, laughing, crying, screaming, slathered in sunscreen, daubed with melting ice-cream and sugar. "I'm not eating a child, Jizz."

"We could just 'ave a small one an' see 'ow that goes."

She glared. "No children. I need chocolate."

"You know, other imps don't 'ave to put up wiv this kinda bullpoop."

"Please," she said. "Fetch me some chocolate."

"And that's not code for sweet, sweet kiddie-flesh, is it?"

"No."

He scowled at her.

"You love me really," she said.

"Course I bloody do, you poof!" He trotted away at speed.

"Who loves you really?" said Caroline.

Jenny gave a start. Caroline was slouched against the wall by the shop doorway behind her. "How long have you been there?"

"Just," said Caroline. "Why? Should I have turned up earlier? Might have caught something juicy."

Jenny sighed. "I was just— I was just remembering something someone said to me."

Caroline smiled. "You're a mysterious one, aren't you?"

"Am I?"

"You're actually a very caring person."

172

Jenny was about to humbly disagree. Instead she switched track. "Why? How do I come across?"

"A cold and self-serving bitch, like me."

"You're not cold and self-serving," said Jenny. "You're ... focused."

"Ha!"

Jenny hitched a thumb towards the shop door. "You not buying anything?"

"No. Nor you?"

"I've got no money. Not much."

Caroline nodded. "Yep. And there's nothing in that shop for me. I'm more likely to get my 'tools' from Ann Summers than a Joss Sticks R Us place like this."

Shazam stepped out with a bulging carrier bag in each hand and an idiot grin on her face. "Can you believe they're doing a summer sale special on crystal balls?"

"Funnily enough," said Caroline. She looked at Shazam's rattling bags. "How many did you buy?"

"Oh, most of this is healing crystals."

"Is someone dying?"

Shazam put the bags down beside Jenny. "Could you look after these while I get the other bags?"

"Others?"

Shazam smiled, a spark of wonder in her eyes. "And Melwyn behind the counter. She's such a friendly person, isn't she?"

"I should imagine that you're her new best friend," said Caroline.

Shazam dashed back inside. While she was presumably buying up the rest of the shop, Dee, Kay and Norma emerged. Norma's capacious bag bulged more than normal. Dee thumbed excitedly through a hardback book she had bought.

"Armadel's Second Grimoire," she said. "It details the exploits of witches through the ages – good and wicked."

"All based on spurious secondary sources," sniffed Norma. "A waste of money."

"Coming through!" called Shazam, emerging with three further carrier bags and a cat unhappy at being jostled about so much.

"Hell's bells," said Caroline. "Did you literally buy everything?"

"Not at all!" said Shazam. "I just snapped up a few bargains. And – get this! – Melwyn says we've been such lovely customers we can have our fortunes read by Zoffner the Astute in his monastic cave for free! Isn't that generous?"

"It's probably the least they can do since you've probably paid their rent for the remainder of the year."

"So, where is this monastic cave of his?" asked Jenny.

"It's in the funfair on the promenade: between the ghost train and the hook-a-duck stall."

"Sounds classier by the minute," said Caroline.

"Let's get this over with." Norma waved them back towards the high street.

There was a thump from a dumpster as Jizzimus returned. Jenny checked to see that the others had left via the alley. "What's this?"

Jizzimus thrust a cellophane-wrapped box of fudge into her hand. The lid said *A Gift from Skegness*.

"Fudge?" she said.

"It's all I could nick from the shop. Look at the fat fucker on the lid—"

"That's the Jolly Fisherman."

"Yeah, the fat fucker. He looks really pleased wiv 'imself. It'll be delicious."

Jenny fought with the cellophane and stuffed a handful of soft fudge in her mouth. "It's not chocolate," she observed, eating it nonetheless.

"It ain't kid flesh either," said Jizzimus.

She skedaddled up the alley to catch up with her fellow witches. The fudge was sweet and delicious, but the stench of children smacked into her again as she re-joined the busy high street. The reek was ingrained into every inch, and the various ice-cream, donut and candyfloss stalls that should have masked it only served to enhance the sweet, forbidden odour, and showcase the sticky little fingers – delicious little fingers – which had pawed every counter and shelf.

She kept her eyes down and followed the others up to a roundabout with a clock tower in the centre, then to the left along an even busier promenade. They reached the funfair without catching any glimpse of the sea. Jenny had no idea such places existed in Britain anymore. She was aware of the gleaming theme parks that dotted the country, which she didn't visit for obvious reasons; she frequently walked past the travelling fairs which appeared in Cotteridge or Cannon Hill park: fungal outgrowths of caravans, security fencing and rickety rides manned by shifty-looking men. Skegness funfair managed to emulate the worst of both worlds: the permanence and scale of the former, the scuzziness and health and safety risks of the latter.

Kay was entranced. "It's like Disneyland," she said.

"With added chip wrappers," said Caroline.

"I don't believe the waltzers at Disneyland look like they might give you tetanus, poppet," said Dee.

A rollercoaster juddered overhead and Jenny automatically drew Kay away from its killzone. "Are we going on the rides?" asked Kay.

"Maybe later," said Jenny.

"I am deffo goin' on that big wheel," said Jizzimus.

"Maybe we'll just go on some of the game stalls," Jenny suggested.

Jizzimus cartwheeled over to a tin-can alley stall. "Come on then, guv. Win us a cuddly monkey."

Jenny shrugged amiably and gave the pubescent stall-holder a couple of quid. "Knock down any can to win a prize," he told her.

"And for the big prizes?" she asked.

"Knock down a pyramid with one ball."

"Easy!" said Jizzimus.

Jenny picked up the wooden balls and threw one at the leftmost pyramid of tins. As expected, Jizzimus leapt up onto the board and kicked them down. As a work of deception, it was entirely unsubtle, the cans flying off in different directions, but what was the lad going to say? *Did you have help from an invisible imp?*

He did get as far as "Wow. That was some thr—" before stopping as Jizzimus, ever enthusiastic, begin kicking at the others towers of cans. Jenny quickly threw her two remaining balls in an attempt to cover up the invisible rampage.

"You still only get one prize," said the young man."

Jenny smiled sweetly at him and pointed at an overstuffed monkey in an *I ♥ New York* T-shirt. The young man unclipped it from where it hung and handed it over.

"Did you do that with your mind?" Kay whispered to her.

"Someone has unlocked telekinetic potential," said Norma, who had been watching. "Now, if you please. Let's get this psychic nonsense over with."

"It's here!" squealed Shazam, literally jumping up and down in excitement, her bags of purchases swinging wildly about her.

Between the entrance to the ghost train and the hook-a-duck stall was a section of black plywood boarding, a simple door and, above it, *Mr Richard Zoffner AKA Zoffner the Astute AKA Mystical Holdings PLC – Knock and Enter the Future.*

"Twaddle," said Norma and opened the door.

"It says knock," said Shazam.

"If he's a decent fortune-teller he already knows we're here," said Dee.

"Enter, ladies," called a mellifluous voice from the darkness.

"He knew we were ladies," Shazam whispered in excitement.

"Because he can hear us," said Norma.

"Mr Astute," Shazam called in. "Do you want us all at once or one at a time?"

"Whatever. It's groovy. The future has room for all," called Zoffner the Astute. "Although I do only have four chairs."

"I'd like to look around the fair," said Kay.

"I'll keep an eye on her if you like," said Dee.

Jenny made a doubtful noise. "No big rides," she said.

"We might even go see the sea," said Dee.

Caroline led the way into the darkness of Zoffner's 'cave': a deep and winding plywood recess built into the space between the surrounding rides and stalls. She followed a trail of fairy lights along the ceiling to a vaguely octagonal chamber. Chairs were arranged around a circular table. Cards, I-Ching sticks and rune stones were placed on the ornate tablecloth and, seated before them, was a white-bearded man. His was not the wispy white beard of some Gandalfesque mystic, nor was it a fulsome Santa beard. His was the beard of a man who had lost his razor some weeks ago and hadn't got round to buying a new one.

"Anywhere?" said Caroline, gesturing to the seats.

Zoffner adjusted his turquoise spectacles. "Anywhere you like, wild child. But choose carefully."

"Oh?"

"For the right chair will allow great and mystical insights."

"And the wrong chair?"

"Is a bit wonky, child."

Norma, Shazam and Jenny squeezed in behind her. The four of them filled the small space. The toy monkey Jenny had won on the stall was squashed between her and Shazam. Beetlebane clawed at its felt head irritably. The black moggy looked like it had not yet recovered from its sauna torment the day before.

"Right, Mr Zoffner," said Norma, "we're here because my deluded friend here is under the—"

Zoffner held up his hand. "No words, foxy lady."

Caroline smirked and Norma bristled.

Zoffner picked up the deck of cards. His shuffle appeared sloppy and his dealing was clumsy but Caroline noted they tumbled and fell from his hand into a perfect five card tarot spread.

"Let the cards speak."

He turned the first one over and looked at Caroline. "The Seven of Cups, wild child. Debauchery and betrayal. Corruption of purpose."

Jenny snickered, apologising immediately.

"Now, this does not have to apply directly to you. You once had a calling to serve a higher power but have turned away from it. And I dig that. Fight the man. But others have turned away from it too and they are not your friends."

"I see," said Caroline thoughtfully.

"Clear as mud," sniffed Norma.

Zoffner turned over a card for her. Poorly drawn men and women stepped from crypts in the ground as an angel sounded its trumpet overhead. "Judgement. Very groovy. But do you stand in judgement over others or do others stand in judgement over you? I sense you are a forceful and sensuous woman—"

Norma leaned forward and slapped him on the check. "Vulgar!"

"—And spontaneous," he added, entirely unfazed. "I'm sure that has got you into trouble more than once." He tapped the card. "But there is resurrection, a chance for rebirth and renewal, my foxy one."

He looked at Jenny. To Caroline's eyes, Jenny seemed nervous.

"Secrets to hide, Jenny?" she said.

Zoffner turned over her card. A tower split by a violent lightning bolt with a person falling from it. "Oh, you are a fiery one," he said. "That's all fab and groovy. It can mean a violent change in you, or in your life. It can also mean a more physical kind of destruction. I'd keep my eye on where the fire exits are if I were you."

"Now, it's me!" said Shazam. "What can you tell me?"

He smiled at her and maybe, for a moment, there was a bit of a Santa Clause twinkle about him. "Oh, I can tell you're a person with a deep interest in the occult."

"I am! I am!"

"And you just want to immerse yourself in all things magical."

"I do! I do!"

Jenny gave Shazam's many and visible One Stop Sorcery carrier bags a meaningful tap with her toe.

"Okay, fiery one," conceded Zoffner the Astute. "Let's see..." He turned over Shazam's card. It was the Fool, chased off a cliff by a dog.

"The Fool," said Jenny neutrally.

"There's a cute doggy," said Shazam.

"Danger surrounds you but you do not know it," said Zoffner.

"Ooh. I got a shiver up my spine. Did anyone else?"

"You have recently had a very narrow escape from a fate worse than death."

"Have I?"

"But you were entirely oblivious to it."

"It'll be that tractor on the main road," suggested Jenny. "I told you it was very close."

"And another has suffered the fate you escaped," said Zoffner.

"Who?" asked Caroline.

"Poppycock," said Norma.

"The cards speak true, foxy lady."

"I don't think we should trust a grown man who spends his days in a cardboard cave."

"You think truth needs to be dressed up in finery and luxury?"

"The man's a fraud," Norma insisted.

Zoffner the astute flipped the final card to an image of a venerable cloaked figure. "I'm a magician."

"A mountebank!"

"I'm more of a beachcomber on the shores of reality." He picked up Shazam's fool card. "I will tell you this truth: you are about to have a terrible shock that will cause you great upset."

"Am I?" said Shazam.

"And the only guidance I can give is to look within."

"Within what?"

"Exactly."

"He's definitely got that mystical hippy thing going on," Caroline said approvingly.

"Tie-dye t-shirts and John Lennon glasses do not a mystic make," snorted Norma.

"Where's your cat, Shazam?" asked Jenny.

Shazam's hand flew to her neck. "Mr Beetlebane!"

Everyone looked on the floor but it wasn't easy, or indeed possible, to discern a black cat on the dimly lit floor of a black-painted room.

"He was there a minute ago!" panicked Shazam.

"Well, he can't have gone far," said Jenny.

"Oh, he's run away. He's not been himself since the sauna!"

"We'll find him, Cobwebs," Caroline assured her.

"But what if he's run off? What if he's got on the rollercoaster?"

"Cats are not well known for enjoying white-knuckle rides," said Jenny.

"Or if he got in the gears of some ride! Or... or..."

Caroline put her arm across Shazam's broad shoulders. "Let's go look. We'll all help."

Caroline guided the trembling, purple-clad witch out towards the daylight. Jenny followed, laden with Shazam's shopping and the over-sized monkey.

"See what you did!" Caroline heard Norma snap at the fortune-teller. "You've upset that poor gullible idiot of a woman."

179

"What did I do but tell her the truth?" Zoffner replied calmly.

"Truth! You know nothing of augury and soothsaying!"

"Are you doubting my methods?"

"You have no method!"

Missing cat or not, Caroline was glad to be out of there.

"I've never seen the sea before," said Kay.

Dee had taken her pink plimsolls off and was scrunching her toes in the sand. The sun was out and she'd unfastened two of the buttons on her cardigan. "Is it what you expected it to be?" she asked.

Kay made the audible equivalent of a smile. "It is and it isn't. It's so—"

"Large?"

"So—"

"Mysterious?"

"Brown."

"Ah."

"I thought the sea was meant to be blue."

"I'm sure it is, somewhere," said Dee. "Here – well, it's not quite estuary, but all the muck flows out of the Humber and... It's not pollution, just good, honest, healthy brown."

"Surely, people don't swim in it," said Kay doubtfully.

Dee looked around at the English holidaying public arrayed across the beach, baking their skin to an alarming pink, flicking their cigarette butts into sand where their kids played, chugging down cans of Liquid Lightning or Special Export lager and eating trays of deep fried something-or-other.

"I don't think we can apply conventional standards of ... health and safety or common sense to the holidaying Brit," said Dee, trying to be charitable. "Mad dogs and Englishmen and all that."

"And you keep donkeys on the beach?" said Kay. "I thought I saw donkeys in those badger insides."

"And a cat and a monkey, as I remember."

"I thought, why would I see a vision of donkeys, and here they are." Kay looked at Dee. "Why are there donkeys at the seaside?"

"Oh, everyone likes donkeys," said Dee, automatically drifting towards them.

"I like donkeys – I grew up with donkeys – but I don't expect to see them by the sea."

"They always look so sad, don't you think?" said Dee. "They were always a favourite at the Shelter for Unloved Animals."

Kay pointed at a toddler being lifted into a saddle. The toddler shook the reins. "Children ride them? You have rollercoasters and spinning rides, yet people choose to ride on donkeys?"

"I suppose it's a tradition. Ah, who's a handsome boy, yes, he is!"

This last was directed at a grizzle-chopped donkey whose collar declared him to be called Little Jimmy.

"Four pound a go," said the dead-eyed youth tending to the dozen or so beasts.

"I don't think I want to ride him, poppet," she said with a smile. "I'm a bit too big."

"S'all right," said the youth. "They can cope. They love it. Had a bloke here yesterday. Twenty stone easy. Rode Donny here up and down, up and down. He coped. He loved it."

Dee looked at the indicated donkey. She made a near invisible gesture of spellcasting. "Did you enjoy carrying the fat man around, my sweetness?" Dee asked the fuzzy quadruped.

The donkey shook its head and snorted.

"It doesn't understand English," said the youth, bored now. "It's four pound a go."

"Donny did not enjoy carrying the fat man around," said Dee.

Another donkey, further back, snorted too.

"And Merrill says you sometimes let two people ride at once." The donkey snorted again. "And do you own an electric shock collar?" said Dee, her voice rising with her anger.

"A shock collar?" said Kay. "Like 'Zap! Zap! Bad dog!'? That's terrible."

A third donkey brayed.

"And Marie says that you fed them rotten carrots yesterday," said Dee. "Although I would argue that's less serious than the shock collar thing. Sorry, Marie."

"Don't know what you're talking about," said the youth.

"You need to treat these donkeys better," she said, as calmly as she could.

"Shove off, woman. Some of us have to make a living."

"These donkeys deserve better!"

The youth brought his face close. "I said, shove off," he whispered unpleasantly.

Dee did not do anger well. She had the general temperament of a loving lap dog: a Yorkshire terrier perhaps, or maybe a King Charles spaniel; and she knew quite well she struggled to express any kind of fury or indignation without sounding ridiculously hysterical. Men simply ignored her or, worse, patronised her.

Sometimes, actions spoke louder than words.

Donny was the nearest. Dee reached out her hand. All at once the stitching on his bridle and harness came apart. Strips of leather and pieces of metal fell to the beach.

"What the frick?" said the youth.

Dee stepped towards Merrill and his saddle and bridle also fell away. Dee made sure she stepped firmly on the collar of fiddly looking electronics as she moved through the herd. The youth dashed to a pile of chairs, buckets and other equipment and drew out some rope.

"Hey," said Kay. "I think there's a big sack of carrots *waaay* over there."

She touched the noses of the freed donkeys and a faint cloud of sparkles appeared over their heads. Donny gave a joyful *hee-haw* and set off at a gentle donkey trot along the beach. Dee watched Merrill, Marie and Little Jimmy follow him.

"What's going on?" the distraught youth yelled. "What you doing?"

Dee smiled sweetly at him and magically dismantled the remaining donkeys' saddlery. She lifted the only donkey rider out of her saddle and passed the toddler to her father, moments before Wayne donkey's harness simply fell off.

"Nasty accident waiting to happen," said Dee. She gave Wayne's rump an affectionate pat as he ran off in search of imaginary carrots. The youth ran off after them, but with one length of rope and more than a dozen donkeys to catch, there wasn't much he could do.

Kay grinned at Dee. "That was fun," she said. "What next?"

"Stop, stop, stop!" Caroline held out hands to restrain her friends. They came to a halt by a donut stand between the dodgems and the Rock and Rollercoaster ride.

"Have you seen him?" asked Shazam. She had settled into a low-level state of panic: a permanent tiz.

"Just stop," said Caroline. "Let's just think for a minute. Think where Mr Beetlebane might be."

"Where would a cat go in a funfair?" said Jenny.

"A cat that, as far as I'm aware, has barely enough energy to crawl from Shazam's shoulder to her lap and back. He can't have come this far."

"Oh, he has a playful side, too," Shazam argued. "He's not on the dodgems," she added.

"Of course, he's not," said Jenny. "He's a cat. He wouldn't be able to reach the pedals and steer at— Shazam, what happened to your arm?"

Shazam's arm, from shoulder to fingers was wrapped in a cloud of candyfloss.

"I thought to myself, where would Mr Beetlebane hide? He does like his comfort. And I thought, he'll just want to curl up somewhere warm and snuggly. And I saw the big pot of candyfloss."

"Going round and round?" said Caroline.

"I just panicked and reached in," said Shazam.

"I bet the stall owner wasn't happy."

"She charged me a fiver." Shazam angled her head round and took a big bite from her upper arm. "Stress eating," she explained.

Norma Looney was furious. For a start, the charlatan Zoffner the allegedly Astute refused to admit that his fortune-telling act was simply that: an act. Additionally, the man remained entirely unruffled by her clear, precise and pointed arguments. In a manner that defied logical expression, Norma believed anyone she chose to have an argument with should at least have the common decency to get angry, burst into tears, or plead for forgiveness. Being all polite and calm and reasonable at her was ... well, it was just rude.

"But your tarot deck..." she said.

"What of it?" asked Zoffner.

"It's not even a proper deck. You've mixed Waite-Smith cards in with cards from the Crowley Thoth deck and— What's this? A business card for a taxi company!"

"Sometimes, our future has a taxi in it."

"But it's just so unprofessional."

"It's what the customer wants."

"But it's people like you who give real and genuine practitioners a bad name!"

"Oh." He smiled, not condescendingly but with interest. "And you are a genuine practitioner?"

"As it happens," she sniffed, "yes."

"Then you'll know, foxy lady, that it doesn't matter what tools I use. A great psychic needs nothing more than—" he closed his eyes as though dredging up the words from the depths of his mind "— than their *wits and intuition*. Wouldn't you agree?"

"Flimflammery and chicanery," she said, even as she recognised the words as her own.

"Why," said Zoffner softly, taking her hand in his, "I could divine your entire future from nothing but the lines of your hand." His fingertips brushed lightly across the back of her hand.

She snatched her hand away. "But you can't!"

"That's just negativity," he said.

"You're a man!"

"Thank you for noticing."

"You shouldn't be able to do any kind of magic."

"Magic, is it?" he smiled.

"Well, what do you call it?"

Zoffner the Astute shrugged, his rainbow tie-dye shirt rippling across his pot belly. "I simply open my mind to the realm of what might be. And I listen. That's an undervalued skill in this day and age. Listening. The cosmos sings, you know."

"Sings?" Norma scoffed.

He shifted his chair closer. "It does."

Before Norma knew it, he had hold of her hand again.

"Listen," he said and cocked an ear.

She held back her considerable – and entirely justified – annoyance and, with a loud huff, also cocked her ear to listen. She heard the intermittent shrieks and cackles from the ghost train. She heard the shouts of impolite teenagers and ineffective parents. She heard, faintly, the caw of seagulls, the bray of donkeys and the distant voice of a man yelling, *"Jimmy! Donny! Come back!"* She heard the clack-clack-clack of a rollercoaster climbing its ramp.

"Go out for dinner with me," whispered Zoffner the Astute.

She recoiled and considered punching the man. "What did you say?"

"Me?" said Zoffner. "Nothing, foxy lady. That was the cosmos talking."

"You asked me to go out for dinner."

"Oh," he nodded, embarrassed. "That's the cosmos. It's always trying to set me up on dates." He shook a fist at the sky. "Leave me alone, cosmos! I'm happy being a single – recently divorced but not bitter – financially solvent, surprisingly bendy middle-aged man with his own house and a two-for-one meal deal voucher for the local Harvest Fayre pub!" He returned his attention to Norma. "I mean I'm flattered, but I don't think you're my type."

"Well, quite!" she said. "And, um, why am I not your type?"

He spread his hands. "It's your mind. It's too closed. Unwilling to plumb the mystical depths of the universe."

"That's not true," she said. "I plumb the mystical depths of the universe all the time. But at least I do it with some rigour and degree of professionalism."

"Is that so?"

Zoffner gathered the tarot cards into a single pile, cut and riffled them together. "Then let's see which of us is the better mystical depths plumber."

Jenny led the way into the First Plaice restaurant bar.

"What are we doing in here?" asked Shazam.

"Getting fish and chips," said Caroline.

"Mr Beetlebane's not in here!"

"I'm going to get us a table," said Jenny. Jizzimus had raced ahead and was mucking about at the cutlery and condiments table, unscrewing but not removing the lids of the salt and pepper dispensers.

"We can't rest until we find him!" insisted Shazam.

Caroline squeezed Shazam's arm – the normal one, not the one covered in candyfloss. "I'm sorry to have to do this," she said.

"Do what?" said Shazam.

Caroline gave a near imperceptible flick of her wrist. "Mr Beetlebane is fine."

"Mr Beetlebane is fine," Shazam repeated.

"He's just having a nap somewhere."

"He's just having a nap somewhere."

"Now, have a sit down and I'll get you some grub."

"I will have a sit down and you will get me some grub."

"Excellent," said Caroline.

Jenny had dumped the shopping bags and the surprisingly weighty monkey on a long seat. Shazam sat down next to them.

Jenny gave Caroline an amused look of appraisal. "You'd never use that hypnotism shtick on me, would you?"

"Heaven forfend!" said Caroline, unconvincingly. "Fish and chips all round, yeah?"

"I fancy 'avin' some of those Jedi mind trick skills," said Jizzimus as Caroline went to the chippy counter. "I'd be 'avin' some balls-deep fun wiv that." He jumped onto the table and intoned deeply, "Look at my swinging dong. You are gettin' 'orny. Very ... very ... 'orny."

First Plaice occupied a unit in the arcade of shops, fast food joints and amusements that encircled the funfair. One set of windows overlooked the runaway train and teacups of the funfair; on the opposite side, they looked out on the sandy beach and the end of Skegness Pier. The best thing about First Plaice, as far as Jenny was concerned, was it was all but empty and there was wasn't a single stinking child in sight.

"I'm hungry," she admitted.

"I'm so-so," said Shazam.

Jenny regarded Shazam's pink and sticky arm, and the pink sticky beard she had also acquired. "You have just eaten a ton of candyfloss."

"I 'ad a little nibble too, while she weren't lookin'," said Jizzimus.

The fish and chips arrived before Caroline came back. The waitress plonked three oval platters piled with cod, chips and mushy peas on the table, and a small mountain of knives and forks. Steel knives and forks.

"Don't you do the little wooden fork things?" Jenny asked her.

"Only for takeaway," said the waitress.

"You can eat the chips wiv your fingers," said Jizzimus. "An' the fish. I'll 'ave the mushy peas."

"I don't like mushy peas anyway," said Jenny. "They look like some kind of bacterial infection."

"Oh, I'll have those." Shazam happily scooped them off Jenny's plate onto hers.

"Greedy bitch stole my peas," sulked Jizzimus.

"I thought you weren't hungry," said Jenny.

"Yes, but it's mushy peas, isn't it?" said Shazam. "Can't let them go to waste."

The monkey next to Shazam fell over as though lunging for the precious peas. Shazam righted the monkey and tucked in.

Caroline appeared.

"Where've you been?" asked Jenny.

"Bought you a present." Caroline passed a folded t-shirt to Jenny. "You've got a big rip in that top. I saw this at the stand next door, thought of you and..."

Jenny unfolded the t-shirt. "Thank you, Caroline, that's very thoughtful. Oh, and look—" She turned the printed front to show Shazam: *WHORE IN TRAINING.*

Shazam snorted with laughter and sprayed her plate with mushy peas.

"You thought of me?" said Jenny.

"Yup," said Caroline.

"Thanks."

Dee and Kay bought ice-creams from a man on an old-fashioned trike with a front-mounted ice box. They sat down on a concrete bench at the point where the promenade met the sand, the funfair behind them. To their left, on the other side of a sea front car park, was Skegness Pier. A mile or more out to sea, rows of sluggish wind turbines turned.

"Is it brown all the way out?" asked Kay.

Dee licked her rum and raisin cone thoughtfully. "I'm sure it turns blue, or at least a respectable grey, before it gets to the other side. Didn't you see the sea when ... when you were brought over to England?"

Kay stopped nibbling the flake in her 99. "How much do you know?"

"Not much, sweetness," Dee replied. "I only know what I saw the day you came into my shop. And, yes, Caroline told me that someone had – sold you, was it?"

Kay nodded.

"I don't know the details," said Dee and then, thinking, "Does Jenny?"

Kay shook her head. "I don't want to get her into trouble by telling her more than she needs to know. I was transported in a box, a big plastic box yeah, from Porto to England. In the back of a lorry like—" she waved her hands at an articulated lorry in the car park "—like that one. Hardly any air. There was just a crack in the side of the box." She held her hands, together as though in prayer, an inch or two apart. "And, you know, all I could see through that crack was – oh, God! It's him!"

"Who?" said Dee, swivelling around.

Kay pressed herself up against Dee and pointed to the articulated lorry in the car park. "Him!"

Dee looked. The lip-enhancing cream had worn off and the man's facial burns had healed a mite in the intervening week and a bit, but there couldn't be many bald-headed men with a face that was fifty percent glazed ham pink.

"What's he doing here?" said Dee.

"It can't be good," said Kay. Dee could hear the fear in her voice.

"Are you sure he's a policeman?"

"He had a badge. And he brought the police to Jenny's house."

"What's he doing here? Is he looking for you?"

"It can't be a coincidence."

The two witches lowered themselves, using the back of the bench as cover, and watched. The policeman walked to the rear of the lorry, talking to a man in crumpled overalls who Dee assumed was the lorry driver.

"What do you think they're talking about?" said Dee.

"We could sneak over and find out," said Kay. "Caroline knew a spell to change her appearance. Can you...?"

"I wish," said Dee. "I don't think they're friends, do you? Looks like the copper is telling the other one what to do, like he's his boss or something."

The lorry driver went to the rear doors and flung one open. He gestured inside, talking all the while.

"Is he dropping something off? Or picking it up?" said Dee. "Ow!"

Kay had gripped her arm painfully. The teenager's eyes were wide with alarm.

"Look."

"What?"

"Look!" Kay was pointing frantically. "The boxes in the truck. The big plastic boxes!"

"You mean...?"

Kay nodded grimly. "We have to rescue them."

189

Jenny returned from the toilets, modelling her dubious new t-shirt. "What do you think?"

"It fits," said Shazam kindly.

The monkey keeled over as though in appreciation. Shazam set it upright.

"Totally suits you," said Caroline.

"Dunno why it says 'in trainin'," said Jizzimus. "Reckon you could turn pro any time."

"Thanks," said Jenny. "Just so you know, I am wearing this ironically."

"If you wish," said Caroline. She pushed aside her finished fish and chips. "Now, I suppose we had better try to find Cobwebs' cat."

"Mr Beetlebane is fine," said Shazam. "He's just having a nap somewhere."

"Ye-es," said Caroline. "Maybe we ought to find him, all the same."

"Where shall we look?" said Jenny.

"This is meant to be a fortune-telling trip," said Caroline. "Maybe we ought to divine where ol' Beetlebum is."

"And when that fails, we go look," agreed Jenny. "Okay. What method shall we use?"

Shazam rummaged through her carrier bags of purchases. "Zoffner the Astute said we should look within so— Ah!" She pulled out a large box.

"*My First Ouija Board,*" Jenny read.

"It's purple and got cats on it," said Shazam, as if that was all the justification she needed.

Zoffner took the card from the top of the deck and turned it over. He gave it the most cursory of glances. "You are here, in Lincolnshire, under some form of duress."

"Isn't everyone?" said Norma.

"Some of us think the place has mellow and rustic charm."

"Like a pig pen." Norma flipped the next card. The Three of Coins. "You lied about having your own house. You live in a caravan."

"Don't be bound by preconceptions. A caravan is a house."

"It has wheels."

"They're both punctured."

"It's not a house," she said firmly.

Zoffner flipped a card. "You see yourself as champion in the fight against evil."

"One tries."

"You ... you believe in wicked witches?" He blinked. "*Actual* wicked witches?"

"No need to sound like that," she retorted. "You're the fool for not believing."

"And who is Lesley-Ann Faulkner?" he asked.

"A wicked witch."

His fingers brushed the edge of the card. "So why do I see a trippy flaming tree monster?"

"It's a long story."

"They take an age to bring out the food at the local Harvest Fayre pub. Maybe you'd like to discuss it over—?"

Norma turned another card and said, without even looking at it, "Your wife got the real house in the divorce settlement."

"It was always in her name. I don't believe in property. She was the sensible one."

"You don't say."

Zoffner flipped a card. "You— Oh." He peered at the card closer, lifting his tinted specs to see it better. "You have met a wicked witch recently. Today, in fact."

"Have I?" said Norma. She leaned in to peer at the card. He smiled softly at her.

"Didn't you know that, Norma?"

She gave him a fiercely irritated look. "I— where does it show that?"

He turned over another card to cover the previous one. It was the Queen of Cups. Norma looked at it.

"Your wife was a witch?"

"What can I say?" said Zoffner. "I'm drawn to powerful and foxy ladies."

Norma was flustered. Her undergarments suddenly felt too tight. Restrictive rather than supportive.

Zoffner flipped another card. "You have been lonely for a long time, Norma. You were sent away somewhere." He looked at her in surprise. "Were you in prison, Norma?"

She put her hands over his and the cards to stop him. "I'm not lonely," she said, stiffly. "There's a difference between lonely and alone."

His gaze met hers. "Not much difference. Trust me."

"No," she said quietly.

"The great thing about two lonely people," said Zoffner, "is that they can each offer what the other needs most."

"That's very astute."

"Groovy."

They cleared the table and set out the *My First Ouija Board*. The three women each put a finger on the glass pointer.

"How does this work?" asked Caroline.

"Is it even witchcraft?" said Jenny.

"Of course, it is," said Dee. "We just ask a question and the board tells us the answer."

"I don't believe in ghostly spirits giving us answers from beyond," said Caroline. "It's stupid."

"No, it's our unconscious minds that reach out and divine an answer using the ideomotor effect," said Shazam.

"You mean our fingers push it," said Jenny.

"Yes." Shazam cleared her throat. "Ouija board. Is Mr Beetlebane still alive?"

The pointer, with no perceptible effort, glided over to *YES*.

"Is he hurt?"

The pointer flew to *NO*, despite Jizzimus trying to stop it by standing on the board.

The monkey toy fell over.

"That monkey keeps falling over," said Jenny.

"Shush," said Caroline. "This is fun."

"Is he close?" asked Shazam.

The pointer drifted near the *YES* then the *NO* and then moved towards the letters.

"*I*," read Shazam. "*N*. In. He's in somewhere. *S*."

The fallen monkey shifted on the seat and twitched its shoulders.

"Okay. That monkey just moved," said Jenny.

Caroline looked. "No. That monkey did not just move."

"It did!"

"Shhh," said Shazam. "*I. In Si... D.* Inside? He's inside somewhere."

The monkey's torso rippled.

"Look!" said Jenny.

"What?" said Caroline and then, "Shit!"

The monkey rolled over onto its back.

Shazam gave a little squeal. "It's possessed!"

The monkey's T-shirt heaved and pulsated.

"It's goin' all alien chest-burster," said Jizzimus, hiding behind Jenny.

"This is insane," said Caroline.

The monkey gave a final heave and a long black limb shot out from under the t-shirt. For half a moment, Jenny thought she was witnessing the hatching of some monstrous spider egg before getting a grip on herself. "It's the cat!" she shouted in relief.

With a *Meow!* Mr Beetlebane crawled out from inside the monkey, covered in white foam stuffing.

Jizzimus chortled. "And that, my girl, is 'ow babies is born."

Shazam dragged her scruffy mog onto her lap. Jenny inspected the huge rip in the monkey's belly. "He must have crawled inside while we were with Zoffy-whatsisface."

"We've had him with us all this time," said Shazam.

"Look within," said Caroline with a sigh. "Do you think he knew all along?"

Jenny shrugged. "Well, that's enough excitement. Maybe we ought to try to find the others. I wonder where Kay and Dee are."

Shazam plucked a cube of foam from Mr Beetlebane's ear. "Let's ask the Ouija board."

"I found that last experience a little freaky," said Caroline.

"It got results," said Shazam.

"Fine," sighed Jenny.

Jizzimus had dragged the monkey toy under the table and was busy disembowelling it, muttering something about "If the cat can do it—"

Jenny put her finger on the Ouija pointer. "Ouija board. Where are Dee and Kay?"

The pointer hesitated a fraction and then drifted off.

"*B*," said Shazam. "Beach. No. *U. R. N.*"

"Burns unit?" said Caroline.

"*E*," said Shazam. "*D*. Burned. *M. A. N.* Man."

The pointer stopped.

"Burned man," said Jenny. "Is that the name of a pub?"

"Or is it she's with a man who's been burned?"

Jenny suddenly tightened with fear. "I know a man who was burned recently."

"So do I," said Caroline.

Kay gave a jump, got one knee onto the trailer's floor, and levered herself into the back of the truck. Dee stayed outside, nervously keeping guard. She realised she really, really needed a wee.

"Hurry," she hissed.

"Are they still in the cab?" Kay hissed back.

Dee poked her head round the side and looked along the length of the trailer. The driver's door was shut. "Think so."

There were eight crates in the back. Eight potential trafficked individuals. Kay struggled with the interlocking lid of the nearest. With far more noise than Dee would have liked, threw it open. "It's empty." She opened the next. "Empty!"

"Maybe they all are," said Dee.

"Just keep an eye out."

Dee popped her head around the other side of the truck and saw the shaven-headed policeman coming towards her. A barrage of half-formed warnings, ideas, doubts and flight instincts rattled through Dee's brain. She dared to hope he didn't recognise her from their ten second encounter in the charity shop.

Loud enough for Kay to hear, she said: "Oh, hello. I wonder if you could help me."

"What were you doing back there?" he demanded.

Dee stepped towards him. In the narrow space between the truck and the car next to it, he wouldn't be able to get past without squashing her aside.

"I was looking for someone to help me, poppet," she said. "I was looking for the, um, the pier."

He gave a little, irritated shake of the head. "And?"

"And I wondered if you knew where it was."

He looked at her as though she was stupid. That was good. If he thought she was stupid then he might not suspect she was up to anything. He jerked a thumb at the building directly behind him. "That's it."

Dee made a show of looking at it intently. "Is it?"

"It says Skegness Pier on the side. In lightbulbs."

"Oh. I did wonder. Is it the only pier?"

There was a thump of trainers on tarmac, Kay jumping out of the lorry. The policeman's eyes flicked; he'd heard it too.

"Excuse me." Gently but implacably he pushed her aside.

Dee stumbled to her knees. She put a hand on his feet and silently mended his shoelaces: mended them into a single mass of woven thread. The policeman shoved her up and out of his way. Dee was not a cruel person, but the look of confusion on his face as he fell over his own feet was delightful to behold.

She dashed to the trailer doors.

"They're all empty!" said Kay.

"We have to go!" urged Dee.

"You!" yelled the prostrate policeman, staring furiously up at Kay.

Under the table, Jizzimus merrily ripped the stuffing out of the monkey, finishing the job that the cat had started. Above, his mistress and the other two tiresome witches chatted on and on. They seemed awfully excited.

"Doug Bowman was my DS when I was a detective constable," Caroline was saying. "I saw him for the first time in ages the day before I came to the Hall. He wanted to know if I fancied a change of job. When I saw him the following morning, he had this nasty burn on the side of his face."

"'Ere goes." Jizzimus wriggled under the monkey's t-shirt, through the rip Beetlebane had made, and slotted his arms and legs into the cavities he had excavated in the toy's arms and legs.

"This Doug Bowman," said Jenny, her voice trembling. "Was he bald? Like, his head shaved?"

"That's right," said Caroline. "A shaved gorilla in a suit. What's wrong?"

It took a bit of wriggling and gouging for Jizzimus to scoop out two eyeholes. When he had, he rolled clumsily to his feet. "Ta-dah! Look at my monkey suit!"

Jenny ignored him utterly. "The burned bald guy. That's the man who chased us, Kay and me. When I rescued her."

"Rescued her?" said Shazam.

Jenny sighed heavily. So did Jizzimus. What was the point of going to the effort of creating his own amazing monkey outfit if no one was going to appreciate it?

"Fine!" he snapped. Unnoticed he ran under a row of tables, out into the car park and towards the pier.

Dee wasn't one of life's runners. It wasn't that she was necessarily unfit – although a love of late-night, cream-filled snacks did count against her – and she was all in favour of practical clothes and footwear for the woman on the move, but nature had seen fit to give her a body that was thoroughly non-aerodynamic. Kay ended up all but dragging her as Dee scuttled along, trying to keep up, spurred on by the shouts of the shoe bound policeman.

Their choice of direction to run could have been better. If they had headed up the slope of the car park, they could have tried to escape into the town centre, the floral gardens, even to a police station. But they had run down the slope. To the right were fast food stands and souvenir stalls, to the left, the wall of the pier building and, ahead, the beach and the sea.

"Oi!"

Dee looked back. The policeman had discarded his shoes and was now running after them barefoot. The truck driver, less enthusiastic, was jogging along behind him.

"Did you see that?" said Kay.

"He's – taken – his – shoes – off," panted Dee.

"No," said Kay. "The monkey."

"What?"

"The monkey. It just ran across there."

Dee saw nothing and, frankly, felt that the appearance of a monkey, however bizarre, was not a priority right now. "Up there!" she gasped, pointing.

Where the pier building ran out of solid land and became a wooden promenade on iron pillars running down to the sea, there was an access ramp. The two witches dodged left, round the last car in the car park, and up it.

"And we ran out of there as fast as we could," said Jenny.

"You must have been terrified," said Shazam.

"Shocked," Jenny agreed. "But not as shocked as I was when he turned up at my house the next morning with a bunch of coppers."

"He's not a cop anymore," said Caroline. "He was fired... *We* were fired."

"You?" said Shazam, giving her a curiously wounded look, like a child who's been told that the toilet isn't the expressway to goldfish heaven. "What for?"

"Bowman is a shifty character. I was ... weak."

"You are anything but weak," said Jenny.

"I'm a good actress. Point is, he's not on the force but he's still got friends. And, whatever dodgy work he's up to, he's still got some clout when he needs it."

"And the Ouija board told us that Kay's with him now," said Shazam.

"Well, he can't be here," said Caroline. "There's no reason for him to be *here*."

There were a number of temporary stalls and toddler rides along the pier boardwalk. Dee and Kay skulked behind a waffle stall near the very end of the pier and tried to look inconspicuous. Kay peered cautiously around the edge of the stall.

"What you doing?" said the woman on the stall.

"Hiding," said Kay.

"Well, go bleeding hide somewhere else."

"He's coming this way!"

Dee did her best to look without being seen. The policeman was indeed making his way along, searching in and around every conceivable hiding place.

"He's going to find us," said Kay.

Dee tried to envisage their capture or arrest. Determined souls though they were, witches or not, it didn't bode well.

"Didn't I tell you to piss off," said the stallholder.

"We really are hiding," said Dee.

Kay was no longer beside her. She looked round and saw Kay, still in the shadow of the stall, standing by the railings, eyes closed and arms stretched.

"What are you doing?" Dee whispered. She looked over the rails. The brown sea chopped and rippled below them. "It can't be more than four feet deep. You can't jump."

"I'm not," said Kay. Without opening her eyes, she pointed up the beach to where a certain youth was still trying and failing to recapture his lost donkeys. "I'm calling for help."

As Dee watched, a faint haze of rainbow light reached out from Kay's hands towards the donkeys.

If Jizzimus has known that being visible would be so much fun – and a visible monkey at that – he would have done it long ago. His appearance along the seafront and inside the pier amusements brought shrieks, gasps, shouts and laughs. Those who weren't horrified by an ambulatory toy monkey could be heard exchanging knowledgeable theories.

"It's just a hologram."

"It's animatronics."

"It's got that mini-me bloke in it."

Not one person even thought to suggest the obvious: that a witch's familiar was wearing the monkey's skin like some plush toy serial killer. But people were stupid; the obvious never occurred to them.

Jizzimus ran on through the pier's bingo hall and café, wondering if he could pull a similar stunt with the badger roadkill they'd found earlier on the side of the road.

"I can see you! Come out. Now!"

Dee looked round the stall. The policeman was there, a fat metal bar held casually in one hand.

"Are you playing silly buggers with these two?" asked the waffle stall woman.

The policeman flashed some ID at her. "Police." He looked at Dee. "And you're under arrest."

"What for?" said Dee.

"Let's start with assault." He wiggled bare toes. "Beatriz, come out here."

Slowly, fearfully, Kay stepped out beside Dee.

"You've been very naughty," said the policeman. "Given us all quite a headache. Turn around and put your hands behind your back."

Dee turned. The policeman gripped her wrists and bound them. The cable-tie squeaked as he tightened it.

"Aren't you meant to do that caution thing?" said the woman on the stall.

"What?"

"That 'anything you do say will be taken down in evidence' thing."

The policeman laughed. "All right. Beatriz Santos, I am arresting you for assault. You do not have to say anything but it may harm your defence if you do not mention when questioned something which you later rely on in court. Anything you do say may be given in evidence."

"We're not going to court, are we?" said Kay.

He leaned in so only Dee and Kay could hear. "No."

Kay stamped back. By luck and good judgement she found his toes.

The policeman howled in pain and anger. Kay stamped again.

"We look for them now," said Caroline, decisively. "Whether it is Doug Bowman or not; whether they're in real danger, we find them. What are you doing, Jenny?"

Jenny was looking under the table as though she had lost something. Under the table was a pile of foam stuffing, although the monkey toy seemed to have disappeared. Jenny stood and walked to the door leading to the car park and picked up a rough cube of foam that had found its way over there.

"Do you know where they are?" said Shazam. Jenny wasn't listening. Caroline and Shazam followed her out into the car park.

"Kay saw something in that dead badger," said Jenny. "A cat and a monkey and—"

"Donkeys," said Shazam.

"That's right," said Caroline.

"No. Donkeys. There."

Caroline followed Shazam's gaze to where a pack or herd or a ... whatever the collective noun of donkeys was trundled up the beach and onto a walkway leading onto the pier. There was no one driving them and they moved with an unnatural sense of purpose.

"You don't suppose...?" said Caroline.

The witches ran after them.

There were screams and shouts as Jizzimus burst out of the pier building and onto the boardwalk. "Tha's right," he roared. "Look a' me! Jizzimus Monkeyflesh O'Crackerjack!"

Then he realised the screams and shouts weren't for him. A drove of donkeys was trotting onto the boardwalk and towards the end of the pier. Jizzimus felt very conflicted and put out.

Rampaging donkeys were something he very much approved of; normally he would take great delight in a scene like this. But he was dressed up and ready to cause mischief and these donkeys were stealing his thunder. It was like being a pyromaniac out to cause a night of arsonist mischief, only to find that everywhere was already on fire.

However, Jizzimus was always ready to improvise. If someone had stolen his thunder, the only thing to do was to claim it back.

With a short sprint, he dashed towards the trampling donkeys, leapt, back-flipped off the knee of one and landed on the back of another. "Onward!" he yelled.

His donkey army – possession being nine tenths of the law – rumbled on. Deck chairs were crushed. Stalls were knocked astray. Children were snatched from the hoofs of death by terrified parents.

He saw three figures at the end of the pier. The fat and stupid witch, Dee, was lying on the ground by the railings where she had been shoved. The stinky child-witch, Kay, was bent over as though she had just been gut-punched. Both had their hands tied behind their backs. Jizzimus recognised the third figure too: the man with an iron bar that he'd clubbed Jenny with, and the burned face Jenny's witchfire had given him in return.

"Oi! Fuzz!" yelled the imp-monkey in fury. "My name is Maximus Jizzimus Meridius. Commander of the armies of the north! Father to a murdered son! 'Usband to a murdered wife! And I will 'ave my vengeance in this life or the next!"

Too late, the policeman saw the donkeys charging at him. They filled the boardwalk side to side and were not slowing. Eyes were wide with alarm, the copper dodged this way and that, looking for an exit. There was none and, as Jizzimus bore down on him, he backed up against the railings.

Jizzimus gripped his donkey's fuzzy mane and ran up onto its head.

The donkeys bashed into the last stall. As it crumpled, a woman inside cried, "Oh, me waffles!"

Within his costume, Jizzimus thrust out his tiny claws to savage the man.

On the floor, Kay raised her hands behind her back. Rainbow light filled the air. The donkeys braked abruptly, hoofs skidding to a halt inches from her. Jizzimus flew forward, wrapped himself like a facehugger around the bastard copper's head and pitched over the railing with him.

With a triumphant cry of *"This! Is! Sparta!"* Jizzimus rode him down into the sea before it got all soggy and salty, and considerably less fun.

Jenny barged her way through the donkeys milling about the boardwalk, indifferent to the danger of getting physical with a dozen large, confused beasts. She pushed past the last and went to her knees beside Kay. "You all right?"

"I'm fine," said Kay. "It was him, the policeman."

"Bowman," said Jenny.

A pinpoint of imperceptible witchfire was enough to melt through the plastic ties around Kay's wrist. Jenny rolled Kay over and hugged her fiercely. "Did you call these donkeys?"

"Yep."

"That was amazing!"

"Did you see the monkey?" said Kay.

"What monkey?" said Shazam.

Dee rubbed her wrists once Caroline had freed them. "I didn't see a monkey."

"There was definitely a monkey," said Kay.

Jenny looked over the railings. Doug Bowman spluttered and flailed unhappily in the shallow sea. Jenny considered the huge satisfaction she would get from pouring witchfire down on the man. She would happily boil away the oceans to put him out of her misery but a public display of wicked witch powers would have been unwise. There was no sign of the monkey toy, but Jenny thought she could make out the tiniest of figures doing a concerted doggy paddle by the shore.

Jizzimus caught up with them as they exited the pier, shivering and wiggling his finger in his droopy cow ear to get the seawater out. "Did you see me, boss? I took that fucker down to Chinatown. Boom!"

Pretending to bend and scratch her knee, Jenny picked him up and placed him on her shoulder. She gave him a loving squeeze.

"Where's Norma?" said Dee.

"We left her arguing with Zoffner the Astute," said Caroline.

"It did get a bit heated in there," admitted Shazam.

They stopped by the entrance to Zoffner's monastic 'cave' in the funfair and looked around. Caroline knocked on the door. "Mr Astute! Norma! Are you still in there?"

"Wait a moment!" Norma yelled in tremulous reply.

"Norma?"

"I said wait!"

Several minutes later, Norma emerged, fiddling with the cuffs of her tweedy jacket.

"You look a little red-faced there, Norma," noted Shazam.

"It's a warm day, Miss Jaye," Norma replied.

"Perhaps you and Zoffner the Astute were having a lively ... debate," suggested Caroline.

"Indeed," said Norma stiffly. "Now, are we heading back to the minibus?"

"I think we ought to," agreed Jenny.

As they walked out of the funfair and up towards the clock tower roundabout, Jizzimus whispered in Jenny's ear. She grinned. "So – Norma...?"

"Yes, Miss Knott?"

"How good was he then? You know, marks out of ten?"

"Pardon?" said Norma, alarmed.

"Zoffner. The world's *greatest* fortune-teller."

"Oh," said Norma, much relieved. "No, that man is a mere paddler in the sea of magic."

"Well, I thought he was amazing," said Shazam. "He knew everything we asked him."

"Yes," said Norma with restored condescension. "I think that any questions you might have can be adequately answered by true professionals such as myself."

"Is that so?" said Jenny. "Then I have a question."

"Yes?" said Norma.

"Weren't you wearing a woollen vest when we came out this morning, not a tie-dye one?"

# Chapter 6 – Bewitched

Dee unfolded the map onto the table in front of them. The map immediately fell apart along its fold lines, so she shuffled the pieces into position. Caroline, Jenny, Shazam and Kay pored over it. They had convened in Jenny's hut. It was one of the few huts that hadn't exploded, burned down, or been destroyed by a bewitched rat-woman.

"If ever Little Chef opens a museum you should send them this." Caroline indicated the aged map.

Dee shrugged. "It was in my car when I bought it. Does the job."

"Long as the job is to find places that used to be Little Chefs on roads that were bypassed thirty years ago, yeah."

Jenny traced a finger across a couple of faded sections. "So we know that Doug Bowman took Kay to Birmingham. Wait—" She lifted her gaze and looked at Kay. "Or would you prefer Beatriz now?"

Kay shrugged. "I don't miss my old name. I mostly used to hear it when I'd done something wrong."

"Same here," said Caroline.

"I don't think it matters what name you're born with," said Shazam. "Sometimes we have to find our own true name."

"And you're sticking with Shazam?" said Caroline.

"Why? Don't you like it?"

"No, no, it's fine, Cobwebs. Gotta say, it does sound like a drain cleaner. *Shazam! And the clog is gone!*"

"S'true," said Jizzimus who was, for reasons, known only to himself, fashioning a wig out of cobwebs he'd gathered off the floor.

Jenny gave Jizzimus a gentle kick and Caroline a fierce nudge.

"It's a lovely name," Caroline insisted.

"You hate it," said Shazam.

Caroline sighed and gave a magical flick of her wrist. "Shazam is the loveliest name in the world," she said.

205

"Shazam *is* the loveliest name in the world," agreed Shazam.

"And Kay is a lovely name too," said Dee, just in case she was feeling left out.

"I didn't even pick it," said Kay. "Jenny did."

"No," said Jenny. "I asked you what your name was and—"

"You asked who had done this to me," said Kay. She held her palms an inch apart and put her eye to the gap. "All I could see out of that crate was a letter K and a number one, printed on the side of some packing."

"Kay Wun," said Jenny. "I'm an idiot."

"Also, true," said Jizzimus, who had given up on the cobweb wig and was now eating it like candyfloss.

"I didn't know what it was or where I was," said Kay, "apart from being in some sort of lorry. But I looked at it – *K1* – and concentrated on it for hours and hours while I was shut away. It was like a mantra of freedom. I think I'll stick with Kay."

"Do you think you came here via Skegness?" asked Shazam.

Kay shrugged.

"Is there some sort of harbour there?" said Jenny.

"No. There's a port in Boston to the south, but I don't think it's big enough for lorries and containers and things."

"What about this road here?" said Dee, carefully sliding a wayward section of map back into place. "The A16. It comes straight down from Grimsby and Hull. Those are definitely places where boats go."

"So why go to Skegness?" said Caroline. "There must be faster ways of getting to Birmingham."

"Maybe it's a stopping off point, or a place where they swap vehicles," said Jenny. "I mean, who would go to Skegness for people trafficking, or whatever this is?"

"Doug Bowman is a sleazeball who'd sell his own granny for a fast buck," said Caroline. "People trafficking would be right up his alley."

"I thought you said he was your friend," said Jenny.

"I make bad personal choices. It's my thing."

"Are they taking girls for sex?" said Dee. "Do those crates get all wrapped up like Christmas presents and delivered to pervy old men?"

206

Caroline couldn't help smiling. "You even make sex trafficking sound twee and cosy."

Dee made a noise like an angry tomcat and sent the map fluttering across the table as she slammed her hand down. "They'd soon regret it if they tried it with a witch! Filthy buggers!"

"Yes, they obviously didn't realise they'd taken someone who might unleash a donkey army upon them," said Jenny with a wink.

"Seriously though, we need to stop them," said Kay. "Other girls might not be as lucky as me."

"We should call the police," said Shazam.

"And tell them what?" said Jenny. "We have no hard evidence."

"And they'd have a lot of questions for Kay that can't be answered without revealing we're witches," said Caroline. "Besides, Bowman might have enough contacts to kill any investigation."

"Then what do we do?" said Shazam.

"It's obvious," said Caroline.

"Is it?"

"I'll contact Doug Bowman."

"What?"

"Maybe meet up with him. He doesn't know I'm anything to do with this."

"That sounds a bit dangerous, poppet," said Dee.

"Why is it that only wicked witches get to use that witchy fire stuff?" said Kay as Dee folded the map pieces back into a pile. "Times like this, a bit of fire power would be bloody handier than healing ointments, stage hypnotism and animal control."

"Oh, don't be jealous, sweetness, not even in jest," said Dee. "When a witch is wicked, she does terrible, terrible things."

"A little wickedness can be fun," said Caroline.

"Amen, sister," said Jizzimus.

I've been reading Armadel's Second Grimoire," said Dee. "Honestly, it would make your toes curl."

"Really?"

"That Elizabeth Báthory who Norma mentioned, *she* killed over six hundred women so she could bathe in their blood."

"Dee, you shouldn't believe all that," said Caroline. "These things always get so exaggerated."

"No, it said in the book. *Sanguinem veneficae bibit.* That's Latin for 'the witch drank their blood.'"

"More likely some poor disturbed girl who killed a couple of people, max. Women serial killers are very rare. And how's *anyone* going to kill over six hundred people?"

"She was a noblewoman, she summoned young women and they came," said Dee, peeved at Caroline's dismissal. "Anyway Kay, good *will* prevail without the aid of witchfire, and you've got your friends here to help you."

They filed out of the hut and crossed the grass to Effie's main hut.

Jenny asked: "Your book, does it mention other magical creatures? Like trolls?"

"No, it sticks firmly to the facts," said Dee.

"Yeah, but facts about trolls."

"No mythical beasts in there at all. The only unusual creature in it is a witch's imp."

Jenny sighed. "I saw something in that dyke. And I don't mean your flaming tree monster."

"What did it look like?" said Dee.

"Like a tumour with a face and a grudge. And it was way too big to be an imp."

"How do you know how big an imp is?" asked Kay, skipping up behind Jenny.

"Um. I assumed," said Jenny. "Aren't they normally depicted as being about the size of a cat?"

"There are some lovely woodcuts in the book," said Dee. "And yes, the imps are shown as smallish ugly things."

"Not 'avin' that boss!" Jizzimus danced with rage. "You tell 'er there's imps wiv massive knobs and film star looks, *Tell 'er!*"

"Imps sort of grow with the age and wickedness of the witch," said Dee. "How big was this thing you thought you saw?"

"*Thought* I saw?" said Jenny, affronted.

"Was it before or after you were hit by the car?" asked Kay.

208

Lesson time.

"Morning class," said Effie brightly. She was wearing a t-shirt that declared she was *Mellow Yellow*. "It's the final week of our course. Hasn't the time flown?"

"Practically galloped," said Shazam.

"And although we will be doing a formal evaluation, feedback and circle time session on Friday, I'm sure you'll agree that it has been a roaring success."

"Most educational," agreed Dee.

"I will be meeting with Mrs du Plessis this evening and, as well as extending our thanks for the use of her facilities, I will be proposing plans for the next round of witch training. My team has already been scouring the country for new recruits."

"By team, she means that long streak of reefer madness, Madison Fray," whispered Caroline.

"And I can only see this academy of witchcraft going from strength to strength."

"An academy, is it now?" said Norma.

"Perhaps," said Effie smoothly, "Today we're going to look at a very useful set of magical tools for your magical toolbox. Let me show you something."

Caroline surreptitiously nudged Norma. "Has Zoffner put his magical tool in your toolbox recently?" she whispered.

"Don't be filthy!" whispered Norma in reply, turning a vibrant red colour.

Effie had turned on the projector and focused the image. It showed a document covered in spidery writing on the cusp of being totally illegible, even with the grainy image expanded to fill the wall. The thing that drew the eye immediately, however, was the embellished star in the bottom right corner.

"Now, this photograph is of a parchment found under a beam at Gelli Bach farmhouse in Wales. It was hidden there for a very good reason. Anyone want to guess what that might have been?"

"Is it a protection spell?" asked Shazam, her eyes bright with recognition.

"Yes it is Sharon, well done!" said Effie. "The pentagram illustrates the intended—"

"It's got six points. It's not a pentagram," said Norma.

"The six-sided pentagram—"

"Shouldn't it be a hexagram then?" asked Jenny.

"No," said Effie, without much certainty. "The point is, it's a spell of protection. A spell to act against the effects of other spells. Now, what business applications can we all see for this type of spell?"

"Oldest trick in the book," said Caroline promptly. "Witches cast spells and witches sell protection *against* spells. My grandfather used to do something similar with foxes."

"He'd cast spells on them?" said Shazam.

"He was a gamekeeper. He'd work summers south of the river, catching foxes on farmers' land and releasing them north of the river."

"And the winter months working north of the river and sending them south," said Norma. "Scandalous behaviour."

"Oh, I bet there were plenty of witches who stepped into both roles to keep things ticking over," said Caroline. "I know I would."

"Succinctly put Caroline," said Effie. "But we can't always be sure who might be on the other end of such a transaction, which is why we're going to practise those skills. Your next set of practical tests will focus on spells and counter spells. You'll be pitting your wits against each other."

Jenny watched as Effie brought out two shoe boxes and jiggled them.

"Wits, boss," said Jizzimus. "Not your strong point."

"We need to make sure that we conduct this exercise on a level playing field," said Effie, "so we will each draw a name out of here. The name that you draw out is the person you will target with your spells."

"Do we get to choose the spells?" asked Caroline.

"No, you do not! I have selected a set of spells that will confirm success without causing any lasting harm. You will select them from this other box, but I have them all listed here." She changed the slide on the projector.

"Victim to be given green hair," read Shazam. "Victim to do everything a chicken might do."

"I saw this video of a woman layin' chicken eggs," said Jizzimus. "I think they were eggs. Coulda been ping-pong balls."

"Victim to speak nothing but the truth," Shazam continued. "Victim to speak in backslang." She put her hand up. "What's backslang?"

"It's where you say words backwards," said Effie. "Used in the past by market traders to discuss things without alerting customers. They might have said something like *the teebar's a bit off today* for example."

Shazam looked at her blankly.

"It's *rabbit*, Sharon. If they said that the rabbit was a bit off then no customers would buy it. That's the point: it was used as a code."

"But people don't eat rabbit," said Shazam. "Rabbits are pets."

Dee shuffled in her seat and looked as if she too might have thoughts on the matter of eating rabbits.

"Piece o' cake, this," said Jizzimus. "Should I nip up there and add in a couple? Summat like *Victim to make themselves available as a tasty snack*? Make things a bit more interestin'?"

"You are going to take a name from the box," said Effie "And make sure you keep it to yourself. You will also take a spell from this box."

"It's a bit like Secret Santa," said Dee cheerfully.

"Now obviously this is a test that will rely on your initiative, but if anyone's got any tips they'd like to share with the group, now's the time. You'll be free to come and go as you please for the next two days while you carry out this exercise."

"Well I'm just glad that I've stocked up on talismans," said Shazam. "I've got an adjustable ward-stopping stick, a glow in the dark warning pentangle and even an individual sleep-safe protection unit."

"I saw that in the shop," said Caroline. "It's a mosquito net with sequins on it. Honestly, Cobwebs, you should save your money!"

"Well I for one will rely on my powers of foresight," announced Norma. "I'll be untouchable if I see you coming. Whoever you are!"

"I don't think you'll be untouchable, Norma," said Kay. "You'll just have a bit of an advantage."

"How does that work, then?" asked Caroline. "If you know what's going to be done, and who's going to do it, how can you stop it? It would mean that your prediction was wrong."

"Interesting paradox, isn't it?" said Effie with an approving nod. "Norma, how would you respond to that?"

"I like to think of the future as a moveable feast," said Norma, obviously warming to a pet subject.

Jenny ignored Jizzimus as he twerked across the floor, miming his own version of a moveable feast.

"If I see the future, as I so often do, it's the most *likely* future at that particular moment. There is no reason at all why it can't change if I choose. Hypothetically that is."

"Hypothetically. Do you seriously mean that you've never tried?" asked Caroline, incredulous.

"It simply means that I have never tried hard enough," sighed Norma. "Things do have a way of asserting themselves in the most *unexpected* ways."

"Absolutely," said Caroline. "Fate is fate. There *is* no free will."

"And therefore no moral responsibility?" Jenny smirked.

"Got it in one, Jen."

Kay straightened in her seat and stared intently at Norma. "Well I like the idea that we can change our future. Surely this would be a great time to try, while we have something that we can control?"

"Like what?"

"Why don't you look now, into the future, I mean, and see who your target's going to be?"

There was a ripple of interested noises from around the room.

"But then we'll know who she's got," said Shazam. "Which will be unfair."

"We can gather the names back in and do the draw again afterwards."

"Very well," said Effie. "Norma? Are you able to give us a prediction or do I need to pop the kettle on for a brew first?"

Norma gave Effie a brief, stern gaze before looking round and pulling an ancient box of Scrabble from the board game pile in the corner. "This will serve well enough." She took out the bag of Scrabble tiles and gave it a shake. "Right, let's see the name of the person who is to oppose me in the coming days!"

She upended the bag and the tiles clattered onto the table. Everyone stood up to see better as they landed. Jizzimus swung from the ceiling light to get the best view. Jenny craned to read the name on the table, but her attention was immediately drawn to Norma who gasped and turned pale.

"What is it?" said Jenny.

Norma's hand covered her mouth, as though stifling a scream.

"Who's Lesley-Ann Faulkner?" said Caroline.

"Interestin' that," observed Jizzimus from above. "Dint we meet 'er in the spa? Stroppy mare wiv the intravenous cocktail treatment?"

Jenny could see that the only tiles which had landed face up clearly spelled out the name.

"She's a made up wicked witch," said Dee.

"Made up?" said Shazam.

"Yeah, out of wood and stuff. We were using her combat training."

But the expression on Norma's face, the wordless horror in her eyes, spoke of something far worse than an effigy used for target practice. Norma backed away from the offensive letter tiles, shaking her head, hand over her mouth as though stifling a scream.

Effie held up her hands. "It seems as though Norma's skills have let her down today."

"I'm sorry," said Norma. She turned and fled from the room.

"Bloody hell," said Caroline softly.

"What could have gotten into her?" said Kay.

"She said sorry," mused Shazam. "She never says sorry."

"She says apologies are for the weak."

"That time she dropped her bee-typewriter thing on my toes—"

"—she said it was your fault for having such freakishly huge feet."

"Class, I'm sorry for the distraction," interrupted Effie. "This is all most unfortunate. Lesley-Ann Faulkner is someone who belongs firmly in Norma's past and most certainly will not be causing any more problems for her in the future."

"This sounds like a story we all need to hear," said Caroline.

Effie was adamant. "I don't think so."

"Is this to do with all that unspoken stuff between you and Norma?" asked Jenny.

"Because she's only here because of the threat of disciplinary action or somesuch, isn't she?" said Caroline.

"Is Lesley-Ann Faulkner a wicked witch?" asked Dee. "I mean, a real one."

"I've already told you there are no such things," said Effie. "Not anymore."

"But Norma would disagree," said Caroline.

"So, maybe we ought to know about her – wicked or not," said Kay. "In case, she turns up and tries to cause trouble for Norma."

"That's not going to happen," said Effie.

"How do you know?"

"*Because she's dead!*" Effie's jaw was trembling. Despite her t-shirt's assurance, she was far from mellow. She turned away from them all and scooped Scrabble tiles back into the bag with shaking hands. "Lesley Ann-Faulkner is dead. And Norma killed her."

There was a silence, and it seemed as though nobody knew quite where to look.

Effie cleared up the tiles, pulled the drawstring tight and only then looked each of her students in the eye. "Norma Looney is one of my oldest friends, but her delusion regarding the existence of wicked witches drove her to—" Effie shook her head. "She spent years gathering so-called proof of wicked witches, focusing on this harmless eighty-something woman in a care home in Eastbourne."

"And Norma...?" said Shazam. "She...?"

"Pushed her off Beachy Head. A senseless crime for which Norma has spent the last nine years in prison." Effie held out the shoe boxes. "Now. Your targets for the counter-spell exercise."

Everyone took a name from one box and a spell from the other.

"If it's all the same to you," said Effie, "I'll go and make sure that Norma has everything she needs. Enjoy the challenge everyone."

Jizzimus rolled his eyes and pointed as she left. "Bleedin' witch murderer. There's only one thing Norma needs and that's a damned good—"

Jenny cleared her throat loudly. The others were gathering their things, ready to leave. They paused and looked at her.

"I didn't want to say this in front of the others, but when I was in the spa I saw someone called Lesley-Ann Faulkner. Maybe Norma's prediction wasn't so wide of the mark after all."

"Interesting," said Caroline. "Did she look like someone who'd managed to survive a fall off Beachy Head? I'd have thought that was beyond the powers of most spas."

"What is this Beachy Head?" asked Kay.

"A cliff. A big cliff."

"Well it was quite a few years ago," said Jenny. "If she survived then she'd be, er, better by now."

"No, it just can't be true!" squeaked Dee. "There can't be a wicked witch right here at the spa. There just can't be! Surely it's someone else with the same name or ... or identity theft or something?"

"The woman in the spa was no way in her eighties," said Jenny. "Thirties more like."

"Well, there's only one person who can say for sure," said Shazam, trying to calm Mr Beetlebane who was agitated by the raised voices. "Norma needs to get a look at this person in the spa."

"I don't think Norma wants to revisit that chapter of her life," said Jenny.

"Zoffner the Astute did say her spontaneous nature had got her into trouble before," said Shazam.

"And that there had been a resurrection," said Jenny thoughtfully.

"Dee, you're the only one of us Norma has any time for," said Caroline. "Can you persuade her to go and have a look?"

Dee gave a reluctant nod.

"And I guess we'd all better swot up on our spells and counter spells," said Jenny.

"Yeah," said Shazam. "Particularly if we have to use them to fight off a real wicked witch."

They all sloped out of the hut and across the lawn. Jizzimus gave a low whistle as he ambled across the grass in front of Jenny.

"They really don' like wicked witches this lot, do they? Gunna have to watch yer back, guv. Anybody suggests a nice clifftop walk, you make yer excuses, yeah?"

There was an ancient payphone in the annexe restaurant. George was cleaning out the coffee machine behind the bar. Caroline gave him a playful smile as she dialled and wondered how she had got through the bulk of a three week course without yet having her wicked way with him.

Doug Bowman picked up on the second ring. "Yep?"

"Guess who."

Bowman laughed. "Caz. You know what, I was just thinking about you."

"Thinking about me?"

"A bit," said Bowman.

"Which bit were you thinking about?"

Another laugh. "Cheeky. You know I only like you because of your winning personality."

"Oh, yeah. Sometimes when I'm wearing a low cut top, blokes can't stop staring at my winning personality."

"I see you quit waitressing."

"Been spying on me."

"Dropped into the café a couple of times. My boss, Kevin, his office is just round the corner so..."

"You're still doing ... whatever it is you're still doing?"

Bowman grunted. "I am."

There was a hiss of steam from the coffee machine. George looked at Caroline and gave a simple mime to ask if she wanted a coffee now he'd finished cleaning the machine. Caroline nodded and gave a more complex mime she hoped conveyed the concept of a skinny latte with sugar.

"Last time we spoke, you suggested there might be an opening in your company," Caroline said to Bowman.

"I thought you weren't interested,"

"I was distracted."

"I recall there was a naked man in your hallway."

"The whole naked man thing," she said. "Yeah, I confess I'll always get distracted by that sort of thing. I'm not distracted now and, yeah, I'm interested if there's still a job on offer."

"There might be. You available to meet up?"

"I suppose so,"

"Lunchtime today?"

Caroline looked at the clock. Birmingham was three hours away by car, if she could get hold of a car. "I'm a little busy right now. I could be in Birmingham by, what, three-ish?"

Bowman hummed it over. "I've got a dinner thing tonight."

"A date?"

"God, no. A bunch of old biddies. A work thing. No, I can do three o'clock. The scene of the crime?"

Caroline laughed. "Our great bust? For old time's sake. Three o'clock."

She hung up as George brought over what appeared to be – miracle of miracles – a skinny latte with sugar. Caroline looked at her spell and counter-spell challenge papers. She had until three o'clock to cast a sleeping spell on Jenny Knott, avoid whatever spell one of the other witches had lined up for her, acquire some wheels and get to Cannon Hill park in Birmingham.

"Looking thoughtful," said George.

"A lot to do," said Caroline.

"Anything I can help you with?"

Caroline smiled. "Do you know, I think there is."

Jenny sat on a garden bench trying to absorb the challenge Effie had given her. She had drawn Kay's name and the *Victim to do everything a chicken might do.*

"We're talkin' peckin' corn, cluckin' a lot and crappin' all over the yard," said Jizzimus helpfully.

Despite the weeks of training, Jenny wasn't confident in casting any kind of spell that didn't involve blasting things with green witchfire. "I don't know if I can do this," she said.

"Course you can, guv. It's all about mind over matter."

"But spells and counter spells and..." She threw up her arms. "Maybe I need something to help me focus. Like Dee and her songs."

"If you're gunna start doing the hits from *The Lion King*, I'm outta here."

"Maybe just a simple song," she said.

"Easy, go for a classic," said Jizzimus, who was ripping apart the flowers in a nearby pot. "*Who let the dogs out!*"

"No, I wanted something a bit more tuneful," said Jenny. Her protest was lost as he launched into a strident round of shouty barking noises. Jenny sighed and realised if she went for the same song as Jizzimus then she might just be able to tune him out for a few vital moments. She tried to hum the song, but quickly found that it sounded more like a coughing fit.

"You all right?"

She jumped at the sound of George's voice, wondering how long he'd been listening to her tuneless grunting. "Er, yes thanks. Throat's a bit dry, that's all."

George sat down beside her and reached into a pocket. "Terrible shame the way we parted company the other day," he said.

"Hmm?"

"You know: you and me..."

"...Running butt naked in the moonlight?

He smiled shyly. "Yes. That. Did you get a lot of teasing for that?"

Jenny looked at him. "No more than I'd expect. It wasn't my finest hour."

"Oh, I don't know. You were pretty fine."

"But not the ideal ending to an evening."

Jizzimus stood in front of the bench, rolling his eyes at Jenny. "Yer on form wiv the witty repartee boss. Jeez. Look, 'e's gunna ask fer an action replay now. Practise sounding like a sex kitten and not a ... a sex hippo will ya?"

"I was thinking," said George, "that it might be nice to try and start over."

"Start over?"

"Get things off on a better footing. What do you think?"

"I don't know," said Jenny. "I've got a few things I need to concentrate on at the moment. I could do without the distraction."

"Well how about this: I'll be here on this bench with a bottle of wine and two glasses in an hour. You can come and share a drink with me or you can leave me to drink the lot on my own."

"Drinking in the daytime. How decadent."

218

"It's your choice." George stood, ready to leave. "Although I urge you to think of the hangover I might give myself." He headed off towards the witches' huts at the end of the garden.

"Boss, you losing yer marbles? Gunna need a search party for your mojo, seriously! That lad wants to get it on wiv you!"

Jenny wasn't listening. Her attention was drawn to two figures about twenty yards away. One of them was Caroline, who seemed to be weirdly fascinated by her own breasts. Her hands were inside her shirt and she lifted the collar so that she could peer down at them. Jenny could quite clearly see her fingers working around inside her bra, exploring and tweaking. Jenny shook her head. Caroline's behaviour didn't shock her any more.

"Now there's someone who knows 'ow to make their own entertainment," said Jizzimus with approval.

But Caroline hadn't noticed Shazam creeping up behind her on the lawn, brandishing a glitter and fairy lights wand that Jenny recognised from the One Stop Sorcery Shop. Caroline jumped as Shazam made contact with her back and uttered *"Ut viride"* in triumph. Caroline turned around and Shazam ran off, giggling. She appeared momentarily confused but gave a small shrug and went back to her delighted appraisal of her breasts.

"'Ere, boss, she must be really liking what she sees in there. She 'asn't even noticed her 'air's turned green!"

Dee side-stepped the hive and typewriter outside Norma's hut, and tapped on the door.

"Go away unless you have goggles," came Norma's voice.

Dee chose to ignore her, and pushed the door open. Inside, Norma was wearing a full welder's mask and protective gloves. Iron shavings covered the floor. Sparks flew in all directions, and the smell of hot metal hit Dee as she saw Norma leaning grimly over a workbench, apparently welding strips of metal together.

The welder abruptly cut out. The sparks faded along with the loud electrical thrumming of the welder. Norma's head came up and, obviously irritated, she banged a red button on the device by her side. She raised the face mask.

"Damned electrics on the fritz! Can't you see that I'm busy?" she snapped. "It takes a good deal of concentration and skill to use an arc welder."

"Aren't you worried about fire?" asked Dee.

"Frankly Dee I've got bigger fish to fry. If I burn this hut down, I'll move to another."

"What are you making?" Dee wondered where Norma had managed to get all of her materials. It looked as though there was an old garden incinerator and an ornamental lamp standing in line to be recycled.

"It's an experimental approach to our current challenge," replied Norma. "When it is finished, I shall demonstrate."

A bee droned in through the open door, landed on the ornamental lamp and ran a little figure of eight.

Norma huffed. "Him? Here?"

"Who?" said Dee. Norma silenced her with a gloved finger.

The bee did another little waggledance.

"What? Now?" she exclaimed, annoyed.

Dee was about to attempt another question when she heard the nearing chimes of an ice-cream van playing a slightly frenetic version of *We're Off to See the Wizard*. Norma threw her gloves aside and charged out, pushing Dee before her. A battered ice-cream van had driven all the way down the lawns, gouging tyre tracks into the grass where it had drawn up by Norma's hut. Faded and slightly misshapen cartoon characters adorned the side of the van beneath a painted heading of *Lolly's and Ice-Cream's*.

"Do you think he got lost on the way to the seaside?" said Dee.

"If only," muttered Norma.

The serving window slid open and a white-bearded man in a *Grateful Dead* t-shirt leaned out. "Can I tempt either of you groovy ladies to a Fab lolly?"

"You most certainly cannot, Mr Zoffner," said Norma. "I would prefer it if you did not turn up unannounced on private property in your ridiculous and badly punctuated vehicle."

"Badly punctua—?" He looked at the painted signage. "Maybe the van belongs to the lolly and ice-cream."

"Piffle."

"Or maybe it's painted that way to provoke those with closed minds and fixed opinions and remind us that rules are there to be broken."

"A horrible notion."

This was the first time Dee had actually seen Zoffner the Astute in the flesh, and he was exactly as she had imagined him. She found it considerably harder to imagine that Norma had supposedly had a romantic dalliance with the man.

"What are you doing here?" demanded Norma bluntly.

"I was drawn."

"Like a moth to a flame, eh?"

Yes, thought Dee. That was about right. He the delicate flappy thing and she the business end of a blowtorch.

"I knew you needed me," said Zoffner. "So I had to come."

"Ha. Dream on. Now clear off. Leave me be and go sell your ice-creams somewhere else."

Zoffner frowned. "What makes you think it's an ice-cream van?"

"It has the words *Lolly's and ice-cream's* on the side of it."

"So you believe everything you read, do you, foxy lady?"

"You offered us a lolly," said Norma.

"And you believe everything you're told? Perhaps this only appears to be an ice-cream van but, in reality, it's the command centre in the global fight against dark forces."

"Is it?" said Norma.

"No, it's an ice-cream van." From beneath the counter Zoffner produced a wafer cone topped with a fat blob of vanilla ice-cream. "For you, my dreamy lady," he said to Dee. "I love the cardigan."

Dee was never one to say no to free ice-cream. As a little girl, while other children were taught to fear strangers offering them sweets or the chance to "see some puppies", Dee always harboured a deep disappointment that such individuals never seemed to target her. She had once fashioned a sign saying, *I like sweets and guinea pigs* and stood with it at the side of the road; but her mum had spotted her, ripped up the sign, and given her a clip round the ear for good measure.

221

As Dee reached for the ice-cream, Zoffner cast a handful of sprinkles over it. He drew squiggly lines in those which fell on the counter and contemplated their mystic meaning. "Your friend, Caroline, needs your help. You wish to cast a spell on Shazam and will find her out on the lawns feeling very pleased with herself. Go now, be swift."

Dee did as she was bid. She had an ice-cream and had a challenge to complete. True, she'd had no opportunity to ask Norma about Lesley-Ann Faulkner, but ice-creams came first and there was time enough for talk later.

Jenny regarded the large protective circle she had drawn in chalk on the floor of the teaching hut. She had only created the simplest of magic circles before. Some of the mystical and esoteric symbols were a bit wobbly and scuffed. Jenny hoped that simply made them even more mystical and esoteric.

"Now I'm safe from all offensive magic," she said. "I think. As long as I stay in this circle."

"You mean you're trapped in 'ere," said Jizzimus.

"I've got nothing better to do today," she replied, tartly.

"There's a man out there who wants to jump your bones and ply you wiv booze. That's better than sittin' in an 'ut playin' Jenny No Mates."

"I don't need a man. Or booze."

"Flamin' 'eck, boss. Never saw anyone more in need of jiggy time than you. Why yer not over there already wiv a whip, a feather and a pot of lube, I'll never know!"

Jenny peered at Jizzimus. "Working on the imp porn again?"

He shook his head sadly. "All I can say is, it's a good job I've got a vivid imagination. If I relied on you fer inspiration the potential imp porn world would be in a very sorry state."

"I might pop down and see George," Jenny said. "But *just* for that drink, and then straight back to my protective circle."

She strolled to the garden bench, deliberately not looking at Jizzimus, who was acting out some of his imp porn fantasies in an attempt to inspire her. By the wall of the unstable stable, at the other end of the house, Jenny could see Caroline, looking more dishevelled than before. Her blouse hung open and she caressed her breasts, a faraway smile on her face. She was clearly oblivious that her recently greened hair had been joined by a pair of ram's horns.

"Caroline?" Jenny called, frowning. "Are you all right?" There was no response.

"She's a strange one isn't she?" said George, appearing at her side. "So glad you came!" He waggled the wine and glasses he'd brought, as promised.

Jenny glanced at Caroline over her shoulder, then followed George to the bench. She accepted a glass of wine and settled back, thinking.

"Here's to stimulating company," said George. They clinked glasses.

"I never saw you as the wine-drinking type," said Jenny.

"Oh? Am I not refined enough for you?"

Jenny held the glass up to the light.

"It's a fine bottle," said George.

"Is it?"

"From Mrs du Plessis's own cellar. Bottoms up."

Jenny didn't take a drink. "I'd love to know more about gardening," she said, indicating the nearby flower beds. "It must be great to know the names of plants and how to look after them. I bet it's a really fulfilling job."

"It is," agreed George. "But I can't imagine anything more fulfilling than being a witch. You can do all sorts of amazing things. I've heard that Kay charms animals. I bet everyone loves her for that."

Jenny stood and strolled to the flower bed. She pointed to a tall spiky flower. "What's this one called?"

"What you playin' at, boss," said Jizzimus. "Stop yapping on about the flowers, 'e's gaggin' for it!"

"It's – oh, it doesn't always matter what it's called. I tend to go more by families and, you know, species," said George. "Drop more wine? Oh, you haven't even started that one."

Jenny shook her head in despair. "Jesus Christ, Caroline! Is there no depth you won't plumb?"

George looked sheepish for a moment. As he well might, Jenny thought, with Caroline inhabiting his body.

"How did you know it was me?"

"Who else would do it?" yelled Jenny. "You've only got to look at the state of the poor sod who's occupying your body to know that something weird's going on."

"Hey, that's one happy camper! He's having loads of fun with my body. I'll admit I had a few minutes' recreation with this one as well." George-Caroline gave a little pelvic thrust, which made Jizzimus whoop in approval.

"And what's in this?" said Jenny, splashing wine from the glass. "What spell were you to target me with?"

"It's a simple sleeping draught."

"You need to swap back now!" said Jenny. "It's freaky and wrong and you know it! Would you actually have slept with me just to win this challenge?"

"And to mess with your head a little," grinned George-Caroline.

"Before or after you'd Rohypnolled me, you gender-bending git?"

"Hey. It's not too late, you know. We could share a beautiful experience. I'm sort of interested to know how it feels from the other side."

Jenny cast around for something blunt to hit him-her with but she felt conflicted. Who would suffer, George or Caroline? "I'm going," she Jenny.

Jizzimus capered on the bench. "Come on boss, this situation is crying out for a hilarious breakup line. How about *I'm going to find myself a real man*? No, don't work for you? Try *Come back to me when you've found the real you* then. No?"

Jenny started off across the lawn. She stopped dead when she heard George-Caroline calling out to Caroline-George, who was engaged in acts of confused but now frantic self-love by the unstable stable.

"Want to try something fun?" called the witch. "Bet you're curious to see what it might be like to—"

Jenny stormed back to where the masturbation-addled Caroline-George knelt and dragged her-him to her-his feet. "Come on. I need to take you somewhere safe until you're back to normal. Well, as normal as possible, given that you have green hair, a pair of horns, and a tail. And of course you're naked. And sex-starved. No wait, that last bit *is* normal."

As promised, Shazam was to be found out on the lawns, by the line of birch trees which made a bit of a pleasant suntrap in the morning. She was reclining contentedly on the grass with Mr Beetlebane curled up on her legs. Kay sat beside her, munching through a paper bag of sweets.

"You've got an ice-cream," observed Kay.

"I have," said Dee.

"Was that a real ice-cream van?" Kay nodded towards the vehicle down by Norma's hut.

Dee gave her ice-cream a thoughtful lick. It tasted okay. "I think so. Aren't you working on the challenge?"

"I was, but the power keeps going off in my hut, so I gave up." Kay held out the bag. "Want a sweet?"

Dee took one and put it in her bag for later. "That'll be Norma's welder: making the power go off."

"Did you see Caroline?" said Kay. "Shazam gave her green hair. And horns. And a tail."

"A tail?"

"I hit her with the green hair spell and she did nothing about it," said Shazam. "So, I went to town with every other spell I knew."

"She did nothing to defend herself?" said Dee. "That doesn't sound like Caroline."

"What doesn't sound like Caroline?" asked Caroline, strolling up. She was notably tailless and lacking both green hair and horns.

Shazam sat up quickly, causing Mr Beetlebane to complain loudly and cling onto her skirts with his claws. "Removing the spells after I cast them is cheating, isn't it?" she said.

"I've not removed any spells, Cobwebs" said Caroline, serenely. "But if you mean the hair, horns and tail I think you'll find that Jenny is currently tending to a bewildered handyman who happens to be sporting all three."

Shazam frowned.

"A body swap?" said Dee.

"A swapping of outward forms, yes," said Caroline.

"Well, I'll be buggered," said Shazam.

"Sadly, I'm no longer equipped to help you with that particular request," said Caroline cheerfully. "But I do have a favour to ask of you and Dee."

"Happy to help," said Dee.

"I'd like to borrow your car."

Dee's boundless generosity faltered a moment. "Mustapha?"

"Your car's called Mustapha?"

"Lots of cars have names," said Dee defensively.

"Yes, although lots of cars are not called Mustapha. Could I borrow – it – him – it?"

Dee believed in loving people and animals, not things, but Mustapha had been her first car, her only car, and his little quirks and habits – which the garage insisted on calling "widespread and dangerous faults" – only made him seem like a living being. But Caroline had asked and Dee believed in nothing but generosity. "You will be careful with him?"

"I'll bring it back with a full tank of petrol and won't drive it any higher than seventy."

"Seventy?"

"Sixty."

"And how can I help?" asked Shazam.

"You're coming with me," said Caroline. "I'm going to meet Doug Bowman."

Kay shuddered.

"We all want to get to the bottom of this," said Caroline. "I'm meeting him in Birmingham. He doesn't know I know you, kiddo. *And* he's never seen Shazam before."

"Ooh," said Shazam. "Is this a covert op?"

"Well as much as it can be when your clothes are covered in cat shaped sequins."

Dee fished around in her bag and passed her keys over. Caroline inspected the key fob. "Who's Terry the Boss-Eyed Tortoise?"

"He's the mascot of the Shelter for Unloved Animals."

"Do *Ugly Animals Need Love Too?*"

"They certainly do, poppet."

"Not just a decent beauty regime?"

Caroline tossed the keys in the air, caught them again and headed off up to the annexe and car park. "Not a jot above seventy," she promised.

"Sixty," Dee called at her receding back.

Shazam made to follow; Dee put a hand on her arm. "Three things. Could you make sure Caroline brings that car back in one piece."

"Of course, Dee."

"And herself."

"Of course."

"And..." Dee sang a snippet of *A Whole New World*, gave a little hand-jive and smiled. "Gotcha."

Shazam smiled at her. "I'm wearing my protective anti-magic vest from One Stop Sorcery. You can't harm me with your *sleps*."

"Sleps?" said Dee.

"Your *kigam sleps*." Shazam attempted to glare at her own mouth. "Oh, that's just annoying. They assured me it would work. I've a good mind to write them a strongly worded *rettel* and demand a *dnufer*."

"And you'd be right to do so," said Dee. "Enjoy Birmingham, poppet."

Initially, Jenny had been uncertain what to do with a befuddled man in a woman's body. Even when Caroline had cancelled her glamour and given George his body back, he was still in possession of lurid hair, curly horns and a prehensile tail; and profound confusion regarding his own sexual anatomy. The answer eventually came in the sleeping potion Caroline had put in the wine. Jenny steered him to the teaching hut, plonked him in the centre of the protective chalk circle she'd drawn, plied him with enchanted booze and left him there to sleep it off; secure in the knowledge he would be safe from other spells.

She sat by and watched over him. By early afternoon she thought she could see signs of the spells wearing off: a lightening of the hair colour, a shortening of the tail.

"An' when are you gunna ride 'im like a locomotive?" asked Jizzimus.

"He's unconscious."

"All aboard the overnight sleeper train! Callin' at Moist Valley, G-Spot an' Climax Central!"

"You're disgusting. A: I'm not going to rape a sleeping man and, B: he isn't... Well, if he's asleep, he's hardly going to be, you know, standing to attention."

"We would like to inform our passengers that today we will be runnin' a reduced service."

"Knock it off, Jizz."

"Customers will 'ave to use our manual relief replacement service due to prudes on the line."

There was a knock on the door.

"Yes?" said Jenny, too loudly.

"Only me," called Kay. She pushed inside. "Sorry, Jenny, I thought you were talking to someone." She looked at the sleeping transformed gardener. "I'm not interrupting something am I?" she asked with a crooked smile.

"Definitely not," said Jenny.

"Too bloody true," sulked Jizzimus. "Doesn't want to eat children. Doesn't want to 'ump sleepin' dudes."

"That weird hippy wizard has turned up and is helping Norma with her latest project. I thought you ought to come down."

"Do they need help?"

"Not really," said Kay, rustling around in her bag of sweets. "Thought you just might want to watch and laugh."

Jenny shut the teaching hut door behind them. They went down to Norma's hut, where an ice-cream van was parked on the lawn.

"Ladies, thank you for coming," boomed Norma. "I want you to be the first to admire my newest invention. Step inside!"

Jenny followed Kay inside. Dee and Zoffner the Astute were already there. The air held a thick tang of acrid smoke. Zoffner was fiddling with the industrial contraption on the table, in such a way as not to draw Norma's attention. The contraption was formed of solid metal straps which criss-crossed each other to create a distorted balloon shape. It looked like a perverse art project fusing a hanging basket with an iron maiden. Dee glanced at Jenny and gave a small shrug, indicating she didn't know what it was either.

"Nice handiwork, Norma," Dee said. "Where did you learn to weld?"

"One can learn a great many useful skills in prison," said Norma. She caught their expressions. "I know Effie told you all. It is important, as always, to use one's time productively, and I did just that."

"Great work, Norma," added Jenny. "What is it?"

"It's a psychic resonance defuser," said Zoffner.

"It's no such thing," said Norma. "This is a prototype Faraday cage corset."

"That's what I said, foxy lady."

"And what is that, exactly?" asked Jenny.

Norma sighed as if they were exceptionally slow pupils. "You're familiar with the usual concept of a Faraday cage, yes?"

Jenny, Dee and Kay shook their heads in unison.

"It is a metal enclosure used to protect whatever is inside, whether it is delicate electrical equipment, or in this case, me, from an electromagnetic discharge."

"An electromagnetic discharge," said Jenny.

"Yes, like lightning," said Norma.

"Or magic," said Zoffner.

"Such as any puny incantations my, ahem, colleagues might try to cast on me."

"Would it protect against witchfire?" asked Dee.

"Witchfire?" said Zoffner, with a broad, disbelieving smile.

"I should think so," said Norma primly. "Although I wouldn't want to put it to the test just yet. You will notice there are hooks here, and here, that will fasten to my usual undergarments. I'm at the stage of development where I need to do a fitting. I require two volunteers to lift it into place for me. No, Mr Zoffner, you can keep your hands to yourself. Dee, Jenny – help me."

Time slowed for Jenny. She was being asked to handle a large piece of ironwork. Norma might as well have asked her to juggle balls of acid. She tried delaying tactics.

"The gaps are quite big, Norma. Won't the magic be able to get through?"

Norma rolled her eyes. "Magic doesn't have a *size*, Miss Knott. The apparatus disperses all approaching magic at a fundamental level."

"Diffuses its psychic resonance you mean?" suggested Zoffner. "I do believe we sell anti-magic vests at our shop. They're much lighter and flattering to the female form."

"They don't work," said Dee. "Trust me."

"'Ere, boss!" said Jizzimus as he peered down at Norma's contraption from a roof beam. "That thing's made out of iron! You can't touch that, you'll get all blistered an' 'orrible. Want me to bite them all until they run away?"

Jenny gave a tiny shake of her head. "Kay, would you mind helping Dee with the corset?" she said.

"Frightened of a bit of heavy lifting?" said the teenager.

"I've just pulled my wrist. Hurt it somehow."

"Let me take a look," said Dee. "How did you do that?"

"Well," said Kay, "I did just find Jenny in the classroom with a man who was lying there with—"

"Enough chit-chat—!" Jenny interrupted. "Come on. Give Dee a hand."

With a squeak of wheels and a clonk of the suspension, Caroline swung the car into the park entrance opposite the Edgbaston cricket ground and, moments later, a parking space that a family-filled people carrier might or might not have been edging towards.

She flung off her seatbelt. "Ten to three. Time to spare."

Shazam still gripped the glove box, her knuckles white. Mr Beetlebane was wrapped around her neck like a terrified furry choker.

"You're a bit of a nervous passenger, eh, Cobwebs?" said Caroline.

"So *tsaf*," whispered Shazam. "So very, very *tsaf*."

"I know we're going a teeny bit faster than Dee wanted—"

"Teeny *tib*?" Shazam consciously disengaged her fingers from the dashboard. "She said don't go over sixty, not drive so fast you go back in *emit*."

"Emit?"

"I mean *emit*. *Emit*! Oh, blast this *esruc*!"

"Pfff. Dee will never know, long as the engine doesn't blow." Several warning lights lit up on the dashboard and steam curled around the edges of the bonnet. "We'll do this thing and give this baby some time to cool down. Now, you remember the plan."

Shazam nodded. "The *nalp* is that you talk to him and get him to tell you about this *elpeep* trafficking operation. For some reason, you're doing this by a pond in a *krap*."

"And your role?"

"To hang around as backup, keeping a low profile."

"Might be best if you wait behind in the car for a moment, and follow us afterwards." Caroline passed her the keys.

Caroline got out. The River Rea separated park from car park. There were two bridges across it: one leading directly into the Midland Arts Centre building, and further on a humpbacked bridge which led into Cannon Hill Park proper. Caroline crossed the humpbacked bridge and walked round towards the larger of the two ponds.

There were dozens of geese and ducks on the pond, a stand renting out pedalos at the near side, a large playground off to the right, and no sign of Doug Bowman. The 'scene of the crime': the biggest bust of hers and Bowman's careers. Unfortunately, the crime was theirs and they were the targets of the bust. They were foolish enough – arrogant enough – to not think that the man they were selling police forensic files to might be a wired-up police informant. They had sat on that bench just there, put the papers in his hand and blabbed their stupid hearts out.

"I always remind myself," said Doug Bowman, appearing behind her, "if those papers hadn't got lost, and the recordings hadn't got scrambled up, as if by magic, then you and I would be, this moment, in little six by eight cells."

"Instead of enjoying the life of bent ex-coppers," she smiled.

"Free agents," he said.

"Oh, that makes it sound so much better."

"It's great, Caz, just the thing for someone like me. Someone like you too."

"Like me?"

"We're mavericks, you and me," said Bowman. "We can't be doing with the nine to five. We've got the flair to hold our own in a world where the stakes are much higher. We'd have been pirates in the old days, I reckon."

"Which is all very well, until we get caught." She gave him a meaningful glance. "And we did, didn't we?"

He laughed and nodded towards the boating lake. "Come on, let's go and play pirates. We need to have a chat, so we might as well, eh?"

Caroline nodded her approval. "I like the sound of this job already. It's not every day you get to conduct business meetings in a pedalo."

Dee and Kay had positioned Norma inside her Faraday cage corset and worked on the various clasps and bolts that secured it in place. Zoffner stood in the doorway, appraising his metal-clad lady with one eyed closed and thumb outstretched, like a fine artist.

"I think there may be a teensy flaw in your design," he said.

"Codswallop, man," Norma replied.

"The universe speaks only truths."

"All my calculations are correct. You've checked them yourself. I'd like to see any spells get through this armour."

Dee reflected that not only spells but muggers, molesters, mortar fire and psychotic polar bears would struggle to penetrate this iron bodice. She knew this was a very serious endeavour, and that Norma's device might well be useful in the fight against evil witches, but nonetheless Dee couldn't help bursting into fits of giggles. One of the many fundraising events that had been held for the Shelter for Unloved Animals was a Family Fun Sports Day. One of the activities they had arranged was sumo wrestling in foam padded suits. Of course, the main purposes of sumo suits was to hinder the competitors and provide a hilarious spectacle for those watching. The sumo wrestlers would bump into each other, get knocked off their feet and rolled around on the floor, all the while looking like ungainly mushrooms. The more Dee tried not to think of Norma's metal overcoat in the same way, the more she couldn't help herself and started laughing again.

"Are you all right, Dee?" demanded Norma. "You look very red in the face."

"It is quite warm in here," said Jenny, standing well clear of the operation.

"I think it's mostly secure now," said Kay. "Shall we go outside?"

"Good idea," said Norma.

Zoffner and Jenny backed out ahead of her. Norma followed.

With a jarring clang she discovered, in her surrounding cage, she was too wide to fit through the doorway. "Oh. That is most unfortunate."

"The universe speaks only truths," said Zoffner.

Caroline and Doug Bowman pedalled across the boating pond in a huge fibre glass swan. Caroline didn't turn around to see if Shazam was following, but a couple of times she thought she heard the sort of yowling that might be made by a cat who was very unhappy to be surrounded by water.

"So, we bring them. Ports, airports, whatever suits. And then deliver them to our customer," said Bowman.

"One customer?" said Caroline.

Bowman nodded. "It's a specialist product."

"Who's the customer?" she asked.

Bowman just smiled.

"Drugs?"

"A mug's game, and the margins are too small."

"But contraband?"

"If you like," said Bowman.

"So, it's smuggling."

"I like to think I offer an end to end logistics solution for customers with very niche requirements."

"That's because you're full of shit, Doug," smiled Caroline. "You always could write up a report that made you sound like a shining star. What would my role be, exactly?"

"I need some more brains around the place, Caz. We got the trucks and the drivers. They all come courtesy of Kev."

"Kev?"

He gave her a look, not suspicious, but the next best thing. "Yeah. Kev. He runs the show. My problem is we've had some critical failings, and I can't cover them all. We had some goods go missing recently."

"Oh?"

"Warehousing and storage is a problem. Our product is ... delicate. And volatile. Security and handling need tightening up."

Caroline nodded with interest. "So the hours and the pay would be what, exactly?"

A smile spread across his caveman face. Caroline knew what it meant. They'd had a saying back on the force when it came to paying someone off. *"As soon as they ask how much, it's in the bag. The rest is just negotiation."*

Jenny had succumbed to Dee's infectious giggles. Norma, strapped into a metallic hamster ball, had tried to get through the door by tilting and wriggling and only succeeded in getting wedged in the door frame at an angle.

"I think we can get her loose if you push from the inside and Mr Zoffner tugs from this side," suggested Jenny.

"You will do absolutely no tugging," Norma warned him but the cut-price mystic paid her no heed. He grabbed a pair of struts either side of her body and there was nothing she could do about it. He even stole a quick peck on the cheek while Norma was trying to see what Kay and Dee were up to behind her.

"See?" said Jizzimus. "Zoffner the Well 'Ung knows what to do wiv someone when they're incapacitated."

"Right," came Dee's voice from inside the hut. "You pull hard on the count of three. Kay and I are going to give a gentle barge – we just need a little run up."

"Okay," said Zoffner.

"One."

"This is not a good idea," said Norma.

"Two."

"You're going to bend me all out of shape!"

"Three!"

There was a clatter of feet, a thump of bodies, a groan of metal and something went *sproing!*. Norma flew out, Zoffner underneath her, and rolled off across the lawns, towards the hedges and the hives.

While Caroline appreciated the ironically uncool as much as the next person, paddling around a kiddies' boating lake in a huge swan was literally and metaphorically getting them nowhere.

"Pedalling's playing havoc with my heels, shall we go and get a cuppa?" she said to Bowman. "And then you can fill me in on the finer details of this job. Or do I need to meet your boss first?"

Bowman, who was looking at his phone, laughed. "You forget, I've known you for years Caz. You do everything in heels. You drove here in them, right?"

She nodded.

"So how do you know Dee Finch?" he asked.

"Dee Finch?"

"I'm not stupid, Caz."

Caroline was speechless for about a quarter of a second. "My, my, Doug!" she said coyly. "Have you been snooping on me?"

Doug wasn't smiling. "You know Dee Finch."

"She's a friend. Well, more of a victim I've cultivated who thinks she's my friend."

"Interesting," said Bowman. He stopped pedalling. The swan began to drift in a circle.

"Well your friend, victim, whatever, is someone of interest."

"Why?"

"I think she might know where those missing goods of mine have got to. And she is one of those critical failings that need tidying up, if you get my drift."

Caroline breathed out slowly. She gave a tiny movement of her hand. "Dee Finch is of no interest to you, and we should probably get back."

"Dee Finch is of no interest to me, and we should probably get back," said Bowman with a nod.

Caroline's attention was snatched away by the yowling of a cat. She turned to see Shazam's bottom sticking up in the cockpit of another swan: trying to retrieve Mr Beetlebane from a hidden recess. Unfortunately, the swan was heading directly for the boat she and Doug were in.

"Hey! Hey, get out of the way!" she yelled. She leaned over the side in an attempt to push the other swan aside. She misjudged and toppled overboard, plunging into a cold and black world. She surfaced, coughing and pushing green slime from her face. The water wasn't deep: she could stand, although her feet pushed into what felt like mushy silt on the bottom.

Doug Bowman, still in the swan, was yelling furiously. "I don't know what sort of fucking hypnosis shit you're pulling, Caroline, but I'm not having it!" He pulled earphones from a pocket and stuffed them in his ears. "I'm not listening to another word you say until I've got you where I can control you!" He put on a pair of sunglasses too, as though he thought they might shield him.

Caroline murmured soothing cantrips under her breath, but either his anger or his defensive efforts prevented them from working. Unfortunate. She turned to Shazam, who was now at least sitting up in her pedalo; Mr Beetlebane apparently recovered from his hiding place. Caroline tried a step towards the pool's edge;, it looked a very long way away. The silt sucked at her feet. She realised that walking rapidly ashore before Doug Bowman could get his hands on her wasn't going to be an option.

"Need a lift, Cobwebs," said Caroline. It was a risky gambit, given that it brought Shazam into the metaphorical line of fire and relied on her pathetic pedalo skills. Caroline wondered if she might benefit from a little remote control assistance.

"You are a co-ordinated and confident driver," she said, "and you're not at all worried by the angry looking thug who's chasing us."

"Can't hear you, you fucking witch!" yelled Bowman triumphantly.

"Hey check me out, Caroline!" shouted Shazam, turning the ungainly pedalo with as much speed and precision as was possible. "I'm a co-ordinated and confident *revird* and I'm not at all worried by the angry looking *guht* who's chasing us!"

Caroline hauled herself into Shazam's pedalo as she drew by. Once she'd done slipping and sliding into the seat, she joined in the pedalling. She saw the man who hired out the pedalos was standing at the edge, watching with his hands on his hips.

"Oi, mate! The pedalo behind us is on fire. You need to act very quickly," she called.

As she and Shazam neared the edge, she risked a glance behind. Doug Bowman was keeping pace with them, but now a small dingy with an outboard motor powered towards him. As Caroline and Shazam scrambled out of the pedalo, a shout went up from the pool. Caroline turned briefly: the man in the dingy was spraying Doug's pedalo with a foam fire extinguisher.

"Make sure the fire is properly out," said Caroline. "You need to empty the whole thing!" She and Shazam ran for the cover of the trees.

If there hadn't been a modest-sized coven of witches standing by, the encounter between human bowling ball Norma Looney and one of the garden hives might have ended very badly. As it was, Kay and Dee employed their best animal charming skills to mollify the hive, while Zoffner rolled an indignant Norma away from the enraged swarm. Once Norma was safely out of range and on to her feet again,

Zoffner tried to aid in calming the hive by breaking out a kazoo and performing a few soft and soulful bars of *Kumbaya*.

Jenny, with no gift for animal magic, no ability to touch iron and no desire to contribute to Zoffner's musical efforts, decided that she could do nothing of value and simply stood by, trying to look both inconspicuous and encouraging. Jizzimus, on the other hand, danced gaily among the bees and sang lustily along with Zoffner with his own rendition: "Someone's crying, m'Lord. Kiss my arse! Oh-oh, Lord. Kiss my arse!"

Once the bees were encouraged back into the hive – with Kay's promise the damaged panels would be repaired the next day – Norma had the gall to declare her day's efforts "One hundred percent successful."

"I defy you all," said Norma. "Cast a spell on me. Go on. Try."

Dee shrugged. She tried to magically heal the scuffs on Norma's elbows without success. Kay threw a nimbus of mind-control magic at her but it dissipated long before it touched. Jenny, eschewing the mind-focusing powers of *Who Let The Dogs Out*, tried to blast her with the chicken-mimicry spell she had lined up for Kay; it died without effect.

"Not bad, Norma," said Kay, taking a sweet from her much depleted bag and offering round the rest.

"Not bad?" said Norma. "I received a premonition this morning that I am once again to face a most wicked witch. I may need this magical equivalent of a bullet-proof vest."

"More like a tank than a vest, innit, guv?" snorted Jizzimus.

"Perhaps I should check that premonition," said Zoffner. "It could be wrong."

"You'll do no such thing, man."

"Jenny saw Lesley-Ann Faulkner in Eastville Hall the other day," blurted Dee.

"She what?" exclaimed Norma.

Jenny slowly unwrapped the sweet Kay had given her. "I only saw a woman with that name on her medical wrist-thingy. But she was clearly far too young to be this woman you met."

Norma *hmmed*. "There are dark means by which a wicked witch can rejuvenate herself."

"What kind of dark means?" asked Kay.

Norma took a sweet, unwrapped it and popped it in her mouth. "Dark *dark* means, Miss Wun."

"That's kind of vague," said Kay.

"Oh, I know," said Norma. "I often keep things to myself. I think it's to give myself an air of mystery and authority when, in reality, I'm constantly beset by doubts and fear." Norma's eyes widened and she slapped a hand over her mouth. "I didn't mean to say that," she whispered in horror.

"Seems your magical corset isn't one hundred percent spell proof," said Kay.

"Oh, it's one of the challenges," said Jenny, comprehending. "Victim to speak nothing but the truth. You've been got, Norma!"

"But I don't see how that's possible," said Norma.

"It's the sweets," said Kay proudly. "I think I've got you all now."

They all stopped sucking and crunching their sweets for a long moment.

"My caravan is being repossessed next weekend," said Zoffner.

"Sometimes when I'm alone," said Dee, "I like to pretend I'm a horse and gallop around the house." She closed her eyes. "Sometimes I tuck my dressing gown cord into my pyjamas and pretend it's my tail."

Jenny spat out the sweet into her hand, distraught.

"What's up, Jenny?" said Kay. "Anybody would think you've got secrets you want to keep from us. Any more naked strolls in the moonlight you'd care to mention?"

"No!" Jenny squeaked.

"Come on. Time to share!"

"I can't share! I can't. You'll all find out that I'm a wicked witch and I've got an imp!" howled Jenny.

Four frozen faces stared at her.

The silence was eventually broken by Zoffner. "I really love that caravan," he said.

Norma, without taking her eyes off Jenny, punched him in the arm to shut him up.

"It's a spell!" declared Dee. "Obviously a spell. Someone's made you think you're a wicked witch or made you say the opposite of what's true—"

239

"I *am* a wicked witch," said Jenny. "My imp's name is Jizzimus. He's standing right there. My beauty regime is mostly a battle with warts. I can—" She held up her hand and flickering witchfire danced across her fingertips.

"But wicked witches...," Dee sputtered. "Those horrible things they do..."

"Like eating children?" said Jenny. "I try really, really hard not to. They smell so delicious. It's a daily battle."

For a woman in a metal cage, Norma waddled really fast. Before Jenny knew it, the older witch had crossed the gap between them and stabbed something into the back of her hand. The iron nail burned like nothing Jenny had experienced before. She tore away with a yowl of pain, staggered back and fell heavily to the ground.

"I should kill you right now!" said Norma.

"No!" yelled Kay. She put a restraining hand on Norma's cage and looked down at Jenny. "Am I a child, Jenny? Would you have eaten me?"

"I've only ever wanted to keep you safe until—"

"Would you have eaten me?"

Jenny sniffed and brushed the tears from her cheeks. The back of her hand blistered where the nail had touched it. "I hope not," she said.

Dee stepped forward beside the other two. Hers was the expression of a kicked puppy. A puppy that had not only been kicked but lied to, betrayed and sold to an unscrupulous butcher. "Go," she said simply.

Jenny opened her mouth to argue, to question, but there was no ambiguity, no argument to give. She crawled to her feet and, with a final backward glance at the women who for a short time had accepted her as an equal, left.

Movement in pond-soaked jeans and high heels was not easy but Caroline had no desire to hang around.

"We've got to get you dried off," said Shazam.

"We've got to get back to the others," Caroline replied, shuffling along at speed towards the car park.

"But you'll get Dee's *rac* seats all wet," said Shazam. "Look. Let's go inside the arts *ertnec* and stick you under a hand dryer for a *tib*."

Caroline shook her head and made for the humpbacked bridge. "Bowman said all the 'goods' they brought in were for one client."

"So?" said Shazam.

"That's not normal. And he knew I knew Dee. I can't see how."

"Maybe he did see you together in Skeggy."

"But he didn't. No, there's something else. Can you drive? I'm all ... yuck." Caroline unlocked the car and passed the keys to Shazam. She grimaced as she squelched into the passenger seat.

"Dee is not going to be pleased," said Shazam. "You're going to get her *rac* all *tew*."

"Her car," said Caroline. "Damn it. This is her car. That's how he—"

Something touched her side and a sensation, so intense and encompassing that it defied understanding, made her black out. When she came to a moment later, Bowman's hand was on her shoulder and her body was no longer hers to control.

The bastard had Tasered her! He had hidden on the back seat and Tasered her!

"Now," he was saying to her, "you so much as utter a word, you so much as moan, I will zap you into a coma. *You*," he said to Shazam. "You are going to drive."

"Where?" said Shazam. Caroline could hear her trying to sound brave and controlled and failing.

"Back to where you came from. Back to wherever I can find Dee Finch and Jenny Knott."

"Eastville Hall?"

Bowman coughed and then laughed. "Eastville Hall? They're at Eastville?"

"Um. Yes?"

Bowman gave Caroline's shoulder an affectionate squeeze. If she could, she would have squirmed. "That is just un-fucking-believable." He chuckled. "Take me to Eastville Hall, driver."

241

Caroline, though she could barely feel her lips let alone talk with them, shouted out at Shazam. She wanted to cry, *No! Don't! We can't take him to Dee and Jenny. And Kay. The man's a monster!* However, all she managed to produce was an incoherent "Nnnngh!"

"I warned you," said Bowman wearily. He stuck the Taser in her side again. Searing white agonies overwhelmed her and pushed her down into unconsciousness.

# Chapter 7 – The Wicked Witch

Jenny packed what few belongings she had into a small bag. Most of what she owned, most of what she was wearing, had been given to her or magicked up by Dee. The realisation made her want to toss everything away, to tear off her clothes in self-loathing, but pragmatism overcame emotion. Besides, they'd already seen a naked Jenny fleeing shamefacedly into the night and no one would spare her a second glance this time.

"I say, fuck 'em all," fumed Jizzimus, giving one of the bed pillows a damned good kicking. "Fuck 'em all and come back an' murder 'em in their beds later."

"We're just leaving," said Jenny, holding back a sob.

"Back to Brum, guv?"

"I don't know."

"Wiv a stop off at a school for some drive thru snackage."

"Just shut up!" she snapped. "Just shut up! Can't you see this is killing me?"

"What is?" said the imp innocently.

Jenny flung a hand out at the wall to indicate and encompass the lawns beyond, the huts, the witches who had been her friends. *Had been.* "I was happy here! For a week or two. A few days. I was happy!"

"Well, I like messing aroun' wiv morons as much as the next imp," said Jizzimus.

Jenny held her tongue. She was angry. There were things she could say. Cruel things. She held her tongue for all of five seconds and then spoke in a quiet and terrible voice.

"Jizzimus. I would trade you in, every inch of you, for one more day with those women. They made me feel normal."

She threw herself down on the bed. A second later, Jizzimus clambered up and sat beside her.

"But you're not normal," he said eventually. "You're frickin' awesome, boss."

Jenny reached out and scooped him up, and hugged him to her chest.

"If you're tryin' to smuvver me to death wiv your devil's macaroons, I keeps tellin' you: you need to get a boob job first."

It was an old joke between them but it was enough to make her laugh. A desperate and hollow laugh but it was a laugh nonetheless.

She sat up. She possessed a small bag of clothes, a tiny amount of cash, no phone and no purse. She had no real means of getting away from this isolated fenland village apart from walking. Not even a friend to call on—

She rooted inside the pocket of a pair of jeans in her bag and produced a much crumpled and folded business card:

KEVIN CARTER-KING
END-TO-END LOGISTICS SOLUTIONS

"Is 'e the one wiv the swimmin' pool full of gold?" asked Jizzimus.

"Metaphorically."

"Cor. Never swum in metaphorical gold before."

She went to the payphone in the annexe restaurant and was glad to find neither George nor any of the witches there. She had change enough for the phone but, cast now into the role of wicked witch, she didn't see why she had to pay. She cast an incantation of opening on the payphone, heard it click inside and dialled the mobile number.

"Go for Kevin," said Kevin. There was the humming background noise of a car engine.

"Hi Kevin. It's Jenny."

"Jenny? Jenny! Long time, no hear. How's things?"

"Hmmm. Ups and downs."

"More downs than ups at the moment?" he suggested.

"Not enough up and down action at all, if you ask me," said Jizzimus.

"I'm actually in a bit of pickle at the moment," she said.

"Anything I can help with?" asked Kevin.

"I'm that obvious, aren't I?"

"Hey," he said happily. "You're a friend in need. I'm a friend in deed. What can I do?"

"I'm at this big house way out in the sticks in Lincolnshire. I've got to get back home and I wondered if you could buy me a bus ticket or, if I get a taxi to the nearest train station, you could—"

"Which bit of Lincolnshire?"

"What?"

"I'm actually over the east side of the country right now. A work thing. No rest for the wicked and all that. Just driven past Grantham. I could swing by and—"

"I couldn't ask that."

"I insist. Now, where are you?"

She told him. He said he'd put it in the satnav. As she hung up, she told herself she was being a complete sponger but then why did she feel so relieved?

She took her bag and walked out onto the driveway to wait. The long summer evening was beginning its slow descent from blue day, through yellow afternoon into red-lit evening. After some time, a car pulled into the driveway. It was too small and old to possibly be Kevin's. Perhaps it was Caroline and Shazam returning. At least she could say a goodbye to them without them ever having to know what she really was.

The car slowed beside her. Madison Fray, Effie's nephew, his hat once again aflame with illusory phoenix fire, looked out the open window. The car exuded a powerful herbal smell. Jenny was surprised he could drive while so high.

"Oh, it's you," she said.

"It often is," he replied. "Running late as usual."

"Not seen you around here for a while."

"Oh, I've been on my travels," he said in mysterious tones. "Here, there and everywhere with my little questionnaires." He slapped a pile of papers in the passenger seat next to him.

"More witches."

"More courses. Aunt Effie's meeting with Mrs du Plessis this evening. Going to propose a – and I quote – 'A rolling programme of courses for the modern and progressive witch' and I know she wants to see who might be attending."

"Can't be a worse shower of dur-brains than this current lot," suggested Jizzimus.

"That's ... that's great," said Jenny. "Could you possibly give Effie my thanks when you see her. She's been nothing but kindness these last few weeks."

"You're not leaving, are you?" he said.

"I'm just..." She tapped the edge of the door. "Just say thanks, yeah?"

She waved him off and ambled up to the where the driveway met the road just as a black Bentley came into view. It pulled into the drive beside her.

"Small world," said Kevin.

"Course it'd seem small to 'im," said Jizzimus, jumping in beside Jenny. "He's got a beer belly as big as a planet."

"I can't tell you how grateful I am," said Jenny.

"I'm just happy you chose to call me," he said.

Kevin continued down the driveway.

"There's a place you can turn round down the side of the house," she said.

"Actually," he said, "I'm popping in to see the owner. It's just a work thing."

"Oh," she said, and then, "Small world, indeed."

"You know Natasha?"

"I've met her."

"She's mentioned you." He parked the Bentley.

"I'm not sure I like the idea of people talking about me," she said.

"All good I assure you," he said. "She says you have potential. I assumed you were working here."

She got out with him.

"Or maybe you ought to be." He gestured to the large front door of the house.

"I'd kind of made my decision to leave this place," she said, going inside anyway.

Jenny had only seen the entrance hall and reception briefly on her hurried way out the other morning. Now, she had opportunity to take in the obligatory sweeping staircase, the de rigeur crystal chandelier, the clichéd oak panelling and the stereotypical chequered floor tiling. The designers of Eastville Hall had clearly shopped at Stately Homes R Us and created something that was superficially impressive yet comfortingly familiar to anyone with National Trust membership.

"All we need is a butler," said Jenny.

"I'm sure he's around somewhere," said Natasha du Plessis, gliding up beside Jenny. She was wearing a simple black cocktail dress and wore it with a style that Jenny knew she would never possess.

Jenny had to physically stop herself from curtseying. "Mrs du Plessis."

"It's Natasha, Jenny, please. Mr Carter-King, a delight to see you."

Natasha held out her hand and Kevin actually kissed it, as though he was a medieval knight.

"*He* can call me Mrs du Plessis."

Kevin laughed as if this was perfect jolly fun.

"He tells me that you were thinking of leaving us," she said to Jenny.

Jenny grimaced. "This course... it just wasn't working out."

Natasha nodded deeply in complete understanding. "But I did tell you there are other ways to become the best witch one can possibly be. Could I show you something?" Jenny felt Natasha's guiding hand pressed against the small of her back. "Mr Carter-King, go play a little while. Jenny and I will join you shortly."

"Yeah, jog on, fat boy," said Jizzimus.

With the lightest pressure of Natasha's hand, Jenny allowed herself to be whisked away down a corridor lined with stuffed animal heads.

Caroline, whose thoughts had been mindlessly wandering dream hills and vales for some time – although frequently returning to *why are my trousers wet?* – came to a fuzzy focus as hands hooked under her armpits and hauled her up.

"Come on, Caz," Bowman was saying, far away. "Put a bit of effort in."

He got her arm over his shoulder and hoisted her upright. There was gravel beneath her feet although her feet didn't feel like doing anything about it.

"You," said Bowman and Caroline somehow knew he wasn't talking to her. "Get inside. That door there. No silly business or I will mess you up."

"Okay," said Shazam.

*Shazam's here*, thought Caroline. *That's nice. I like Shazam.*

There was a loud meow and patter of paws on gravel.

"Leave it!" snapped Bowman. "In. In there."

The gravel underfoot gave way to stone.

"Down those stairs."

Caroline felt a hand helping her from the other side. It was Shazam. *Good old Cobwebs.*

*Why are my trousers wet?* she wondered.

"No, it's jammed," said Dee.

"Then you're doing it wrong," insisted Norma.

"Here," said Zoffner, returning from his ice-cream van with a very large adjustable spanner. "A few twists with this and everything will be fab and groovy."

Norma turned around to bring the awkward catch of her corset into the light from the hut. Zoffner fiddled with spanner and catch.

"Have you free in no time, my love," he said and performed a series of grunts and gasps that had no visible result. "No, it's jammed," he concluded.

"You said you'd have me free in no time," said Norma.

"Time is an illusion, foxy lady."

"I'm going to punch you in ten seconds. Shall we see if that's an illusion?"

Kay approached silently out of the shadows, grabbed the spanner still attached to the corset, and with a single violent wrench snapped off the catch. The corset fell apart in two halves on the lawn.

"Well done, Miss Wun," gasped Norma. "That device was beginning to chafe something awful."

Angrily, Kay weighed the adjustable spanner in her hand.

"Still upset, poppet?" said Dee.

Kay, her lips a grim line, nodded.

"As you should be," said Norma, attempting to rearrange her gusset as much as a woman could in polite company. "Miss Knott deserves nothing but our contempt."

"I'm not angry with Jenny!" snapped Kay.

"Aren't you?" asked Norma, unruffled.

"No! I'm angry with—" She hurled the spanner down with such force that it bounced off the lawn and cartwheeled into the gloom. "I'm just angry, okay?" She put her head in her hands and growled in fury. "Jenny was nice to me," she said. "*Nice*. She and Dee brought me here to protect me. This doesn't make sense. The world should make more sense. It's not fair!"

"Life isn't fair," said Norma bluntly.

"It's rarely made sense to me, poppet," added Dee.

"If I may," said Zoffner, hands outspread like a performer taking the stage. "Life *is* confusing and infuriating. Why did my ex-wife change the locks on the front door? What meaning was to be divined from finding my clothes scattered all over the front garden? Mysteries. Only later would I find out that these were instructions from the cosmos."

"Most people use a divorce lawyer," muttered Norma. Zoffner ignored her.

"Those strange events set me on the most fab and groovy path that I now ride, dear girl. This crazy universe appears to be nothing but chaos but, when you open your heart and inner eye to its workings, you see that improbable chance and sublime serendipity want all of us to join the dance."

Something was approaching them rapidly across the lawn. Even in the dark, it was quite clearly Mr Beetlebane. He was making an ululating yowl like a demented ambulance siren.

Kay turned and caught him as he flew out of the darkness. He ran up her chest, circled her neck and shoulders three times and then shoved his face in hers and gave a single, short but insistently loud *meow!*

Kay resisted for a moment and then met his gaze. "She's what?"

*Meow!*

"What? Here?"

*Meow!*

Dee cast a quick spell so she could get up to speed on the goings on in the life of a cat. She listened to Mr Beetlebane's distressed explanation and translated for any non-cat-speakers present.

"They went to the park. Caroline drove very fast. They met the man with the burned face. He knows that Dee and Jenny are here. And he brought them here because—"

"Because?" said Norma.

"He is here," said Kay. "His chief, his pride leader. His boss."

Dee nodded in agreement with the interpretation.

"Whoever Bowman is working for, they're here. They've been here all this time."

"That's one hell of a coincidence," said Dee.

"Serendipity," Zoffner corrected her.

Natasha followed Jenny into the drawing room. Here too, trophy animal heads looked down on them, as well as on the chaises longue and plush carpets. Jizzimus scaled the fireplace to harass a stuffed weasel on the mantelpiece. Natasha closed the door behind her. It was a thick age-darkened door with a jewel-cut lump of quartz for a door handle; it closed with the finality of a cell door.

"Your dress looks nice," said Jenny.

Natasha smiled and gave a girlish swirl. On such a noble-looking woman, the action appeared balletically beautiful. "We are having a celebration dinner tonight. Celebrating Effie Fray's success in attracting so many witches to Eastville Hall."

"And Kevin? How do you know him?"

"The spa business has such specific needs. He's been a godsend." Natasha ran her fingers along the top of an armchair. "But Effie's little course for witches has failed to … meet your expectations?"

"It's not the course," said Jen. "It's me."

"I agree," said Natasha.

"I'm sorry?"

"It is you. You are not like the other women out there, are you?"

Jenny felt an abrupt coldness form in the pit of her stomach; a suspicion. "Um. We're all different aren't we?"

"But you don't fit in. They've rejected you, haven't they?"

No words came to Jenny. She decided she was better off saying nothing anyway.

"For a group so used to persecution across the ages, you would think witches might be less hasty to judge others. A couple of them, I notice, are obsessed with so-called wicked witches."

"Um. Yes?" said Jenny.

"She's got your number," said Jizzimus.

"Actually, they thought that one of your guests might be a wicked witch." Jenny forced a laugh to demonstrate how ridiculous she thought the idea was.

"*One* of my guests? No," said Natasha. She cupped her hands and a ball of green witchfire burst into life. "Not *one*."

Norma rummaged around in the drawers and shelves in her hut, stuffing mystical packages, implements and amulets into her pockets and into the waistline of her skirt. Dee watched her from the doorway.

"So, when the, um— When Lesley Ann Faulkner went over Beachy Head, did they recover a body?"

Norma turned and stared at her. "No they didn't, but that's not unusual. I was grassed up by a local chaplain who walks up there to try and discourage suicides."

"So it is possible that the Lesley-Ann Faulkner in Eastville *is* your Lesley-Ann Faulkner?"

Norma snatched up a tiny jam jar and strode out of the door. Dee barely avoided being trampled. Outside, Kay stood, holding Mr Beetlebane closely. Zoffner sat cross-legged on the floor, blowing bubbles from a bottle.

"This is no time for bubble blowing, Mr Zoffner," said Norma imperiously.

"There is always time for bubbles."

"Terrible deeds are afoot!"

"Are the bubbles making them any more terrible?"

"I take it we're going into Eastville Hall," said Dee.

"We?" said Norma who clearly hadn't even considered the possibility of teamwork.

"You and me," said Dee. "Mr Zoffner can stay here and look after Kay."

"I don't need looking after," said Kay.

"But maybe I do," said Zoffner. "I've got bubble mixture in my eye."

"Excuses," said Kay.

"And I'm a coward." He looked at Norma. "A lover not a fighter."

"Good," said Dee as though that settled it. "What's our plan, Norma?"

"We can't rely on the police to help us. We know Miss Black and Miss Jaye are being held prisoner in there. We also suspect there's a wicked witch in there, too. Our plan is we go in and have a look. We find our friends and we bring them out."

It all sounded rather decisive, rousing even, then Norma spoiled it by stamping her foot, turning in a circle while wiggling her behind and making a high-pitched buzzing sound. Norma held up the jam jar and Dee just managed to see the bee which had flown into it. Norma screwed the lid on.

"What's that?" said Dee.

"Plan B," said Norma. She addressed Zoffner. "If our mission fails and we are unable to return, I will release Barnaby here and he will come warn you. You are both to get in that ludicrous vehicle and drive far away from here."

"Hang on a moment, my lovely," said Zoffner and dashed inside the hut.

"Unable to return?" said Dee nervously.

"We may have to fight a wicked witch, Miss Finch. They are not easily killed."

"But maybe this woman isn't a wicked witch anyway."

"Maybe. I'll be able to check with my file."

"Oh I didn't realise you had one," said Dee. "Can I read it?"

Norma pulled out a sharpened iron file and held it up.

"Oh. That kind," said Dee.

Zoffner reappeared with a bulging paper bag, which he pressed into Norma's hands.

"This had better not be some soppy love token," she told him firmly. She opened the bag and looked inside. "Oh. That's actually quite clever."

Jenny's brain bounced and spasmed from one thought to another.

Her initial thought was *Oh, God! It's a wicked witch!* Quickly followed by *But I'm a wicked witch too!* and *But maybe she's a genuinely wicked wicked witch.*

She got a grip on herself. *But how many genuinely wicked wicked witches have you met?* "You have wicked witch guests?" she said aloud.

"We tend to think of ourselves as just witches," said Natasha.

"Of course," said Jenny.

"You have been living with a label hanging over you your entire life. You're not a demon. You're not a monster. You're not a second-class citizen. You are a witch like them but one with certain skills, certain needs and—" She glanced around. "Your imp is in here with you?"

Jenny nodded.

"Is he abusing the weasel on the mantelpiece?"

"Yes."

"Ain't doin' nuffin'," said Jizzimus, leaping away from the stuffed animal.

"Imps are so predictable," said Natasha.

"Is your imp here?" asked Jenny.

"Malunguibus is too much of a handful. He's penned up with the other imps in the stable. But most of the time, I let him roam free."

"Ah, that's why it's out of bounds. The unstable stable."

"Partly."

"There are other imps?"

Natasha nodded. "There are currently nineteen of our sisters staying at Eastville Hall, each with an imp. Consider this isolated rural house as a retreat, a haven for our kind."

"And I thought it was just a spa."

Natasha smiled and Jenny couldn't help but smile back. The warmth of that smile, the certainty that oozed from every pore; maybe this was what people felt like when they met the queen.

"Be assured, they are all paying guests," said Natasha. "They travel from across the globe to this place."

"Surely, there are other covens – er, meeting places."

"Yes, but we do offer something special here." Natasha opened a sideboard cabinet and took out a crystal sherry glass. "What's the one thing that our kind cannot control?"

"We can't touch iron," said Jenny, realising why the room's door handle and every door handle in this old house was made of non-metallic material.

"That one we can work round," said Natasha. "Gloves are surprisingly convenient. It was a shame when ladies evening gloves fell out of fashion."

"Evenin' gloves?" said Jizzimus. "How old is this bint?"

"No, I refer to our one uncontrollable drive." Natasha placed the sherry glass on a round table and then produced a medical sample tube from her purse. A dark red liquid sat within.

Jenny felt her chest tighten. "Is that—?"

"Blood?" said Natasha. "Yes."

Jenny waved it away. "I don't."

"I gather as much." Natasha unscrewed the lid. "Do you think any of us *like* drinking children's blood? Eating their flesh?" She poured the blood into the sherry glass. "At Eastville Hall, we are proud to offer an alternative."

Jenny sniffed. It wasn't children's blood. She could smell children from a mile away and their blood was a glorious reek to a wicked witch's nostrils. This blood didn't smell of children but it wasn't ordinary blood either. It smelled—

"Is it even blood at all?"

"Trade secrets," said Natasha, "but you can tell that this is not from any child. This is a guilt-free vintage and it does more than satisfy your cravings." She slid the glass along the table in Jenny's direction.

Jenny reached for it and then paused. "Why are you offering me this?"

"You don't want it?"

"I mean, why are you being so kind?"

Natasha chuckled. "Suspicious to the last. It comes with the territory. Think, Jenny. Effie Fray started this witch training course project because she feared *her* kind were dying out. How much rarer and more threatened must *our* kind be. I'm not offering this to you. I'm asking you to join us."

"Wahey," said Jizzimus, who had jumped down to the floor to inspect the glass of blood more closely. "An invitation to the wicked witch club. Yer aboutta become a made man, a wiseguy."

"There are nineteen of us here tonight," said Natasha. "I would gladly have you be recognised as the twentieth. Speaking of which: I have a celebration dinner to attend. I'm going to leave you here with that. If you don't wish to join us and take your rightful place, then you know where the door is. You are free to leave with only my best wishes. I hope you will decide otherwise."

Natasha turned and left the room.

Jenny looked at the bloody glass.

Caroline came to her senses. It felt like ... it felt like one of those videos of a skyscraper being demolished, only played in reverse. It was confused, loud and painful but, when it was over, she was awake and whole.

"My trousers are still wet," she said and opened her eyes.

She was slumped against an unremarkable and unfriendly brick wall in a small square room almost entirely composed of unremarkable and unfriendly brick walls. Something about the quality of the dank air and the light filtering through a brick grille on the wall told her that she was underground. The only breaks from the unfriendly brickwork were the small grille, a stout door and the presence of Shazam crouched beside her. She had Caroline's hand in hers.

"Hardly a romantic location, Cobwebs," muttered Caroline.

"I tried to cast a healing spell on you."

"It worked. It really worked."

Caroline was surprised to note that they weren't cuffed or chained up in any way. Probably spoke volumes about the stoutness of the door.

"I'm frightened," said Shazam.

"We're alive," said Caroline.

"Mr Beetlebane ran off. I don't know where he is or what's happened to him."

Caroline cast about the cell. "Well, wherever he is, he's probably doing better than us. Still, this is cosy, isn't it? A bit of quality seclusion time, just the two of us."

"And the creepy piece of stone," said Shazam.

"Excuse me?"

"The creepy stone," said Shazam, pointing.

A piece of sharp white rock sat on the concrete floor next to Caroline. She was surprised she hadn't spotted it already. "I've seen creepier stones."

"But look what it's written!"

On the wall above the stone, words had been scratched into the brickwork in clumsy block lettering:

HELLO.

HELP ME.

I'M TRAPPED.

IS ANYONE THERE?

HELLO. I'M TRAPPED.

"It's odd," agreed Caroline, "but hardly creepy. It's not as if the stone itself wrote— Ah."

With an uncertain wobble, the white stone rose off the floor, bumped gently into the wall and scratched out the word:

HELLO.

"Okay," admitted Caroline. "That is one creepy stone."

Dee and Norma stood in the shadows a little way back from the main entrance to Eastville Hall.

"Right, our first challenge will be to get past the receptionist or whatever," said Norma. "We've got two choices. Either we create a distraction by smashing something loudly out here, or we can try and bluff our way in as potential clients and then incapacitate her somehow."

"Or," said Dee, slightly worried by Norma's disregard for collateral damage," we could let ourselves in through the back door."

"There's a back door?" asked Norma.

"Yes, by the stables on the other side. I'm sure I've seen George going in and out that way. Come on."

They went round to the rear of the building, which was nothing like as picturesque as the front. Ugly air conditioning units clustered on the wall, and a mess of sealed bins lined the short walk down to the stable block. The stables mirrored the annexe where the witches' rooms were: forming the other arm of the building. There were gaps in the roof tiles, windows either boarded or covered in rusting wire grilles. The brickwork sagged. The only things that appeared well maintained were the doors, and they were bolted shut.

"I can't see a back door," said Norma.

"Sure there is," said Dee. "Along there."

They went through the stable yard.

"Psst," hissed Norma.

Dee, a fraction ahead, turned. "What?"

"I heard a moaning sound from in there," Norma pointed at a barred and bolted double door.

"What kind of moaning sound?" said Dee.

Norma made a throaty groan.

"Old beams settling in the evening?" suggested Dee.

"It didn't sound like beams settling. It was more like a growl."

"George uses one of these as a workshop. And as a cider brewing thing. Maybe it was just a power tool winding down."

"It wasn't a power tool."

"A gurgling cider vat thing?"

"No."

"Maybe a mixture of all three?"

"No, Miss Finch. It sounded like ... like zombies."

Dee gave her a look. "I'm sure I don't know what zombies sound like. But—" she added "—I have found an entrance." She gestured at a door round the corner. It was open, only guarded by a chain curtain for keeping flies out. "Looks like it goes to the kitchen."

"Then let us enter," said Norma, squaring her shoulders. She pushed through the chains with Dee close behind and they stepped into a large industrial kitchen. In a world of sizzles and clattering pans, a half dozen kitchen staff chopped, cooked and prepared plate after plate.

One middle aged man, in chef's whites that were thoroughly smeared with brown, held up his hand. He was either in the middle of making something messy and chocolatey, or had just returned from a day of bog snorkelling. "What you doing in here?"

Dee had a moment of panic, She tried to attempt the kind of mind control enchantments Caroline excelled at. She flicked her wrist and hummed a snatch of *Whistle While You Work*.

"We work here. We're waiting staff."

"No you don't."

"Yeees, weee aaaare," said Dee in what she hoped were mesmeric tones.

"Oh, really?" said the chef. "Then where's your uniforms?"

"Um. Theeese are our uniforms. Look into my eyyyyes. You will seee that these aaare waitress unifooorms."

"Listen, madam," said the chef, completely unhypnotised, "if you and your mum are trying to sneak outside so you can have a crafty fag before dinner, you can't come through here. You need to go back out, up the stairs to the main corridor, take a left and you can go stand out on the terrace."

"Oh," said Dee. "Oh. Thank you."

"What do you mean, 'and your mum'?" demanded Norma.

"Come on, *mum*. This way." Dee took her hand and dragged her away.

"I'm not old enough to be your mum!" snorted Norma, once they were out of the kitchens and in a corridor that had the Spartan look of a place reserved for staff rather than clients.

"How old are you?" asked Dee, looking up and down the corridor and wondering where to go next.

"A lady never reveals her age."

"Okay," said Dee. "Do you remember the moon landings?"

"Yes."

"You're old enough."

Norma humphed. She spotted a trolley of cutlery and put her hand on it. "This is interesting."

"It is?" said Dee.

"Plastic cutlery."

"Saves washing up?"

"It is not disposable, Miss Finch. This is high quality stuff. Look around, you will notice that nearly everything is made from non-ferrous materials. What does that suggest to you?"

"Wicked witches?" whispered Dee, eyes wide.

Norma nodded. "Come on, let's move."

They made their way further along the corridor and up a small flight of stairs, to where the floor was carpeted and the décor much richer.

"I think that's where Reception is. These must be offices," said Norma, indicating a pair of rooms to their left. She tried the handle on the first and the door opened. The office was a fairly standard if vintage design, containing an oak desk and a side table with a coffee machine. Dee spotted something and touched Norma's elbow, pointing at the desk. She stepped past Norma to take a look. The desk was fairly empty apart from a computer monitor and a blank notepad, but propped against a pencil pot was something she recognised.

Aren't those...?"

"Sabrina's permanent PK potential rings!" breathed Norma.

Dee picked them up. Yes, one of them even had a smear of plaster on it from when it had e        mbedded        itself        in        the restaurant ceiling, days ago.

"Why on earth would they be here?" said Norma.

Jenny sat and looked at the glass of blood. Or not blood. Or near-blood. Or whatever it was.

"Are you gunna drink it or not, guv?" said Jizzimus.

"I don't know," said Jenny.

"You don' fink it's poisoned, do you?" Jizzimus hopped onto the table, leaned over the glass and lapped at the blood with his tiny tongue. "Tangy. Kinda familiar. Defin'ly not poisoned."

Jenny still didn't take it. "The thing is," she said, "I've resisted all these years. I've never once eaten a child."

"'Part from that teenager in the shop."

"Yeah, but he was shoplifting. and it was just a nibble."

"You nearly et an 'ole finger."

"The *point is*, I've resisted. Why would I need methadone if I've never done heroin?"

"You're sayin' we should do heroin?" said Jizzimus.

"No, Jizz."

"I've always wan'ed a try a bit of skag. Bit of 'orse. Chase the dragon an' all that. Reckon it'd be well cool."

"Be sensible for once, Jizzimus."

The imp wrinkled his ugly nose in distaste. "Tried it once, didn't rate it. I still say you should drink it."

"Give me one good reason," said Jenny.

"Well, for one, you're drooling."

"Am not." Jenny put her fingers to her lips. She was salivating, true, not exactly drooling but— She dug in her pockets for a tissue. As she pulled one out, Kevin's business card fell out with it. She picked it up and was about to stuff it in her pocket again when something made her stop.

Her right thumb covered the last two letters of Kevin's surname. She stared at the card. She placed her left thumb over the beginning of his name until only two letters were visible: KI

"Kay Wun," she said softly.

"What about 'er?" said Jizzimus.

"When she was in the crate, on the way over here. All she could see through the gap in the crate were a letter and a number printed on something inside the lorry. *K1*. But it wasn't *K1*. It was a *K* and an *I*." Jenny turned the card round to show the imp. "It was one of Kevin's lorries."

The creepy shard of stone settled to the cell floor again where it proceeded to do absolutely nothing.

"Is that it?" said Caroline.

"It'll do it again in a bit," said Shazam.

"But *why's* it doing it?"

"I don't know," said Shazam. She looked at the words on the wall. "Maybe it's lonely."

Caroline brought her face down to the stone. "Hello?" she tried.

The rock didn't reply.

"Hello, my little rocky friend."

Nothing.

Caroline picked the stone up. It vibrated – it *fizzed* – in the palm of her hand. "Curious sensation," she said.

"You should be careful," said Shazam. "Maybe it's cursed."

"I'm sure it's fine."

"I'm just saying that if your head spins round and you start vomiting pea soup over me, I'm going to lose it big style."

Caroline stared at the stone. It appeared to be leaning, tugging her hand towards the door. Caroline got to her feet and let the stone lead her. The stone stopped when her fingers touched the door.

"Yes," she said. "We'd like to leave too."

Caroline considered the door. Despite its stoutness, it appeared to have only one lock and a fairly standard mortice lock at that.

"We could try to pick it," suggested Shazam.

"Lock picking without the right tools is far harder than people think," said Caroline. She patted her damp pockets for something they could use but she had nothing. "Unless you have some hair grips conveniently stuck in your barnet?"

Shazam put a hand to her impressively vertical hair. "This is all hairspray and wishful thinking. Sorry."

Caroline touched one of the cat sequins on Shazam's top. They were a good two to three inches high and made of thick foil. "May I?" she said.

"May you what?"

Caroline ripped the sequin off and rolled it into a long thin tube. It tried to resist and spring back into shape but, once she'd flattened it against the wall, it held its shape as a matchstick length of pliable but strong metal.

"Maybe," said Caroline and tore another cat sequin off Shazam's top to make a second lockpick.

"Okay," said Jizzimus, putting his forefingers to his temples to focus his brainpower. "Try me again."

"Kay was in one of Kevin's lorries. She saw part of the logo from inside her crate."

"Surely there's loadsa businesses wiv a *KI* or *K1* in their name."

"True. But Kevin's freight business runs all across Europe and one of his vehicles could have brought her all the way over from Portugal. He could even have flown her in freight via Birmingham airport."

"Sure."

"Doug Bowman was in Skegness with a lorry that had probably come in from a local port— Fuck!" she exclaimed.

"What?"

"How did Doug Bowman know Kay was at my house?"

"Lucky guess?"

"What if there was CCTV in that warehouse? What if Kevin saw it? He'd recognise me. He knows where I live."

"The twat," said Jizzimus.

"And Kevin has some sort of business arrangement with Natasha du Plessis."

"Uh-huh."

262

"He's bringing people here." She swallowed hard as a thought occurred to her. "Those ghosts. Those ghosts of young women down by the dyke. Dead women."

"Dead women. Check."

"But some of them seemed very old. Like centuries."

"Yes?"

"This definitely isn't child's blood," she said, pointing to the glass.

"Nope."

"And ordinary blood, from an adult I mean, wouldn't have any beneficial effect for wicked witches."

"Correct."

"So this is something else?"

"Indeedy-do."

"Blood from women, not children, but not ordinary women either."

"Nope," said Jizzimus.

"So, what makes Kay special? What's the difference between ordinary women and women like Kay?"

Jizzimus shrugged.

"She's a witch, Jizzimus! A witch! Natasha du Plessis is trafficking witches!"

"Oh," said the imp and then frowned. "What does she want wiv witches?"

"Witches' blood," said Jenny, picking up the cup. "Damn it. And we were told. We were told!"

"When?"

"Zoffner the hippy and groovy guy. The day after Shazam and Sabrina had been at this spa and Sabrina mysteriously decided 'to quit', he told Shazam that she had just escaped a fate worse than death."

"And what was that?" said Jizzimus.

Jenny threw the glass aside. The glass snapped in two as it landed. The blood made a dark stain across the carpet. "Sabrina never left. She never left at all."

In the office, Dee weighed the silver rings in her hand. "I can't imagine Sabrina would have left them behind when she went."

"When we were told she'd left, you mean," said Norma.

A movement at the door caught Dee's eye. She instinctively stuffed the rings in her pocket just before a woman entered the room.

"Oh. Can I help you ladies?"

The woman, her warm amber eyes sparkling, radiated a maternal authority. Dee felt a guilty blush creeping up her neck, knowing they'd been caught red handed.

"We were just looking for a price list," said Norma.

"A price list?" asked the woman.

"Yes. Er, we heard good things about the rhassoul mud massage," said Norma.

"And you felt compelled to enquire at this time of evening?"

"Seized by an impulse," said Dee with a big smile.

The woman smiled back. "I always act on impulse. To do otherwise is unnecessary self-denial. You're not guests here, though."

"No," said Norma, "I'm—"

"Norma Looney," said the woman. "And you'd be Dee Finch. Part of Effie's group. That's a fetching cardigan, Dee."

"Thank you."

"I like the..." The woman pointed directly at the pocket containing the silver rings. "The little rats sewn onto the pockets."

"They're hedgehogs."

"Of course they are. I'm Natasha."

"A pleasure to meet you, Mrs du Plessis," said Norma and held out her hand to shake. Natasha du Plessis plucked a folded leaflet off a stand and placed it in Norma's outstretched hand.

"Our prices."

Natasha opened the door, indicating with a sweep of her arm that they should leave the room. But as the two witches made to leave, she stopped them. "What things?"

"Sorry?" said Norma.

"What good things? About the rhassoul mud massage?"

"Oh," said Norma. "Just that it was very, ahh—"

"—muddy," offered Dee.

Good!" smiled the woman. "We always enjoy feedback. Now, if you'd follow me..."

As they emerged from the office, a man hurried up to Natasha. "I've brought back Black and Jaye and put them in the basement room next to—"

Dee and Bowman recognised each other in the same instant. Bowman gawped. Dee froze.

Norma shoved Natasha hard into Bowman, pulling Dee back into the office. She had the door shut and a filing case wedged against it a split second before something hammered violently on the other side.

Jenny stood up. It was a bold and decisive kind of standing up. Her mind was in turmoil and confusion and it felt good to do something decisive even if it was only standing up. "Here's the plan."

"I loves a plan," said Jizzimus. "Does it involve cunning disguises?"

"No. We're going to get out of here and—"

"I want one of them rubber face disguises like Tom Cruise."

"We need to rescue Sabrina."

"You know, like when Tom Cruise rips his face off and you see it's not really Tom Cruise."

"Or maybe I ought to warn the others first," she wondered.

"Actually, I'd just like to rip Tom Cruise's face off. Hang on, why are you gunna warn those evil cocknoshers what just unfriended you?"

Jenny gasped as a thought struck her. "Effie is having dinner with Natasha right now!"

"A right slap up feast, yeah. Ideal opportunity to sneak out."

"And Madison just brought her all those completed questionnaires."

"And?"

She stared at her imp, wishing he was quicker on the uptake. "All those names and addresses of witches. Witches whose blood Natasha du Plessis can drain. We have to get that list. That's priority number one."

"We're going to the feast?" said Jizzimus.

Bowman was throwing himself against the door but – God bless the building standards of their historical forebears – the wood was showing no sign of giving.

"That's him!" said Dee. "The bent copper."

"And she's got our friends in the cellar," said Norma.

"Mrs du Plessis? But she seemed so nice."

"You heard him!"

There was a bang and some muffled voices from the other side followed by a polite knock. "Norma? Dee?" it was Natasha. "Would you open the door please?"

Neither moved to open it. Norma had drawn her file with one hand and held her bee-in-a-jam-jar in the other. Dee was considering possible escape routes.

"We'd just like to talk," said Natasha.

"And lock us up too?" shouted Norma.

"It's all just a misunderstanding," said Natasha reasonably.

"Misunderstanding?"

"You do know you have wicked witches staying here, don't you?" shouted Dee.

Norma waved her iron file around, gesturing at the plastic filing cabinet, the stone doorknob and the distinct lack of any iron or steel office paraphernalia in the room. "Yes, Miss Finch. She knows."

Jenny walked along the corridor, nodding and smiling at the staff she passed. There seemed to be some sort of thumping and commotion

266

going on somewhere to the rear of the house and the staff were, thankfully, more than a little distracted.

Trying to guess where she'd keep a dining room if she owned a stately home, Jenny progressed through the huge house. When she found an open door from which candlelight and polite conversation radiated, she performed a smug but entirely imaginary victory dance.

"Look," she said, pointing to a serving trolley covered with a heavy cloth. "Perfect."

Checking there was no one in sight, she ducked under the cloth and curled up on the bottom level of the trolley. "This never fails to work in movies," she whispered as Jizzimus hopped up beside her.

"You and I watch different movies," he said.

After what seemed like an aeon of wiggling, poking and experimental prodding, Caroline levered the lock tumbler round a quarter turn, a half turn and— Click!

"Oh, well done," said Shazam. "I'm impressed."

"Thank you."

"I thought you were just pretending you could do it. You know, to keep my spirits up."

"Cheers, Cobwebs."

Despite the eager gyrations of the creepy stone in her hand, Caroline did not move with haste. She eased the door handle down and opened the door slowly. There were no assailants waiting for them on the other side, but nor was there freedom.

It was another subterranean room, differing from the cell in a number of key aspects. For a start, it was longer by a good twenty feet. Furthermore, the door at the far end appeared considerably more formidable than the one they had just come through. Additionally, the floors and walls were not bare concrete or brick, but covered in clean and shiny white tiles. There was a window, quite long but only six inches tall, high up on one wall. Most noticeable of all, the room contained a dozen hospital beds, each with a woman bound to it.

"My creepy-o-meter has just gone up a notch," said Caroline.

Many of the women appeared to be asleep or drugged. A number of them looked pale and unwell. Of those few who were awake, some only looked at Caroline with sad and weary eyes. A couple attempted to raise themselves, to speak, to draw her attention. Caroline realised they weren't only bound to their beds with restraints: flat, jaw-encompassing gags were fastened across their mouths.

"Oh, this is some Guantanamo Bay shit," whispered Caroline horrified.

The suddenly-less-creepy-than-everything-else stone tugged at Caroline's hand, pulling her along the row of beds, past a parked wheelchair and trolleys of medical equipment.

"We're not just leaving them here," Caroline told it. But the stone had no intention of leaving.

It pulled her to the foot of a bed. The woman there was awake, staring with furious intent, her fingers weaving magical circles, plucking at the stone she was controlling with her telekinetic spell.

When someone came along and wheeled the trolley into the dining room, Jenny felt thrills of both fear and excitement. She gave Jizzimus a silent thumbs up. He gave her a crazy double thumbs up in return. Below the inch-high gap between floor and concealing cloth, Jenny could see chair legs and shoe heels.

"Can I top up your drink?" asked a waiter.

"No thanks," said Effie Fray's voice. "Otherwise I will be three sheets to the wind before the starters have even, well, started."

"I am sure that Mrs du Plessis will be along shortly," said a woman.

"She is a martyr to her work." That was Kevin Carter-King. "Top up me, feller. Toot suite if you will."

"Ah, speak of the devil," said another woman.

There was a rustle from the direction of the door.

"Do forgive me all," said Natasha. "A minor emergency in the office."

There was good-natured laughter.

"I will be joining you all in just one moment but I wonder if – Lesley-Ann, Agatha – would you be able to help me with something. I have need of your talents."

With a scrape of chairs, two women made their apologies and rose.

Jenny twisted round to look at Jizzimus and presented a very clear mime to indicate that he should sneak out and get the pile of questionnaires from Effie, wherever they might be.

"You want me to twiddle my fingers, emerge from my burrow an' draw down the rain an' shove it in my pants?" he said.

Jenny scowled and tried again.

"Go out? Go out and stick it up 'em? Dig? Turtle? Touching cloth? Look around? Look around. An' then what? Yank? Pull? Pull down the...? Is it knickers? Knickers? I can do knickers. Awright, awright. Keep yer 'air on. Not pull down knickers. Get something? Fetch something? Fetch what?"

Jenny gave him a furious tight-lipped glare.

"The papers?" he hazarded. "The spikey-haired bint's papers? Right. No problem." He slipped out under the cloth.

Shazam took hold of Sabrina's hand, killing the spell on the piece of stone in Caroline's hand. "Oh, dear, what happened to you?" said Shazam. "How long have you been here? Who did this?"

Sabrina gave her a look which clearly and patiently said, *I'm wearing a gag. I cannot speak.*

"I know," said Caroline, sympathetically. "But her heart's in the right place. What is all this stuff, Cobwebs?"

Shazam looked at the sigils and symbols drawn on the bonds and gags in what looked like permanent marker. "Oh, that's Montesque's Nullification Ward. It's mentioned in Mr Zoffner's book. It renders the object impervious to magic. These straps can't be moved, destroyed or affected by magic."

"Then how do we get her bonds off?"

Shazam unbuckled and unwound the restraint on Sabrina's wrist. "Without magic, silly." She rolled her eyes at Sabrina. "I know. But she does try."

The office window was stiff, possibly even varnished shut. With a bit of magic mending Dee managed to twist the handle and force it open. Although the office was notionally on the ground floor, the sloping of the land towards the rear of the house meant it was a good eight feet or more to the ground.

Before Dee could express her concerns, Norma said, "You first then."

"I thought you'd all be for staying and fighting," said Dee.

"Regrouping and recharging," said Norma. "Our girls are in the basement and we can't get to them from here."

She unscrewed the jam jar and shook the bee out the window.

"Now go," said Norma. Dee didn't know if Norma was talking to her or the bee but she hoiked her less than athletic legs up onto the window sill, stood unsteadily and jumped. She screamed a little as she leapt, thinking it perfectly reasonable in the circumstances. She hit the grass and rolled in a move she hoped was like an expert paratrooper, but suspected was more like a sack of spuds falling over. She came up poised and alert, remembering to move aside a second before Norma landed heavily in the spot where she had just stood.

The bee had already disappeared.

"Can bees fly at night?" asked Dee.

"Bees have a very can-do attitude," said Norma. "And if we don't make it back, how else will Kay know we're in danger from wicked witches?"

Jizzimus scaled the curtains to get a good view of the room. There was a sheaf of papers sticking out of Effie Fry's handbag. He could hop over and get them now, but he'd likely be noticed. He needed something to make everyone look in the opposite direction. A wooden clock on the mantelpiece caught his eye.

"A bit of ding dong action to draw the ladies' eyes," he said and leapt effortlessly over to the mantelpiece.

There was a little door in the back of the clock. Jizzimus opened it and surveyed with glee the row of little hammers and chime bells.

"Move over Big Ben. See 'ow a true pro does it."

Effie looked up. "Does that clock always play that, er, tune?"

"I can't tell what tune it is," said that fat wanker, Kevin Carter-Wotsit.

"It sounds a little bit like *Who Let the Dogs Out?*," said Effie. "But that can't be right, it's an antique clock."

Out on the lawns, green fire exploded from the building, aimed at Dee and Norma. Dee ducked. Norma clapped her hands and shouted, *"Pharpus!"* A sudden gust of wind ripped past Dee and blew the fire sideways before it could strike them. There was a shout behind them: Dee saw a woman running towards them along the rear of the building, witchfire in her hands, ready to hurl. From somewhere else, Bowman shouted.

"Flanking us," said Norma. "Run!"

They fled down the long lawns.

Oh!" said Effie. "Did anyone else hear that?"

"Hear what?" said Natasha.

"A sort of bang from outside. An explosion. No?"

"Probably the pipes," said a woman. "The plumbing in this place thumps and rattles like nobody's business."

"Now, now, Bette. Any and all complaints must be presented to the management in writing."

The assembled wicked witches laughed. Before it had faded, Jizzimus had ducked under the trolley cloth and hopped up next to

Jenny's curled up body, clutching a bunch of papers bigger than himself.

Jenny gave him the biggest smile and would have kissed him if there was room to reach him. Jizzimus piled the papers against Jenny's side and leaned on them with one elbow. There was a victoriously smug look on his face.

With perfect timing, hands took hold of the trolley and wheeled it from the room. All they had to do was wait for the trolley to stop, hop out when no one was about. and go warn the other witches.

The trolley came to a halt. Jenny stayed still and quiet. There were feet stood beside the trolley. They didn't look particularly like the feet of waitressing staff. That pair looked like work boots and that pair looked far too elegant to be—

"You can come out now, Jenny," said Natasha.

"What shall we do, boss?" said Jizzimus. "Shall I open a can of whup-ass on them?"

Jenny momentarily considered doing nothing, but the trolley was hardly a hiding place and they knew she was there. She considered coming out fighting, but it wasn't possible to spring into a fighting pose when she was presently curled up on her side in the foetal position.

"Now, if you would," said Natasha. "I am neglecting my guests."

"Okay," said Jenny and rolled out onto her hands and knees.

Natasha du Plessis's expression wasn't one of anger. If anything, she looked disappointed. Bored and disappointed. George the handyman who, curiously, was wearing his amber-tinted carpenter's goggles gave her a little smile of greeting.

"I take it you've decided not to join us," said Natasha.

"It's witches' blood," said Jenny as she stood.

"The cornerstone of our ethically sourced diet. Not to mention, the basis of our rejuvenation therapies. *Sanguinem veneficae bibit.*"

"Watch out, boss, she's speakin' Latin. That's demon-summonin' shit that is."

"No," said Jenny, thinking. "Dee mentioned it. It means 'The witch drank their blood', or something."

"I can see you've not had a classical education," said Natasha. "It's 'She drinks witches' blood'."

"Yes, but..." Jenny stared at Natasha's face. She had suspected on their first meeting Natasha was a bit older than she appeared. Jenny realised that she was wrong. Natasha du Plessis was *a lot* older than she appeared.

"The papers, Jenny," said Natasha and held out her hands.

"You're harvesting witches."

"Harvest is an interesting word," said Natasha.

"The only reason you gave Effie free use of the place was—"

"So we could select those we needed. We don't want to wipe out witchkind, do we? Just a strong and stable population to feed from."

"And these?" said Jenny, clutching the papers tightly.

"All farmers tag their herd."

Jenny produced witchfire in her free hand. "I'll burn them."

As quick as a striking snake, Natasha reached down and grabbed Jizzimus around the waist, pinning his tiny arms to his side.

"Oi!" he yelled. "You can't do that. I'm invisible!"

Natasha blinked and smiled. For the first time Jenny noticed Natasha's amber eyes were the same colour as George's goggles.

"Magic contact lenses?" said Jenny.

"Give the papers to me, Jenny, or I'll rip his little legs off."

"You can't kill an imp. They're indestructible. Sadly."

"Yes," said Natasha. "That's true."

She glanced at George. Before Jenny even saw him move, he'd socked her across the cheek with a powerful fist. She gasped in shock. He came at her immediately with a right uppercut. It slammed her jaw closed and knocked all sense from her.

Dee was not enjoying fighting real wicked witches. They were scarier than wicked witches made of animated wood – although, in all honesty, on a par with giant flaming tree monsters. Not that they were doing much fighting: mostly running. Dee felt she had made it quite clear to the universe that she wasn't built for running; it was jolly unfair of the universe to throw her into situations where running was required.

There were at least two witches chasing them, although they were only identifiable by the blasts of witchfire being flung. Some of the blasts were wildly off target, some seemed to be deliberate misses, but some had come bloody close. When she had time to stop and look, Dee wanted to check if the back of her cardigan was currently aflame.

"I think," she huffed, "that they're toying with us."

"Or driving us," said Norma.

"Or maybe—" *huff!* "—these are their best shots."

Above the pounding of blood in her ears, Dee heard the sound of ice-cream chimes. A glance across the lawns and she could see the headlights of Zoffner's van making their way towards the side of the house. Zoffner and Kay were at least making a getaway.

A long thin blast of witchfire reached out from the darkness, across the grounds and found the ice-cream van with unerring accuracy. The van exploded in yellow flame, tossing the chassis up into the air in a brutal arc of destruction.

Effie beamed at the other women around the table. They were all so genuinely enthusiastic about her success with the witch school. She'd known from the start it was a good idea, and the fact that she'd answered so many questions was proof she was right. She glowed with the inner satisfaction of a job well done; and the effects of more alcohol than she was used to. Perhaps it also had something to do with the proximity of Mr Carter-King, who was delightfully attentive to all of the ladies. He was telling them a hilarious anecdote about an employee who'd climbed into an open lorry to sleep off the effects of his stag party and had woken up halfway across the North Sea. Mr Carter-King – Kevin as he insisted – put his hand on Effie's arm several times during the telling.

There was a loud and unmistakeably clear bang from outside. Effie saw ripples in her water glass. "Oh! Surely you heard that?" She turned to Natasha. "A loud bang? A boom even. From outside?"

"I dropped my spoon," said Bette. "Silly me! So sorry if it startled you, Effie. So what happened when he realised that his trousers were gone too, Kevin?"

Effie gave them all a weak smile and gazed at the after-tremors in the water.

"No!" screamed Dee, skidded to a halt and, fuelled by an instant rage, turned to fight. "You bitches are gonna pa—!"

Norma almost slammed into her. She grabbed Dee's arm and hauled her onward.

"Don't be an idiot, woman!" puffed the older woman.

"They killed them!"

"So? Anger won't give you magic powers!"

"But Zoffner... Kay..."

"In here!" Norma steered her sideways and all but shoved her through the door of the large teaching hut. They were plunged into near complete darkness. Even in the countryside, low levels of light gave some shape to the darkness. In here, they were stumbling in blackness with only the grey outlines of the windows for reference.

"What are we going to do?" said Dee.

"We stop. We think. We—"

However stunning the third suggestion was going to be, it was interrupted by the hut doors exploding inwards. Burning matchwood scattered across the room. Two shapes approached out of the darkness, witchfire in their hands. Norma looked down at her feet and then their assailants.

"We stand our ground," she said with a new confidence.

Dee tensed. Her bladder wanted to empty and her legs wanted to run – even though they clearly didn't like it – but she did as Norma said and held her ground. Two witches entered the hut. One had hitched up her long skirt and tied it off to one side. She was also barefoot, Dee noticed.

The witch noticed Dee's gaze. "You try running in heels," she said.

The other, the one with short orange hair, exclaimed in delight when she saw Norma. "It *is* you."

"Miss Faulkner," said Norma stiffly. "You've changed."

Lesley-Ann put fingers to her cheeks and gave her a dimpled grin like some Forties starlet. "I've taken a dip in the fountain of youth. You like it, Norma?"

Norma tilted her head. "I preferred it when you were dead and broken and drowned. It's a matter of taste."

Lesley-Ann Faulkner's expression hardened. "I owe you a long and lingering death."

"We belong dead," said Norma and held her file out like a fencing blade.

Lesley-Ann laughed. Both palms raised she unleashed a torrent of witchfire at them. Dee braced herself and prepared to be barbecued alive.

Free of her gag, Sabrina worked her jaw and licked dry lips. Her skin was pale. As Caroline helped her sit upright, it was clear she was very weak. Sabrina could barely raise a hand to gesture at the other beds.

"... Them too..." she sighed.

Caroline gave Shazam the nod and the sequinned witch began moving from bed to bed, untying the bound women.

"Water," said Sabrina.

Caroline looked about but there were no taps or jugs. There were pouches of saline solution by the bedside, however. Caroline ripped one open, spilling much of it, and offered it to Sabrina.

"It's going to be a bit salty, sorry."

Sabrina gulped at it nonetheless. Caroline stared at the drip pouches and cannulae taped to each of Sabrina's arms. "What the hell's been going on here?"

Sabrina pushed the water pouch aside. "Ur, she's been perfecting her technique."

"What technique?" said Caroline.

276

"An iron-poor diet for her cattle. Chelation treatment of our blood. The discovery that she can intravenously inject the stuff rather than bathe in it."

"Who?" said Caroline.

"Elizabeth Báthory?" said Shazam as she worked on another woman's bonds.

Sabrina nodded.

"What? That maiden-murdering witch Dee mentioned?" said Caroline. "But she must be like hundreds of years old!"

"Ur, four hundred and fifty something," said Sabrina. "I'd love to see her imp."

"Her imp?"

Sabrina swallowed weakly. "The older and more wicked the witch, the bigger the imp."

It was gratifying to see Lesley-Ann Faulkner and her evil barefoot companion as surprised as Dee felt. Lesley-Ann blasted them again but the flame struck an invisible barrier and flowed over and around them in a wide arc.

"That's dead impressive, Norma," gasped Dee.

Norma tapped her foot. Dee looked down. There was a large chalk protective circle drawn on the hut floor. "The symbols are very badly drawn," said Norma, "and I can't tell if *that* is meant to be the dread sigil *Odegra* or an invocation to the *Ogdru Jahad*. Very sloppy. Probably Miss Knott's work. Still, it's holding."

"So we're safe in the circle?" said Dee

As if to prove the point, the barefoot witch blasted them again, to no effect.

"Safe from all magic," said Norma.

"I could throttle you with my bare hands," said Lesley-Ann.

"You're welcome to try," said Norma and gave a flourish with the tip of her file.

The wicked witches exchanged a look. They backed out of the hut, closing the doors behind them.

"Well, that showed them, didn't it?" said Dee.

There was the loud but flat roar of flame from outside.

"What are they doing?" said Dee.

Flames appeared at the windows, to the left and the right of the door. Fresh flames rapidly appeared at the windows further round.

"They're burning the hut down around us," said Norma flatly.

"And the magic circle will protect us?"

Norma's expression was not reassuring.

Jenny came to in a dark and tumbledown barn-like room. The musty smell in the air, fifty-percent chemical works, fifty-percent abattoir, almost smothered the scent of fresh wood shavings. Jenny was lying on a hard surface, held in place by ropes across her upper thighs and chest. Above her were gloomy rafters and dilapidated tiles. Turning her head to one side, she saw tubs of chemical cleaner stacked on top of rolls of plastic sheeting. Turning the other way, she saw a dusty collection of gas canisters, Caroline's apple spirits still and a couple of bottles filled with the potent clear liquid.

"Jizz," she called. "You there?"

"Jizz?" said George from somewhere behind her head. "Is that the name of your imp?"

"Where is he?"

"Mrs du Plessis has him in the house."

"If you hurt him—"

George stepped into view and looked down at her. His eyes were barely visible behind the amber goggles. "I'm not going to hurt him," he said. "At least not directly."

"What are you going to do with me?" she asked.

His smile became tight, pained even. "I like you," he said. The word *but* didn't need to be said. It was written large in every syllable.

"And I like you," she said. "You should let me go."

"I follow orders," said George simply. "There are many parts of this job I don't like."

"Like being a lackey to a house full of wicked witches?"

"But there are perks."

"Yeah?"

"I work outside. I get to see the changing seasons. And there's a quality of life here, a work/life balance that many would envy."

"Oh, good," said Jenny, deadpan. "And do you like this bit? The tying up of helpless women?"

He shook his head and Jenny immediately hated him. It was the headshake one might give in response to "Would you like sugar with that?" or "Did you see *Eastenders* last night?" It was a headshake devoid of doubt; empty of any moral qualms.

"When the girls can't give blood no more, I have to bring their bodies out here. They don't weigh a thing. Just skin and bone. I put the body on here and cut it up so it can be divided up evenly between them."

Mentally skirting the words *cut it up* for a moment, Jenny asked, "Them? Between who?"

"I forget," said George, amused. He slipped off his goggles and positioned them over Jenny's eyes.

A score of creatures looked down at her from the rafters. Hideous, ogreish creatures with monstrous teeth. Bull-headed creatures. Hobgoblins that looked like a five-year old's drawing of a pig. Some were as gnarled and twisted as rotten trees. Others were slick and ill-formed, like wax figures next to a fire. They were imps, every one of them. Many were as small as Jizzimus but some were notably larger: hulking demon-chimps. But one of them, too large to climb up into the rafters, towered over them all. Its squashed nose sniffed hungrily and a leering smile broke out on its face as it recognised her from their encounter in the dyke.

"That'd be Malunguibus you're looking at," said George. "I try not to get on his bad side."

Jenny understood: she was in the stables. The out of bounds, unstable stable. Where the imps lived, and where George kept the power tools for cutting up wood and such. And the plastic sheeting for the bodies. And the bleach for cleaning up after the imps had eaten their fill. *It's amazing how quickly we get through this stuff*, he had said to her.

Jenny suddenly felt quite light-headed. She raised her head as best she could and looked down at her feet.

Yup. She was strapped to a length of wood on top of a mounted table saw. The saw blade was positioned just ahead of her feet, set to slice her neatly up the middle. Well, not so neatly. She imagined there was going to be a lot of blood; and more besides.

The situation would have been a laughable cliché – as hackneyed as being tied to railway tracks or suspended over a pit of crocodiles – if it wasn't actually happening to her.

George took the googles from her and the imps were invisible once more. She could still feel their presence, their malevolent and hungry gazes.

"I am sorry about this," said George. "I do like you."

"You like me but you're going to watch me fed through a saw?"

"No," he said. "I'm going to wait outside."

Waving away a bee that had buzzed into the stable, George reached down for a button. The saw whirred loudly into life. The board beneath her moved forward with almost imperceptible slowness. Jenny yelled at George but he was already hurrying out the door.

# Chapter 8 – What a world! What a world!

Kay stood next to Zoffner, both staring at his wrecked ice cream van.

"It's part of my personal philosophy to avoid any attachment to material goods," said Zoffner, "but that ice cream van and me, we go back a long way."

"It could have been worse," said Kay. "We could have been inside it. I'm impressed you saw what was about to happen and pushed us out in the nick of time."

"I didn't foresee these events, sweet young thing, I was reacting to the warning light on the dashboard which normally precedes a major malfunction. Such as this."

"Well, it wasn't wrong," observed Kay.

The van was upside down on the road. Fluid from the engine mingled with melted ice cream to form a greasy puddle. Zoffner approached the open window and dragged out a tub of ice cream which had been miraculously preserved.

"Are you hungry?" asked Kay, slightly incredulous at Zoffner's skewed priority. "It's just that, you know, your van has been trashed by an unexplained explosion and we're standing in the line of fire."

"I'm not hungry," smiled Zoffner. "Our industrious friends might be, though." He waved above his head to indicate a swarm of bees. He opened the ice cream, set it down on the ground and scooped out a tiny chunk with the side of his thumb, holding it aloft. "Come and enjoy, little stripy friends. You look as though you have much to tell us."

Dee and Norma stood back to back in the burning hut. The heat from the walls was intense and Dee eyed the flames creeping across the ceiling. It wouldn't take long before the hut collapsed and covered them both in burning debris.

"So, is there a spell for occasions like this?" she asked Norma. "A fire extinguishing spell or a ward for protecting against falling ceiling beams?"

"No, Miss Finch, there is not."

"That's a shame," said Dee, who was quite a master of the understatement at times.

"A witch must use her initiative," said Norma. "Let us think what we might use. I am in the unfortunate position of not having my handbag. It is outside the circle. What do you have in your pockets?"

Dee felt her way through the contents of both pockets. "I've got an emergency biscuit, a pair of reading glasses, four charred acorns—"

"Charred acorns?"

"Yes. I got them from Lesley-Ann Faulkner."

Norma pointed to the burning door. "Lesley-Ann Faulkner?"

"No." Dee did her quickest and worst ever impression of a monster tree. "Lesley-Ann Faulkner. They're kind of full of monster tree energy." She passed them to Norma. "Would probably only take a small growth spell to nudge them into life. Oh – and I've got Sabrina's lifting rings! Can we use those?"

"We most certainly can," said Norma. "We will need to apply them to something that will enable us to levitate."

"Fly out of here, you mean?" Dee was filled with sudden excitement. "Like broomsticks?"

"I'm not sure it has to be broomsticks."

Dee was already looking around the shed for anything like a broomstick.

"Any over there?" asked Norma. "There's an unfortunate lack of anything except garden paraphernalia on this side."

"There's nothing," said Dee. "Could we make a workbench fly?"

"No," said Norma firmly, "we need something that we might point and steer. The fabled use of broomsticks is not an accident, I feel."

"Wait!" Dee closed her eyes as she tried to remember.

"What?"

"In the cupboard. We were doing the amulet challenge and Jenny said—" She dashed over to the smouldering cupboard door and hauled it open. "Ah-hah!"

Kay looked at Zoffner. "Did you get all that?"

Zoffner smiled. "I've always been a student of body language rather than linguistic detail. Bees are so expressive. So, we have problems, yeah? Was there something about an aeroplane and a bear? His name is Lucius, yes?"

"Um, no," said Kay.

"Or Timothy?"

"The bees say that Caroline and Shazam are trapped in a basement room and Jenny is strapped to a saw table in the stables."

"Oh. Bummer. A saw table?"

"And the saw is running."

"That's all very, *Sho, Goldfinger, you exshpect me to talk,* isn't it?"

"I've no idea what you're talking about."

"But it's definitely a bummer. And you're keen to rescue this Jenny even though she's a wicked witch?" asked Zoffner.

"Hell, yes. She's a wicked witch, but she's my friend," said Kay firmly.

"That's beautiful," breathed Zoffner.

"I'm glad you think so."

"No," said Zoffner, pointing urgently at an imperious figure hurtling through the sky. "That there! That's beautiful."

"I think yours must be easier to steer!" yelled Dee, as she veered dangerously through the top branches of the birch trees edging the lawn. She was riding a petrol-driven hedge strimmer while Norma's steed was a folded garden parasol: a much sleeker beast. Once the anti-gravity rings had been slipped over both ends of each item, and the command given, the two unlikely vehicles had shot forward. Dee barely had time to angle her ride upward and hold on before it moved. She was now faced with the very real possibility of crashing from the sky in a mess of broken bones if she didn't quickly get better at handling her new ride.

"Up here!" commanded Norma. Dee wobbled unsteadily as she rose to join Norma. For some reason, the magic rings were also providing power to the strimmer itself, and the hedge-cutter blades whirled behind Dee like an outboard motor.

Dee wobbled even more as a scream heralded a blast of witchfire aimed up at them. Fortunately, it was clear Lesley-Ann Faulkner and her barefooted crony simply didn't have their range.

"Have you ever ridden a bike or a skateboard?" asked Norma.

Dee was unable to answer for a moment: she was picturing Norma on a skateboard. "Um, a bike. Not recently, mind."

"Well if you can recall anything of that experience, you will remember that it's essential to keep your head up and look where you're going. If you focus on the non-aerodynamic qualities of your broomstick, or indeed on the ground, you will find great difficulty. Head up and eyes forward, Miss Finch!"

Dee spotted Zoffner standing stood on the lawn gazing up at them. Norma gave him a slightly saucy wave.

"Focus, poppet," said Dee. "They have Caroline and Shazam held prisoner."

Norma nodded curtly and signalled that they should approach the hall from opposite sides. Dee dropped down to fly across the front façade of the house, looking for clues.

Kay raised an eyebrow at the sight of her colleagues flying on items of garden equipment, but a shout from behind made her look aside. Doug Bowman was running across the lawn towards her.

"Stop right there!" he yelled. "You've given me no end of trouble, girl." There was an object in his hand – the Taser. Kay remembered it and almost froze in terror.

"I got a lot on my plate right now," snapped Bowman. "But you're one problem I can put right straight away."

"Now, see here, young man," said Zoffner reasonably. "There's no cause for all this negativity."

"Step away, grandad," said Bowman, a vicious grin on his face.

Kay *almost* froze in terror at the sight of the man who'd held her captive. Instead, she embraced that part of her which had spent time exercising her powers in the company of new friends. She gave Bowman a serene smile of her own. He faltered, hesitated, raised one hand against what was about to come.

"Too late," said Kay.

A bee buzzed across his face. He stopped to swat it away. Then there was another, and another; all too soon there was a swarm of them, forming a cloud around his head.

"Well played child," said Zoffner. "I abhor violence but ... well played."

"Let's go," she said. "Jenny needs our help."

They left Bowman screaming and flailing, and hurried up to the house.

Caroline and Shazam had freed the other women from their gags and bonds. They busied themselves pulling out cannulae, urging the women to sip fluids once they were free. Few of them had the strength to stand, some were barely conscious. They remained on their beds, their dull eyes enlivened slightly with a glimmer of hope. Caroline looked at them and knew she was not equipped to rescue them all.

"What about the door?" asked Shazam, who sat next to Sabrina, gently helping her to flex her limbs.

"I can get through it, although it's going to take longer than the other one. Especially with sequin based lock picks," said Caroline.

"Look there," said Sabrina, pointing at a set of drawers. "I'm sure there are tools in there that might be more suitable."

Caroline looked through the drawers; they were full of medical paraphernalia. She pulled out some long metal stabby things. She tried to imagine what they might be used for in a medical context, but stopped herself. It was just plain terrifying. They did, however, look as though they might pick a lock more efficiently than a sequin. As she approached the door, a shadow fell across the window high above them. A familiar face appeared: a grim smile of satisfaction on it.

"Norma!" Caroline cried. She attempted a mime to convey the situation: lots of weakened women, no means of rescuing them from a locked room. Norma responded by stepping backwards and kicking in the window.

"You look as though you could do with a hand," said Norma as she toed the leftover glass aside.

"The window's too small and this door is locked."

"Right-o, Miss Black," said Norma with surprisingly good cheer. She placed something on the window sill. "You might want to stand back."

"Why? And why are you holding a picnic umbrella?"

"Stand. Back," said Norma. "*Ösgön!*"

Caroline tripped backwards as a small sapling appeared on the window sill. She dragged a young and bewildered witch out of the way as the sapling grew rapidly. Caroline had seen ruined buildings with trees growing through them; where roots and branches had relentlessly pushed bricks and mortar aside. She had not, however, seen it accomplished at a million times the normal speed. In an explosion of shattered brick and snapped timbers, a near full-sized oak tree took hold and transformed the narrow window space into a cave-like opening in the ceiling of the room.

Effie looked up at the swinging ceiling light, and the woman around her. Was no one else noticing this? Did they not feel the tremor that had run through the room? Was no one going to mention anything?

"Everything all right, Effie?" said Natasha.

"Oh, um, yes," said Effie.

"I think the staff are being a bit noisy upstairs, aren't they?"

"Are they?" nodded Effie politely and raised her glass. "Cheers."

"Wow," said Shazam, gazing at the tree-wrought hole. "That was like magic."

Norma started to climb through the hole.

"Watch out Norma, it's quite a drop from—"

Caroline ended up sitting on the bed next to Shazam and Sabrina as Norma swooped down into the room on a bizarre, flying parasol.

"Nice ride, Norma!" said Shazam. "I suppose the umbrella bit is used as an air brake."

"*Nustoti!*" commanded Norma. The parasol was at once lifeless in her hands.

"Ur, let me guess," said Sabrina. "Have you used my permanent PK potential rings?"

"Yes we did. Interesting story about where we found them." Norma looked properly around the room for the first time. "Perhaps you already know some of the details, though."

"Elizabeth Báthory is here," said Caroline.

Norma pursed her lip. "The crooked cop. His employer—?"

"Is Báthory."

"She must be very old. What on earth must she look like?"

"Ur, she looks somewhat like a cousin of mine," said Sabrina. "Cheekbones you could cut yourself on, but the eyes ... golden, loving."

"Well then, I believe I *have* seen her."

"You have?" said Shazam.

"Natasha du Plessis is Elizabeth Báthory, rejuvenated." said Norma.

Sabrina nodded.

Norma lowered her voice. "And does that anti-aging technique rely on draining the life force out of all these poor souls?" She looked across at the other beds.

"That *sorceress* has had centuries to perfect it," said Sabrina.

"We need to move this lot," said Caroline, walking around the beds to assess the freed captives. All of the witches were now conscious, but still very weak, their eyelids sagging. "We need a way to get these girls to safety. And none of them are climbing up to that hole. How good are you at flying that thing, Norma?"

287

"Proficient, heading towards excellent," said Norma. "What do you have in mind?"

"Get over here, Cobwebs," said Caroline. "We're going to try something out on you."

"Why me?" asked Shazam.

"Because if it goes horribly wrong, you're more likely to bounce than any of these girls." Caroline whipped a sheet off a bed. "Lie down on this, we're going to wrap you up for transport."

Jenny tried to extract her mind away to a happy place. If she thought about the saw blade that was now vibrating the edge of her shoes, the gorge rose in her throat. Maybe it would actually be better to choke on her own vomit than to bear the agony of a saw ripping her in half?

"That's right," she said out loud. "Cheery thoughts, Jenny."

Something in the rafters chuckled.

"*Nustoti!*"

Dee stepped off her levitating strimmer onto the balcony. She'd flown along the front of the house several times before deciding to investigate that weird jerking silhouette in one of the upper windows. It had looked like a guinea pig throwing shapes in an illicit rodent rave.

She pushed aside the net drapes to discover that the thing in the cage was a small and unbelievably hideous gargoyle: part goblin, part cow, part STD scrapbook and all manner of hideous.

"Ugly animals need love too," she murmured as she approached.

"'Old yer 'orses" said the creature. "A bit of 'ot lovin' sounds smashin' but we ain't been introduced yet."

Dee gasped, automatically rifling through her handbag, thinking of all the lessons that Norma had taught her. "It's an imp! It's an imp!" she whimpered.

What did she need to defeat the imp of a wicked witch? That must surely be what this creature was. It was tiny, but that didn't mean it wasn't harmful, and she needed to be very careful. Could it ensnare her with its voice? She wasn't sure why else it would have manifested itself to her.

"Not listening, not listening," she chanted under her breath.

"Gawd, yer a bit 'ot under the collar aintcha?" said the imp. "I know it can be a shock to see such an 'andsome and well 'ung imp such as myself for the first time, but you really need to get over yourself. Jenny's in trouble."

"Jenny?" she blinked. "You're her imp."

"Jizzimus Ruff-Diamond Parallelogram at your service. Or at hers anyway. Although that might all change shortly as I will become an ex-imp as soon as these bleeders carry out their murderous plot."

"Jenny's still here?"

"Darn tootin', sister. Let me out of here and I'll take you to her. Reckon you could take me to 'er on your sky-rocket. I ''as been wavin' at you fer ages."

Dee's hand hovered over the cage's lock and she fixed the imp with a firm gaze. "I'm choosing to believe you, imp. If you corrupt and ensorcell me once you're out of here, I want you to know that I will be very, very disappointed," said Dee.

"I ain't ensorcelled no one. S'vicious rumour."

"Anyway, aren't you meant to be invisible?"

"Yeah, but I can switch." He gave a grunt and a tiny fart and was gone. "See?" said an invisible voice. Another grunt and miniscule trump and he was back again. "Ta-dah, biatch."

"Is the flatulence strictly necessary?"

"Nope. Jus' a special bonus for the ladies," he said with a click and a wink.

Kay ran with Zoffner into the stable yard and hung back in the shadows when she saw George was there. He hung his goggles on a wall peg and went through the chain curtain into the kitchens.

"You're not dead!" exclaimed a voice behind Kay.

Kay turned and saw Dee approaching her, a hedge-strimmer in her hand and something that looked like a zombie turd on her shoulder.

"But the ice-cream van—" said Dee.

"We weren't in it," said Zoffner.

"That was lucky."

"The universe watches over us all, my dreamy lady."

"Oh," said the turd thing in apparent recognition. "It's Gandalf Grey-pubes, the one who speaks bollocks in a cardboard cave for a livin'."

"My fame grows ever further," said Zoffner.

Kay pointed at the weird creature. "You've been busy."

"Long story," said Dee. "You probably won't believe this, but I've got Jenny's imp here and he says Jenny's in trouble."

Kay nodded at the creature. "I thought they were meant to be invisible."

"Shall I show her?" said the imp.

"Not now, poppet. But Jizzimus says that all the other witches imps are in that stable and *they* are invisible."

"That cum-burger George uses magic goggles to see 'em," said Jizzimus.

Kay ran over to the wall peg and snatched up the goggles.

"But Jizzimus says we should let him go in first," said Dee. "He has a plan."

"Plan wiv a capital Fuck Yeah," said Jizzimus.

The creature beckoned and they walked further into the stable block. The distant buzzing of a saw guided them to the correct building, but when Kay approached the doorway she stopped, her brain struggling to process what she saw before her. Were these all witches' imps? How could there be so many, and what on earth was the big one? She was only dimly aware of the small creature scampering past them.

Sabrina was the last of the witches to be airlifted out of the dungeon ward.

"Time to go, Sabrina," said Caroline.

"Ur, I don't want to go out in a shroud," said Sabrina.

"Let's call it a sling," said Caroline carefully.

"No, thanks."

"It's no time to get picky, posh-knickers."

Sabrina fixed her with a hard stare before casting around the room. Her eyes settled on a wheelchair by the wall. Norma's face appeared in the hole in the ceiling and gave Caroline a stern look when she saw her next fare wasn't ready to go.

"Problem, ladies?" she asked.

"Ur, not at all," said Sabrina.

"As long as that thing can take the weight," said Caroline.

The saw blade was between Jenny's knees now. She was generally unhappy about this.

Something landed on her chest.

"Jizzimus!"

"Shut it, wench!" he said.

"Quick! I haven't got long!"

"I'm not 'ere to rescue you, you piss-poor excuse for a wicked witch!"

"But—"

"If I let you go, these other imps 'ere would just tie you up again."

A low chortle in the cobwebby darkness confirmed this.

"And damned right, an' all!" spat Jizzimus. "I've 'ad it up to 'ere wiv you. *Ooh, look at me. I'm Jenny Knott. I don' eat ickle kiddy-winks. I jus' eat vegetables an' fart all night. I don' smoke. I don' do drugs. I don' have sex wiv random strangers in lay-bys. I won' even fund my imp's sure-fire imp porn business!* You're a fackin' joke, woman!"

"Jizz," she trembled, "I'm sorry I've not been the best—"

"Shut it, you slag. I'm jus' gunna sit back and watch you get sliced up like sushi and then go solo."

"Fool," a deep voice laughed from the darkness.

Jizzimus whirled. "Who was that?"

A shadow fell to the ground, suddenly visible. It leered with a face that was more scar tissue than skin, apparently held together by pus.

"Me, Clappoxian," it snarled.

"An' you dare call me, Jizzimus Girthmighty, a fool?"

"I do. You're a worm, and a brainless worm at that. Soon as she dies, so do you."

Jizzimus gave him a look of utter contempt. "Is that what you think?" he spat. "Is that what you think? Little baby's gunna die wivout 'is muvver?"

"It's fact," said Clappoxian. "You can't change the world."

"You know nuffin ''bout the real world," said Jizzimus. "You wouldn't survive five minutes out there. Fancy being kept in a stable like a bunch of slave monkey losers!" There was a low growling sound from the other imps. "Tell you what," he continued. "I bet you all have some sort of imp groomer who comes round and shampoos your scales and trims your claws, like show poodles. When you're a street imp you learn to do stuff like this."

There was a change in the noise the saw made. Jenny strained to look up. Jizzimus stood over the blade and was holding out a hand, claws extended. The tips splintered in the path of the blade.

"See, proper hard, that is! I wouldn't even care if it cut my fingers off. None of you lot would have the brass balls to do that, eh, eh?"

As Jenny watched, Clappoxian stepped forward and pushed Jizzimus out of the way.

"Little punk!" it growled. "You got no idea who you're dealing with!"

Clappoxian thrust his hand into the saw blade and sliced it off at the wrist without a moment's hesitation. He guffawed and picked up the amputated appendage for all to see. Jenny knew that for imps, bound as they were to the life of their witches, such self-mutilation wasn't permanent. That didn't stop it being stupid.

"Zat is nussing!" declared another imp, dropping down and becoming visible. "Vatch me cut my leg off!"

With a roar of pure aggression, it lifted its leg onto the saw blade. The leg flew off into a corner and the imp shouted in pain and triumph, toppling over as he lost his balance.

Jenny stared at the curious new dynamic rippling through the group of imps. It would not be true to say it took her mind off the saw blade: between her thighs and heading north. Whatever Jizz's plan was, she hoped it was going to reach fruition soon. In something like the next thirty seconds, she reckoned—

Imps were popping into visibility left, right and centre, seizing the opportunity to show how tough they were by mutilating, amputating and generally knocking themselves silly. One was head-butting the rafters. Another had found the spare circular saw blades and was trying to fit as many as possible in his mouth. A third had picked up Caroline's apple moonshine still and was repeatedly smashing it against his face.

Then the largest of them, the hulking Malunguibus, stepped forward. He aimed a callous and dismissive kick at the one-legged imp struggling on the floor. When he spoke, it was a deep grinding sound: a rockslide modulated into something that barely qualified as speech. "You wrong. I show you. Nobody beat Malunguibus."

The giant imp lowered his monstrous head. He thrust it into Jenny's lap, his neck across the saw blade. Jenny felt the splatter of his bodily fluids up her legs, but the blade only partly penetrated his neck. He gave a gargling grunt and pressed down harder. The saw stuttered and jammed. The motor beneath her whined as it struggled for purchase. Malunguibus jerked his head up in disgust and the blade came completely away, embedded deeply in his neck.

Jenny released a huge breath she hadn't realise she'd been holding. The saw was broken. But she was still strapped to a table, at the mercy of her enemies and her enemies' imps.

Malunguibus turned to the group of imps and gave another gargling grunt, clearly expressing his triumph and superiority over all other imps.

"Aw, dat's just impressive," said one imp and tried to get the clapping started; not easy as he had successfully removed both hands moments earlier.

While some continued to savagely attack their own bodies and others crowed and cheered for their near headless leader, Jenny felt hands on the ropes binding her.

"Soon have you out of here, my fiery one," whispered Zoffner.

"Now, where is stupid little imp?" demanded Malunguibus.

"Stupid? Moi?" called Jizzimus from atop a ceiling beam. "All I see is a bunch of pussy-whipped morons. Look at that one! 'E's trying to eat 'is own foot."

"You will regret calling us mor— Oi!" yelled Malunguibus.

As the last of Jenny's bonds were loosed, Malunguibus tried to grab her. She rolled aside and hit the floor ready to run. Dee and Kay were in the doorway. Kay snatched up a bottle of apple hooch and clonked a nearby imp on the head. Dee sang a brief snatch of an up-tempo disco number and wiggled her hands in what Jenny recognised as one of her mending spells. Mending?

Malunguibus was lunging after Jenny when the saw blade in his neck started up.

Dee's look of grim satisfaction turned to dismay as the saw mended beautifully. The blade spun through Malunguibus's neck as if it were an extra part of him. Malunguibus glanced down, grunted in approval, and resumed his charge.

The delay had given Jenny and Zoffner the precious seconds they needed. They tumbled out into the stable yard with Dee and Kay. A second later both Malunguibus and Clappoxian slammed into some invisible barrier across the doorway.

Dee stared in surprised.

"They're penned in," said Jenny, catching her breath. "Magically."

Clappoxian hurled the still at them through the barrier, leaving a trail of apple hooch. It smashed harmlessly on the ground.

Jenny looked at her saviours. "How did you know where to find me?"

"Your imp told me," said Dee.

"The bees told me," said Kay.

Jenny looked from Kay to Dee and back again. "Have we got some catching up to do?"

"Not until you tell your imp to get off my shoe," said Kay, lifting her goggles to pull an expression of distaste.

The flying parasol struggled with the weight of the witch and the wheelchair beneath it. Norma had the parasol angled straight up but it was still only rising at a crawl. Caroline climbed up by herself, using a bed, then a shelf, then the roots of the magical oak to reach the opening. She hauled herself out into the night air to find Shazam tending to the other witches on the lawn.

"That was fun," said Shazam. "Like a fairground ride."

"You've been to some rubbish fairgrounds," said Caroline. "What now?"

"The minibus," said Caroline. "It's just round the corner. We get everyone loaded up and out of here. To the nearest hospital for preference."

Shazam pointed into the sky. "Why are they still rising?"

"Because I can't angle the damned thing down!" Norma yelled from on high.

Caroline glanced up. Norma was drifting over the roof of Eastville Hall with a wheelchair swinging precariously from the end of her parasol. Green witchfire flew up towards the wheelchair. Sabrina gesticulated wildly and the fire flowed harmlessly around her.

"Catch!" yelled Norma.

Caroline was almost struck in the face by a bulging paper bag. As two figures, green fire at their fingertips, ran towards them across the lawn, she looked in the bag.

"Cool beans," she grinned. "Cobwebs! Get this lot to the minibus! Now!"

"Nere you are, noo gucking 'itches."

Jenny and her rescuers had been so intent on the enraged imps and generally being glad to be alive, they had not noticed Doug Bowman staggering towards them across the stable yard, Taser in hand.

Jenny had any number of things she wanted to say, powerful and hurtful things. They were all relegated to second place at the sight of Bowman. Who *inflated your face?* she wanted to ask, or *How are you even still standing when your entire body is so swollen?* In the end she settled for "What happened to you?"

"'Ees."

"'Ees?"

"Vees! Allergy. Gucking hur's."

Curiosity satisfied, Jenny curled her fist into a ball of witchfire. Bowman, inflated like a Cabbage Patch Doll though he might be, was still fast. He lunged forward and grabbed Kay by her collar.

"Li'l girl caused 'e no end of 'rouble."

He held the Taser up to her neck. Kay twisted away and swung the bottle of hooch at him. Bowman parried with the Taser, smashing the bottle. Kay stumbled. Zoffner ran forward to assist. Bowman met him with a savage punch, sending the mystic reeling with a bloody nose.

Bowman growled. Maybe he was saying something and the bee venom was closing up his mouth and throat. Or maybe it was just a growl.

Bowman growled and activated the Taser. A mistake: his hand and arm were coated in highly flammable spirits. The growl became a scream as his arm ignited. He flapped and spun. Kay scrambled away into Jenny's arms.

Bowman made another mistake. Even in his panic, he remembered to drop and roll on the ground, to put the fire out. Unfortunately, he rolled on the spot where the still had smashed.

Dee pulled Zoffner away from the flaming eruption. Kay pushed at Jenny, pushed her further and further away, far beyond the fire's reach.

"It's okay," said Jenny. "It's okay."

Kay's dirt-streaked face met hers. "Gas canisters," said the young witch simply.

Jenny looked up. The flammable hooch had left a trail. The fire was snaking from Bowman's self-immolation towards the stables.

"Oh, crap," said Jenny.

"Fireworks!" yelled Jizzimus.

Above Caroline's head, Norma was struggling to keep her parasol and the dangling wheelchair under control. Off to her right, Shazam urged, cajoled and carried the freed witches towards the minibus. In front of her were two wicked witches. A spurt of green flame shot at Caroline's face and she managed to turn away in time to suffer no more than a touch of instant sunburn.

Caroline felt distinctly under-prepared for the task in hand. Her police training had covered combat techniques and riot situations, but failed to address a situation where your assailants could fry you with witchfire. Here she was, armed with a paper bag as a one-shot defence. A paper bag, and a hard-ass attitude.

The ginger-haired witch brought a fiery hand back like a baseball pitcher winding up. She didn't get chance to unleash: at that moment, something exploded at the far end of the house, sending debris and flame into the air and a tremor through the ground.

Caroline saw the wheelchair dangling beneath flying parasol tip – caught by the blast. It struck the roof of the old house and plunged straight through, Sabrina still on board. The sound of roof tiles shattering was quickly followed by the less defined sounds of many other things being smashed.

The initial explosion rocked the dining room, knocking over wine glasses and jolting a mounted gazelle's head askew. Effie opened her mouth to exclaim but was distracted by a tremendous crash from upstairs. Speckles of plaster dust fell onto the table, There was a second, closer series set of crashes.

"Don't tell me no one heard that!" Effie yelled.

297

"I think our pest problem is still with us," said Natasha, giving meaningful glances to her lady guests.

Effie wasn't sure how to respond to that. She never got the chance, as a wheelchair, an occupied one at that, burst through the ceiling and landed in the centre of the table.

Caroline recovered from her shock a fraction of a second before the wicked witches.

"Agatha! Get her!" screamed the red-haired one.

Caroline lobbed the paper bag as Agatha prepared to unleash her fire. The bag split in mid-flight, and a cloud of iron filings and other sweepings off Norma's shed floor showered over the woman. A red shotgun blast pattern instantly erupted over the wicked witch's face and exposed arms. The redhead threw up her hands to shield herself from the poisonous iron. Caroline pegged it towards the minibus.

Seconds later, one of the wicked witches evidently had the idea to clear the cloud of burning iron fragments with witchfire. Perhaps they had missed that particular high school chemistry experiment, or they didn't care. Whichever, a flash of light as bright as day illuminated Caroline's way to the minibus as the wicked witches briefly turned themselves into the world's largest sparkler.

Madison Fray, wearing a flaming hat and a stunned expression, stood beside the minibus. "Is something happening?" he asked.

"Yes," said Caroline, with a flick of the wrist. "You're going to drive this minibus as quickly but as safely as you can to the nearest hospital."

"Yes," he said, "I am going to drive this minibus as quickly—"

"Just get in!"

Caroline looked for signs of Norma or the wheelchair-riding Sabrina. She saw none, Deciding a dozen birds in a bus was worth two in the sky she jumped into a passenger seat.

"Drive, Madison!"

"Seatbelts everyone!" shouted Shazam in the back. "Now, has anyone seen my cat?"

With a shout of "*Veikti!*", Dee kicked off from the ground and rode her strimmer above the ruin and smoke to where Norma circled a hole in the roof. Even flying round in the night sky, they could each read the other's expression.

"Report, Miss Finch," said Norma.

"Rescued Jenny from the stables. Lots of imps, many of them in little pieces. That wicked policeman blew himself up. Effie Fray is still in the house. Oh, and Kay and Zoffner are not dead. Repeat, not dead."

Norma allowed herself a moment of wide-eyed ecstatic joy at the news her possibly/possibly-not boyfriend wasn't toast before snapping back into her usual officious manner.

"We rescued Miss Black, Miss Jaye and eleven other witches from some awful blood farm. Unfortunately, I dropped Sabrina down that hole— The fiends!"

Norma was looking across the roof towards the driveway. The minibus had reached the road and was turning south towards Stickney village. What had caught Norma's eye were two women jumping into cars to make their pursuit. By firelight and reflected headlights, one of them was clearly Lesley-Ann Faulkner.

"Go," said Dee.

Norma looked at her.

"Go," Dee insisted. "We'll find Effie and Sabrina. Go keep them safe."

Norma folded herself over her parasol like a hawk preparing to dive and shot off towards the cars.

On the stable yard – some of which was aflame and much of which was less vertical than before – Jizzimus bounced on Jenny's shoulder.

"Glad you're not dead an' everything boss, but we're not out of the woods yet."

299

"Okay," said Jenny.

"Let's hurry it up a bit, eh? You'll 'ave no end of mad ole baggages on yer tail in a minute. You'll be the entertainment in between their main course an' their puddin' if you 'ang around."

"We need to get inside."

"Inside?" said Kay, who was helping Zoffner hold a tissue to his bloody nose.

"Effie's in there, and the list of witches."

"What list?"

Dee came in to land, leapt from her flying strimmer and jogged to a halt. Despite everything else, Jenny laughed. "The look on your face."

"What about it?" said Dee.

"You've never looked happier. I think you were born to fly."

Dee blushed.

"So what's the plan?" asked Kay.

"We need a distraction."

"You mean, apart from one end of the house being on fire and the other having a giant tree growing out of it?" said Dee.

"A distraction from us taking the fight to the wicked witches."

"I think that can be arranged," said Zoffner, blinking as he tried to gaze at his own broken nose.

At Natasha's command, several of her guests had run from the dining room, in search of – as far as Effie could work out – some *pest* or other. The rest turned angrily to the witch who was still sitting in her wheelchair atop the dining table.

"Sabrina," said Natasha coldly.

"Elizabeth Báthory," said the young witch, colder still.

Effie glanced at Kevin. It was relief to see someone else with as little idea what was going on as herself.

Natasha flung her hands forward and poured – was that witchfire? – onto Sabrina. Effie dropped to the floor and crawled behind her chair. It was turning out to be a very confusing and ultimately disappointing evening. Effie had worn her favourite

Rolling Stones T-shirt especially, and now she had red wine and Marie Rose sauce all over it.

"Priorities, Effie," she chided herself, clinging to her paltry shield as the table cracked and splintered under the continuous blast of witchfire.

Dee stood on the lawn with Zoffner the Astute, ready to carry out her part of the hastily arranged plan. She was tasked with summoning the bees to create a distraction in the dining room, and then flying up to join Kay and Jenny in the final assault.

Dee's bee-lore was not as advanced as it really should be. She concentrated hard to recall what Norma had taught her. She tapped a foot and gave a brief experimental spin.

"Groovy," said Zoffner. He mimicked her movements, embellishing them somewhat. His bee dancing was halfway between a goose step and a raver in full ecstatic flow. Dee found it so mesmerising that she unconsciously stepped along with it. Remarkably, a few moments later, a bee swarm hummed over their heads, a thousand black bodies against the night.

Zoffner smiled at her in encouragement. "Shake it, dreamy lady."

Another swarm came from a different direction.

"Shake it yourself, poppet," said Dee.

Several more swarms joined the first. Before long, bees filled the sky. As one they plunged towards the house. Dee and Zoffner paused in their dancing to watch.

"Where are they going?" asked Dee. "I thought I was telling them to go down the chimney and enter the dining room."

"Oh were you?" said Zoffner. "I was doing Mr Mistoffelees from *Cats*."

A piercing, terrified meowing filled the air. Something the size and shape of Mr Beetlebane, if he were surrounded by layers and layers of bees, took to the air. The strange, buzzing cat-shaped bundle headed up the roof.

"Oh, that's not good," said Dee.

The bee-cat collective rose up to the chimney stack and disappeared inside, with a long trailing cloud of bees in close pursuit, swirling around like an emptying drain.

"But it will certainly be a distraction," said Zoffner philosophically as Dee mounted her strimmer.

Madison, enchanted, drove as fast as the narrow fenland roads would allow.

"Do you know where you're going?" Caroline asked him.

"Boston," he said. "Twenty minutes tops."

There was a sparkle of light in the wing mirror.

"Caroline!" called Shazam.

Caroline tumbled over the front seat into the rear. The headlights of two cars in convoy were rapidly catching up with them. "That's Dee's car," she said.

"Mustapha?" said Dee.

"What's going on?" shouted Madison.

"Nothing, handsome. Just you keep driving. Aunty Caroline will deal with this." She had no idea how.

Eventually, the huge dining table gave way under the heat of Natasha's witchfire. The legs buckled, the tabletop cracked in two and the whole thing fell flat to the ground.

"My leg!" screamed Kevin Carter-King from somewhere.

Effie coughed and waved away the wood smoke.

Surprisingly, Sabrina in the wheelchair was entirely unharmed. Natasha and her guests appeared surprised.

Sabrina rolled her neck. "Ur, it is as almost as if I had cast Cherlindrea's Seat of Sanctity on this contraption."

"There's no escape," said Natasha.

"I'm perfectly happy here," Sabrina replied in the satisfied tones of a woman who had all the time in the world.

Jenny and Kay grabbed what weapons they could as they ran round the house. They reached the front door holding a garden fork and a pair of shears. Jenny was uncomfortable in such close proximity to lumps of iron and she'd rather have been armed with the fork than the unwieldy shears she'd picked up.

They watched the bees vanish into the various chimneys of the house.

"I wonder what that funny noise is," said Jenny.

The unholy screeching echoed up from the chimney, like a tortured soul in a well.

"Do you think they're distracted yet?" said Kay.

"Distracted?" said Jizzimus. "Let's see, someone dropped an angry witch through the roof in a wheelchair. They've got every bee in the land in there by the looks of it and *somehow* a banshee is in the chimney. I should fucking cocoa."

"We get in there," said Jenny, "grab Effie and Sabrina and any other innocent bods we find, get out and hightail it out of here."

Dee swooped down to join them on her flying strimmer, giving Jenny the giddy notion that they could be filming the opening sequence for a television gardening makeover show, or a really terrible new superhero franchise.

"We going in or what?" said Dee impatiently, killing the power as she stepped off.

"Just waiting for you, Rambo," said Jenny.

Effie often felt life was a play she had come into halfway through. She had never felt it more than now; but she was slowly putting the pieces together.

Natasha was a wicked witch. Most, if not all of her guests, were wicked witches. Sabrina had been her prisoner but was now freed. The bizarre explosions outside, the structural shift in the house that had warped floor boards here and there, and the unnerving yowling coming from the chimney were still mysteries to her, but she was prepared to accept them as such for now.

She ducked again as Natasha tried another experimental blast of witchfire at the wheelchair.

"Ur, you tried that," said Sabrina, dismissively. "It didn't work. Wicked witches: no imagination."

"Please, someone," whimpered Kevin from ground level somewhere. "My leg—"

Natasha ignored him and moved round the edge of the room until she was standing over Effie. "Get out of the chair or I burn this one to a crisp."

"Please don't involve me," said Effie.

"Do it," sneered Sabrina. "The woman's a fool."

"She's an innocent bystander," said Natasha.

"Exactly," said Effie. "Don't mind me. Be about your business. I'll just—"

Effie was cut off by the arrival of what she could only describe as a flying cat covered in bees. It burst out of the fireplace, loose insects blossoming in its wake. Screaming like a rollercoaster full of screech owls, it lapped the room with no care for what lay in its path.

Life was indeed like a play she had come into halfway through, and that had taught Effie one thing: don't sit there gawping, get on with it.

As wicked witches stared or swatted at the stinging insects, Effie picked herself up and ran for the door. In the corridor outside, floorboards had been pulled up and thrust aside by an unexplained oak branch which hadn't been there earlier. Effie paid it no heed, vaulted over the gap in the floor and ran for the stairs, where she met Dee, Jenny and Kay coming the other way.

"Oh girls! We need to leave this place, you've no idea how strange things have become!" She looked at the assorted gardening implements they were toting. "Or maybe you have a pretty good idea."

"Get out of here, Effie," said Jenny. "Run."

"Wait!" said Dee, rummaging in her handbag for a moment. She pressed a six inch nail into Effie's hand. "If Natasha or any of her friends come after you, use this on them."

Effie looked stricken, but she clasped a hand around the nail and ran for the door.

"Everyone as far forwards as possible," said Caroline, assisting a pale teenager to a seat nearer the front. "Utch up. Get cosy."

It took Agatha three attempts to get her range on the minibus. After charring a telegraph pole and setting a hedgerow aflame, her third shot from Dee's car found the rear of the minibus. Windows smashed and one of the back doors lost a hinge. It swung loose.

The minibus swerved but Madison kept it on the narrow strip of tarmac between the hedgerow and the dyke. The rear of the minibus was now an open target. One well-timed blast would fry them all.

"I'll deal with this," said Shazam who had produced a crystal ball from God knows where.

"Hardly time for fortune-telling, Cobwebs," said Caroline.

Shazam leaned over the back of the last chair. With powerful arms that were more than the bingo wings they appeared, she lobbed the crystal ball at their pursuers. A headlight popped. Tyres screeched. For the time at least, their pursuers fell back.

Jenny, Kay and Dee approached the dining room.

"That'll be one of my acorns," said Dee proudly as they sidled past an oak branch growing through the massive rent in the floorboards.

The noise from within the dining room was a deafening cacophony of buzzes, roars and yells.

"I'm guessing Operation Distract 'em with Bees worked," said Kay.

Jenny pushed the door open. It was difficult to see clearly, with the density of bees in the room. They circled the room at speed: a dense, buzzing fog. The half-dozen wicked witches in the room –

and Natasha was not among them – were using their witchfire to try to clear the bees. All they managed was burning a handful with a brief electrical pop before a thousand more took their places. They couldn't have done a better job of antagonising the bees if they had smeared themselves in honey and thrown personal insults at their queen.

An empty wheelchair sat in the centre of the demolished dining table. To one side, Sabrina crouched in a defensive position and was magicking bowls, plates and anything within range to fly at the beleaguered wicked witches.

A serving dish whizzed through the air and smashed over the head of a witch, spilling broccoli and cauliflower every way. A wicked witch attempted to retaliate but the yowling thing that was Beetlebane in a bee flight suit buzzed the woman savagely and drove her back.

The trio advanced, trying to look menacing with their unlikely weapons.

Dee called out. "Sabrina! We need to get you out of here!"

"Good!" said Sabrina. "I'm running out of crockery based missiles."

Jenny had to duck as the last of these spun over her head. She saw movement from the corner of her eye. Kevin Carter-King was on the floor, crawling for the wheelchair. There was a dark and ragged wound on his leg.

"Kevin," she said flatly.

"Jenny," he croaked. "You've no idea how great it is to see someone normal. Can you believe all this, eh?"

Jenny was stunned. "You wretch!" she said with something between pity and contempt. "This is your doing. All yours."

A wicked witch had managed to battle her way through the bee cloud to reach Sabrina and the rescue team. Kay jabbed savagely with her garden fork and the woman fell back as four searing holes bubbled on her thigh.

Kevin hauled himself up into the chair and began wheeling himself to the door.

"Bastard nicked a wheelchair boss," said Jizzimus. "That's low, that is. You should report 'im to Stephen Hawkin' or summat."

306

Kay thrust her hand up into the bee cloud and a stream of rainbow-coated bees flowed past her fingertips and towards Kevin. The swarm amassed behind the wheelchair and leant their power to his efforts. He was suddenly accelerating out of the door. There was a crunch and a crash and a whimper.

"Come on!" urged Dee. "Let's stick together and get out of here!"

Jenny hooked her arm through Sabrina's. The group formed a tight cluster as they made for the door. Once through, Jenny helped Sabrina past the massive hole in the floor. The wheelchair lay off to one. Kevin Carter-King lay awkwardly among the joists and timbers in the gap under the floorboards.

He reached out to Jenny. "Give a friend a hand, eh?"

Jenny shook her head and moved on.

Kay and Dee looked down at him.

"Please, Jenny," he called.

"You ask for help? Now? How can you do something so evil, be immersed in it, and not see what you're doing?"

"Don't be like that. We can make it all better."

"Of course we can, sweetness," said Dee. With a song and a wave, she mended the hole in the floor.

Caroline called forward to Madison. "Slow at this second corner. Just for a moment."

"What's the plan?" said Shazam.

"Plan is a strong word," said Caroline.

As the minibus slowed on the sharp bend, Caroline pushed herself out the rear door. She had pictured herself landing with a parachute roll but her onward momentum sent her tumbling backwards: bum, shoulder, chest.

"Undignified," she said, picking herself up off the tarmac. But she was unhurt.

The one working tail light of the minibus trailed off in one direction. Dee's car, Mustapha, rounded the bend in the other. The second car, further behind, was not yet visible.

Caroline flexed her wrists. She took a deep breath. "I am a bloody big tractor," she said. "I am a bloody big tractor." There was an impenetrable hedge to one side of her and a deep dark dyke the other. If this didn't work it was going to be a dive into the drink for her. "I am a bloody big tractor and I'm pulling onto the road— Now!"

The car swerved to avoid a non-existent tractor. It bounced over the verge, cleared the ground entirely for an instant and, as it slid past Caroline, rolled down into the dyke. It smacked into the water upside down.

"One down," said Caroline. She turned back to the road and the Bentley that was rapidly approaching. "I am a bloody big tractor," she said. "I am a bloody big tractor and I'm pulling onto the road—Now!"

The Bentley didn't budge.

"Now."

The Bentley was on her, fat headlights blinding her.

*"Big fucking tractor!"* she screamed and prepared to dive aside.

Something barrelled out of the sky, grabbed her outstretched hand and snatched her away, still screaming.

"Damn it! Can't hold you!" yelled Norma.

They tipped, wobbled, mostly cleared the top of the hedgerow and came down hard in a field of something that was both soft and spiky. In the dark, Caroline couldn't tell what it was.

She sat up. Her arm was dislocated from when Norma had grabbed her. Dislocated or ripped off at the joint. It hurt too much for her to check.

There was a clap and a ball of pale fire in Norma's hand.

"Bennu's Something-something Light," said Caroline, surprised how weak her voice sounded.

"Phoenix Fire," said Norma, placing it on the ground beside Caroline. She tutted. "I blame the EU."

"What?"

Norma lifted the flap of a ruined pocket in her tweed jacket. "They used to make things to last." She scouted about on the floor, gathering a pile of pins, nails, charred acorns and herb bundles. She deposited them all in Caroline's lap. "Ah-hah!"

She held aloft a woodworker's file that had been sharpened to a wicked point. "I need to check that witch in the ditch is dead."

"But the other car..." said Caroline.

Norma touched her hand. "You gave them a head start, Miss Black. They'll be fine." She stood. "You did well."

"That's the nicest thing you've ever said."

Norma scowled at her and ran off into the night, leaving Caroline in the small circle of light.

As Jenny, Kay, Sabrina and Dee hurried along the corridor, the double doors leading to the entrance hall slammed shut in front of them.

"No," said Natasha.

The three witches turned to see Natasha behind them.

"Dog willies!" said Jizzimus with feeling.

As Natasha moved her hands, the corridor around her cleared of bees, excluded by an invisible bubble of her making. The bees buzzed angrily, but it sounded as though they were in another room. Natasha sighed loudly.

"You girls have passed the point of being a tolerable diversion. You have caused material damage to a successful operation, and I'm afraid you will need to be disposed of. Put down, like diseased beasts."

Natasha's face, her beautiful face, was marked with angry red bee stings. They were blemishes on perfection. Dee – who had always favoured the ill-favoured, always loved the ugly creatures in the world, always been drawn to the lop-sided, the weak and the plain – Dee saw, by the same token, absolute beauty could be the personification of evil. Those elegant cheeks, those gentle eyes. Every bit of the woman had been paid for in the blood of innocents.

"How old are you?" said Dee.

"Four hundred and fifty seven. And I've dealt with more pernicious pests than you."

A side door from the stairs flew open. A trio of hulking imps burst through, visible to all and larger than life. One, with the face of the ugliest goat in the herd, opened its extendable jaws and began slurping bees out of the air. The one Jenny recognised as Clappoxian, his severed hand now reattached, clambered up the animal trophy heads on the walls to the ceiling and leered down at them. The third imp was Malunguibus, Natasha's imp, the saw blade stuff whirling quite merrily through and around his neck, like a hardcore Elizabethan ruff.

"I thought we blew them up," said Dee.

"Idiot," sneered Natasha. "You can't kill an imp!"

"Cos we're 'ard as fuck," said Jizzimus proudly.

"But we can kill their owners," said Sabrina. She reached out and summoned the overturned wheelchair to her. It knocked Natasha's legs from under her as it slid past. Malunguibus roared as his mistress fell.

"Aw did the wickle imp's mummy get a boo-boo?" said Jizzimus. Malunguibus whirled on him but Jizzimus was already running through the beast's legs and away.

Dee jabbed at the goat-faced imp with her still-buzzing strimmer, slicing his beard and a chunk of his goaty chin away.

Clappoxian leapt down on the witches, his bulk smashing Kay aside. Out of fear as much as rage, Jenny opened her hands and pumped witchfire into his face. She stopped when she heard him laugh.

"Witchfire doesn't work on imps, child!" snapped Natasha.

Natasha swung her hands out and magically whisked the witches' legs out from under them. Jenny's breath was knocked from her. Kay came down hard and smacked her head off the skirting board. Sabrina tripped over the wheelchair in front of her. Dee had to roll aside to avoid getting cut by her own dropped strimmer.

The goat-headed imp lunged down at Dee. She grabbed the handle of the strimmer. *"Veikti!"*

The flying strimmer took off, dragging Dee out of the imp's reach. Within the length of the corridor she managed more by luck than skill to angle the strimmer up and take to the air, doubling back on herself and gaining what little height the corridor allowed.

Dee looked at the row of trophy animal heads on the wall: dead, stuffed, but still holding a glimmer of the life they once had. She gave a mind-focusing wiggle, bringing her hips and feet into the spell while her hands were occupied with steering.

The first to move was some sort of long horned antelope. It gave a startled glance around the room, then focused on the ancient witch and imps below. A fox's head chomped its jaws a couple of times, as if getting used to the idea of moving again. Finally a tiger fixed its predatory amber eyes on the goat-imp and licked its lips.

The imp looked nervous. Dee liked that.

She had given the animal heads as much animation as was possible to something without limbs. It was largely a question of getting them to fall into the right place. The long horned antelope gave a plaintive bleat, piercing Malunguibus in the arm as it flung itself clear of the wall. A wolf burst forward with surprising energy and fixed its jaws across the shoulder of Clappoxian, growling and chewing ferociously. The tiger pivoted out of place and, jaws wide, landed mouth first on top of the goat-imp's head. It made a sound like someone chewing a giant gobstopper – a gobstopper made of flesh and bone and which screamed like a trapped animal.

"Score one for the kitty!" yelled Jizzimus, punching the air. "Now if that tiger would just get on wiv it an' eat the 'ead 'oncho we can get out of 'ere!"

However, Malunguibus was not fazed by the antelope attack. He wrenched the reanimated ruminant out of his arm and fed it, snout first, into his whirling neck-saw. The antelope head exploded in a burst of tanned hide and stuffing.

Clappoxian ripped the wolf's head away – along with much of his shoulder – and flung it at Jenny. She batted it aside with open palms, giving Clappoxian time to grab her in a muscular grip and slam her to the ground. She still held the shears but her trapped elbow prevented her angling them round to use them on the imp.

Beside her, Sabrina, who had been tending to the unconscious Kay, directed a telekinetic nudge at a couple more heads – a ram and some sort of polecat-weasel-badger – and they leapt from their positions onto Malunguibus. Their effect was sadly negligible. The giant troll pounded, pulverised and shredded them in short order, before pinning Sabrina to the ground with his massive foot.

Dee yelled out, but should have been more mindful of her own safety. Malunguibus reached up with his gorilla arm and tumbled her from her strimmer with a fingertip. Dee fell into his rough claw as the strimmer, riderless, shot up against the ceiling and skittered along the coving like a fly trying to get out of the wrong side of the window.

Jenny struggled futilely under Clappoxian's bulk. Suddenly, the shears were ripped from her hand by a powerful, unseen force. Natasha's smile increased. The shears were reversed, the metallic tips brushing Jenny's forearm. She screamed as blisters erupted along her skin, and pain seared through her. She could hear hisses of delighted glee from Clappoxian.

Natasha cooed. "Come now Jenny, it's just a little iron. It's not as if you're about to lose a finger, is it? Hmm. Perhaps you are."

The shears opened and the maw of the vicious tool crept along Jenny's hand, flesh sizzling in its wake. She closed her fist to protect her fingers. Natasha tutted, and Jenny could feel her fist opening, even though she fought it: fingers splaying against her will.

"Don't you dare 'urt my guv," yelled Jizzimus, giving up on gnawing at Clappoxian's face. He flung himself at Natasha. Before he was halfway towards her, Natasha bunched her fist, snapped it open, and Jizzimus exploded into a hundred chunks of imp flesh with a sound no louder than a damp cloth ripping.

Norma didn't bother looking for a gap in the hedgerow. She took the view that the plant kingdom was entirely subservient to humanity and it would not be proper to let plants think otherwise. Armed with that attitude, a parasol, a file and layers of protective tweed, she pushed through and onto the narrow road.

Dee's car lay upturned in the dyke on the other side, sunk up to its wheel arches and steaming gently.

Water was historically regarded as a fine way to deal with witches. Water or fire. Better still both. Non-wicked witches did not have access to witchfire but a can of hairspray and a butane lighter were a fine substitute. Norma crawled a little down the bank and sprayed the car's underside with flame. And, yes, there was enough leaked oil or petrol on the underside for the fire to take hold.

"Tried to burn me, you cow?"

Norma whirled. The witch, soaked and dripping with black silty water, rose from the dyke bank. Agatha unleashed a bolt of fire. Norma had only time enough to raise the parasol in front of her. The fireball burned the parasol cloth and pressed on with enough impact to push Norma head over heels, down the other side of the car, and into the dyke.

Water gripped her like an icy cloak. Norma twisted and righted herself, feet brushing through snagging weeds. She fought for the surface, weighed down by sodden clothing. She breached the surface once and immediately sank again. Coming up a second time she thrust out the parasol she still gripped and jabbed its base into the bank like a piton.

She coughed and spluttered and tried to gain some purchase.

A hand grabbed the parasol. "Tried to drown me?" shrieked Agatha. She took hold of the parasol with both hands and wrenched it from Norma's grasp. Norma flailed for something to hold onto. She grabbed the front bumper of the car and tried to pull herself up. Agatha raised the parasol to stab at Norma's hands.

"You're not going anywhere!"

"You are," said Norma. "*Veikti!*"

The parasol shot upwards, taking Agatha with it. Perhaps if she'd had the wherewithal to let go in the first second, she might have survived the fall, but Agatha instinctively hung on as it flew straight up. Her yell of surprise tailed off like a screaming firework.

Bracing herself against the burning car, Norma crawled up the bank and flopped onto the roadside. She rolled onto her back and looked up. A shadow passed over the clouds, hundreds of feet above.

"*Nustoti!*" she shouted.

The shadow fell. Partway down, the parasol popped open. If Agatha hadn't burned most it away, the umbrella might have slowed her fall.

But probably not.

Natasha stepped over Jizzimus's remains towards the witches, one unconscious and the other three in the mighty grips of imps.

With no warning, the goat-imp vanished from existence with no more fanfare than a popping soap bubble.

"Agatha," said Natasha.

The tiger head rolled to Natasha's feet, and immediately latched into her ankle. Its jaw was immensely powerful. Bones splintered and blood gushed but Natasha remained standing. She blasted the disembodied cat head with witchfire until it was a blackened husk; healed her ankle back into alignment with an audible crackling of bones.

She turned to Jenny, her smile gone. "I'm disappointed, Jenny. A traitor to your own kind."

She nodded to Malunguibus. With slow and measured malice he ground his foot into the witch on the floor and squeezed the life out of the one in his hand.

Even in the dark, Caroline knew that the figure approaching from her left was not Norma. Norma Looney moved like a Sherman tank. This person moved like a fox. Or a devil.

Caroline tried to shift herself round to see the woman better but the pain in her arm had intensified with time, not eased. She looked at her injured arm. Blood ran freely down from the back of her hand. Her fingers were a swollen and mashed mess of flesh. A couple of them looked ready to fall off.

"Where is she?" The red-haired witch stalked across the field, witchfire coating her hands like gloves.

"Who?" groaned Caroline.

"Norma Looney. She was here."

"And you are?"

"An old friend."

"Ah," said Caroline, understanding. She moved without thinking and hissed in pain.

Lesley-Ann Faulkner's nostrils twitched and the witchfire died a little. Caroline gave her a fearful look.

"She's gone off somewhere. I'd go look for her if I were you."

"But she'll be back, won't she?" smiled Lesley-Ann. She couldn't take her eyes off Caroline's wounded hand.

"Norma tells me you're eighty or ninety something."

"Did she?" Lesley-Ann crouched beside Caroline and sniffed.

"That's right," said Caroline, dropping a nervous tremble into her voice. "And I just wanted to com – compliment you on your beauty regime."

"That's nice."

The wicked witch lifted Caroline's hand. Caroline grunted in genuine pain. Lesley-Ann bowed her head, licked the blood from the back of Caroline's hand and then, quick as a pouncing cat, put Caroline's finger in her mouth and bit down hard.

Caroline screamed, long, loud and pure and Lesley-Ann ground her teeth into the joint and ripped a fleshy mouthful away. Lesley-Ann stood and stepped back. She looked very pleased with herself. She dabbed at her bloody lips with her fingertips.

Lesley-Ann Faulkner swallowed.

"That's what I love about desire," said Caroline.

The wicked witch looked at her, uncomprehending.

"You refused to see an illusory tractor, but give you a helpless witch covered in yummy, sticky blood and—" Caroline looked pointedly at her own hand on the ground. There was no blood, no missing finger, just her hand, whole and unharmed.

"Oh, little trickster," said Lesley-Ann, half-amused, half-incensed.

"But it does make me wonder what you really ate just then. *Ösgön!*"

Lesley-Ann Faulkner opened her mouth to say something but no sound came. There was something stuck in her throat, growing. Her eyes widened.

Like the goat-imp before him, Clappoxian winked into nothingness. The weight on Jenny vanished. She rolled to her feet.

Natasha, sour-faced and tired, reached out. The shears flew into her hand. "This ends."

Jenny nodded. "*Nustoti!*"

The strimmer, blades whirling, fell from the ceiling into Jenny's hands. She thrust it directly at Natasha's throat. Natasha grabbed at the shaft to hold it off but Jenny had youth and fury on her side. She shoved with all of her might, backing Natasha up against the wall.

Witchfire blackened and melted the shaft where Natasha held it.

"You're a wicked witch. Like us." Natasha's sudden fear gave Jenny strength.

With a shove, Jenny thrust the hedge-strimmer forward and decapitated Natasha du Plessis. The ancient witch's head dropped to the floor at Jenny's feet.

Malunguibus vanished.

Dee dropped to the floor with an "Oh, flip!" Sabrina, free from the imp's foot, breathed deeply and coughed.

Jenny looked at the remains of Elizabeth Báthory. "I'm not a wicked witch," she told it. "I'm a fricking *awesome* witch."

"Hell, yeah," mumbled Kay, opening her eyes.

Norma found Caroline where she'd left her. Or at least it was where she thought she'd left her.

"Was that oak tree there before?" said Norma.

"Well, it could hardly have appeared by magic," said Caroline.

Norma looked at it a little more closely: at the rags of bloody material wrapped around it. "And why does it appear to be wearing a dress, Miss Black?"

Sabrina picked up Natasha's head.

"What are you going to do with that, sweetness?" asked Dee.

"Ur, I'm going to take it outside and find a hammer. Then I'm going to take the pieces and burn them. Then I am going to take the ashes and scatter them. And then I am going to curse the ashes."

"Good," said Dee. "That sounds ....thorough. And that's to stop her coming back from the dead, is it?"

"Ur, she's already definitely dead," said Sabrina. "But it will make me considerably happier."

Dee walked outside. She walked slowly. She'd cast all the healing remedies she knew over her friends and herself, but that didn't mean there weren't still some aches and pains and the certainty that she'd feel like a tenderised steak in the morning.

Out on the front lawns, Kay was casting rainbow glows over the swirling masses of bees and sending them off to their natural homes. Zoffner the Astute stood beside her, not actually helping but generally sending out positive waves into the aether. With an exhausted mew, Beetlebane dropped out of the sky and into Kay's arms.

A big black Bentley turned into the driveway. Norma stepped out and went round to the passenger door to help Caroline. Norma had apparently been for a swim, fully clothed. Caroline had her arm in a makeshift sling and looked like she'd been dragged through a hedge backwards. Zoffner ran over and gave his love an unrestrained hug.

"Get off me, man. I'm all wet," said Norma.

"Everything all right, poppets?" called Dee.

"Terrific," grunted Caroline. "Madison and Shazam have the girls at Pilgrim Hospital. The wicked bitches?"

"Dead or fled."

"Bowman?"

"Crispy fried," said Kay.

"Couldn't have happened to a nicer guy."

"But there's still this one," said Jenny, coming round the corner of the house, hauling George by the scruff of his neck. The barman-cum-gardener-cum-accessory-to-mass-murder came pleading and sobbing.

"Look, I'm sorry. I'm really sorry. They made me do it and I never enjoyed it."

Jenny tossed him down onto the gravel drive and filled her hands with witchfire.

Caroline tried and failed to conceal her surprise. "Jenny's a ... a, you know."

"She's our friend," said Kay.

"And she's kind," babbled George. "I'm willing to learn the error of my ways. I was just following orders. You've opened my eyes to what I've done and if you give me a chance I will show you I—"

Jenny recoiled in disgust. "How many?" she said.

"How many?" said George.

She pointed across the fields. "I've seen them. The girls. Dozens of them. Hundreds. Centuries' worth of murder. How many?"

"But I wasn't responsible for it. Not for it all."

"I know what to do," said Sabrina. She put her hands momentarily to the grisly head beneath her arm. She came away with two slivers of amber at her fingertips.

"What's going on?" said George.

"I'm opening your eyes."

She waved her hands and the amber contacts floated across and, with no resistance, inserted themselves over George's eyes.

"What? What's going on?"

George glanced about him, sucking in a breath as he did so.

"Who are they?" he said and pointed at nothing at all in the middle distance. "What are they?"

"Ghosts," said Jenny. "Yours."

George whirled around, trying to find a view that he could cope with. He became more and more agitated as he realised that there wasn't one. He clawed at his eyes but the lenses wouldn't come free.

"I think maybe you want to go a long way away, George," said Jenny. "It could be that the women don't follow."

George ran for it. He ran down the drive at a full sprint, a terrified sob coming from him.

"Well, girls," said Effie Fray, "I think you've done an outstanding job."

"How long have you been standing there?" said Dee.

"Long enough. You've demonstrated teamwork and many inventive uses for your skills. I would like to make sure you all get your certificates of competence, even though the future of the training facility is somewhat uncertain, given the possible withdrawal of our main patron."

"Possible?" said Sabrina, jiggling the head beneath her arm.

Caroline couldn't help but laugh, not stopping even when Effie gave her a look of haughty disapproval.

"Yes, Caroline? Something amuses you?"

Caroline tried to compose herself, but Dee chipped in.

"I think we can all imagine a world where you keep the witch school going here."

"Maybe a spa business as well?" suggested Kay.

"All you need to do," said Dee, ticking off on her fingers, "is find a need, open your mind to marketing opportunities, watch your operating expenses and face the future."

"Embrace the foof," said Caroline.

"You might have noticed that it's not my building," sniffed Effie. "And the police will be all over the place when these girls tell their story. I'd never get away with just moving in."

"The story that these girls need to tell will be based upon everybody's best interest," said Caroline, with a brief practice flexing of her hand.

"The far wing of the house is currently on fire," said Effie.

Norma cracked her knuckles. "Nothing we can't handle."

"Listen to the universe, groovy lady," said Zoffner.

Effie relented. "Well, it certainly seems like a foofy enough idea to me."

A hand tugged at Jenny's leg. Jizzimus was balancing against her as he attempted to screw his leg back on.

"Some assembly required, guv."

She swept him up and hugged the tiny horror like he was hers and hers alone. His arm fell off and she had to stop hugging him to pick it up.

"Dunno whether to stick myself together wiv super glue or stitch myself up and get some quality scars, boss. Bitches love scars."

"So," said Effie, in the diffident British tones of one trying to adapt to the unusual, "you'd be our resident wicked witch, Jenny?"

Jenny gave her an amiable shrug.

"What a world it would be," said Effie, "if witches, both good and ... well, all witches could come together in peace."

"What a world indeed," said Norma with wry scepticism.

"And this," Effie waved her hands to vaguely indicate the invisible imp on her shoulder, "would be your imp?"

"His name's Jizzimus," said Jenny.

Effie smiled and reached out to delicately shake his hand. "A pleasure to meet you, Jizzimus."

"That's not ... um. That's not his hand," said Jenny.

"Hilarious," said Jizzimus.

# Acknowledgements

We are indebted to members of THE Book Club (TBC) for kindly donating their names to this novel. We were unable to use names from all of our willing volunteers, but our thanks to everyone and the following are the ones that we used:

Jenny Knott
Dee Finch
Caroline Black
Norma Looney
Natasha du Plessis
Kay Wun
Sabrina Holder-Eckford
Sharon Jaye
George Slingsby

A special thank you to Ellen Devonport who came up with the book's title.

Printed in Great Britain
by Amazon

59271079R00192